CHARLATANS

ALSO BY ROBIN COOK

ROBIN COOK

CHARLATANS

MACMILLAN

First published 2017 by G. P. Putnam's Sons,
an imprint of Penguin Random House LLC, New York

First published in the UK 2017 by Macmillan
an imprint of Pan Macmillan
20 New Wharf Road, London N1 9RR
Associated companies throughout the world
www.panmacmillan.com

ISBN 978-1-4472-9855-7 TPB

Printed and bound by CPI Group (UK) Ltd, Croydon, CR0 4YY

Visit **www.panmacmillan.com** to read more about all our books
and to buy them. You will also find features, author interviews and
news of any author events, and you can sign up for e-newsletters
so that you're always first to hear about our new releases.

To my extended family and friends

CHARLATANS

PROLOGUE

Due to the seasonal tilt of the earth's axis, the dawn of June 27 came swiftly to Boston, Massachusetts, in sharp contrast to mornings in the dead of winter when the sun's arc was low in the southern sky. Starting at 4:24 A.M., progressively bright summer light quickly filled the streets of the Italianate North End, the narrow byways of elegant Beacon Hill, and the broad boulevards of stately Back Bay. At exactly 5:09 A.M., the sun's disc appeared at the horizon out over the Atlantic Ocean and began its steady rise into a cloudless early-morning sky.

Of the varying spires of the Boston Memorial Hospital, known as the BMH, the first to catch the golden rays was the very top of the central, twenty-one-story Stanhope Pavilion. This modern glass tower was the newest addition to the mishmash of structures comprising the famous tertiary-care Harvard teaching hospital that overlooked the Boston Harbor. Its clean silhouette was strikingly different from the older, low-rise, red-brick buildings dating back more than a hundred and fifty years.

The state-of-the-art Stanhope Pavilion had every modern hospital accoutrement, including a suite of twenty-four of the most up-to-date operating rooms, called "Hybrid ORs of the Future." Each bristled with

1

high tech and looked like it had been designed as a set for a *Star Trek* movie, far different from the old standard operating rooms. The entire suite was oriented in two radii of twelve rooms around two central command stations. Windows provided direct visual contact of each OR interior by OR supervisors to augment closed-circuit TV monitors.

Within each of these new hybrid ORs, capable of supporting a wide variety of surgical procedures, from brain surgery to complicated heart surgery to routine knee replacement, a number of large and exquisitely adjustable utility booms hung from the ceiling and supported various types of state-of-the-art medical technology. The suspension system allowed all the equipment to be instantly available yet kept the floor open to maximize movement of the personnel and speed up the transition between cases. One boom supported the anesthesia station, another included a heart-lung perfusion system, a third had an operating microscope, and a final C-shaped boom supported a biplane digital imaging and navigating system that used a combination of infrared light and X-rays to provide real-time three-dimensional images of internal human structure. Each OR also had multiple banks of high-definition video screens plugged into the hospital's clinical information system so that patient data and medical images such as X-rays and sonograms could be displayed instantaneously by voice command.

The rationale for all this super-modern and inordinately expensive equipment was to increase the efficiency and efficacy of the surgery as well as enhance patient safety. Yet on this beautiful late-June day all this modern technological wizardry and rational design was not to be a guarantee against unintended consequence and human foibles. Despite the good intentions of all the dedicated personnel of the BMH surgical department, a human disaster was in the making in Stanhope's hybrid operating room #8.

As sunlight filled the drop-off area for the Stanhope Pavilion at 5:30 A.M., cars and taxis began to line up at the entrance beneath the porte-cochere, their doors opening and passengers emerging with overnight bags. There was little conversation as these soon-to-be inpatients and their accompanying family members entered the hospital and took the elevator up to "Day-Surgery Admitting" on the fourth floor. There had been a time in years past when people were admitted the day before their scheduled elective surgery, but that perk had mostly fallen by the wayside, thanks to health insurance company dictates. The extra night in the hospital was deemed too expensive.

The initial surge of patients represented the first cases of the day. Other patients scheduled as "to follow" cases were instructed to arrive two hours before the time their surgery was estimated to begin. Although the length of operations could be approximated to a reasonable degree, it was never certain. If there was to be an error on timing, it was always to the hospital's benefit, not the patients'. Sometimes this caused the patients to have to wait for extended periods in holding areas. This could be a problem for some, as all patients were instructed to take nothing but a small amount of water by mouth starting at midnight the night before.

On this particular day, one of the "to follow" cases was an open right inguinal hernia repair on a strapping, healthy, intelligent, and gregarious forty-four-year-old man named Bruce Vincent. Since the operation had been estimated to begin at 10:15 A.M., he had been told to arrive at Surgical Admitting at 8:15. Unlike other patients scheduled that day, he wasn't concerned about his upcoming procedure. His comparative nonchalance wasn't just because of the relative simplicity of his procedure but had more to do with Bruce's familiarity with the BMH. For Bruce, the hospital was not a mysterious, scary netherworld, because he'd been coming there most every day for twenty-six years. He had been hired by the BMH right out of Charlestown High School, where he had been a popular local sports celebrity, to join the hospital's security department. It had been a legacy gesture: Bruce's mother had been an LPN at the hospital for her entire career and his older sister was one of the hospital's RNs.

But being an employee and thereby accustomed to the hospital environment was not the only reason for his comparative sangfroid that morning. What truly made him calm was that he had, over the twenty-six years of employment, befriended almost everyone, including doctors, nurses, administrators, and support staff. In the process, he had learned a lot about medicine, particularly hospital-based medicine, to the point that it was a common joke among the staff that he was a graduate of the nonexistent BMH medical school. Bruce could discuss surgical technique with orthopedic surgeons, malpractice concerns with administrators, and staffing problems with RNs, and he did all of this on a regular basis.

When Bruce had been told he was to have spinal anesthesia for his upcoming hernia repair that was going to take maybe an hour at most, he knew exactly what spinal anesthesia was and why it was safer than general anesthesia. For him there was no mystery involved. And on top of that, he was extremely confident of his surgeon, the legendary Dr. William Mason. Bruce was well aware that the mercurial Dr. Mason, who was known behind his back as "Wild Bill," was one of the most famous surgeons at the hospital. Dr. Mason himself saw to it, making sure that it was common knowledge that patients came from around the world on a weekly basis to take advantage of his skilled hands and incredible statistics. Dr. Mason was a full Harvard professor of surgery, chief of the Department of Gastrointestinal Surgery, and one of the associate program directors of the hospital's famed surgical residency program. His subspecialty was the very demanding surgery of the pancreas, an organ tucked away in the very back of the abdomen that was notoriously hard to operate on because of its peculiar consistency, digestive function, and location.

When Bruce told people that Dr. Mason was going to do his hernia repair, everyone was shocked. It was common knowledge that Dr. Mason hadn't done a hernia repair since he had been a surgical resident more than thirty years ago. The professor prided himself on doing only the most complex and difficult cases involving the pancreas. Some had been mystified enough to ask Bruce how he had managed the impossible, getting Mason to do what he certainly considered a piddling operation fit for a surgical neophyte and well below his dignity. Bruce had been happy to explain.

Over the years, Bruce had enjoyed persistent advancement in the security department, thanks to his unabashed commitment to the hospital combined with his outgoing personality. He loved his work, and because of his attitude and the fact that he seemed to know everyone by name, everyone loved Bruce Vincent in return. They also liked that he was a family man who had married another outgoing and popular BMH employee from the food-service department. Together they had had four children, one of whom was an infant. Since the Vincent kids' pictures continuously graced the cafeteria bulletin board, it seemed to the entire medical center community that they were the quintessential hospital family.

Although Bruce's popularity ratings had been high from day one, they soared when he had been elevated to take over the hospital's problematic parking division. Due to his efforts, the seemingly intractable difficulties had melted away, especially after he convinced the hospital board to build a third multistory garage specifically for doctors and nurses as part of the Stanhope project. On top of that, Bruce was never one to hide out in his "parking czar" cubicle. Instead, he was always available in the trenches, anticipating problems from the crack of dawn to late afternoon with a smile and personalized comment. By his example, all the other parking employees were similarly dedicated and personable. And it was in this capacity as a hands-on supervisor that Bruce had managed to befriend the otherwise rather aloof Dr. William Mason.

The whole hospital knew when Dr. Mason got his red Ferrari four years ago. There were some jokes behind his back about a mid-life crisis, because along with the flashy sports car he had become overtly flirtatious with several of the OR department's younger and attractive women, mostly nurses, but also one of the female surgical residents. Bruce heard the buzz about Dr. Mason's behavior and off-color comments but dismissed them as envy. And as far as the Ferrari was concerned, instead of thinking of it as inappropriate and out of place among the tamer and more conservative Volvos, Lexuses, BMWs, and Mercedes, Bruce lavished it with praise and even offered daily to personally park the car in a special protected place to avoid door dings. So when Bruce learned from his Charlestown GP that he had to have his hernia repaired, a problem he had had for some time but which was now giving him mild intermittent problems, particularly with his digestive system, he simply asked Dr. Mason if he would do it. Bruce popped the question on the spur of the moment one morning when he took the Ferrari's keys. To everyone's surprise—even Bruce's, as he later confided—Dr. Mason agreed on the spot, promising to squeeze Bruce into his jam-packed schedule of celebrities, business mavens, European aristocrats, and Arab sheiks whenever Bruce wanted.

Despite being scheduled for surgery that very morning, Bruce had still appeared at his parking office at five as if it were a normal day. And just as he had done for years, he greeted the staff as they arrived. He even parked Dr. Mason's Ferrari. Dr. Mason was a bit taken aback to see him and said as much, wondering if his own memory was failing him.

"I'm a to-follow case, so I don't have to be at Surgical Admitting until eight fifteen" was Bruce's simple explanation.

Yet Bruce's dedication to his job wasn't without consequence on this particular morning. After handling a problem generated by an employee who had failed to show up or call, Bruce was late getting to Surgical Admitting on Stanhope 4.

"Bruce, you are almost forty minutes late," Martha Stanley said anxiously. She was head of Day-Surgery Admitting. She didn't usually do intakes herself, but she had been waiting for Bruce to show up. "You were supposed to be here at eight fifteen. We've already heard from the OR, wondering where the hell you were."

"Sorry, Miss Stanley," Bruce said sheepishly. "I got held up by a staff problem in the garage."

"Maybe you shouldn't have worked this morning," Martha said with a disapproving shake of her head. She had been surprised to see him in his usual uniform when she pulled into the garage early that day, as she was aware he was scheduled for an inguinal repair. She opened the folder and riffled through its contents, checking that the history and physical were there, along with the most recent blood work and an ECG. She turned her attention to the computer screen to be sure all the same material was there. "In case you don't know, Dr. Mason is a bear about waiting, and he has two other big VIP pancreatic cancer cases this morning."

Bruce flashed a remorseful, almost pained expression. "Sorry! I'm sure he hates to wait. Maybe we can speed this admitting process up a bit. My operation is no big deal. It's just a hernia repair."

"Every case is important and has to be done by the book," Martha mumbled as she made an entry into the EMR, the electronic medical record, "but we do have to get you up there sooner rather than later. You haven't eaten anything, have you?"

"I'm having spinal anesthesia," Bruce said. "Dr. Mason's fellow, Dr. Kolganov, told me I was to have spinal when he did the history and physical."

"It doesn't matter what kind of anesthesia you're scheduled to have. Have you eaten anything? You were told not to eat after midnight. That is the same for everyone."

"No, I'm fine. Let's get the show on the road." Bruce glanced at his watch as his heart skipped a beat. A sudden fear swept over him that Dr. Mason might change his mind and refuse to operate on him. That was the last thing Bruce wanted.

"Okay," Martha said with a touch of reluctance. "You have a negative history and physical by Dr. Mason's fellow, so maybe we can leapfrog the junior surgical resident going over it and adding his two cents. There has been a kind of rush here over the last half hour, so I know he's got his hands full, meaning it would take quite a while for him to get to you. Which side is to be operated on?"

"Right side," Bruce said.

"Do you have any allergies?"

"No. None."

"Have you ever had anesthesia?"

"No. I've never been a hospital patient."

"Excellent." Then Martha called out to one of the attendants tasked to take patients into the changing area where they would get out of their clothes and put on hospital gowns. She handed Bruce's folder to him. "Good luck," she added to Bruce. "And next time be on time!"

Bruce gave her a thumbs-up and a guilty smile, and followed the attendant.

After getting out of his clothes and struggling into the hospital gown, Bruce lay down on a gurney and pulled a sheet up under his armpits. Another nurse appeared, dressed in surgical garb, one of the few nurses he didn't know. She introduced herself as Helen Moran and asked the same questions Martha had asked. Then she marked Bruce's right hip with an indelible marker after confirming with him the side to be operated on. "My orders are to move you along at top speed," she said. "I'll let anesthesia know you are on your way over. They have been looking for you."

Bruce nodded. He felt progressively embarrassed at having been late to Admitting and appreciative of the extra attention he was getting because of it. He figured it was due to a large degree that Dr. Mason was his surgeon. An orderly appeared just after Helen left, unlocked the gurney, and then maneuvered it out into the hallway. His name was Calvin Wiley. Bruce didn't know him, but he knew Bruce. "You are a VIP," Calvin said as he wheeled the gurney along the tortuous route toward the operating suite. "I was told you were one of Dr. Mason's patients and I was to get you up to the surgical holding area on the double."

"Hardly a VIP," Bruce responded, but he was pleased. As he had assumed, having Dr. Mason as his surgeon was a major plus. He just hoped his being late wouldn't screw things up.

Calvin deposited Bruce in the pre-anesthesia holding area in a cubicle defined by curtains. As soon as he left, two nurses appeared: Connie Marchand and Gloria Perkins. Bruce knew both of them, because both commuted to and from the medical center by car. After a bit of banter, mostly about Bruce's children, Gloria left. Connie went over the paperwork, checked the inked X on Bruce's right hip, and went through the same questions Martha and Helen had asked. Satisfied that all was in order, Connie gave Bruce's arm an endearing squeeze and told him that she would let anesthesia know that he was there. "I imagine one of the anesthesiologists will be by right away," Connie said. "We've gotten a few calls about your whereabouts. Dr. Mason doesn't like to wait."

"So I hear," Bruce said. "My bad! Sorry! I was a bit late to Surgical Admitting. Will everything be okay?"

"It should be all right," Connie assured him.

A few minutes later the curtain was pulled aside and a youthful woman with arctic-blue eyes and tanned skin came to Bruce's side. She was dressed in blue scrubs, including a hood that completely covered her hair. In a direct and pleasant fashion, she introduced herself as Dr. Ava London, one of the staff anesthesiologists, and then added: "I will be helping Dr. Mason take care of you this morning, Mr. Vincent, while he fixes your hernia. I must say it is a pleasure to meet you. I've heard that you are quite a popular guy and that the darling photos I've seen on the cafeteria bulletin board are your children."

"I oversee hospital parking," Bruce explained, already liking this attractive and personable anesthesiologist. "I am surprised I haven't met you. Are you new to the staff?"

"Relatively new," Ava said. "But it is coming up on five years."

"That is not new," Bruce said, a tad chagrined, as he prided himself on his knowledge of the medical center's staff. "I guess you don't use the garage."

"No need. I'm able to walk to the hospital," Ava said as she looked through the paperwork on the clipboard at the foot of Bruce's gurney. "I live nearby, on Beacon Hill." She immediately noticed there was no corroborating note by a junior surgical resident. She asked Bruce why.

"Martha Stanley felt there was no need, because Dr. Mason's fellow had done the history and physical just a few days ago. Truthfully, it was my fault. I was late getting to Surgical Admitting. They wanted to get me over here ASAP."

Ava nodded. A fellow, having already completed his surgical residency, was certainly more qualified than a junior surgical resident. She glanced through the history and physical. It was totally negative for any medical problems except the run-of-the-mill inguinal hernia. Satisfied that all was in order, she put the clipboard back onto the gurney and reestablished eye contact with Bruce. "So it seems you are in good health."

"I think so. Can we speed this up? I don't want Dr. Mason upset that I was a bit late checking in."

"It is important to do this right. I need to ask you a few questions. I see there is no history of medical problems, particularly no problems with your heart and lungs."

"None."

"And you have never had anesthesia?"

"Never."

"And you haven't eaten since midnight."

"Dr. Mason's fellow said I was going to have spinal anesthesia."

"That is correct. Dr. Mason's secretary specifically let us know that the doctor requested spinal anesthesia. Are you okay with that? You know what it is?"

"I do. Actually, I know most of the anesthesiologists and nurse anesthetists, who have told me all sorts of things about anesthesia."

"An informed patient! That's helpful for sure. But you realize we have to have consent to use general anesthesia in case there is any problem with the spinal."

"What kind of a problem are you talking about?"

"The chances of a problem are very small, but we have to be prepared. For instance, if the surgery takes longer than expected and the spinal begins to wear off, we must be prepared to give you general anesthesia. For that reason, we need consent just to cover all the bases. That's why we are interested in whether you have any problems with your lungs."

"No problems with my lungs."

"How about reflux disease?"

"I'm fine! Really, I am. Are you sure we are not holding Dr. Mason up?"

"There is no problem about holding up Dr. Mason, believe me. Now, let's talk about the spinal. Do you know that we have to put a needle in your back to enable us to give you the anesthetic agent?"

"Yes. I know all about it. Dr. Mason's fellow gave me the complete rundown and assured me that I won't feel anything."

"That is correct. You won't feel any pain during the operation. I will make absolutely sure of it. But tell me: Do you have any back problems that I should know about?"

"Nope. Back's fine."

"Good. What will happen is that when we get you in the room, you will be asked to sit on the side of the operating table with your face and head resting in a support. You will feel a pinch when I put some local anesthetic into the skin of your lower back before putting in the spinal needle. Once the medicine has been introduced into your spine, we will help you lie back down on the table. Now, a question for you: During the operation, do you want to be awake and possibly watch if Dr. Mason is okay with it, or would you prefer to be asleep? Either way, you definitely will feel no pain, and I will be with you for the whole procedure."

"I want to be asleep! I don't want to watch anything." As comfortable as Bruce was with being in the hospital, there was no way he wanted to watch someone cut into him.

"Okay, fine. Then you will be asleep. Now I ask again, have you eaten anything since midnight?"

"No."

"And you have no known allergies to any medication?"

"No allergies."

"And you are not taking any drugs, prescribed or otherwise?"

"No drugs."

"Excellent. Now I will start an IV and get you down to the operating room. I've been told Dr. Mason is nearly ready for you. Do you have any questions for me?"

"I can't think of any," Bruce said. For the first time, a slight shiver of fear raised a few hackles on the back of his neck. The reality of what he was facing was finally sinking in: He was in the hands of the surgical team and no longer in control of his life.

Dr. London started the intravenous line with such skill and rapidity that Bruce was surprised when it was done. As comfortable as he was with the hospital environment, he fully admitted he never liked venipuncture and always turned his head to the side. "Wow!" he commented. "I hardly felt that. I guess you have started a few IVs."

"A few," Ava said. She knew she was good at it, just like she knew she was good at anesthesia in general. She was also sensitive to her patients' mental state and detected a slight shift in Bruce's demeanor. "How do you feel? Are you anxious?"

"A bit nervous," Bruce admitted. His voice, which had been strong and self-assured, now wavered slightly.

"I can give you something to calm you down if you would like," Ava said, hearing the hint of anxiety.

"I would like," Bruce said without hesitation.

With a syringe and a medication vial she had in her pocket for this very reason, she quickly gave Bruce four milligrams of her favorite pre-medication drug, midazolam. Then she disposed of the paraphernalia she'd used to get the IV going, released the brake on Bruce's gurney, and without waiting for an orderly, pushed Bruce out into the main room, heading for the OR suite.

"I can feel that medication already," Bruce admitted as he watched the recessed ceiling lights pass overhead. The fear he'd had moments earlier had miraculously already vanished. He felt the need to talk. "When do I get to see Dr. Mason?"

"Soon. I was told he is waiting on us, which is why I'm taking you down to your operating room myself without waiting for an orderly."

If someone had asked him, Bruce would have said he felt a little tipsy as he entered OR 8 and glanced around at the scene. Almost a year ago he'd had a tour of the new hybrid operating rooms when they had been completed, so he wasn't surprised by the exotic cream-colored booms hanging from the ceiling or the banks of video monitors or the window looking out at the central desk. As the gurney was guided alongside the operating table, he saw that the scrub nurse was already gowned and masked and busy arranging instruments. He didn't recognize her with so little of her face visible, but he did recognize the tall circulating nurse, Dawn Williams, who he knew drove a white Ford Fusion. She recognized Bruce in return.

"Welcome, Mr. Vincent," Dawn said cheerfully as she came around the end of the gurney to help Ava transfer Bruce onto the operating table. "We are going to take especially good care of you just like you do with all our cars." She let out a bit of muffled laughter.

"Thank you," Bruce said, as he put his legs over the side of the operating table to face the doughnut-shaped support for his head. His eyes scanned the room for Dr. Mason, but the surgeon was not there. "Where is Dr. Mason?"

"He will be here as soon as we let him know you are all ready for him," Dawn said.

"Is he still in on his first case?" Ava asked as she and Dawn helped position Bruce with his head in the support. It was a general rule that anesthesia was not started until the surgeon was physically present and part of what was called the "pre-op huddle," when the surgeon, the anesthesiologist or anesthetist, and the circulating nurse went over the case to make sure everyone was on the same page with all the details. Unfortunately, that was not always the situation with Dr. Mason and a few other members of the surgical hierarchy who were known to flaunt some of the rules in favor of maximizing their productivity. The problem was: They got away with it.

"Yes. Dr. Mason is still in OR fourteen," Dawn said, "but the OR supervisor said Mason wants us to go ahead and get Mr. Vincent ready for him."

"Okay," Ava said with resignation. She donned sterile gloves and began the prep of Bruce's lower back. She wasn't happy about starting the case before having laid eyes on Mason, and it wasn't the first time she'd been put in the same uncomfortable position with him. On five previous occasions, he had insisted she start anesthesia before he was even in sight, much less in the room. Ava liked to do things by the book, believing it was key to patient safety, and starting anesthesia before the surgeon was physically present was a definite violation of her sense of good medical practice.

If truth be told, Ava did not like working with the egotistical Dr. Mason. She was uncomfortable that he felt entitled to bend the rules due to his professed superstar status. Intuitively, she knew that if there was ever a problem on a case, he would not take responsibility and that she would undoubtedly have to bear the burden as the fledgling anesthesiologist. Yet as bad as this concern was, it was not the only reason she wasn't fond of working with him. She was one of the few single female anesthesiologists on staff and certainly the youngest, and Mason had come on to her on more than one occasion, just as he had done with some of the female anesthetists and OR nurses. He had even called her at home on several occasions, supposedly about discussing upcoming cases, and suggested he "pop" over since he was in the neighborhood, though Ava had always demurred. Although appalled at this behavior, Ava had not communicated her true feelings, as she was afraid to make an enemy of the man. Nor had she said anything to the chief of anesthesia, Dr. Madhu Kumar, who had hired her, since he, too, was in Dr. Mason's league as a titan in his field, and the two were close. It was Dr. Kumar who did the anesthesia for Dr. Mason's VIP patients from around the world, just as he was doing that day. Yet for Mason's less highfalutin patients who were below Dr. Kumar's interest, such as Bruce Vincent, Mason usually asked for Ava.

The first thing Ava did after the prep of Bruce's lumbar region was to raise a small wheal with local anesthetic at the site where she would place the spinal needle. After checking to make sure the stylet was properly seated, Ava skillfully pushed the spinal needle into Bruce's back. "You will feel a little pressure," she said to him. Within seconds she felt the first pop as the needle penetrated the ligamentum flavum, and a moment later the second pop when it went through the dural covering of the spinal canal. When she was certain as to the proper position of the needle, she introduced the spinal anesthetic bupivacaine. As usual for Ava, the procedure went entirely smoothly. A moment later, she and Dawn helped Bruce lie back down on the operating table.

"My legs don't feel any different," Bruce said. He was clearly worried that the anesthesia wasn't going to work on him.

"It takes a few minutes," Ava explained as she attached Bruce to all the monitoring devices she had at her disposal. When she was finished and everything was entirely normal, including the ECG, breathing rate, and level of anesthesia, she added a proper dose of propofol as a hypnotic. At exactly 9:58 A.M., Bruce Vincent lost consciousness and fell asleep. By reflex, Ava glanced again at the continuous recordings of Bruce's vital signs. Nothing had changed, and she began to relax. The beginning of a case was always the most anxiety-producing for her.

Over the next forty minutes, Ava found herself getting increasingly irritated. Despite repeated inquiries out to the OR desk as to Dr. Mason's ETA and multiple reassurances that his presence was imminent, he still hadn't appeared. As the time dragged on, Ava faulted herself for having started the spinal when she did. Although she was confident the dose she had given could last as much as two hours more, which was plenty of time for a simple hernia repair, she thought it was inconsiderate for the patient to be waiting for the surgeon, who should have been there from the beginning.

"Dawn!" Ava called out finally, her patience at an end. "Go out to the main desk and demand to know exactly what the hell is going on and when Dr. Mason is going to appear! Talk to Janet Spaulding directly. Let her know the patient's spinal has been in place for more than a half hour." Janet Spaulding was the supervisor of the OR and a force to be reckoned with. If anyone could get results, Janet could. She was a fixture in the OR and didn't take grief from anyone.

Ava exchanged an exasperated glance with Betsy Halloway, the scrub nurse, who had been standing motionless the entire time with her gloved hands clasped over her chest. She had the instruments laid out and covered with a sterile towel. She'd been ready for even longer than Ava had.

Ava scanned Bruce's data. Everything was normal, including his body temperature. Ava had Dawn put a warm blanket over him when it had become clear Mason was going to be delayed.

Dawn returned quickly. "Good news," she reported. "Wild Bill will be here momentarily. He is out of OR fourteen. There had been some sort of an unexpected congenital abnormality of the biliary tree in his first patient that required him to spend more time than he'd planned."

"Good Lord," Ava mumbled. She looked over her shoulder and through the window to see if Dr. Mason was at the scrub sink, but no one was there. "So where the hell is he?"

"He went into OR sixteen, where his second team is opening up his second pancreatic patient."

"Which means he is responsible for three patients under anesthesia," Ava said derisively.

"But Janet said he will be here in a second. She promised."

"Where is Dr. Kumar?"

"No idea. Probably going back and forth between the two rooms. He does that sometimes."

"Give me a break," Ava said to herself, thinking it was a good thing the general public didn't know this kind of thing went on in a major teaching hospital. Out of the corner of her eye she saw movement in the scrub room. Turning her head, she saw Dr. Mason putting on a surgical mask while talking and laughing with another younger man whom Ava did not recognize. Ava took a deep breath to calm herself.

Five minutes later Dr. Mason breezed into the room. "Hello, everybody," he said with alacrity. "I want you all to say hello to Dr. Sid Andrews. He is to be my new fellow starting July first, but he generously volunteered to come in today to give me a hand with this hernia repair. It has been a while since I've done a hernia, so I thought it couldn't hurt." He laughed as if he'd just said something absurd about him needing help.

Dr. Andrews had come in behind Dr. Mason, holding his hands up toward the ceiling in front of his chest as surgeons do after scrubbing. He waved to the group. He was a tall, slender man in his late twenties with a face as tan as Ava's. In just about every respect except height he was the antithesis of Dr. Mason, who was stocky and broad-necked, with heavy forearms and particularly large hands and thick fingers, appearing more like a construction worker than a renowned surgeon. He was also more than twice Andrew's age and sported a moderately protuberant belly.

"Sid is an Aussie," Dr. Mason continued as he allowed Betsy to help him on with his gloves. He glanced over to Ava. "Have you ever been Down Under, honey?"

"I have," Ava said. She bristled at being called "honey," as well as the possible double entendre. "Listen! The patient's spinal has been in for over an hour." She was hardly in the mood for off-color repartee, if that was what Mason was intending, or travel chitchat, if he wasn't.

"Ah, always business first," Dr. Mason said in a mildly mocking tone. "Sid, I want you to meet one of our best anesthesiologists here at the BMH and certainly the sexiest, even in her baggy scrubs." He laughed again while he intertwined his fingers to seat them fully into the gloves.

"Nice to meet you," Dr. Andrews said to Ava as Betsy helped him don his gloves.

"Can we get this case going?" Ava questioned.

"She's a pistol, Sid," Dr. Mason said, as if Ava couldn't hear. He stepped up to the right side of the operating table and watched while Bruce's inguinal area was prepped. Sid went to the left side of the table. A few minutes later, amid banter about the glories of the Great Barrier Reef, the two surgeons draped the patient. Ava took the edge of the drapes facing her and secured it over the anesthesia screen with hemostats, all the while ignoring Mason's repeated attempts to get her to join the conversation.

Once the case began with the skin incision, Ava recovered her composure enough to breathe a sigh of relief. She settled onto her anesthesia stool and checked the time. The spinal had been in place for an hour and twelve minutes. She was pleased the patient had not responded to the cutting, meaning the spinal was still totally adequate. She hoped the case would go quickly and without complication. Unfortunately, that was not to be.

The first hint of trouble was a sudden burst from Dr. Mason thirty minutes later. "Shit, shit, shit," he blurted in obvious exasperation. "I can't believe this." Although the two surgeons hadn't spoken about any technical problems, it was obvious they were struggling with something.

Ava stood up and looked down the length of the operating table. She couldn't see into the operating field from her vantage point but could appreciate that Dr. Mason was not happy about something.

"Try to free the damn bowel from your side," Dr. Mason said to Sid.

Ava watched as Sid leaned forward and put an index finger into the incision site. It was apparent he was working by feel.

"Is there a problem?" Ava asked.

"Obviously, there is a problem," Dr. Mason snapped, as if it were an inane question.

"I can't do it," Sid admitted, pulling his hand back.

"Okay, that's it," Dr. Mason said, throwing up his hands in disgust. "You try to do a favor for someone and they punch you in the gut."

Ava exchanged an eye roll with Betsy, as both knew what Mason was implying: Whatever problem had emerged, it was clearly the patient's fault.

"We're going to have to go into the abdomen," Mason said irritably to Ava. "So we are going to need some decent relaxation."

Suddenly the PA system came to life. "Dr. Mason, sorry to interrupt. This is Janet out at the main desk. Both chief surgical residents are requesting your presence in their respective rooms on your two pancreatic cases. What would you like me to tell them?"

"Jesus H. Christ!" Mason fumed to no one in particular. Then, glancing up at the speaker mounted high on the wall, he added; "Tell them to keep their damn fingers in the dike and I'll be in as soon as I can."

"Roger that," Janet Spaulding said.

"If you must go into the abdomen, we have to switch to general anesthesia," Ava said. In a way, she was relieved to switch, as she was becoming progressively worried the spinal might be wearing off. The patient was showing very slight signs that his anesthesia was getting light, with mild changes in his respiration. She gave Bruce another bolus of propofol and then carefully monitored his breathing rate and depth.

"Whatever," Mason said. "That's your problem. You're the anesthetist."

"Anesthesiologist," Ava corrected. In her value system, being called an anesthetist was as bad as being referred to as "honey." Anesthetists were nurses, and anesthesiologists were doctors, with a significant difference in training requirements. "What is the problem? Can you tell me?"

"The problem is we can't reduce this little pesky knuckle of bowel caught up in the hernia," Dr. Mason explained irritably. "So we have to go inside the abdomen. It must be freed up, and that's the only way to do it. Anyway, you probably should have used general anesthesia from the beginning, with the GI symptoms the patient has had."

"Your office specifically asked for spinal," Ava said to set the record straight as she began to get out everything she would need to switch to general inhalation anesthesia. Then, to start the process, she grabbed the black breathing mask that was always within reach and turned on the oxygen supply. Deftly she put the mask on Bruce's face. She wanted to hyperoxygenate the patient for at least five minutes before giving a muscle relaxant. She thought she would use succinylcholine as the paralyzing agent because of its rapid onset and reversal. Then, after the muscle relaxant had been given, she planned on using either an LMA, a laryngeal mask airway, or an endotracheal tube. As she was debating the pluses and minuses of these two methods of managing the patient's airway, her mind registered the last part of Mason's comment: the part about the patient's GI symptoms. She didn't remember any gastrointestinal symptoms in the chart, nor had the patient mentioned any. To be sure, she held the breathing mask with one hand and with the other opened the patient's chart to the history and physical. A quick glance confirmed her suspicions. She had remembered correctly. There was nothing about any gastrointestinal symptoms. Had there been, she might have felt general anesthesia would have been a better choice.

"There was no mention of any GI symptoms in the history and physical," Ava said, interrupting the surgeons' banter, which had now turned to the Australian Outback.

"There had to have been," Mason snapped. "It was the reason the surgery was recommended by the man's GP."

"I just checked the chart again," Ava said. "There is no mention of it in the H-and-P that came over from your office."

"What about the junior resident's note?" Mason asked. "Did you look at that, for chrissake?"

"There is no junior resident note," Ava said.

"Why the hell not?" Mason demanded. "There is always a junior resident's note."

"Not this time," Ava said. "The patient was late to Admitting. Your fellow had done the history and physical just a few days ago. I suppose they thought that was adequate in Admitting. Maybe Admitting was backed up. I don't know all the details except what the patient said. Your fellow also specifically told the patient he was going to get a spinal."

"Whatever," Mason said with a wave of his hand. "Let's not make this anesthesia transition your life's work, would you please! Do the switch so we can get this show on the road! As you heard from Ms. Spaulding, I'm needed elsewhere for a couple of real cases."

"Had you been part of the pre-op huddle, this could have been avoided," Ava said under her breath.

"Excuse me!" Mason thundered. "Are you lecturing me? Do you forget who I am?"

"I'm just making a comment," Ava said, trying to back off. "The purpose of the pre-op huddle is precisely to avoid situations like this."

"Really, now?" Mason questioned mockingly. "Thank you for telling me. I've always wondered what the reason was for those little gatherings, even though I was one of the originators of the idea way back when. But tell me! How long do we have to wait before we can get back to work here?"

"Another minute with the one hundred percent oxygen," Ava said, glad to change the subject. She was already deriding herself for provoking Mason. She wondered what she was thinking. She took a deep breath to clear her mind and switch her total attention to the problem at hand, particularly regarding the airway. With general anesthesia, the airway was the critical component. The laryngeal mask airway was easier and quicker but not as secure or safe. Responding to more of a gut feeling than anything else, she elected to go for the endotracheal tube with its added safety. Later, she would have reason to question why she came to this decision.

Still holding the face mask with one hand, Ava got out the appropriate-sized endotracheal tube, along with the laryngoscope she would use to place it. She tested the suction unit to be sure it was functioning in case it was needed. In the background the low-volume but ultra-high pitch of the oxygen oximeter alarm reassured her that the patient was fully oxygenated. She checked the time. Five minutes had passed. Luckily, Mason had already forgotten the little squabble about the pre-op huddle. He and his assistant were back to talking about scuba diving.

Quickly putting the breathing mask to the side, Ava gave a one-hundred-milligram bolus of succinylcholine intravenously. There was some minor fasciculation of Bruce's facial muscles, but nothing abnormal. Most important, the pulse and blood pressure stayed the same. After tilting the patient's head back, Ava inserted her right thumb into Bruce's mouth to lift his lower jaw as she slid the blade of the laryngoscope held in her left hand under and behind his tongue. Letting go with her right hand, she reached for the endotracheal tube.

Although Ava had used a laryngoscope and placed endotracheal tubes thousands of times, the process always put her on edge, giving her a rush and reminding her why she loved the process of anesthesia even though the vast majority of the time it was routine. The feeling reminded her of the one time she had been talked into skydiving. Her mind was sharp, her senses honed to a razor's edge, and she could feel her own elevated pulse in her temples. Although the patient was more than adequately oxygenated after the 100 percent oxygen, he was now not able to breathe due to his paralysis from the muscle relaxant, so time was of the essence. She had about six to eight minutes to commence breathing for him before the extra oxygen would be used up and he would begin to asphyxiate.

Deftly, Ava advanced the laryngoscope blade into the depression above Bruce's epiglottis and gently but firmly lifted the laryngoscope up toward the ceiling to pull his mandible and tongue forward. A moment later she was rewarded with a clear view of the man's vocal cords and the opening of his trachea. Without taking her eyes off the target, she had brought the endotracheal tube into view with her right hand with the intention of inserting its tip into the trachea when the view disappeared. To Ava's horror, the man's mouth had suddenly filled with fluid and a mixture of undigested food.

"My God!" Ava blurted as her heart leaped in her chest. The man had regurgitated an apparently full stomach, which wasn't supposed to happen, since he had been told not to eat or drink anything after midnight except possibly a bit of water. Obviously, he had ignored the warning and had consequently created an anesthetic emergency of the highest order. Although Ava had never experienced this complication of such a large amount of vomitus with a live patient, she had practiced innumerable times handling such a situation with a simulator and knew exactly what to do. First, she turned the man's face to the side to allow all that could to run out of his mouth while at the same time tilting the whole table to get his head lower than the rest of his body. Then she grabbed the suction device and rapidly sucked out the remainder of the vomitus from Bruce's pharynx. What worried her the most was how much had gone down the man's trachea.

"What the hell?" Mason questioned with alarm when the table unexpectedly tilted. He stepped around the ether screen, glaring at Ava. Dawn, the circulating nurse, leaped off her stool in the corner and came around to the other side.

Ava ignored both. She was too busy. Retrieving the laryngoscope and the endotracheal tube, she repeated the process she had done earlier and this time inserted the endotracheal tube. Once it was in and sealed, she used a narrow, flexible tip on the suction device and threaded it down the endotracheal tube and sucked out as much vomitus as possible, progressively advancing the suction tip deeper into the man's chest. It was at that point that the cardiac alarm went off. A glance at the ECG showed the heart had gone into fibrillation, meaning the heart was no longer pumping. An instant later the blood-pressure alarm went off, meaning the blood pressure was falling to zero. Then the pitch of the oximeter alarm began to decrease as the oxygen saturation fell.

"Call a code," Ava shouted to Dawn.

Betsy immediately spread a sterile towel over the open incision while Mason and Andrews yanked the drapes off the anesthesia screen and folded them down, exposing the man's thorax. While Andrew pushed Bruce's gown up around his neck, exposing his chest down to his belly button, Mason slapped him on the sternum with an open palm hard enough to jar the man's body. Everyone watched the ECG, hoping to see a normal rhythm, but there was no change. Ava continued to suck out vomitus from the man's trachea as far down as his bronchi. Mason hit Bruce's chest again, this time using the side of a closed fist. Still no change. Andrews leaned over the patient and began closed-chest cardiac massage.

The OR door burst open and in rushed several senior anesthesiology residents with a defibrillation machine. Ava yelled that the patient was in fibrillation. Dr. Mason and Dr. Andrews stepped away from the table as the two new arrivals went ahead and immediately shocked the patient. To everyone's relief, a normal sinus rhythm reinstituted itself immediately. The pitch of the oxygenation alarm began to rise, indicating an increase in blood oxygen. At the same time the blood-pressure alarm went silent, although the blood pressure rose to only 90 over 50.

Pleased at their success, Dr. David Wiley and Dr. Harry Chung pushed the defibrillator out of the way and joined Ava at the head of the table. As they watched the ECG to make sure the rhythm was stable, she told them what had happened: "Massive regurgitation and aspiration when I tried to intubate. Obviously, the patient had a full meal this morning despite denying having had anything by mouth. He flat out lied to me and the admitting nurse. As you can see in the suction bottle, I've sucked out over three hundred cc's of fluid and undigested food, including bits of bacon and other poorly chewed material." She pulled out the suction catheter and connected an ambu bag to the endotracheal tube. The ambu was attached to 100 percent oxygen. Immediately she began attempting to respire the patient by compressing and releasing the bag.

"Jesus," Dr. Mason complained. "This was supposed to be a simple hernia."

"Has it been about eight minutes since you gave the muscle relaxant?" Harry asked, looking at the anesthesia record and ignoring Dr. Mason.

"About that," Ava said. "I'm hoping we'll be okay in that regard. I gave him a full five minutes with pure O_2 before the succinylcholine."

"How does the resistance feel when you breath him?" David asked.

"Not good," Ava admitted. She was thinking about the raised resistance the moment David brought it up. It was subtle but definite. It was a sensitivity born of experience of breathing for thousands of patients under all sorts of circumstances. With the succinylcholine on board, there should have been very little resistance to expanding the lungs. "To be sure, you try, while I listen to his chest."

David took over the ambu bag while Ava used the stethoscope.

"Breath sounds are terrible bilaterally," Ava said.

"I agree there is too much resistance," David said. "The bronchi must be full of vomitus and seriously occluded. I don't think we have much choice. We are going to have to bronch him."

Suddenly the pitch of the oximeter alarm began to fall again, indicating that too little oxygen was getting into the blood with the bronchial blockage, despite David's efforts.

The door to the OR opened and in rushed Dr. Noah Rothauser, a senior surgical resident who was scheduled to be the super chief surgical resident come the first of July, less than a week away. He was tying a face mask over the top of his head. Practically everyone knew Noah. It was generally felt that he was the best surgical resident the BMH had ever produced. A few jealous colleagues wondered if he was too good, as he had consistently gotten the highest grades recorded on the biannual American Board of Surgery In-Service Exams. He was known to be a tireless worker, extraordinarily knowledgeable for a resident, decisive, and remarkably congenial for a surgeon. As was typical of his commitment, the moment he'd heard about the code while he was in the surgical lounge, he came running to see if he could lend a hand.

The scene that confronted Noah wasn't auspicious. The two surgeons were standing immobilized a step back from the table that was tilted in a head-down position. Their hands were clasped in front of their chests. The patient was supine, naked from his head to his umbilicus, with his hospital gown bunched up under his chin. His color was a disturbing shade of slate blue, and his chest didn't seem to be moving. Three anesthesiologists were grouped around the patient's head, and one of them was yelling for the circulating nurse to get a bronchoscope stat while trying to use an ambu bag.

"What's going on?" Noah asked urgently as Dawn rushed out the door for the bronchoscopy setup. Noah heard the pitch of the oximeter alarm falling, and then at that very moment he heard the blood-pressure alarm go off. By instinct honed from experience he knew that the situation was critical and the patient's life was hanging in the balance.

"We have one hell of an emergency," Ava blurted, confirming Noah's impression. "The patient aspirated a ton of gastric contents and arrested. His bronchi are seriously blocked. He's not getting enough oxygen and has already arrested once."

Noah's eyes darted from Ava and the other two anesthesiologists to Mason and Andrews and then down at the patient. The patient's color was getting worse by the second. "There's no time for bronchoscopy," Noah snapped. By reflex, his intuitive, can-do surgical personality hijacked his mind. Although he was a mere resident in the presence of a celebrated attending surgeon on a private case, he took control. The first order of business was to sound another alarm even before another cardiac arrest occurred, which he guessed was imminent. Turning and looking through the window toward the main desk and knowing that he could be heard if he made enough of a commotion, he shouted mayday three times followed by: "We need a cardiac surgeon, a perfusionist, and a thoracotomy setup immediately!" Then, with no hesitation whatsoever, he grabbed scissors directly off the sterile instrument tray with a bare hand and proceeded to cut through Bruce's gown that was bunched up around his neck. He threw the scissors to the side. "Heparinize the patient while there is still a heartbeat!" Noah shouted to the anesthesiologists. "We have to get him on cardiopulmonary bypass." Still without sterile gloves, as he didn't want to take the time to put them on, he proceeded to prep Bruce's chest with antiseptic, frantically sloshing the dark fluid over a wide area and onto the floor.

Ava and the two other anesthesiologists hesitated for a moment, then fell to work. It was clear to them that Noah was right. The only chance of saving the patient was to get him on the "pump." More than anything else, he needed oxygen, and he needed it now, since his oxygen saturation was below 40 percent and falling. The bronchoscopy would have to wait.

Moments later Dawn rushed back into the room along with another nurse carrying the thoracotomy setup and Peter Rangeley, a perfusionist, who would run the pump. Luckily, in this modern hybrid operating room, the equipment was readily available on one of the utility booms suspended from the ceiling. It was up to Peter Rangeley to prime the system with a crystalloid solution and be sure all the air was expunged from the arterial lines.

Once Noah had the thoracotomy setup available to him after it had been opened by Betsy, he wasted no time, even though a cardiac surgeon had yet to arrive. Still without gloves, Noah took a scalpel from Betsy and made a vertical incision down Bruce's sternum, cutting directly to the bone to save time. With the blood pressure as low as it was, there was little bleeding. Noah then took the pneumatic sternum saw and proceeded to cut through the sternum from top to bottom. Bits of tissue and blood spattered his chest. As he got close to finishing with the noisy saw, the cardiac alarm went off.

"He's in ventricular fibrillation," Ava shouted.

"The cardioplegia solution will take care of the fibrillation," Noah yelled back. "Since he is not breathing, we can't take the time to defibrillate." Then, as Noah put in the sternal retractor and began cranking its blades apart, he shouted up at the PA system: "Have you found us a cardiac surgeon?"

"I'm not sure he is completely heparinized with his heart fibrillating," Ava said.

"Dr. Stevens is on his way," a voice answered over the PA.

"Tell him not to bother scrubbing or it will be too late," Noah yelled back. "I'm in the thorax and looking at the heart." It had taken him less than two minutes to open the chest. The heart was quivering in uncoordinated fibrillation. "Get me some cold saline, Dawn! That might take care of the fibrillation until the pump is ready. How's the pump prep coming, Peter?" Noah reached into the chest with his bare hand and began giving open cardiac massage by alternately squeezing and releasing the slippery organ. He thought it was worth trying to take advantage of what oxygen might still be available in the blood. Brain cells were exquisitely sensitive to a lack of oxygen.

"I'm almost ready," Peter said. He and a colleague had been working furiously to prime and ready the heart lung machine. Both knew time was extremely critical, and they were trying to do in minutes what normally took an hour.

"You heard me about the heparin?" Ava asked.

"I did, but there's nothing we can do about it," Noah shot back. "We'll hope for the best."

Dawn reappeared with a liter-size bottle of cold, sterile saline. Noah advised her to go ahead and pour it over the heart while he was massaging. Gingerly, she started.

"More!" Noah urged. "The faster the heart cools, the sooner it will stop fibrillating."

Dawn poured faster. Pouring cold saline over an exposed heart was a new experience for her, even though she had been an OR nurse for almost twenty years.

"It's working," Noah said. He didn't have to look at the ECG. He could feel the fibrillation abate.

The door burst open and Dr. Adam Stevens, a cardiac surgeon, appeared. He stopped short, momentarily transfixed by the scene of a patient exposed to the waist with his chest flayed open while the circulating nurse was pouring fluid into the wound and a gloveless resident was massaging the heart. Betsy stepped off the stool she was standing on and held out a gown for Stevens, which he thrust his hands into while asking Noah for an explanation. Noah and Ava gave him a quick rundown as Betsy helped Stevens into sterile gloves.

"Okay," Stevens said. "Let's get him on the pump. Are you ready, Peter?"

"I think so," Peter responded.

"Thanks for coming in, Adam," Mason said. "I'm sorry Anesthesia has created this mess. Unfortunately, I am needed elsewhere; otherwise, I'd stay and help. Dr. Andrews is here and can lend a hand. Good luck!" With a final glare at Ava, he left the room. Only Andrews responded with a wave. Everyone else was too busy, but they had heard him.

"Hold up on the massage," Stevens said to Noah. "It's most likely futile, considering the oxygen saturation is so low. By the way: the cold saline was a good idea, not only to stop the fibrillation but also to wash out the wound. Now get a gown and some gloves on! I'll put out some sterile drapes."

A moment later, Noah was back at the opposite side of the table, joining Andrews. By then Stevens and Andrews had the two arterial cannulas, which included one for the heart, and one venous cannula in the operative field, and Stevens was beginning to implant them. He started with the arterial ones first. One went into the aorta, after which the aorta was clamped, and the second one went into the heart for the cardioplegia fluid that would keep the heart from beating and lower its need for oxygen. The final venous cannula went into the major vein leading into the heart. A few minutes later, when Bruce was fully on the heart lung machine, the blood oxygenation and blood pressure rose quickly. "I want him cooled to at least thirty-two degrees centigrade," Stevens told Peter. Peter responded that the patient would soon be at the target, as he was already at 35 degrees and the heart at 4 degrees.

"Let us know when we can bronchoscope him," Ava asked Stevens. By then the two anesthesiologists who'd brought in the cardiac defibrillator had left, convinced Ava had things as much under control as possible. In their place was a pulmonologist, or lung specialist, by the name of Dr. Carl White, who had come in to do the bronchoscopy and clean out the bronchial tubes.

"Go ahead and bronch him," Stevens said. "The sooner, the better. It's to his advantage to be on the pump as little as possible."

The bronchoscopy went well. It was quickly determined that both bronchi had been almost totally occluded with a bolus of undigested bread, which was easily removed under direct visualization. When the blockage was gone, Ava was able to inflate and deflate the lungs with ease. "We're good," she said. She was pleased. The vital signs were now stable, as was the level of acid in the blood, which she had corrected earlier. She had also typed and cross-matched a significant amount of blood, which was on hand if needed, but she doubted they would need it, as there had been very little blood loss.

The mood in the OR, which had been tense, relaxed as Stevens and Noah prepared to take Bruce off the heart-lung machine after being on it for only a little more than ten minutes. At that point Ava had the patient on the ventilator with 100 percent oxygen, and everything appeared excellent, including electrolytes, acid-base balance, and vital signs. The first order of business was to warm the heart and discontinue the solution that kept the heart from beating. This was done by allowing blood at normal body temperature to flow through the heart. Next Stevens gradually undid the clamp across the aorta, which increased the blood to the coronary arteries, helping to warm the heart. At this point, Stevens fully expected the heart to begin beating, as it did in most bypass cases. Unfortunately, it didn't happen. Undaunted, Stevens tried a series of shocks to the flaccid heart, but none worked. He then tried an internal pacemaker, but even that was unsuccessful.

"What do you think it is?" Noah questioned. He could sense Stevens's dismay.

"I don't know," Stevens said. "I've never had a heart that wouldn't even respond to a pacemaker after it was warmed up. It is not a good sign, to say the least."

"There was only a few minutes between the heparin being given and the heart going into fibrillation," Noah said. "So he might not have been completely anticoagulated. Could that be the problem?"

"I guess it is possible," Stevens said. Then, to Ava, he added, "Let's check the electrolytes again!" He was feeling a sense of mounting exasperation. He had tried all the tricks he knew, including having Ava give various heart stimulants and even lidocaine intravenously.

Ava drew another blood sample and sent it off.

"I don't like this," Stevens said after another ten minutes had passed. "I've got a bad feeling here. The heart has got to be in super-bad shape. How long did he fibrillate, Noah, when you were opening him up?"

"I believe just minutes. The cold saline stopped it almost immediately."

Stevens looked over at Ava. "How about the first episode of fibrillation: How long was that?"

"I'd guess two or three minutes," Ava said. "That was how long it took for the crash cart to get in here." She glanced down at the anesthesia record to be sure. "Actually, it was less than two minutes. It wasn't long, because the cardioversion occurred with the first shock."

"That's not a lot of time in both instances," Stevens said. "I'm at a loss. Somehow the heart had to have been significantly damaged not to even respond to a pacemaker. We are running out of options. Also, I've got to get going on my own case."

No one responded to Stevens's last comment. Everyone knew what he was implying: Maybe it was time to give up. The patient could not be kept on bypass continuously.

The PA system came to life. "I've got the electrolyte results," a female voice said. She then read them off. They were all relatively normal, without change from the first sample.

"Well, it's not the electrolytes," Stevens said. "All right. Time for a few more tries."

Over the next few hours Stevens retried all the tricks he knew. There was never the slightest response. "I have never had a post-bypass heart not respond to a pacemaker like this. We haven't gotten so much as a blip on the ECG."

"What about a transplant?" Noah suggested. "He's a relatively young and healthy guy. We could put him on extracorporeal membrane oxygenation to tide him over."

"ECMO is not for long-term care," Stevens said. "The reality is that there are three thousand people waiting for a heart on any given day. The average wait for a heart is four months. It varies according to blood type. What's his blood type, Ava?"

"B negative," Ava said.

"There you go," Stevens said. "That alone limits the chances of a decent match. Also, since this heroic effort was started without sterility, the chances are better than even he'd have a post-op infection. We've given it our best shot, but I'm afraid it is time to face the facts. Turn off the pump, Peter! We're done here."

Stevens stepped back from the table and snapped off his gloves and peeled off his surgical gown. "Thank you, everybody. It's been fun." He sighed in response to his own sarcasm, gave a little wave, and left the room.

For a moment, no one moved. The only sounds came from the pulse-oximeter alarm and the ventilator.

"Well, I guess that's it," Peter said. He turned off the heart-lung machine per Dr. Stevens's order and started to clean up.

Ava followed suit, switching off the ventilator and detaching the monitoring.

Noah stayed where he was, looking down at the flaccid heart that had failed everyone, but mostly the patient. Although he didn't question Stevens's decision that it was time to quit, Noah wished there had been something else to try in hopes of a different outcome for the patient's benefit and Noah's, too. Noah's intuition was telling him loud and clear that there was a very good chance this unfortunate case was going to be real trouble once he became the "super chief" surgical resident in less than a week. As super chief, it was going to fall to him to investigate and then present this death at the bimonthly Morbidity and Mortality Conference, where it was sure to become a hotly debated episode. From what Noah had already gleaned from Dr. London, there was clear fault on the part of the patient for failing to divulge having eaten a full breakfast despite orders not to do so, and for Dr. William Mason for failing to communicate key information, due at least partly to his running two other concurrent surgical cases.

From Noah's perspective, what made the situation so worrisome were two unfortunate realities. The first was that "Wild Bill" was known to be a remarkably narcissistic man, fiercely protective of his reputation, and notoriously vindictive. Dr. Mason wasn't going to be happy to have his role in this unfortunate case made public and would be looking for scapegoats, which might include Noah. Second, Dr. Mason was one of the few members of the surgical hierarchy who wasn't impressed with Noah, and Mason was the only one who overtly disliked him. Dr. Mason had said as much, and as an associate director of the surgical residency program had already tried to get Noah fired a year ago, after they'd had a serious run-in.

Noah glanced over at Dr. London. She returned his gaze. What he could see of her usually tanned face was pale; her eyes were wide and staring. To Noah, she looked as shell-shocked as he felt. Unexpected deaths were hard to bear, particularly when they involved a previously healthy individual undergoing simple elective surgery.

"I'm sorry," Noah said, unsure of what he was apologizing for but feeling the need to say something.

"It was a gallant effort," Dr. London said. "Thank you for trying. It is a tragedy that shouldn't have happened."

Noah nodded but didn't respond verbally. He then followed Stevens out of the operating room.

BOOK 1

1

The smartphone alarm went off at 4:45 A.M. in Noah Rothauser's small and sparse third-floor one-bedroom apartment on Revere Street in Boston's Beacon Hill neighborhood. As a surgical resident at the Boston Memorial Hospital, it was the time Noah had been waking up just about every day except Sunday for five years. In the winter, it was pitch black and cold, since the building's heat didn't kick on until seven. At least now, in the summer, it was a bit easier to climb out of the bed because it was light in the room and a pleasant temperature, thanks to a noisy air conditioner in one of the rear-facing windows.

Stretching his sleepy muscles, Noah padded into the tiny bathroom buck naked. There had been a time when he wore pajamas as he had done as a child. But the habit had been abandoned when he came to appreciate that pajamas were just another piece of apparel he had to launder, and he wasn't fond of taking the time to do laundry, as it required walking a block up the street to a Laundromat and then waiting around. It was the waiting he couldn't abide. As a totally dedicated surgical resident, Noah chose to have little time for anything else, even personal necessities.

He eyed himself in the mirror, recognizing that he looked a little worse

37

for wear. The evening before, he'd had a couple drinks, which was rare for him. He ran his fingers up the sides of his face to decide if he could get away without shaving until after his first surgical case. Often he shaved in the surgical locker room to allow him to get to the hospital that much earlier. But then he remembered today wasn't a usual day, so there was no reason to hurry. Not only was it Saturday, with its usually light surgery schedule, but it was also July 1, the first day of the hospital year, called the Change Day, meaning a whole new batch of residents were beginning their training and the existing residents were advancing up the training ladder to the next level. For fifth-year residents, also considered chief residents, it was a different story. They were finished their training and were off to begin the next stage of their respective careers—everybody except Noah. By a vote of the surgical faculty, Noah had been proud to be selected to do a final year as the super chief resident who would run the Boston Memorial Hospital surgical department on a daily basis like a traffic cop at a very busy intersection. In most other surgical residency programs, a super chief status rotated among the fifth-year chief residents. BMH was different. The super chief was an added year. With the help of a full-time residency program manager, Marjorie O'Connor, and two coordinators under her, it was now Noah's job to schedule all the residents' rotations in the various surgical specialties, their operating room responsibilities, their simulation center sessions, and their on-call duties. On top of that, he was responsible for work rounds, chief-of-service rounds, and all the various weekly, biweekly, and monthly conferences, meetings, and academic lectures that made up the academic part of the surgical department's program. As a kind of mother hen, he also had to make sure that all the residents were appropriately fulfilling their clinical responsibilities, dutifully attending all the teaching venues, and handling the pressures of the job.

Without the usual need to rush to the hospital, Noah opened the medicine cabinet over the sink and took out shaving cream and a razor. While he lathered his face, he found himself smiling. His new job sounded like an enormous amount of work and effort, especially since he would have his own patients and be doing his own surgery at the same time, but he knew he was going to love the year. The hospital was his world, his universe, and as super chief he was to be the alpha-male surgical resident. It was an honor and a privilege to have been selected for the position, especially since on its completion, he was assured by precedent that he would be offered a full-time faculty position. This was huge. For Noah, the opportunity to be a full-time attending surgeon at one of the world's premier academic medical centers associated with one of the world's premier universities was the pot of gold at the end of the rainbow. It had been his goal for as long as he could remember. Finally, all the work, effort, sacrifice, and struggles in college, medical school, and now as a resident were going to pay off.

With quick strokes of the razor Noah made short work of his overnight stubble, then climbed into the tiny shower. A moment later he was out and vigorously drying himself. There was no doubt that it was going to be a very busy year, but on the positive side he would not have any official night call, even though, knowing himself, he'd be spending most evenings in the hospital anyway. The difference was that he would be doing what he wanted to do with interesting cases that he'd get to choose. And equally important, he would not be bogged down with busy work, the typical bane of house officers or hospital residents, particularly surgical residents, since there was always some menial task that had to be done, such as changing a dressing, advancing a drain, or debriding a gangrenous wound. Noah would be able to designate others to do all that stuff. For him, the learning opportunities were going to be off the charts.

The only fly in the ointment, and it was a big fly and a nagging, persistent worry for Noah, was the responsibility he now had for the damn bimonthly surgical Morbidity and Mortality, or M&M, Conference. This conference was different from all the others, since Noah would not have the option of farming out any aspect of the responsibility to other residents. It was going to fall to him and him alone to investigate and then present all adverse-outcome cases, particularly those resulting in death.

Noah's fear of the M&M Conference was not some irrational concern. Since the conference was specifically about cases that didn't turn out well, often involving mistakes and individual shortcomings, blame and finger-pointing in an emotionally charged environment with dirty laundry hung out for everyone to see was the norm and not the exception. Considering the egotistical mind-set of many of the surgeons, the atmosphere could be explosive and a breeding ground for hard feelings, with the potential of creating enemies unless an underling scapegoat could be found. Noah had seen it happen over the last five years, and the scapegoat often was the messenger: the presenting super chief resident. Noah worried that the same could happen to him now that he was super chief, especially considering the Bruce Vincent fiasco. The case had trouble written all over it for many reasons, not least of which was that Noah had been involved. Although Noah had never second-guessed his decision to put the man on emergency bypass, he knew others might.

Adding to Noah's concern, the death of the popular parking czar had the entire medical center in an uproar and gossip was rife. Prior to the event, Noah hadn't even known the man, because Noah didn't have a car and never had any reason to visit any of the hospital's three garages. Noah walked to work, and when the weather was bad, he merely stayed in the on-call facilities, which were expansive and more inviting than his own apartment. He'd seen the kids' photos on the cafeteria bulletin board but had never known whose children they were. Yet now he knew and understood he had been in a distinct minority of not being a Bruce Vincent fan, all of which was going to make the M&M Conference a standing-room-only affair.

The main reason Noah was fearful was that the Vincent case involved Dr. Mason, who Noah knew to be egotistical, quick to export blame, and outspokenly critical of Noah. Over the previous year and a half, Noah had made an effort to stay out of the man's way as much as possible, yet now, with this next M&M coming in less than two weeks, they were on a definite collision course like a certain cruise ship and a giant wayward iceberg. Whatever Noah was going to find in his investigation of the case, he knew it was going to be a diplomatic nightmare. From the little the anesthesiologist had said at the time, it seemed to Noah that a considerable amount of responsibility had to be directed at Dr. Mason, who had been running two other concurrent surgeries. The concurrent-surgery issue alone was an emotionally charged hot-button issue within the department.

Noah ducked back into the bedroom and went to the bureau for underwear and socks. There were only three pieces of furniture in the room: the bureau, a queen-size bed, and a single bedside table that supported a lamp and a stack of medical journals. There were no pictures on the walls or any draperies over the two windows facing out into a rear courtyard. There were no rugs on the hardwood floor. If someone had asked Noah about the decor, he would have described it as spartan. But no one asked him. He didn't have visitors and wasn't there much himself, which was probably the reason he'd experienced a few break-ins since Leslie had left. At first such episodes had bothered him as a personal violation, but since he had almost nothing to lose, he came to accept it as part of city living with lots of impecunious students visiting the tenants above him. Mostly, however, he didn't want to take the time or effort of finding a new apartment. In lots of ways he didn't even consider it a home. It was more a place to crash a few times a week for five or six hours.

There had been a time several years ago when he'd felt differently, and the apartment had been warm and cozy with things such as throw rugs, framed prints of famous paintings on the wall, and curtains over the windows. There had also been a small writing desk covered with framed photos, and a second bedside table. But all that homey stuff had belonged to

Leslie Brooks, Noah's long-term girlfriend, who had come with Noah from New York to go to Harvard Business School after she graduated from Columbia in economics and he in medicine. She had lived with Noah until she finished her graduate degree two years ago, but after graduation had moved back to New York with all her stuff to a great job in finance.

Leslie's departure had taken Noah by surprise, until she'd explained that she had come to the realization over the three years that his professional commitment was such that there was little room for her. Most surgical residents got progressively more time with their families as they advanced up the residency ladder. Not so with Noah. Each year his hours got longer by choice. There had been no rancor on either of their parts when they went their separate ways, even though Noah had been initially crushed, as he had come to assume they would marry at some point. Yet he quickly realized that she was right and he had been selfish with his time and attention. At least until he finished his graduate training, which he thought of as a 24/7 activity, he was metaphorically married to medicine and had spent very little time in her company and in the apartment.

On occasion Noah missed Leslie and looked forward to their monthly FaceTime phone calls, which she made the effort to continue. Each considered the other to be a true friend. Noah was aware she was now engaged, which tugged at his heartstrings when he thought about it. At the same time, he was thankful that she had been forthright about her needs, and he was relieved that her contentment was no longer his responsibility. At least until his residency was over, medicine was his overly demanding mistress. Ultimately, he truly wished the best for her.

From the closet Noah got a white shirt and a tie and went back into the bathroom to put them on. Once he was satisfied with the knot, which often took several attempts, he dealt with his rather thick, closely cropped dirty-blond hair by parting it on the left and brushing most of the rest to the right and off his face. Back when he had been a typical teenager, Noah had been vain and worried about his looks. He had spent a lot of time wanting to believe he was a stud, as a couple girls had referred to him. Although he wasn't exactly sure what they had meant, he had taken it as a great compliment. Now he was not concerned about his appearance other than to look appropriately doctorlike, which he interpreted as being reasonably manicured, with clean, pressed clothes. He despised those residents who thought it a badge of honor to wear wrinkled, bloodstained outfits, especially scrubs, to advertise how hard they were working.

Noah was a bit more than six feet in height and still appeared athletic, even though he'd not had time for athletics since he'd graduated from college. Still weighing in at 165 pounds, he had never gained weight like some of his high school friends, despite not getting much aerobic exercise. He attributed his good luck to rarely taking the time to eat and to having decent genes, thanks to his father, which might have been the only positive thing he got from him. In the looks category, what made him the proudest was his chiseled nose separating emerald-green eyes. The eyes were a gift from his redheaded mother.

The final act of dressing before heading off to the hospital involved his white pants and white jacket, both of which he was known to change several times in the same day, taking advantage that they were cleaned and pressed by the hospital laundry. When he was fully ready, with his computer tablet in his side pocket, he checked himself in the mirror that hung in the living room. The mirror had belonged to Leslie, and why she had left it she had never explained, nor had he asked. Otherwise, the living room was almost as stark as the bedroom. The furniture consisted of a small threadbare couch, a coffee table, a floor lamp, a folding card table with two folding chairs, and a small bookcase. An elderly laptop sat on the card table as the sole remnant of his teenage love of computer gaming. The only wall decorations in the room were a simple brick mantel painted white and the mirror. Like the bedroom windows, the living room windows were bare. They looked out onto Revere Street and the typical Beacon Hill brick buildings opposite.

When Noah exited his building, it was only a little after 5:00 A.M. On a normal day, when he didn't take the time to shave, he always left before 5:00, proof of the efficiency of his morning routine. This time of year, it was a pleasant temperature outside and nearly full daylight, although the sun itself had yet to rise. In the winter, it was another story, especially on snowy mornings. Yet he liked the walk in all seasons, as it gave him time to think and plan his day.

His usual route took him to the left, heading farther up Beacon Hill, which was a real hill and not just the name of the neighborhood. At Grove Street, he switched over to parallel Myrtle Street and continued climbing. As was fairly typical, Noah saw no other pedestrians until he crested the hill, at which time, as if by magic, people materialized, mostly dog walkers and joggers, although a few commuters appeared, too. As he passed the Myrtle Street playground, he was showered with the sounds of summer. Even though he was in the center of a major city, the bird population was considerable and the air was filled with chirps, trills, tweets, and warbles.

As he walked, Noah couldn't keep from fretting about the damn M&M. Why it bothered him so much was his abiding fear of authority figures such as principals, college or medical school deans, influential teachers, and powerful surgical faculty members. In short, it was anyone who had the power to derail his strong urge to be a consummate academic surgeon. He'd always known it wasn't a totally rational phobia, since he had been a top student from eighth grade on, but such an understanding didn't reduce his anxiety. He'd had a fear of authority figures throughout his schooling, but it had ratcheted up in both college and medical school and had even gotten worse during his residency, especially after it had been hugely reawakened when he had been blindsided during his second year.

The unexpected irony for Noah was that his total 110 percent commitment to his surgical residency had not been without problems above and beyond the social sacrifices in relation to Leslie. With a certain amount of dismay, after his first year as a resident he came to realize that there were attendings who thought of him as overzealous, particularly the more openly narcissistic surgeons, such as Dr. William Mason. The super chief at the time, Dan Workman, took Noah aside to explain that it might be better for Noah to rein himself in to a degree. Without naming specific people, he said that there were faculty who thought of Noah as a little too good, too ambitious, and getting far too much acclaim and needing to be humbled.

Noah had been shocked until he came to understand where the animosity was coming from. As a first-year resident, Noah had started interfering with a certain surgeon's private cases because of his attention to detail. By his thoroughness, he had the uncanny ability to discover additional problems when he did routine admitting history and physicals. These discoveries not only got a number of cases canceled but also suggested that the original workup had been incomplete or sloppy, a fact that certain attendings were not happy to learn and had advertised. In many ways, it was yet another example of blaming the messenger.

At first Noah had just dismissed the problem, since he felt confident he was putting patients' needs first, which a doctor is supposed to do. If anything, the criticism spurred him to even greater efforts until he was taken down a peg. With his degree of commitment to excellence and patient care as evidenced by his effort and thoroughness doing routine admitting histories and physicals, Noah spent way too much time in the hospital. He was always there, always available, even when he wasn't on call. Whenever a fellow resident asked him to cover, he always agreed. He didn't even take a day off until literally ordered to do so by the super chief.

Noah knew full well his behavior was in constant violation of the work limits imposed by the Accreditation Council for Graduate Medical Education, known as ACGME, yet he felt the rationalization for the limitations in terms of patient safety did not apply to him. He needed little sleep, rarely felt tired, and, in contrast to more than half the other residents, wasn't married and didn't have children. At the time, he thought Leslie understood and was supportive.

Eventually someone brought Noah's work ethic to the attention of Dr. Edward Cantor, the surgical residency program director. The result was a personal warning, which had a mild effect on Noah for a few days before he switched back to his usual schedule. Then, as Noah would say, the shit hit the fan. On two occasions, he was hauled before the Residency Advisory Board, which was particularly embarrassing since he sat on the board, as voted by his fellow residents, and hence had to recuse himself. On the first occasion, he got another warning and was told that his behavior would put the hospital's total graduate medical education program in jeopardy if the media were to get wind of it.

For a few weeks Noah tried to restrain himself, but it was difficult. For him, being in the hospital was like an addiction. He couldn't stay away. Three weeks later, Noah was back in front of the Residency Advisory Board, whose faculty members were furious. To Noah's absolute horror, on this occasion he was threatened with dismissal and told that from then on he was on probation such that a third violation would result in his walking papers.

Noah had indeed been taken down a notch. From then on he proceeded with extreme care and devised all sorts of inventive strategies, such as signing out from the hospital and leaving from one door only to enter another. Luckily, as time passed, the threat of dismissal lessened. By the time he finished his third year, he began to ease up on all his machinations of eluding attention because senior residents were not followed as closely as junior residents. As for a vacation, he hadn't taken one and no one seemed to have noticed.

Now it was 5:26 A.M. when Noah entered through the main entrance of the Stanhope Pavilion. As he always did, he felt a shiver of excitement just coming through the door. Every day was a new experience; every day he saw something he'd never seen before; every day he learned something novel that would make him a better doctor. For Noah, arriving at the hospital was like coming home.

2

The very first thing that Noah did every morning after coming through the revolving door was board one of the elevators and head up to the surgical intensive-care unit located on Stanhope 4, the same floor with the operating rooms. Visiting the SICU was always number one on his agenda, whether he slept at home or in the surgical on-call facility, which was also on Stanhope 4. For obvious reasons, the patients in the intensive-care unit were the hospital's sickest and most needy.

Like the Stanhope operating rooms, the intensive-care unit cubicles were arranged in a circle, defined by glass partitions, with a central desk from which the nursing supervisor could see into each cubicle by merely turning her head. The night shift supervisor was Carol Jensen, a certified critical-care nurse. She was no-nonsense like all the other supervisors, particularly when she was tired, and toward the end of a shift intensive-care nurses were always tired. It was one of the most demanding jobs in the entire hospital.

"You are a ray of sunshine, Dr. Rothauser," Carol said as Noah came in behind the counter. The central desk, like the room, was circular.

"It is always nice to be appreciated," Noah responded cheerfully. He took a seat in one of the swivel desk chairs. He understood what Carol mostly meant by her flattering metaphor: namely, that his arrival augured the ending of her shift and she would soon be on her way home. At the same time, he took it as a compliment. Noah had been told on more than one occasion, and even by Carol herself, that he was one of the nursing staff's favorite residents. She'd explained that everyone appreciated that he was always available at a moment's notice and was always cheerful, no matter the time of day or night, in contrast with other house staff who could be downright surly if they were exhausted, which they often were when on call at night. Even when Noah was in surgery, he'd made it known he didn't mind talking over the intercom for an emergency consult on a patient. For nurses, particularly critical-care nurses like Carol, doctors being reachable was enormously important because problems could arise quickly and critical decisions had to be made or patients suffered. But what Carol didn't say and what Noah was blissfully unaware of was that most of the other female nurses thought Noah was a bit of a mystery. As one of the more attractive, unattached male residents, he never gave even the slightest sexual spark or engaged in double-entendre wordplay, which was otherwise relatively rife within the hospital culture.

Noah's eyes roamed around the unit. He saw that each cubicle had a nurse, some more than one, and all were busy. The patients were all totally bedridden, many with respirators as the only sign of life. For Noah, the fact that there were no doctors present was revealing and reassuring. "Looks like you have things wonderfully under control," he said. The other reason nurses liked Noah was because he was appreciative of their role and the work they did. Noah often asserted that the nurses did nine-tenths of the work in the hospital and that residents were there merely to help.

"It has been a better night than usual," Carol said.

"Any problems that I should know about?" Noah asked. He redirected his attention to the unit supervisor. He was surprised that she was staring at him.

"I don't think so," Carol said. "Let me ask you a question: How is it your white coat always looks so clean and pressed?"

"I change it often," Noah said with a laugh.

"Why, exactly?"

"I think patients appreciate it. I know I would if I were a patient."

"Curious," Carol said. She shrugged. "Maybe you are right."

"You'll be getting several new surgical residents today," Noah said.

"Don't remind me."

For nurses, July 1 was often a difficult time, especially in intensive-care units, where there was a steep learning curve for first-year residents. For a week or two the critical-care nurses joked that they had to direct almost the same amount of attention to the residents as they did to the patients to make sure the residents didn't do anything untoward.

"Let me know if there are any problems," Noah said.

Carol merely laughed. There would be problems. There always were.

"I mean any problems above and beyond the usual," Noah added.

In the unit, Noah had two of his own patients whom he had operated on, both disaster cases that had had surgery at community hospitals and that had to be redone. Both patients had been airlifted in dire straits into the BMH and were now on respirators. Noah spoke with the nurses taking care of each one, checked the patients themselves briefly, particularly their sutured incisions and their drains, and then glanced at their SICU charts that hung off the ends of their gurneylike beds. Noah did all this in minutes but with attention to detail to be sure he wasn't missing anything. While he was in the second cubicle, residents assigned to the SICU began arriving; their faces reflected their fatigue.

In terms of residents, the SICU was a kind of miniature United Nations. Critical Care had evolved into a specialty of its own, with its own residency program. At the same time, it was felt appropriate to continue to rotate junior surgical residents through the unit to gain the experience that it could provide. It was the same with anesthesia. What this meant for Noah was that a certain amount of diplomacy was necessary, as he technically did not have power over critical-care residents or anesthesia residents.

Lorraine Stetson and Dorothy Klim were the two surgical residents who had been assigned to the ICU for the previous month, and seeing Noah, they immediately came in to join him. Although the number of female surgical residents had climbed dramatically over the last ten years, it was rare for both ICU surgical residents on the same rotation to be female. Lorraine was a first-year resident who had miraculously transformed overnight into a second-year junior resident, thanks to it being July 1. Likewise, Dorothy was now a third-year senior resident. Noah got along well with both women, although Dorothy often made him feel uncomfortable. He didn't know exactly why but assumed it had something to do with her appearance. In his mind, she looked more like a movie actress playing a role than a real surgical resident, even though he admitted such a thought was sexist.

"I'm sorry we were not here when you came in," Dorothy said.

"Why?" Noah said. "Everything is copacetic here, and SICU rounds don't start until six."

"Still, I think we should have been available when you arrived."

"No problem. It doesn't matter. What matters is that you will be passing the baton to a brand-new first-year resident by the name of Lynn Pierce. Also to Ted Aronson, whom you obviously know. I want you to let me know if there are any problems whatsoever, particularly with Miss Pierce." For first-year residents, starting off in the ICU before getting their feet wet in the program was often stressful for everyone.

"We met Lynn Pierce last night at the Change Party," Lorraine said. "I think it is going to be fine. She's actually excited about being thrown into the deep end of the pool. Those were her exact words. She thinks she lucked out."

The famed Change Party was a yearly surgical department event held at the nearby Boston Marriott Long Wharf hotel on the evening of June 30, no matter what day of the week it occurred. The party's main purpose was to send off the fifth-year residents with a fun-filled event that included a number of irreverent homemade videos, generally mocking the attending staff of BMH but in actuality celebrating them and the institution. As a command performance, Noah had attended the celebration, as he had previous Change Parties, but such gatherings weren't his cup of tea. To be sociable and try to relax, he'd had several drinks, which had made him feel less than top-notch this morning.

Although the Change Party was to acknowledge the residents who were leaving, it was also secondarily an opportunity to welcome the twenty-four first-year residents who were about to join the BMH family. Only eight of the twenty-four were categorical residents, meaning they were expected to stay for all five years of surgical training. The other sixteen were planning on finishing only a year or two of surgical training before going on to various surgical subspecialties, such as orthopedics or neurosurgery.

During the course of the evening and despite generally feeling like a fish out of water, as he always did in large social situations, Noah tried to introduce himself to a few of the incoming surgical residents, a couple of whom he had met when they had come for their interviews before being accepted. One of them was Lynn Pierce, and he had been impressed with her, although she'd had a similar effect on him as Dorothy, making him wonder if physical attractiveness was now a criterion for the program.

"Are you going to stay for SICU rounds?" Dorothy asked.

"No," Noah said. "Seems there is no need, and I have a lot on my plate before the welcoming ceremony this morning. And you guys are planning on attending, right? Remember, everyone is expected to show up."

"We wouldn't miss it for the world," Dorothy said with a smile. "That is, unless the roof falls in here in the SICU."

"Don't count on it," Noah said. "Be there!"

The welcoming ceremony was as preordained as the Change Party but a lot less fun. It was supposed to welcome the first-year residents, but Noah saw it more as an opportunity for the departmental bigwigs to hear themselves bloviate. Over the years he had come to understand that there was always a lot of posturing and jockeying going on in the front office of top academic surgical programs, and the surgery department at the BMH was no exception. Competition was the name of the game in medical academia, particularly in the surgical arena, and it never stopped. Luckily, Noah considered himself good at it.

As had been the case for the last four welcoming ceremonies he had attended, Noah was not looking forward to it. The first one had been different because he had been eager to start his residency. He had been so eager that he had found most of that June five years ago to be almost intolerable. The days had seemed to drag by from medical school graduation until July 1, despite his having been busy finding the Revere Street apartment and setting it up with Leslie.

From Noah's perspective, this year's welcoming ceremony was going to be more trying than usual. He was not going to be allowed to sit passively and persevere as he had the previous four years. As the new super chief resident, he was going to be asked by Dr. Carmen Hernandez, the chief of surgery, to say a few words. Unfortunately, this wouldn't happen until after the chief and then Dr. Edward Cantor, the surgical residency program director, had exhausted everyone with long, boring speeches about the history and importance of general surgery and the BMH in the development of modern medicine. Noah knew that by the time he was introduced, the audience would be close to comatose.

Of course, Noah understood it made sense for him to address the group, since he was the new residents' day-to-day boss. The structure of the surgical residency program was as simple as it was medieval. The first-year residents were the serfs, or, according to in-house parlance, the "grunts," Noah their liege lord, Hernandez the king. Each year the residents ascended the rigid ladder, with increased perks and responsibilities.

Noah had never been fond of public speaking, particularly in a formal setting. He was fine if not brilliant in informal settings, such as on surgical rounds, considering his command of the medical literature to back up any point he was trying to make. The reason public speaking bothered him stemmed from his competitive quest for academic excellence, which he thought was put at risk in such a circumstance. He always had the fear that his mind might go temporarily blank or he'd inadvertently say something outlandish. It wasn't necessarily a rational fear but real nonetheless, similar to his fear of social engagements like the Change Party. To make matters worse, he had been so busy preparing to assume the role of super chief that he hadn't planned his remarks. He was going to have to improvise, which only increased the likelihood he'd say something inappropriate in front of the surgical hierarchy.

Leaving the SICU well before 6:00 A.M., Noah took an elevator up to general surgery on the eighth floor. Work rounds with junior and senior residents weren't scheduled until 6:30, giving Noah time to check in with the night-call senior resident, Bert Shriver, a solid, dependable resident. Like everyone else, Bert had risen in stature overnight, if only in name. He was now a fifth-year chief resident. He gave Noah a quick rundown of the night. There had been two surgeries, both appendectomies that had come in through the ER, and the patients were doing fine. With all the surgical inpatients, there had been no problems whatsoever. There had been one consult from the internal medicine floor to do a cut-down on a patient who needed an IV but had no superficial veins.

"You'll be at the welcoming ceremony, right?" Noah asked. As the new super chief, he was now responsible for no-shows.

"Wouldn't miss it for all the tea in China," Bert said with a grin. "Can't wait to hear whatever pearls you have conjured up."

Noah gave him the finger and an exaggerated dirty look.

Still with time to spare before general work rounds would begin, Noah used the phone in the nurses' station to call the OR to see if anything had been scheduled behind his back. He had checked the evening before, prior to the Change Party, and had been told no surgeries would be scheduled until 10:30 A.M. His concern was that if surgeries had been scheduled overnight, which needed resident helping hands, it would be up to him to supply them. He was happy to learn that no cases had been added. For once, word had apparently gotten out so that the entire surgical department knew about the welcoming ceremony. Noah was pleased on one hand and a bit more nervous on the other. The implication that the ceremony might be even better attended than usual added to his anxiety about speaking.

Noah next went around to check in on his three private patients whom he had operated on. He thought it important for him to visit each at least twice a day to have direct, personal, face-to-face contact. Though he would see them again on work rounds, that was different, as it would be with the whole resident team. Noah had never been a patient himself, but he was sure that if he were, he'd want to have a few private moments with his doctor every day. His attitude about the importance of communication was one of the many reasons he was so popular.

Two of the three patients were still asleep when Noah entered their rooms, and Noah had to wake them up. During his first couple years as a surgical resident, Noah would not wake patients, thinking he was doing them a favor by letting them sleep. A dressing-down by a patient made him change his mind. Patients truly valued the personal, one-on-one time.

All three patients were doing fine, with one scheduled for discharge that afternoon. Noah spent a little more time with him to let him know what he could and could not do. He also assured him that he would see Noah and not another resident in the clinic for follow-up. The man had been a patient of the BMH for years and knew the ropes. Sometimes when residents rotated onto different services they didn't get to follow patients they had taken care of on previous rotations. Noah had always made sure that didn't happen to him. It was one of the benefits of the sheer number of hours Noah spent in the hospital, which married residents with families simply couldn't do. Noah was never bothered by this added effort; in fact, he thought the opportunity gave him a leg up.

Work rounds went especially smoothly for a number of reasons, primarily because there were no problem cases that needed extended discussion as to future course of action. Another reason was that it was Saturday, when it was rare for attending surgeons to show up and try to turn work rounds into a variation of chief-of-service rounds, whose goal was teaching or at least pontificating. Work rounds, by definition, were a time to merely review the chief complaint, what had been done so far, and what was going to be done that day or in the near future, and then move on to the next patient.

The final reason the work rounds proceeded apace that morning was that the junior residents who did the actual presenting were now all second-year residents and knew the ropes. Presenting cases was a learned skill, which all had mastered, except for Mark Donaldson, who was obviously either not prepared or, worse yet, had somehow failed over the year to grasp an appropriate sense of what was important and what was not. Noah spared him the embarrassment of calling him out on the spot, which had been a typical pedagogical surgical-rounds teaching method honed by some attendings to the level of torture. Noah had hated it when he was a junior resident, even though it had rarely been directed at him. Nonetheless, Noah had vowed never to do it as he rose up the ladder. With the belief that persuasion was a far better teaching method than ridicule, he planned to take Mark aside at some appropriate time, probably later that day, and have a heart-to-heart discussion.

Since it was Saturday and there were to be no chief-of-service rounds, Noah had a bit of free time. The welcoming ceremony wouldn't commence until 8:30 and it was now 7:00. After reminding all the other residents about attending the welcoming ceremony and after entering his progress notes on his three patients in the electronic medical record, or EMR, Noah took the elevator down to administration on the third floor.

In sharp contrast with the rest of the hospital, which operated on a 24/7 basis, the administration area was all but deserted on a Saturday morning.

Noah's destination was the surgical residency program office, which was at the far end of a carpeted hall where all the graduate medical education offices of the various specialties were located. When he got to his office door he fished out the lone key he had in his pocket. It had been dutifully handed over to him a few days ago by Dr. Claire Thomas, the outgoing super chief responsible for shattering a few significant glass ceilings. She had been the first African American woman to be the BMH surgical super chief and was, as of that very day, the first African American woman on the BMH surgical faculty. Noah knew she was going to be a hard act to follow, as everyone liked and respected her, including Dr. Mason. She had never been chastised in front of the Residency Advisory Board by the program director, Dr. Cantor.

Using the key, Noah opened the door. He stepped over the threshold and closed the door behind him. For a moment, he just stood there and surveyed the room. There were five desks. One was for Marjorie O'Conner, the surgical residency program manager. She ran the show from a bureaucratic standpoint. Another smaller desk was for the coordinator, Shirley Berensen. Her area of concentration dealt with managing the complicated evaluation requirements to make sure the program retained its accreditation and residents reached appropriate milestones. Another desk was for Candy Wong, also a coordinator, who oversaw the equally complicated issue of resident duty hours and the on-call schedule. Miss Wong had been the person whose attention Noah had spent so much effort avoiding after he had been threatened with dismissal for violating duty hours when he was a junior resident. For Noah, there was a certain irony that now he would be working closely with her.

There were two more desks, both smaller than the coordinators'. One was for the secretary, Gail Yeager, and the other for Noah. Looking at them, Noah had to smile. The irony here was that he and the secretary were probably going to be the busiest people in the surgical residency program and yet had the least impressive real estate. But the worst part, from Noah's perspective, was not the size of his desk, which had no significance to him, but rather that his desk was completely out in the open, meaning there was no privacy whatsoever except after hours and on weekends. For something like the conversation he needed to have with Mark Donaldson, the venue was completely inappropriate. For such situations, Noah was going to be forced to improvise.

Two days ago when Claire had given him the key to the surgical residency program door, Noah had brought in office supplies, along with a significant amount of paperwork, including his very initial ideas for the choices of faculty mentors for each of the new first-year residents. Every new resident was assigned a faculty mentor. Even though Noah had never utilized his mentor other than enjoying a few pleasant dinners at the man's home, he still thought the program had merit. There were always a couple of first-year residents who found adapting to the role of a surgical resident challenging. Being a resident was a world of difference from being a medical student.

Sitting down at the desk, Noah took advantage of the preternatural stillness of the deserted office. He got out the list of first-year residents and the list of faculty members who had volunteered to be part of the mentor program and went back to trying to match them. Quickly it became apparent that there was too much guesswork involved, because Noah knew very little about the new arrivals. The only thing he knew for certain was their genders and the medical schools they had attended. On the other hand, he knew the faculty members reasonably well, maybe too well in some instances.

When Noah had done what he could, he turned to managing and planning the plethora of meetings and conferences. Of particular concern was the weekly basic science lecture, since it was going to be the first conference under his tutelage and was fast approaching in less than a week. The basic science lecture was held every Friday at 7:30 A.M., and he had yet to decide on a subject for the first meeting, much less a lecturer. What he didn't admit was that he was avoiding even thinking about the even more worrisome and problematic M&M Conference.

Time went by quickly, and before Noah knew it, the alarm on his cell phone went off, shocking him back to reality. It was quarter past eight. He'd set the alarm in the rare eventuality he wasn't called, texted, or paged for some problem someplace in the hospital, which was what he fully expected. During the early morning, there was always something that happened that needed his attention. Certainly, had he stayed on the surgical floor, he would have been inundated. Taking full advantage of the peace and quiet, he'd made progress and had now outlined the first three basic science lectures and had emailed appropriate potential lecturers to ask if they would lend a hand.

After putting away his paperwork, Noah headed out the door. His destination was the Fagan Amphitheater in the Wilson Building, which was reached by a pedestrian bridge located on the second floor of the Stanhope.

3

"Thank you, and welcome to the best surgical residency program in the world," Dr. Edward Cantor said with a wry smile to acknowledge he might be exaggerating to a degree. He was a tall, slender, angular man, fit and assertively intelligent. He picked up his notes from the Fagan Amphitheater's lectern and sat down in the chair he had vacated twenty minutes earlier. It was one of five in the amphitheater's pit. The others were occupied by Dr. Carmen Hernandez, chief of surgery, and Dr. William Mason and Dr. Akira Hiroshi, both associate surgical residency program directors. The fifth chair was noticeably empty.

The welcoming ceremony had started precisely at 8:30 A.M. as scheduled. Noah had entered from the second floor prior to its commencement with several minutes to spare and looked down into the pit to see Dr. Hernandez waiting at the lectern for 8:30 to arrive. The chief was a compulsive man, especially about time. The room was built as a typical half-circle medical-school amphitheater, with tiers of seats rising from the half-circle pit or arena a full story below, making it look like an ancient Greek or Roman theater. The room was nearly full, with the twenty-four newly minted and obviously eager first-year residents sitting front and center in the first row. They all had on glaringly white, highly starched coats similar to Noah's. Over the whole scene was a surprisingly loud buzz of conversation as a testament to the room's fine acoustics.

As Noah had begun to descend one of the amphitheater's two rather steep stairways that divided the seating into thirds, his arrival caught the attention of the chief of surgery, who waved up to him and gestured toward the only empty chair in the pit. Noah had quickly signaled that he preferred to sit in the audience. It had been a snap decision predicated on his seeing that the empty chair was next to Dr. Mason. As nervous as he was about speaking in front of the packed amphitheater, Noah had no interest in compounding his anxiety by having to relate to his least favorite attending, so he took an aisle seat in the twelfth row. The fact that the empty chair was also next to Cantor's also played a role. After the man had threatened to dismiss him for spending too much time in the hospital as a junior resident, Noah had never felt at ease in his presence.

The program progressed just as Noah had predicted. Dr. Hernandez carried on for almost a half-hour, letting Noah's mind wander to all his newly acquired responsibilities. Unable to avoid observing Mason down in the pit, wearing one of his typical expressions of disdainful disinterest when he was not the center of attention, Noah had found himself mostly worrying about the damn M&M Conference and how the hell he was going to navigate the minefield he knew it represented. He had successfully avoided thinking about it all morning, until Mason's presence made it impossible.

After the chief of surgery had spoken, the program director followed suit in an equally predictable fashion, enough to make Noah marvel that no one in the audience fell asleep. He could tell that Dr. Mason was not finding the program particularly stimulating, either, as he was constantly fidgeting in his seat and crossing and uncrossing his heavy legs.

The moment Dr. Cantor had taken his seat, Dr. Hernandez got up and returned to the lectern. After adjusting the microphone down to accommodate his height, he cleared his throat and said: "Now I want to intro-

duce to you our brand-new super chief resident, Dr. Noah Rothauser."
With that he gestured up toward Noah.

As Noah got to his feet and began descending the steep stairs that lead
down into the pit, he could feel the hairs on the back of his neck stand up,
as well as his pulse begin to hammer in his temples. There was a smattering of applause and a few teasing catcalls and some playful laughter in the
audience. Noah was popular not only with the nursing staff but also with
his fellow residents. One of the reasons was practical: If ever anyone
needed someone to cover for whatever reason, everyone knew Noah never
turned anyone down regardless of the hour or the day of the week.

Noah kept his eyes down and concentrated on avoiding a fall, as that
would be a scene he'd never live down. Not only were the amphitheater's
stairs abnormally steep, there was no handrail. Once in the pit, he walked
directly to the lectern, feeling himself blush. Dr. Hernandez had returned
to his seat.

After adjusting the microphone up, he still hunched over, then raised
his eyes to gaze directly at the twenty-four brand-new first-year residents.
He started to speak, but his voice came out in an otherworldly squeak,
making him clear his throat. When he began again, he sounded relatively
normal, at least to himself.

"I would like to add a welcome to you all," he said while he made eye
contact with each new resident in turn and gained confidence as he did
so. "I had planned on giving a long, detailed speech about the history of
surgery, but I believe that has been adequately covered by our own es-
teemed surgical professors, who are giants in their respective fields."
Noah briefly turned and nodded toward Hernandez and Cantor, both of
whom smiled contentedly as the audience tittered in relief. Noah avoided
looking at Drs. Mason and Hiroshi, although he had nothing against Hiroshi, with whom he never had much interaction.

"Instead I would just like to say you are about to begin the most exciting and demanding part of your extensive training, and leave it at that.

I would like to add that I wish I could say my office door is always open for whatever reason you might have to pay me a visit, but unfortunately, I do not have an office."

A few chuckles rapidly grew to a round of real laughter as a reaction to the pomposity of the previous speeches. Noah found himself smiling, too, although he worried that his off-the-cuff attempt at humor might offend Dr. Hernandez. A quick glance reassured him when he saw the chief was at least smiling.

"Office or not," Noah continued, "I will always be available for whatever reason. Don't be shy! I'm easy to find. Surgery here at the BMH is a team effort, and we expect everyone to be a team player. You all got your initial rotation assignments, so after the coffee and doughnuts served next door in the Broomfield Hall, we are off to the races. Thank you! And let's have a fabulous year."

Noah turned and faced Dr. Hernandez, who had risen to his feet. He was a square-built man, in some ways similar to Dr. Mason but a smaller version, with darker, thicker hair, an olive complexion, and a heavy mustache. In contrast to Dr. Mason's bluster, he exuded an air of quiet confidence, which he maintained no matter the challenge in either the operating room or the boardroom. "I hope you didn't take my attempt at humor as a complaint," Noah said.

"Not at all," Dr. Hernandez said. "It was unexpected, which made it funny. But you do have an office . . ."

"I have a desk," Noah corrected. "Not an office."

"I see," Dr. Hernandez said, before his attention was hijacked by an attending surgeon who pulled him aside for a quick consult.

Noah noticed several of the new residents, including Lynn Pierce, coming down into the pit and heading in his direction. He couldn't help but notice Lynn was wearing a very striking yellow summer dress under her white coat. With a minor wave of panic, Noah glanced back at the exit, but before he could beat a retreat, he felt a tap on his shoulder. He turned to face a nurse dressed in scrubs whom he had seen on occasion but with whom he had never spoken.

"Dr. Rothauser, I'm Helen Moran."

"Hello, Helen," Noah said.

"I don't want to take much of your time," Helen said. "I know you are busy, but I wanted to speak to you briefly about the Bruce Vincent case. I am one of the few people who didn't personally know him, but I participated in getting him admitted. Rumor has it that he was a victim of the concurrent-surgery process. Is that true?"

Taking a deep breath, Noah tried desperately to organize his thoughts and figure out what to say. In truth, he didn't want to say anything, as he had been trying to avoid even thinking about Bruce Vincent, but now, gazing into the indignant eyes of Helen Moran, that clearly wasn't an option. Obviously, he was already being drawn into the minefield he was dreading. There had even been a few unflattering articles about concurrent surgery in the lay press.

"I have yet to investigate the case," Noah said vaguely.

"I hope the case is going to be presented at next week's M&M Conference."

"I'm sure it will be," Noah said. "It was tragedy, which certainly needs to be aired to see if we can learn anything to keep it from happening again in the future."

"Didn't Dr. Mason have two other cases going at the exact same time? That's what I heard."

"I will be checking in on that for certain," Noah said.

"I hope you do. I happen to know that was the situation, and I personally think that concurrent surgery shouldn't be allowed here or anyplace. Plain and simple. Not in this day and age."

"I'm not fond of the practice myself," Noah said. "Now, if you can excuse me, I have to get over to Broomfield Hall."

While Noah had been briefly speaking with Helen Moran, the covey of first-year residents that he had seen approaching had grouped themselves around him. The moment he was free, a batch of simultaneous questions erupted about the on-call schedule. Jokingly, Noah held up his hands as if he needed to protect himself, then pointed toward the exit. "How about we all go next door and get some coffee? I promise I'll answer all your questions."

As Noah watched Helen recede in the direction of the door, there was another tap on his shoulder. This time it was significantly more forceful, causing Noah to have to take a step forward to maintain his balance. With a twinge of irritation, he spun around to complain, but then swallowed his words. He found himself facing Dr. Mason. The man's expression had changed from boredom to a scowl.

"I heard what you said to that woman," Mason growled. "Let me tell you, my friend! You'd better tread lightly about this Vincent case or you are going to be in big trouble." To emphasize his point, Mason stabbed Noah a number of times in the chest with one of his thick index fingers.

"Excuse me?" Noah managed. He'd heard Mason clearly but needed a moment to process what was obviously a threat.

"You heard me, you freaking Goody Two-Shoes. Don't you dare turn this Vincent disaster into a cause célèbre against concurrent surgery. If you do, you'll be messing with the most powerful surgeons here at the BMH who need double booking to meet demand of their services. You hear what I am saying? And let me remind you: The muckety-mucks in Admin feel the same, since we bring in the cold cash to run this place. You got it?"

"I hear you," Noah managed. He stared into Mason's unblinking black eyes. The man had his considerable chin tucked back like a boxer's. "I will investigate the case thoroughly and present the facts dispassionately. That's all."

"Bullshit, my friend. Don't take me for a fool! You can skew the facts whatever way you please. But I am warning you, Anesthesia screwed up, plain and simple, by giving the wrong anesthesia, compounded by the patient himself, which should have been discovered by Admitting. Keep it simple or, believe me, you are going to be looking for work."

"I will not skew the facts," Noah said, gaining a smidgen of confidence. He knew intuitively that Mason was in the wrong in trying to dictate the outcome of the M&M Conference. Yet as a realist, Noah also knew he was now deep into the proverbial minefield.

"Really?" Mason questioned superciliously. "Well, let me tell you a fact. Bruce Vincent was alive when you came flying in and sliced open his chest like the cavalry arriving at the last second. The only problem is you killed the patient. That is a fact."

Noah swallowed. His mouth had become dry. There was some truth to what Mason was saying, but had Noah not "sliced" into Vincent's chest, Vincent would have been dead in about three or four minutes. It had been a gamble, but a gamble that had not paid off. Still, someone could make the argument that Noah had been too rash, and that maybe the patient should have been merely defibrillated externally and bronchoscoped as an emergency.

"You'd better think about it long and hard!" Mason growled. He poked Noah a final time, hard enough to force Noah to take a step back. Then Mason turned on his heel and churned angrily through the crowded pit and out of the amphitheater like a speedboat in a packed harbor, leaving Noah in his turbulent wake.

4

A light rain was falling as the late-model black Ford van with its snub nose and rakish headlights pulled over to the curb on a dark residential street in Middletown, Connecticut. There was no lettering on the non-descript, workaday vehicle with Maryland tags. The headlights switched off, but the engine kept running to keep the air-conditioning functioning. There was only one pedestrian visible down near the end of the street, walking a small white dog. He quickly disappeared into one of the homes, leaving the street deserted. Lights were on in many of the modest two-story houses that lined both sides of the street, although mostly on the second floors. It was bedtime in most of the households.

There were two men in the van's front bucket seats, dressed in light-weight summer suits with black ties: George Marlowe's was dark gray; Keyon Dexter's was black. Both men were in their late thirties, athletic appearing, and were clean cut in a military fashion, with short hair and closely shaved faces. Both had been in the Marines and had been deployed to Iraq, where they had met in a special cyber unit. Keyon was African American, with medium dark skin; George was Caucasian and blond. They were staring out the windshield at a Craftsman-style house with tapered columns supporting a hip-roofed porch two houses down and across the street from where they were parked. Incandescent light spilled out of the first-floor windows, but the overhead porch light was off and the second floor was dark.

"Check and see if he is online now," Keyon said from the driver's seat. "And while you are at it, recheck the GPS coordinates. We wouldn't want to be arresting the wrong dude."

They both chuckled at such a suggestion as George opened his laptop, booted it up, and then let the fingers of both hands rapidly type on his keyboard. He was clearly adept at keying his laptop.

"He's online," George said presently. "Probably trolling and causing mischief as usual. And we've definitely got the right house." He closed the computer, reached around, and put the machine on one of the rear seats. The back of the van was filled with sophisticated electronic surveillance and computer equipment.

"So now we get to see the real Savageboy69," Keyon said.

"My guess is that we are not going to find a stud," George said. "Ten to one he's going to be a boring, colorless, middle-aged guy."

"You got that right," Keyon said. "I'd wager him being a real candy-ass despite his online persona." They both laughed again. They knew that in current lingo, *Savage boy* was the same as *Fuck boy* in the world's teenage smartphone "connected culture" and in rap lyrics. Neither man could define the term precisely, although both knew exactly what it meant, something like the way they thought about the concept of pornography, which they also struggled to define but felt they knew when they saw it.

"I'm hoping he's home alone," Keyon said. "That will make things a lot easier and cleaner."

They had already run the house through a number of databases to find out the current owner. It was Gary Sheffield, age forty-eight, who was divorced five years ago and worked for an insurance company as a statistician. He had no criminal record and no children.

"Are you ready?" George said.

"As ready as I'll ever be," Keyon said. He turned the van's ignition off. Suddenly there was the sound of crickets, particularly when they opened the van's doors. It was a warm summer night. The rain had stopped. From all directions came the hum of window air conditioners.

They walked quickly, but not too quickly, climbing the three steps of the house and positioning themselves on either side of the front door. They were professionals and had done this many times. George rang the bell, and the chimes could be heard through the door.

They waited. Just when George was about to ring the bell again, the overhead porch light came on. A moment later the door opened a crack and an eye peered out. "Can I help you?" Gary Sheffield said.

"I believe you can," Keyon said. "Are you Gary Sheffield?"

"I am," Gary said. "Who are you?"

"l am Special Agent Dexter of the FBI, and this is Special Agent Marlowe," Keyon said. He held up his badge so Gary could plainly see it. George did the same. "We need to talk to you for a few minutes."

The door opened fully. The blood had drained from Gary's face. "What do you need to talk about?"

"We are part of the Cyber Action Team of the FBI," Keyon said. "It has been brought to the Cyber Division's attention that there has been significant felonious online activity perpetrated from this location. It needs to be investigated."

"What kind of felonious activity?" Gary said in a hesitant, tremulous voice. He was, as his visitors assumed, of medium height, corpulent but not obese, with blotchy skin and thinning hair. He was not a stud.

"That is exactly what we have to talk to you about," Keyon continued. "Now, we can arrest you and take you to the FBI field office, or you can let us in and talk with us and perhaps clear up this problem. It's your choice, sir."

Gary backed away, still holding on to the front doorknob.

Keyon and George entered a small foyer. Gary closed the door. He was visibly trembling. "We can sit in the living room," he managed, gesturing to his left.

"We'll stand, you sit," George said, pointing toward the couch as all three entered the drab room. There was an open laptop on the coffee table displaying a dramatic photo of mountains as a screen saver. There was also an open bottle of beer.

Gary did as he was told. He reached out and shut the laptop.

"First off, I want to ask if you are alone in the house at the moment."

"Yes, I am alone," Gary said.

"Okay, good," George said. "Second, I'd like to ask if you are familiar with cybercrime punishment here in Connecticut?"

Gary shook his head. He visibly swallowed.

"It is considered a serious offense, punishable by up to twenty years in prison."

Gary stared back without blinking.

"Is there any other computer in this house," Keyon asked, "other than the laptop here on the coffee table, a desktop or another laptop?"

"No."

"Good," Keyon said. "Now, we may have to confiscate this machine because what we suspect is that it has been used for serious cyberstalking, harassment, and threats to a thirteen-year-old girl by the name of Teresa Puksar. Does that name mean anything to you?"

"I suppose," Gary said weakly.

George and Keyon exchanged a knowing glance.

"It seems that this online activity," Keyon continued, "has been carried out by an individual whose user name is Savageboy69 and whose Facebook profile is under the name of Marvin Hard. Are either of those names familiar to you?"

Gary visibly swallowed again. He nodded.

"Okay, very good," Keyon said. "We are making progress here. That's encouraging."

"So those are two of your online monikers?" George asked.

Gary nodded again.

"Do you use any other sock-puppet names?" George said.

"I used Barbara Easy for a while, but not for a long time."

"Interesting," George said with a wry smile. "A little gender role reversal. Very clever. Was it rewarding?"

Gary didn't answer.

"Let's get down to specifics," Keyon said. "As Marvin Hard you managed to get Teresa Puksar's IP address and then used it to get her real address. With that you threatened her with swatting if she didn't send you nude pictures. Is that an accurate description of your activities?"

"Should I be talking to a lawyer?" Gary asked hesitantly.

"That is your call, Mr. Sheffield," Keyon said. "But if you want to involve a lawyer at this early stage of our investigation, we will have to arrest you, confiscate this laptop, and take you to the FBI field office. Then, within twenty-four to forty-eight hours, you will be able to make a call to your attorney if you have one. Does this sound like the way you want to go? It's up to you."

"I don't know," Gary admitted. He felt like he was caught between a rock and a hard place.

"As I said at the door," Keyon said, "we would like to clear all this up and be on our way. Arresting you creates a ton of paperwork for us. We'd prefer to avoid it. We need to finish our investigation, make sure you understand the kind of risks you are assuming with your trolling behavior, and make sure you mend your ways. In your favor, you didn't try to meet up with this underage young lady. That's good. At the same time, threatening her is certainly against the law. Exactly what you were going to do with the nude photos is another issue entirely. Luckily, at this stage, we can ignore the child-pornography problem. But there are a few things we need to ask you."

"Like what?" Gary said.

"A key point," Keyon said. "Are you working with anyone else? Have you communicated to anyone anything at all that you have learned about Teresa Puksar in your ongoing chats and messaging with her? Anything in particular that she has revealed to you or you have learned?"

"No," Gary said. "What I do online is private. I don't share it with anyone."

"From some of your messages that I've read, I think that is a wise idea, Mr. Sheffield," Keyon said. "You presented yourself as a twenty-year-old college student to Miss Puksar, but to me you seemed even younger than she. Be that as it may, right now we are mainly interested in one particularly important question: Have you communicated to anyone Miss Puksar's physical address or her IP address? Now, don't answer immediately! I want you to think for a moment, because it is very important. Have you told anyone Miss Puksar's location or anything about where she lives?"

"I don't have to think about it," Gary said. "I haven't told anyone."

"Have you written Miss Puksar's address on any paper or transferred it to any storage device or put it into your contacts? Think, Mr. Sheffield!"

"It is just in this laptop," Gary said, pointing to the machine on the coffee table.

"How about your cell phone?" Keyon suggested.

"There's no address in my cell phone," Gary said. He was beginning to perk up, sensing he was pleasing his interrogators and that this scary episode was coming to an end.

"Show me!" Keyon said.

Gary straightened out his right leg and pulled his smartphone from his front pants pocket. He went into his contacts and pulled up Teresa Puksar. There was a phone number with a 617 area code. He showed the screen to Keyon, who nodded.

Keyon looked at George. There was a moment of nonverbal communication between them as they tried to decide if they were finished with the interview. Each nodded slightly, indicating that he was content, meaning that they had learned what they needed to know. Keyon used his right hand to form a make-believe gun with his index finger extended and thumb upright. He pointed it at George.

George took the hint, and in quick, smooth motion reached under the lapel of his jacket and pulled out a Smith & Wesson .38 Special revolver from a shoulder holster. A fraction of a second later the gun was pointing directly at Gary's forehead. The report was loud in the small room with its unadorned plaster walls and ceiling. The soft-nosed bullet hit Gary in the middle of his forehead, snapping his head back and spraying the wall behind the couch with blood and bits of brain.

With a wave of his hand to disburse the smell of cordite, George reached out and picked up the laptop and the smartphone. "Let's take some other crap besides his electronic gear to make it look like a robbery gone bad," he said.

"Right on," Keyon said as he pulled on a pair of gloves. He rolled the corpse to the side and got out the man's wallet. Then he pulled off Gary's Rolex.

5

Noah walked out of the operating room area by pushing through the double swinging doors and headed into the surgical lounge. He was feeling relatively chipper after having ducked into each OR to check on the residents to see firsthand how they were faring in their surgery assist roles, particularly the first-year residents. Although he was reasonably confident there were no problems, since there had been zero complaints from the attending surgeons or the OR nurses the entire first week, he liked to check himself just to be certain, since he had been the one doing the assignments. There was nothing quite like just wandering into an OR unannounced and listening to the unedited banter between the surgeon and the residents and sensing the atmosphere. A lot could be deduced, especially when it could be augmented by a quick corroborating chat with the circulating nurse. Although a few of the surgeons recognized him out of the corner of their eyes, most didn't. It was as if he was his own undercover agent.

In the surgical lounge Noah felt relaxed enough to grab a cup of coffee and stand by the window, gazing out at the busy Boston Harbor as he drank it. Although most of the activity on the water was commercial, there were a few pleasure boats with people enjoying the summer weather.

For a brief moment he fantasized what it was going to be like once he finished his long, grueling, and totally immersive training in less than a year and attained his long-sought-after goal. Although he loved his role as a surgical resident, he knew he'd been metaphorically imprisoned in the hospital for five years, a fact brought painfully home by Leslie's regrettable but understandable departure. Outside of the hospital he didn't have life, and he was in his mind becoming something of a social recluse. After all was said and done, would he be able to resurrect some normal social abilities and enjoy himself like those people out there boating in the sunshine, or was he destined to always be a medical workaholic? He had no idea. It was going to take a lot of effort and maybe a bit of luck. The hope was that he could somehow meet a woman who would not be challenged by his single-minded commitment to medicine.

Noah sighed and turned his back on the outdoor scene and gazed around at the people who populated his reality. With no surgery scheduled, he could take a moment for the first time since he had arrived at the hospital at a quarter past five to reflect on how things were generally going in his isolated world. Professionally, things were remarkably okay. The morning had been busy as per usual, but without incident. The SICU was quiet and Carol Jensen was even complimentary about Lynn Pierce, the new first-year resident. The on-call senior resident had no complaints about the new junior residents during the night. Work rounds had gone well, and even the first-year residents' presentations were surprisingly coherent and to the point, offering yet another bit of evidence that the Residency Acceptance Committee had done a bang-up job. Even the first basic science lecture that morning at 7:30 was a thumbs-up, according to feedback he'd gotten. And finally, Chief of Service rounds had gone better than he could have imagined. Dr. Hernandez had even given him a pat on the back at the conclusion as a rare but welcome compliment.

Noah felt good enough to treat himself to a second cup of coffee. He couldn't have imagined the morning going any better, or the first week, even though he'd not been back to his apartment for six days. The only minor bumps in the road were a few quirks in the complicated duty schedule, but he and Candy Wong had worked out the kinks to everyone's satisfaction. Noah had even had a chance to talk individually to all twenty-four first-year residents, commit their names to memory, get a feel for their aspirations and interests, and assign them appropriate faculty mentors. So even that burden was out of the way.

After rinsing out his mug, Noah planned on taking full advantage of the current unexpected pause in his responsibilities by changing out of his scrubs and heading for the library to read the journal articles he'd selected for Tuesday's Journal Club meeting. But his plans were quickly undermined when he found himself cornered by the sink. Unbeknown to him, Dawn Williams, the circulating nurse in the Vincent case, had come up behind him, patiently waiting for him to finish with his mug. At almost six feet tall and slightly overweight, she wasn't one to be lost in the crowd, especially when she was standing so close that her nose was within a foot of Noah's. He knew her to be a hardworking, opinionated, and candid OR nurse.

"Do you have a moment, Dr. Rothauser?" she asked. Her voice was hushed and clipped, which Noah immediately interpreted as not a good sign.

"I suppose," Noah said, unsure if he wanted his unexpected tranquillity rattled. The woman was obviously upset. He glanced around. The surgical lounge was busy but not overflowing. At the moment, no one was paying them any heed.

"I wanted to give you my two cents about the Bruce Vincent case," Dawn continued, keeping her voice low. Noah couldn't help but notice she wasn't blinking.

"Should we go somewhere less crowded?" Noah suggested. The mention of Vincent's name was enough to fire up his own pulse. Here was yet another situation that made him wish he had a private office. It was clear that whatever Dawn had to say was meant for his ears only.

"This is fine," Dawn said. "No one is listening."

"Okay. I'm all ears."

"I know you are going to be presenting the case at next week's M&M, so I would like to make sure you are aware that Dr. Mason didn't even appear for about an hour after anesthesia had been started. He wasn't part of the pre-op huddle. That should not happen, plain and simple, and had he been there, the outcome probably could have been different."

"I am aware there was some delay," Noah said diplomatically.

"He had three patients under anesthesia all at the same time," Dawn snapped, her voice rising. When she realized how loud she'd become, she covered her mouth with her hand and glanced around to make sure no one was listening. "Sorry."

"It's okay," Noah said. "I haven't finished my investigation of the case, but I will be talking with everyone involved, including you if you have more to add. Thank you for coming forward."

"I know there is an ongoing departmental debate about concurrent surgery," Dawn continued in her hushed voice. "But this situation with Mr. Vincent was beyond the pale. I just wanted to be sure you knew. I think it has to be brought up."

"I appreciate your telling me your opinion," Noah said. "I will be sure to bring up all the facts about the case, including the delay."

"Thank you for hearing me out," Dawn said. "Mr. Vincent was a wonderful man. His passing is a tragedy that shouldn't have happened. At least that is my feeling. I miss him every morning I drive into the hospital garage. Well, thanks for your time. And good luck. A lot of people are upset about this."

"For good reason," Noah said. "It is a tragedy when anyone dies in surgery, especially a young, healthy person and a beloved part of the BMH community. Again, thank you for speaking with me."

"You are welcome."

With that said, Dawn nodded slightly before turning and walking toward the lounge's exit.

Cursing under his breath, Noah watched Dawn disappear. His sudden aggravation was not directed toward her. His irritation was directed at himself for having continued to put off working up the Vincent case and then fibbing about it, telling Dawn he hadn't finished when he had barely started. He should have begun in earnest right after his mini-confrontation with Dr. Mason in the Fagan Amphitheater. Instead he'd been like the proverbial ostrich sticking its head in the sand, vainly hoping the whole mini-nightmare would somehow miraculously disappear. Since that was not going to happen, he had to get a move on and do the necessary legwork because the M&M Conference was looming the following Wednesday, only four full days away.

Reluctantly giving up a trip to the library, Noah ditched the idea of putting on his street clothes. Instead, to save time, he merely grabbed his white coat and pulled it on over his scrubs before taking the stairs down to Stanhope 2 en route to his all-too-public desk. The idea of heading to the library to prepare for the Journal Club was out the window. The unexpected exchange with Dawn had been the wake-up call he needed. Free time for him was a rare commodity.

He'd briefly started preparing for the M&M after the disturbing exchange with Dr. Mason by writing down all the people associated with the Vincent case, whether he thought he needed to interview them or not. But doing this wasn't a real beginning but rather a way of controlling his immediate anger and anxiety. Once he'd finished, he'd put the sheet of paper away in one of his desk drawers and forgotten about it, which was easy, thanks to the tidal wave of more immediate responsibilities that engulfed him as the new super chief resident.

Arriving at the surgical residency program office, he said a quick hello to everyone. Sitting down at his desk, he found the list, drawing a line through Dawn Williams and Helen Moran, as he probably didn't need to speak with them again. The remaining names were Martha Stanley, Connie Marchand, Gloria Perkins, Janet Spaulding, Betsy Halloway, Dr. Ava London, Dr. David Wiley, Dr. Harry Chung, Dr. Sid Andrews, Dr. Carl White, and Dr. William Mason. He put question marks over Wiley, Chung, Andrews, and White, recognizing that they were only ancillary actors in the drama and talking with them probably wouldn't add anything to the central issue of fatal gastric regurgitation.

The only other name on the list wasn't a specific individual but rather an organization. He wanted to get in touch with the Office of the Chief Medical Examiner. As an operative death, the body had been sent to the medical examiner as a matter of law. What Noah was hoping to learn was why the hell the heart would not start after being on bypass, even with an internal pacemaker. Noah was hoping for an explanation. He was certain the issue would come up at the meeting if an angry Dr. Mason wanted to make Noah the scapegoat.

Next Noah fired up the monitor on his desk and swung out the keyboard. After entering his password, he typed in Bruce Vincent's name to get the man's EMR. There wasn't much, only the entries associated with his recent surgery.

Noah brought up the admission H&P, or history and physical. He recognized the author as Dr. Mason's fellow, someone Noah had met. Although Noah tried generally to avoid Dr. Mason, he couldn't completely when it came to his desire to become adept at pancreatic surgery. On a number of occasions Noah had had to swallow his pride and scrub in with the renowned surgeon to take advantage of his talent and learn his technique. Working with Dr. Mason meant working with his fellow, Dr. Aibek Kolganov, from Kazakhstan. Noah had not been impressed for a number of reasons, and now that he was looking at Bruce Vincent's H&P, he was even less impressed. To Noah it was clearly one of those copy-and-paste jobs that can be found easily on the Internet.

As Noah's eyes ran down the overly extensive list of negatives, he suddenly came across two positives in the gastrointestinal review of systems. One was mild reflux disease, and the other was mild bloating and constipation. But what really caught his attention was that the two positives were in a different font than the rest of the H&P. And by investigating a bit further, Noah could tell that the two positives had been added after the surgery!

Noah stared off into the middle distance, trying to absorb what he had just found. Changing a medical record after an adverse event was a huge no-no from a legal point of view. A short, humorless laugh escaped Noah's lips. He shook his head at the implications. "Not good," he murmured.

"Something wrong?" Gail Yaeger, the secretary, asked to be friendly. She was a sensitive person. Her desk was facing Noah's, with only a half-dozen or so feet separating them.

"Maybe," Noah said vaguely. "Thanks for asking. We'll have to see." Actually, he knew he had a problem. Or, more accurately, he knew the hospital had a problem that might result in a multimillion-dollar lawsuit, and once again Noah would be the messenger if he brought it up. It was yet another potential bomb. Everything about the case seemed to spell trouble.

Returning his attention to the monitor, Noah searched in vain for the junior resident's admitting note to see if reflux and bloating were mentioned. He was surprised there was no note. He groaned. Here was yet another problem. Why wasn't there a resident admitting H&P?

Noah then scrolled to the anesthesia record, which was mostly a computer-derived readout directly from the anesthesia machine. He looked at the recordings of the vital signs and the electrocardiogram. Everything was entirely normal right up until the first ventricular fibrillation episode. On the ECG Noah could plainly see the time of the shock from the defibrillator and that the heart rhythm returned to normal before the second fibrillation event. Soon after that he could see when the heart stopped fibrillating, followed by no electrical activity whatsoever when the iced saline was poured over the quivering organ.

Scrolling down farther, Noah came next to several entries typed in by Dr. Ava London, the anesthesiologist, which had interesting syntax with multiple superlatives and no acronyms or contractions. The first entry was prior to the ultimately fatal regurgitation episode and included that the patient's health was superb with no medical problems whatsoever, and that the patient had absolutely no allergies, took no single drug on a daily basis, had taken no food or drink by mouth since midnight, had never had anesthesia for any reason, and . . . Suddenly Noah's eyes stopped. He'd come across a particularly cogent negative stating that the patient had no history of any digestive system problems like reflux or heartburn, meaning that Dr. London had specifically asked about these symptoms and the patient denied it, just as he had denied having eaten breakfast when he clearly had done so.

Noah knew this was a very significant point that probably exonerated Anesthesia, despite Dr. Mason's claim to the contrary. If the patient had been truthful about either issue, he probably would still be alive. It also called attention to the after-the-fact entry in the admitting H&P apparently done by Dr. Mason's fellow. Noah inwardly groaned. How was he going to present all this without totally alienating Dr. Mason? Unfortunately, he had no idea.

Returning to Dr. London's initial entry, he read that Bruce Vincent had complained of moderate anxiety, mostly associated with concern that he had been extremely late to Admitting and that Dr. Mason might be angry about possibly waiting. Now Noah had to laugh, knowing that Dr. Mason ended up keeping the anesthetized patient and the whole team waiting for more than an hour.

The rest of Dr. London's initial entry was straightforward and clinical about giving the patient midazolam for his anxiety, giving the spinal without any problem using bupivacaine, and putting the patient asleep with propofol.

Dr. London's second entry was a bit more terse and more clinical, mentioning massive regurgitation, extensive aspiration, and sudden cardiac arrest during the placement of the endotracheal tube when the patient was being switched from spinal anesthesia to general anesthesia. She then went on to describe the defibrillation, the blood thinning with heparin, the placement of the patient on cardiopulmonary bypass, and finally the bronchoscopy. She listed all the medications that were tried in vain to get the heart to commence beating. The final sentence gave the time the bypass machine was turned off and the patient declared dead.

Noah took a deep breath. Just reading about the episode brought it back in vivid detail, at least the part he experienced. It had been an extremely upsetting episode for everyone.

Next Noah turned to the nurses' notes and read what had been entered in Admitting by Martha Stanley, whom Noah had known since he'd been a junior resident. Using the usual acronyms, Martha had tersely noted that the H&P, the ECG, and the basic blood work were all in order. She also wrote that the patient had no allergies, no medications, no anesthesia, and was NPO since midnight, and the hernia was on the right side. There was no mention of reflux disease.

There were notes from two other nurses involved in the admitting process: Helen Moran and Connie Marchand. Both indicated in the EMR that they had asked the same questions as Martha Stanley and had gotten the same responses, particularly about Mr. Vincent not having eaten anything. Also, neither of these nurses mentioned possible reflux disease. The only thing unique about Helen Moran's note was that she was the one who had marked Bruce Vincent's right hip with the permanent marker to make sure the surgery was done on the correct side.

Next Noah turned to the operative reports. There were four. The first was dictated by Dr. Sid Andrews and described the attempt to repair the inguinal hernia. That was straightforward until the part about the knuckle of intestine caught up in the hernia and the failed attempts to reduce it externally. The second operative report had been dictated by Dr. Adam Stevens and described putting the patient on bypass. It, too, was straightforward. The third note was dictated by Noah about opening the chest. He didn't need to read that. The final entry was by the pulmonologist, Dr. White, who described the bronchoscopy procedure and the removal of the aspirated material from the patient's lungs.

As a final investigation of Vincent's EMR record, Noah glanced over the blood work, particularly the electrolytes. It was all normal, including the sample taken after the patient had been on the bypass machine. It was frustrating, as Noah still had no idea why the heart wouldn't restart beating after the bronchoscopy. At the time, he had hoped it was a potassium problem, which would have made a certain amount of sense and which could have been addressed. The problem was that by not knowing, he had no idea if there was something they should have done differently.

Noah sat back in his chair. The question was how to proceed and who to talk to first. He couldn't quite decide, but he knew who would be the last person: Dr. Mason. Noah was certain that any conversation with him was going to be confrontational from the start, so he needed to have all his ducks in a row. From what Dr. Mason had said in the amphitheater, it was painfully obvious he was not about to accept any blame and fully intended to see that it was directed elsewhere, mostly at Anesthesia, Admitting, and the patient. With that reality in mind, Noah decided it would be best to talk with Dr. Ava London next to last. He didn't know her well, as he had always found her superficially friendly but distant. Knowing Dr. Mason's intention of using her as a scapegoat was going to make talking to her almost as difficult as talking with Dr. Mason, especially after she had already expressed her opinion that Mason was largely responsible. The idea of being caught in the middle of crossfire between two BHM attendings spelled potential disaster as far as Noah was concerned.

Deciding to start from the beginning, meaning where Bruce Vincent began his fatal admission, Noah stood up with the intention of heading to Surgical Admitting on the fourth floor to see Martha Stanley. He thought it best to just show up rather than call. But his plans changed when his mobile phone buzzed in his pocket. It was Dr. Arnold Wells, a new senior resident covering the emergency room.

"Thank God you picked up!" Arnold blurted. "Noah, I'm over my head here with a flail chest and major head trauma from a head-on collision. It's a disaster. I need help now!"

"On my way!" Noah shouted, shocking everyone in the surgical residency program office.

The fastest route down to the emergency room was the stairs, and Noah took them in twos and threes while struggling to keep his stethoscope, tablet, and collection of pens and other paraphernalia from flying out of his pockets. Although it wasn't far distance-wise, by the time he ran into the ER he was out of breath from exertion. He didn't have to ask where the injured patient was, as one of the admitting clerks frantically pointed to Trauma Room 4. Noah barged through a gaggle of EMTs coming out of the room.

The patient was a mess. His clothes had been cut down the front and pushed to the side. His unrestrained arms and legs were wildly flailing. A large-bore IV was running. The major visible trauma was to the head and face, with the right eye socket empty and bloody and a major gash down to the bone that started in the middle of his forehead and extended up into his hairline. Tiny bits of yellow material could be seen that might have been brain. Arnold was attempting to use a bag-valve mask to provide positive pressure respirations, but the center of the man's chest was bruised and showing paradoxical movement.

"Good God," Noah murmured. His mind was in overdrive, as this clearly was a hypercritical situation.

6

For the second time that day, Noah pushed through the double doors to exit the BMH operating room suite. The first time had been mid-morning, after he'd made his covert check on all the first-year residents who were assisting in surgery. He remembered feeling good that all was going well. This time he felt even better, despite looking like hell and wearing bloodstained scrubs. On this occasion leaving the OR, he was reveling in the unique feeling that he thought surgery and maybe only surgery could provide. He had been sorely challenged with a difficult case of forty-three-year-old John Horton, who arrived at the emergency room at death's door from a head-on collision on Interstate 93. As an obviously intelligent and educated man, as Noah later learned, who worked as an analyst at a major investment firm, John should have been wearing his seat belt in his classic car that wasn't equipped with air bags. Unfortunately, he wasn't. As a result, John's unchecked body had rammed full force at sixty-plus miles per hour into the steering wheel, which fractured and disarticulated his sternum, before catapulting out through the windshield.

When Noah had first arrived in the trauma room, his trained mind had instantly analyzed the situation, and he acted by reflex with the same decisiveness that had propelled him to slice into Bruce Vincent's chest. Instinctively knowing that oxygen would be the determining factor if this patient was going to live, Noah called for an emergency tracheostomy set and ordered the patient to be given IV fentanyl for pain. While Arnold continued to struggle with the bag-valve mask connected to 100 percent oxygen, Noah completed the emergency tracheostomy, then connected a positive pressure respirator. Immediately, blood oxygen levels went up to a reasonable level, giving Noah time to examine the patient with the help of several X-rays. It was immediately apparent the man had multiple rib fractures, a fractured sternum, a fractured skull, and extensive internal injuries.

After stabilizing the patient as much as possible with several units of blood, Noah had him brought up to surgery. With the help of the chief neurosurgical resident, who saw to the skull fracture, and an ophthalmologist, who located the missing eye in the man's maxillary sinus, Noah went into the abdomen to remove a damaged spleen and repair the liver. By then the wealthy patient's private doctor had been located; he, in turn, alerted a private thoracic surgeon as well as a neurosurgeon, both on the BMH staff, who came in and relieved Noah.

Whatever was going to happen to John Horton, Noah had the rewarding sense of knowing that he and Arnold had saved the day and kept the patient alive at the most critical hour. To have the knowledge and skill to accomplish such a feat was what had propelled Noah into medicine in general and then surgery in particular. He knew that such a feeling was mostly denied to those who went into internal medicine. They might on occasion cure someone of something with the right therapy, but it was never so immediate as it was with surgery, and therefore more difficult to take the credit. Whether John Horton was going to live or die Noah didn't know, considering the extent of his head injury plus his cardiac and pulmonary contusions. But at least now the man had a fighting chance, thanks to Noah's intervention. For Noah it was a heady, deeply satisfying feeling that justified all the sacrifices he'd had to make to be where he was.

Unfortunately, Noah's euphoria lasted for only another ten minutes, or at least until he got into the locker room and saw the list of people he needed to talk with about Bruce Vincent protruding from the pocket of his white jacket. Putting on fresh scrubs, he emerged from the men's locker room fully motivated to get back to the Vincent affair. Emergency surgery notwithstanding, he recognized further procrastination was no longer an option. Since he was already on the fourth floor, he headed over to Surgical Admitting.

"I always have time for you," Martha said when Noah appeared at her office door and asked if he might have a word. She was a pleasant but nondescript-appearing woman of indeterminate age with frizzy hair and a florid complexion. Noah appreciated her bent to wear scrubs to advertise she was an integral part of the surgical team, which she was.

"What can I do for you?" she asked once Noah was seated.

Noah outlined what he knew about the Bruce Vincent case and mentioned that he had read her notes in the man's EMR. He told her he had to present the case at next week's M&M Conference and wondered if there was anything she thought he should know.

Martha toyed with a paperclip while she thought about Noah's question. "I suppose you want to know why there is no resident H&P."

"That would be helpful. I noticed it was missing. It is bound to come up."

"We had a number of patients all come in just before Bruce Vincent showed up, so the resident was behind. Really behind. Since Mr. Vincent was forty minutes late, I had already gotten a call from the OR asking where the hell he was. The suggestion was that 'Wild Bill' was champing at the bit, and we all know what that can lead to. To speed things up, I moved Mr. Vincent along without seeing the resident, who never knew about the case. There was a recent H&P by Mason's fellow, which is all that is needed by the book."

"True, but it's accepted practice to have the additional check by a junior resident. This is a good case for the rationale why."

"I understand, but under the circumstances I thought it okay to move him on. The H&P was entirely negative."

"I gather you specifically asked him if he had had anything to eat."

"Absolutely. No question. I always do. He lied to me, that is clear. The question is why, because it had to be deliberate, meaning it wasn't as if he just forgot not to eat. If I had to guess, I'd say it was because he thought he knew more than he did."

"I don't follow."

"He was a bit anxious about being late when I reminded him Mason could be a bear about waiting and that Mason had two big pancreatic cases that morning besides his hernia repair. But about his surgery, Mr. Vincent was cool as a cucumber and mentioned he was scheduled for a spinal, which is why I believe he thought he could get away with eating whatever he wanted. I think this is an example that a little learning can be a dangerous thing. My sense is that Mr. Vincent thought he knew enough about anesthesia to game the system."

"You might be right," Noah said with a nod. He wasn't going to try to guess what was on Bruce Vincent's mind that fateful morning. Yet what Martha was saying made a certain amount of sense, even though Noah believed for a patient to have a full meal before any surgery was suicidal. "What about reflux disease? Did you ask him about that?"

"I didn't. Nor do I generally ask patients about reflux symptoms. Maybe I should, but I think that's an issue for the anesthesiologist to ask so they can gauge the degree."

"Perhaps," Noah said, being noncommittal. It wasn't something he'd thought much about, yet it might be a good issue to bring up at the M&M to keep the discussion away from more problematic areas.

"Did you know that Bruce Vincent was working in the hospital parking garage the morning of his surgery like it was a normal day for him? I saw him myself."

"I didn't know that," Noah said.

"That's why he was late," Martha said. "Supposedly, he had to solve a personnel problem because one of the parking attendants didn't show up. Can you believe it?"

"I can't," Noah admitted. The case was becoming stranger by the minute, as most people were understandably intimidated the morning of their surgery. "Well, thank you for your time. If you think of anything else before Wednesday, please let me know." He stood up.

"Okay. And good luck. I have a feeling this case is going to raise some hackles."

"That's my worry, too. Are you planning on attending the M&M Wednesday morning?"

"I wouldn't miss it. I think it's going to be a full house. At least that's the general word. People are very upset. He was a popular guy."

"Great," Noah said, and moaned. He could feel his anxiety ratchet up a notch.

From Martha's office, Noah walked into the area where patients changed out of their clothes and into patient garb. He again talked briefly with Helen Moran and learned nothing new, although he was reminded she was the one who marked Vincent's right hip to avoid an operation carried out on the wrong side. With the way things were going, Noah thought that operating on the wrong side might have been the only way that the case could have been worse than it was.

In the pre-anesthesia section Noah searched for Gloria Perkins and Connie Marchand. Gloria was off for the day, but he did get to talk with Connie. She told him that she had asked Vincent all the usual questions, as Martha and Helen had, including if he had been NPO since midnight, meaning nothing-by-mouth.

"I assume he denied eating?" Noah said.

"Absolutely," Connie said.

"Anything I should know that you didn't write in the EMR?" Noah asked.

"I don't think so," Connie said. But then she corrected herself. "Come to think of it, I didn't mention in my note that we had gotten several calls from the OR asking where Mr. Vincent was, and each request was accompanied by a friendly reminder that Dr. Mason doesn't like to wait."

"Martha Stanley got the same call. Is that typical?"

"Put it this way: It is not atypical for the OR to check on what was going on if a patient is significantly late. It just doesn't happen very often, because patients are rarely late."

"Then why did you mention it to me?" Noah asked.

"Only because I heard through the grapevine that Dr. Mason ended up keeping the patient waiting for an hour with the spinal in place. Personally, I don't think that's right, and I know a lot of other people feel the same, especially after the OR had called over here looking for him."

Noah felt another unpleasant uptick of anxiety. The case was definitely morphing into an argument against concurrent surgery, which was going to irritate the hell out of Dr. Mason and a handful of other top surgeons, and Noah knew all too well who was going to suffer the consequences.

7

After donning a surgical hat and mask, Noah walked from the pre-anesthesia holding area directly into the OR to check the main OR scheduling monitor that listed the day's surgeries. Each entry had the estimated or actual start time, the patient's name, the procedure, the surgeon, the anesthesia person, the scrub nurse, and the circulating nurse. When the surgery was completed the color changed from blue to yellow.

Noah's goal was to find Dr. Ava London to see if he could speak with her when she finished for the day, which he knew was around 3:00. Although most of the anesthesiologists made it a point to hang around for a time after their shift to socialize in the surgical lounge, he had never once seen her participate during the entire five years he'd been a resident, which he knew happened to be nearly the same amount of time Dr. London had been on staff. Although she was always friendly when they worked on a case together, which had probably happened some fifty times over the years, he thought of her as consistently reserved and private, qualities that Noah respected because he thought of himself as being somewhat similar. Like Ava, he had never availed himself of the surgical-lounge chitchat sessions, even though most of the other residents did. Noah felt uncomfortable talking about his social life because he didn't

91

have one, though he suspected there was a big difference with Dr. London. With her constant tan even in the dead of winter, which she always politely refused to explain or gloat about to anyone, and the fact that she was lean and fit, Noah assumed she had a particularly active life outside of the hospital.

Noah found Dr. London's name in OR 8, the same operating room where the Vincent debacle had occurred. She'd been scheduled to "pump gas," which was the anesthesiologists' humorous description of their job, for a bariatric surgery case that had started at 1:30 P.M. But just as Noah was reading the entry, its color changed from blue to yellow, conveniently signaling the case was over.

Thinking she'd soon appear in the PACU, or post-anesthesia care unit, Noah wandered in. Most of the beds were occupied as a testament to BMH's surgical volume, even on a Friday afternoon. His intention was to wait for Dr. London to appear, which he assumed would be imminent. He was surprised to find her already there, signing off on her patient to the PACU staff. Noah walked over toward the foot of the bed. The patient was enormous. Noah estimated he was well over three hundred pounds. Noah had become good at estimating human weight after his rotation on bariatric surgery as a senior resident. He was well aware that handling such patients was an enormous challenge for the nursing staff.

Noah listened while Dr. London gave the last of her instructions to the PACU nurse and then did something that surprised him. She gave her mobile number with the comment that if there was any trouble whatsoever to give her a call. Noah was impressed. Such personal follow-up was not the rule, as there were always in-house anesthesiologists available 24/7.

When Dr. London was finished, she abruptly turned and practically collided with Noah. He assumed she was eager to be on her way, which he interpreted as less than auspicious. Since Friday afternoon was the beginning of the weekend in most people's minds, Noah immediately worried he might not get to talk with her until Monday.

"I'm sorry," Dr. London said. Her voice was soft and clear but with a touch of an accent that Noah had never been able to identify.

"Not at all," Noah said. "It's my fault for sneaking up on you."

Dr. London stared at Noah with her striking blue eyes as if surprised by his comment.

"Well, I really didn't sneak up on you," Noah corrected. "But I did want to ask you if I could talk to you briefly."

With a quick glance at her watch, suggesting she might have a pressing engagement, she asked what he wanted to speak to her about.

"The Bruce Vincent case," Noah said. "I have to present it at next Wednesday's M&M Conference. It is important that I get your input."

Dr. London's response was to look back at the nurse taking care of her last patient and then at the other nurses working around the room. She was clearly suddenly ill at ease.

"I have been devastated by the Bruce Vincent case," Dr. London confided in a lowered but emotionally strained voice. Her eyes zeroed in on Noah like lasers. "It was my first operative death. I went over the case a dozen times and found nothing, absolutely nothing, that I could have done differently. Well, that's not entirely true. I could have waited for Dr. Mason to be in the room before starting the anesthesia. But he insists otherwise and is supported by Dr. Kumar. That's the reality, so I don't think I can add anything. I'm certain the outcome had nothing to do with anything I did or didn't do."

"Okay," Noah soothed. He was completely taken aback by Dr. London's unexpected vehemence. She was staring at him with uncamouflaged intensity. "I certainly empathize with you about it being your first operative death. I'm sorry, really I am, and I know it can be difficult. But I have to warn you that Dr. Mason plans on blaming Anesthesia. He told me directly. I would like to avoid what might cause a problem for you and the Anesthesia Department, but I need your help."

"This is not a good place for us to talk," Dr. London said. "Do you have a private office?"

"I don't," Noah said, again wishing such was not the case.

"I don't, either," Dr. London said. "Maybe we can find a place in the surgical lounge. We can at least sit and not stand out like sore thumbs."

"Okay," Noah said, even though he thought the idea ludicrous if she was looking for privacy. But then he remembered on Friday afternoons it was far less busy than during the week, especially in the summer, with a lot of doctors and nurses heading off to the Cape and the Islands.

"I'll meet you there in ten minutes or so," Dr. London said. "I have to finish up here."

When Noah got to the surgical lounge, he realized his first fears were entirely founded. The room had been commandeered for an impromptu party for one of the OR nurses who was going off on a vacation cruise. There were even some bon-voyage decorations draped over the windows. Despite strong misgivings that Dr. London was not going to find the lounge any better than the PACU, Noah pulled a couple chairs into the far corner apart from the main crowd. Most of the revelers were grouped around a spread of snacks on the countertop at the kitchenette end of the room.

As she had promised, Dr. London soon appeared, and Noah could tell that she was not pleased to find a party under way. Nevertheless, she started toward Noah, who had waved to get her attention. He watched her as she approached. The way she carried herself reemphasized his impression of her as being lean and fit, as well as suggesting a certain confidence. At the same time, he again marveled at how little he knew about her, despite all the times they had worked together. The only thing he did know was that she was a highly competent board-certified anesthesiologist on the staff of one of the country's premier tertiary teaching hospitals, which meant she had been seriously vetted. From Noah's conversations with others, his sense was that no one knew too much about her. Although superficially friendly, she was indeed a private person.

"This is not what I had in mind," Dr. London said as she took the seat catty-corner to Noah's while glancing over her shoulder at the merriment.

"At least they are engrossed," Noah said, just as OR supervisor Janet Spaulding spied them and immediately broke from the group and approached.

"Well, I wouldn't believe this if I didn't see it with my own eyes," Janet said. "My two favorite party poopers comparing notes." She laughed to convey that she was teasing. "It's nice to see you two chatting. I don't think I've ever seen either one of you socializing in here. But whatever, please join us. Don't be strangers. We're giving Janice a proper send-off."

"Thanks, but I unfortunately have to get going," Dr. London said before Noah could respond. "I'm already late for an engagement. Dr. Rothauser and I just needed to talk briefly about a case."

"Well, if you change your mind, we have plenty," Janet said, gesturing back toward the food and drink. She half waved before returning to the festivities.

Noah and Dr. London regarded each other. "This is not going to work," Dr. London said as she pulled her bouffant surgical cap off her head, releasing a silky profusion of long, seriously blond-streaked hair from its workday confinement.

As a kind of reflex, Noah sucked in a bit of air and held his breath. With a certain amount of shock, he recognized that Dr. London was a surprisingly attractive woman who obviously cared about her appearance. Seeing her as alluring was something that had never occurred to him before, as he had never seen her without her dowdy head covering and surgical mask. Although there were a few women on the staff who caught his attention on occasion because something about their appearance clicked in what he humorously referred to as his reptilian brain, it had never happened with Dr. London. Why, he didn't know, because suddenly in this starkly utilitarian lounge and hardly seductive environment she appeared rather exceptionally lovely. The halo of mostly blond hair framed a face dominated by intensely blue eyes, a narrow, pixielike upturned nose, full lips, and startlingly white teeth that contrasted with her blemish-free, healthy complexion. Totally unaware of the effect she was having, she used her fingers to tame her hair. Even that seemed coquettish to Noah.

"Can you think of someplace else we can go?" Dr. London asked. When Noah didn't respond, she asked again a bit louder.

"Excuse me," Noah said, averting his gaze. "Someplace else? Let me think—"

"Tell me this first!" Dr. London interrupted. "What exactly did Dr. Mason say to you about me in regard to the Vincent case?"

Noah struggled to reprogram his brain. He felt acutely embarrassed that he was acting like a besotted teenager. He raised his eyes from looking down at his hands in his lap. "Actually, he didn't name you specifically. He said that Anesthesia screwed up by giving the wrong anesthesia."

"He didn't say anything about his office stipulating the anesthesia he wanted or that no one knew the patient had had GI symptoms associated with bowel obstruction?"

"I don't think so," Noah said. He wasn't certain. On the spur of the moment, he couldn't remember. His mind wasn't functioning up to speed.

"I did not screw up," Dr. London said bluntly, with emotion bordering on anger. "As I said, I went over the case with a fine-toothed comb. Except for waiting for him to be physically present before starting the anesthesia, I wouldn't have done anything differently."

"He did say the patient and Admitting people contributed," Noah said, suddenly remembering Mason's exact words.

"That is an understatement, considering what the patient ended up vomiting," Dr. London said. She bent closer to Noah, close enough that he could appreciate her perfume. "He had eaten a huge breakfast. But listen! I'm glad you came to me. With Dr. Mason saying what he did, we definitely have to talk, because you have to present this case very carefully to keep it from becoming a disaster for both of us."

Noah nodded. He was surprised but pleased. He had expected her to be defensive and distant, maybe even wary and unhelpful. Quite the contrary, she was sounding as if she were totally in his camp, seeing the up-and-coming M&M just as he did: a potential calamity.

"Unfortunately, I don't think we should be seen talking together about this here in the hospital, because it could easily smack of collusion or even conspiracy," Dr. London said. "You understand?"

"I do. I hope you understand that I'm going to be on a tightrope, and I need all the help I can get."

"The way I see it, we are both going to be on a tightrope."

"Why do you believe you are on a tightrope?" Noah questioned. He was mystified. "You say you have gone over the case and wouldn't do anything differently. You are a board-certified staff anesthesiologist. Dr. Mason could not do anything to you. I'm different. I'm only a surgical resident, and he already doesn't like me, and he is part of the surgical residency program hierarchy."

"I find him a difficult person to deal with," Dr. London admitted. "Personally, I think the man has a personality disorder, but let's not go into that now. The problem is he and my boss, Dr. Kumar, are bosom buddies. To make matters worse, Dr. Mason is not fond of me, either."

"How can you say that?" Noah asked. "Word has it he often asks for you."

Dr. London waved her hand as if shooing away a bothersome fly. "Let's not get into it now. Here's my suggestion: Are you off tonight?"

"Sort of," Noah said, surprised by the question. "As the super chief, I'm never completely off. There are a chief resident, a senior resident, and a junior resident on call tonight. I just have to be available if disaster strikes."

"Okay, good," Dr. London said. "I live nearby in Beacon Hill. Louisburg Square, to be exact."

"I know Louisburg Square," Noah said, sitting up a bit straighter. "I live on the hill, too. On Revere Street."

"Then we are practically neighbors," Dr. London said. She leaned closer and lowered her voice a bit more. "Here's my suggestion: When you finish here at the hospital this evening, drop over to my house. It is number sixteen. We'll be able to talk freely. What do you say?"

"Thank you," Noah said, taken aback. It was an unexpected offer. He also noticed she said "house" and not "apartment." Single-family homes were the exception on Beacon Hill. "I'll be glad to come by your place. I appreciate your offer."

"You are welcome," Dr. London said, getting to her feet. "Let me give you my mobile number so you can text me if something comes up and you can't make it." She stepped over to the phone table and scribbled her number down on a piece of paper. Noah watched her. He was momentarily dumbfounded. He hadn't expected any of this. When she walked back to where he was sitting, holding the paper out in front of her, he could see from the way she moved that she definitely had an athletic body. It was even apparent in her baggy scrubs, although he had never noticed it before.

"Until later," Dr. London said. "I hope to see you tonight." She handed over the sheet of paper before disappearing into the women's locker room.

For the very first time since Noah had been fretting about the upcoming M&M Conference, he felt a glimmer of hope that he might possibly be able to survive his presentation with minimal fallout. At least now he had a BMH attending who was on his side, even possibly a collaborator of sorts, willing to counter Dr. Mason's interpretation and his apparent desire to divert the conversation away from the real issues. Vaguely, he wondered why she believed Dr. Mason did not like her and whether he'd find out that evening, provided, of course, he could leave the hospital. At least her house was close to the BMH if he had to get back in a hurry.

After checking his watch to be sure he had enough time before afternoon work rounds, he headed back into the OR. His intention was to find the two anesthesia residents, Wiley and Chung. What he wanted to learn was the inside, "resident" scoop on the Vincent case, and whether the general feeling of the anesthesia residents corroborated Dr. London's beliefs about her performance. There was always a resident grapevine that was invariably more truthful than the involved attending's interpretation.

8

It was still light outside when Noah exited his apartment building on his way to Louisburg Square, one of the tonier sections of Beacon Hill and sharply different from his much more modest Revere Street environs. When he'd finally gotten out of the hospital, he had decided to dash back to his apartment to get out of his hospital whites and take a quick shower. After all, it had been fifteen hours he'd been on the go.

Noah had put on a pair of jeans and a polo shirt that were reasonably clean. He chose them because he thought they were flattering. He'd considered wearing his only jacket and a tie but had dismissed the idea as too old-fashioned and proper. As he was dressing he admitted to himself that he was energized but nervous about the upcoming visit with Dr. Ava London above and beyond the need to prepare for the damn M&M. She had unnerved him at their little tête-à-tête in the surgical lounge, and now that he was actually en route he felt the same way. Instead of trying to understand his reaction, he concentrated on the destination. Over the five years he had been in Boston, he had walked through Louisburg Square innumerable times and had wondered what the houses were like on the inside. Now he was going to find out. He was also curious about Dr. London and how she would act in her home environment.

Noah had hoped to be out of the hospital much earlier, and he had become progressively worried Dr. London might have evening plans and change her mind about seeing him. The problem had been a surgical consult that had gone bad, requiring Noah to smooth the feathers of one of the internal medicine chief residents who had requested the consult. It ended up being more of a personality clash than anything else, but it took time for Noah to resolve the issue without causing anyone to lose face. For Noah, it was yet another learning experience to emphasize that diplomacy was one of the major jobs of a super chief resident, a skill that he knew was going to be sorely tested at the M&M.

As Noah walked up Pinckney Street, he thought about what the two anesthesia residents had told him that afternoon when he'd cornered them in the anesthesia office. They said that the case had been a widespread topic of conversation right after the incident, and everyone without exception backed Dr. London's interpretation. For the most part, they blamed the debacle on Dr. Mason's cavalier attitude and willingness to have three patients under anesthesia at the same time while he flitted back and forth from room to room. As Noah trudged up the hill, he briefly wondered if he should mention what he'd learned to Dr. London, as it was certainly supportive, but almost immediately he decided against the idea. Since he was just getting to know her, he reasoned it would not be diplomatic to admit he was spying on her behind her back.

Reaching the square that was actually a rectangle, Noah stopped long enough to appreciate its suddenness as an unexpected oasis in the middle of a warren of brick tenements, brick sidewalks, and black macadam pavement that made up the rest of Beacon Hill. With its soaring elms, it was a true hideaway of lush greenery surrounded by an imposing wrought-iron fence. There were a few children playing on the enclosed lawn, and their shouts reverberated off the brick façades of the surrounding town houses.

Number 16 was on the downhill side of the square, whose long axis was oriented perpendicular to the rise of the hill. After climbing a half-dozen granite steps, Noah faced an imposing mahogany door. Searching for a doorbell and not finding one, he entered the foyer. There he found a bell. He pushed it. When nothing seemed to happen, he was tempted to try it again while suppressing a sudden worry that he was going to be stood up. After all, he'd not provided his mobile number. He'd thought about texting Dr. London earlier to say he would be late but had decided against it, at least partially for superstitious reasons.

Suddenly the door was pulled open fast enough to create a mild breeze that ruffled his hair. Standing in front of him at the base of an elegant carpeted staircase was Dr. London, who appeared far different than he was accustomed to seeing her. Instead of baggy scrubs, bouffant cap, and face mask, she had on form-fitting black yoga pants and an athletic tank top. For fear of making a fool of himself, he glued his attention to the woman's blue eyes to avoid staring elsewhere.

"Welcome, Doctor," Dr. London said with a gracious sweep of her hand, gesturing through an archway immediately to her right. "Please come in!" In sharp contrast to her professional *froideur* in the hospital, she seemed remarkably hospitable. There was not a speck of staff-versus-resident condescension.

"Thank you, Dr. London," Noah managed, glad to be able to redirect his eyes into the room. He found himself in a large, high-ceilinged living room that extended from ten-foot-tall double-hung windows in the home's bow front all the way to the rear of the house, where there were French doors. The decor was restrained Georgian with period moldings. To Noah's eyes everything seemed new, as if it had just been constructed. On the south wall were a pair of period black-marble fireplaces. Partially dividing the room into two spaces were several fluted Corinthian columns. In the section of the room facing the square were two large, dark green sofas facing each other. Between them was a marble coffee table with several stacks of large, colorful books. On the walls were a collection of gilt-framed oil paintings. In the back section of the room beyond the columns stood a grand piano. The air was cooled and dehumidified.

"First and foremost," Dr. London said as she followed Noah, "let's dispense with the formalities. Please call me Ava, and I presume I can call you Noah."

"By all means," Noah said. He allowed his eyes to look back at his hostess, but he immediately redirected them to the surroundings. It was going to take a few minutes for him to adjust to her outfit, which he jokingly thought could have come from a spray can. He had sensed she had an athletic figure. Now he was sure of it. The definition of the muscles of her legs was all too apparent. Same with her arms but slightly less so. Sudden movement on the staircase captured his attention. Two sizable cats streaked down the stairs to race into the room. Both stopped and cautiously sniffed Noah's leg.

"I hope you aren't allergic to cats," Ava said.

"No, not at all," Noah said. He bent down and let each cat smell his outstretched hand. One was grayish-blue with striking yellow eyes, the other gray-and-white striped with blue eyes. "Beautiful cats."

"Thank you," Ava said. "They are my buddies. Yellow eyes is Oxi, short for oxygen, and blue eyes is Carbi, short for carbon dioxide."

"Very clever," Noah said. "Have you had them for a long time?"

"Relatively," Ava said. "I got them from the animal shelter."

"Well, they certainly lucked out," Noah said.

"I think I got the better end of the bargain," Ava said. "Can I get you anything to drink? There is a bar off to the right as part of the library."

"You have a library?" Noah questioned. He didn't know if she was joking or not. Having a library was not part of his vocabulary.

"Of course. This is a rather big house, even though from the front it appears modest. The building's footprint has what is called an *L* off the back."

"*Modest* is not the adjective I would choose."

Ava laughed in a sincere, crystalline manner. "Everything is relative."

"Do you live in the whole house?"

"As opposed to what?"

"Are there apartments?"

"I see what you mean," Ava said with another laugh. "No, there are no rental units. It is a single-family house. I just happen to be a family of one with two cats."

"How many floors?"

"Six."

"Not bad!" Noah said. "It's very impressive. I like the period decor." The house was far bigger than he would have guessed from seeing its façade, which made it look as if it were three stories, not six. He wondered what it would be like to occupy such a place, thinking his entire apartment probably would fit in the room he was standing in.

"Are you interested in architecture and design?"

"I suppose," Noah said, even though he had never given the idea much thought, as evidenced by his apartment.

"Would you like to see the house?" Ava asked. "I would be happy to give you a quick tour. Creating it has been a labor of love for me. Since I spend a lot of time in the house when I am in Boston, I wanted it to reflect me and my lifestyle as kind of a homebody. The renovation has only been finished for less than a year."

"I'd love to see the house," Noah said.

They started on the first, or basement, floor, which was level with the garden in the back. Noah was shown a full guest studio with its own kitchen. Next was a full workout room with several stationary bikes, a treadmill, a half-dozen weight machines, and a rack of free weights. "Here's where I spend six-thirty to seven-thirty every evening I'm in town," Ava said. "Just like I did today. That's why I'm still in my workout clothes. I was afraid to get into the shower, for fear you would arrive the moment I did."

"Do you travel out of town frequently?" Noah asked.

"I do," Ava said. "As often as I can. In fact, almost every weekend. I take full advantage of my freedom. It's one of the benefits of anesthesia as a medical specialty. When I'm off, I am really off."

"Good point," Noah said. "What do you do about your cats?"

"My housekeeper, Maria, comes every day when I'm out of town. She loves Oxi and Carbi."

"Where do you usually go?"

"It depends if it is business or pleasure," Ava said.

"What do you mean 'business'?" Noah asked. The question popped out before he even thought of whether it was appropriate. "Are you on an anesthesia staff at another hospital as well?"

"Not at all," Ava said without offense. "I couldn't do that. Dr. Kumar wouldn't tolerate it. I do consulting."

"Interesting," Noah responded. He wanted to ask more but felt it too probing, and Ava was already climbing the stairs to the next level.

The second floor, which was half underground on the Louisburg Square or front side of the building, housed a large, modern kitchen with all the usual appliances, a dining room, and a full maid's apartment.

"I don't have a maid," Ava said in response to Noah's shocked expression. "When I did the design for the renovation I was thinking of resale as well as my own needs."

"Interesting," Noah repeated. He was more than impressed. Knowing a little about real estate values, he doubted Ava could afford such a manse even on anesthesiologist's salary. Her consulting business had to be extremely profitable. It was either that or she had inherited a fortune.

The third floor was where Noah had entered when he'd come in through the front door, so they continued up the main stairs to the fourth. It was here that Noah was most impressed. The main portion of the house without the back L comprised two rooms. The front and slightly larger room was an inviting, dark green study with several desks, a floor-to-ceiling bookcase, a sitting area with comfortable overstuffed club chairs with ottomans, an expansive coffee table with a number of colorful coffee table books, a collection of framed photographs of Ava in various athletic venues, and lots of light streaming through large windows. Noah could imagine spending a lot of time in such a space.

"Do you mind if I check out your photos?" Noah said.

"Not at all," Ava said. She laughed with pleasure at Noah's interest.

Noah's eyes ran over the entire lot, one more interesting than the last. He could tell most were selfies taken with a selfie stick. There were a few group shots, but the others were solo, with Ava smiling into the camera as if she were as happy as a lark. She seemed to have the same expression in all of them and her hair was always perfect. There was something oddly impersonal about them. "I guess you're quite a sports enthusiast," Noah commented.

"I like sports and travel," Ava said. "Now let me show you another room." She gestured back out into the hallway.

In contrast, the rear room was dark and uninviting until Ava turned on the light. Then Noah's face lit up like a child's at Christmas seeing the decorated tree for the first time. The entire room was devoted to a computer setup the likes of which Noah had never seen except in his dreams. "I'm so jealous," he said as he stepped over the threshold. There were three monitors sitting on a broad desk against the far wall and angled so all three could be seen by someone at the desk with just a minor turn of the head. A bank of electronics, including a server, were on open shelving to Noah's left. Large speakers stood on either side of the desk. Several of the latest virtual-reality headsets sat on top of it. The windows at the rear of the house were shuttered to keep out the light. The ceiling was covered with acoustical tile.

"This is my favorite room in the house," Ava said with pride as she noted Noah's reaction. "I spend every evening in here when I am in Boston, sometimes as much as four hours. I lose track of time."

"I can see why it's your favorite room," Noah said. "I think it would be mine, too, if I had the time. Are you a gamer?"

"Not as much as I used to be as a teenager," Ava said. "But I still play once in a blue moon, mostly League of Legends, despite the misogyny involved. From your reaction, I guess you're a gamer, too."

"I used to be," Noah said. "I played League of Legends when it first came out while I was in medical school, but not since becoming a resident. No time."

"I didn't play when I was a resident, either," Ava said.

"This setup certainly suggests you play more than occasionally," Noah said. "What level did you get to?"

"Silver Two, but I haven't kept it up. Instead, I'm into virtual reality. I also use the system every day for MOCA. Are you familiar with MOCA, Maintenance of Certification for Anesthesia?"

"Of course," Noah said. He knew that the various specialty boards in medicine, such as the American Board of Anesthesia, require its diplomats to recertify every ten years. One way to do it was online, but Noah was aware most people put it off until the last few months and then binged. The fact that Ava was doing it every day was a sign of true commitment. "And you really do it every day?" Noah asked, just to be sure.

"Every day without fail," Ava said. "Even when I'm traveling. I have to be up on all the latest trends. Plain and simple, I make a real effort to be the very best anesthesiologist possible."

"I hear you," Noah said. "I feel the same about surgery. Seems that we are equally committed to our specialties, like two peas in a pod."

Ava laughed in her unique fashion. "Two peas in a pod! I love that metaphor. We share a definite similarity, knowing your reputation. But to be completely honest, the MOCA only takes me about a half-hour a day. What I mostly use this setup for nowadays is social media, which I do most every day. I know it's a bit of overkill for just social media, but what can I say."

"What do you mean by 'social media'? Like Facebook?"

"The entire gamut: Facebook, my YouTube channel, Snapchat, Twitter, Instagram, Tumblr, Pinterest . . . you name it. But mostly Facebook, which certainly dates me. To tell you the truth, social media has become my game of choice. When I was a teenager in the late nineties I got addicted to SixDegrees and AOL Instant Messenger for social reasons to manage my reputation, or so I thought, which in retrospect was a disaster, as it truly took over my life in a bad way. Now I'm addicted to it as entertainment and to stay connected. I'm fascinated by it like a lot of people. It is certainly driving our culture."

"You mean you go on it every day?"

"Usually," Ava said. "And even at the hospital, I occasionally sneak a peek on my mobile in between cases to respond to snaps and tweets. When I'm here in the house, I'm either working out, doing MOCA, eating, or doing social media. What can I say? I'm addicted, I admit, but I tell you, I have learned more about myself doing social media than I would have if I'd spent years doing psychoanalysis."

"Really?" Noah questioned with skepticism. "I think you'd have to explain that to me. I mean, I use Facebook and Snapchat a bit, but I don't think I have learned anything about myself from doing it."

"I'd be happy to explain," Ava said. "But that will take some time. I think we should stick to the M&M problem for now."

"You are so right," Noah said. He felt his pulse rise. As entertained as he was by Ava and her impressive house, it had momentarily slipped his mind why he was there. "Where should we sit?"

"Before we get down to business," Ava said, "would you like to see some of the capabilities of my computer system, particularly in virtual reality? It will only take a moment if you are interested."

"Sure," Noah said. "Why not?"

Ava had Noah sit in the chair in front of the three monitors. Leaning over him, she booted up the system. Noah couldn't help but notice she had not bothered to put in a decent security code, as she awakened the computer by merely typing the number *1* six times. Yet he wasn't surprised. When he'd first entered the building he'd noticed her newly renovated house had a modern and highly sophisticated security system.

For the next sixty seconds Noah was treated to a display of graphics and audio that took his breath away. "Okay, I'm convinced," he said when the demonstration was over. He raised his hands in mock surrender. "It's terrific, and I'm jealous. I've got to have a system like this before I die."

Ava laughed. She was pleased. "I can put you in touch with the people who installed it if you're serious," she said.

"Maybe in a year," Noah said. He could at least dream.

"Anytime you're ready," Ava said. Then she pointed upstairs. "There are two more floors, but it's just bedrooms and bathrooms, boring stuff. But I will be happy to show it to you if you would like."

"Thank you, but no, thanks," Noah said. "I'm overwhelmed as it is."

"Okay, let's get down to work. How about we sit in the office? For just relaxing and chilling, that's my favorite room."

"Sounds good to me," Noah said.

They left the computer room and walked back into the study. It was getting dark outside, and through the elm trees in the square Noah could see that lights had come on in the buildings on the other side of the greensward.

"You didn't say what you would like to drink," Ava said, but before Noah could respond, she added, "Wait a second! What a terrible host. I didn't think to ask whether you have eaten dinner tonight."

"No, I haven't," Noah admitted. There were lots of nights he just skipped dinner when he got back to his apartment from the hospital.

"Nor have I," Ava said. "How about we rectify that? Do you like Thai food?"

"Who doesn't like Thai food?" Noah questioned.

"I'll call down to King and I on Charles Street and order take-out. And if you wouldn't mind walking down there and getting it, I'll have a chance to jump in the shower and become a bit more presentable."

"Happy to go," Noah said. All at once, he realized he was starving.

9

When Noah returned with the take-out food, Ava greeted him at the door dressed much more appropriately in a fitted, tailored white blouse and stylishly distressed blue jeans. The outfit had made Noah considerably more comfortable than the clinging yoga pants and tank top. They had eaten the Thai food at a high-topped counter in the kitchen overlooking the small garden. The conversation had remained away from the M&M problem and concentrated on the issue of why both of them thought it best to avoid social ties with fellow hospital personnel. They had agreed it was far too professionally incestuous and could only create problems in the long run, since the hospital was an inveterate gossip mill.

Following their dinner, they had retreated to the upstairs study, taking glasses of wine and settling into the velvet-upholstered club chairs catty-cornered to each other. Despite a couple drinks at the recent Change Party, Noah rarely drank alcohol, as he was never completely sure he wouldn't be called into the hospital. But given that one of his best chief residents was on call, he was as sure as he'd ever been that he would not be called.

"So," Ava said, once they were ensconced in the plush easy chairs. "How should we begin?"

"I guess I'd first like to follow up on something you mentioned earlier today," Noah said. "You said that Dr. Mason was not fond of you. If I am not being too nosy, could you tell me why you feel that way? I mean, everyone knows he frequently asks for you to be his anesthesiologist."

"You're not being too nosy," Ava said. "But before I explain, I also said I believe the man has a dysfunctional personality. To be specific, I believe he has a serious narcissistic personality problem. Actually, I know he has one. Are you familiar with the symptoms?"

"Relatively," Noah said. He knew a bit about the condition, as did everyone who'd gone through medical school, but his course in psychiatry was way back in second year, some eight years ago.

"Well, let me refresh your memory," Ava said. "I'm up on it, because having to deal with the likes of Dr. Mason has forced me to go back and review the profile. But before I go any further, I need to make one thing clear. What I am about to say is for your ears only. I want to be certain that nothing will be repeated to anyone, especially to anyone at BMH. Are you good with that?"

"Absolutely," Noah said with conviction. He was appreciating Ava London more and more. He had come to her home feeling like a defenseless lone warrior facing an imminent crisis and hoping for a lifeline. Now he was feeling as if he had a comrade-in-arms who was a full BMH attending with skin in the game. There was no doubt in his mind that they could help each other, as she seemed to be socially astute, really smart, and possibly as committed to medicine as he was. On top of that, she was far nicer to be with than he had expected and a pleasure to even look at, especially now that she had showered and donned clothes that he didn't feel embarrassed to appreciate. Noah couldn't help but notice that she had taken the time and apparently cared enough about his visit to put on a touch of makeup, just enough to accentuate her eyes and complexion.

"People with a serious narcissistic personality problem are like bulls in a china shop," Ava said. "They cause all sorts of trouble for most everyone they interact with, especially if someone doesn't feed their insatiable need for admiration or, worse yet, insults or criticizes them. At the same time, they can be very successful, and Dr. Mason is a perfect case in point. He's a truly famous world-class surgeon. There is no doubt about it, and he gets a lot of deserved kudos for his skill, but it is not enough for him. It's never enough for someone with his needs. He might be a fantastic pancreatic surgeon, but he is also excessively arrogant, entitled, domineering, and vindictive, and capable of exploding at the slightest provocation."

"Which is why he has earned the nickname 'Wild Bill,'" Noah said.

"Precisely," Ava said. "He is a walking time bomb."

Noah found himself nodding in agreement. What Ava was putting into words was exactly his take on Dr. Mason and the reason he was terrified about the upcoming M&M Conference. There was no doubt in Noah's mind he was going to be in the unstable man's crosshairs.

"Unfortunately, I am one of those people who have insulted him," Ava said.

"Literally?" Noah asked with astonishment.

"No, not literally," Ava said. "He has tried to come on to me multiple times. He has even called me twice here in my home in the evening, asking to come over with the excuse that he was in the neighborhood and wanted to talk about a patient. I have never been interested in a social relationship with anyone at the hospital, much less someone like Dr. Mason. There was no way I was going to allow him into my life, especially with him being married on top of everything else. I've tried to be diplomatic, but it's hard, because he is so cocky and insistent and incapable of taking no for an answer. I am sure he has taken my continued refusal as an ongoing insult, especially now that he is backed into a corner with this Bruce Vincent case and needs a fall guy or girl."

"I'm sorry," Noah said.

"No need for you to be sorry," Ava said. "The biggest worry for me is that Dr. Mason and Dr. Kumar are really buddy-buddy. I don't want to lose my job, which might happen if Dr. Mason manages to blame the Vincent death on me. Losing my job would be a personal disaster. From my first year in medical school, it has been my dream to be on the BMH staff."

"I'm sorry, because it is sexual harassment," Noah said.

"I agree. Thank you for recognizing it."

"What I find ironic about your story," Noah said, "is that the main reason Dr. Mason dislikes me also has a romantic element."

Ava's mouth dropped open, and she stared back at Noah in shocked surprise.

"Wait a second!" Noah said, holding up his hands as if to ward off an attack. He laughed. "Don't get me wrong. There's no potential romance between Dr. Mason and me."

"Okay," Ava said, regaining her composure. "I don't mean to jump to conclusions, but I suppose you are aware there have been some rumors about you and your social preferences. You are considered a very eligible bachelor, but it is noticed you don't flirt with any of the available OR women."

"I'm aware of the rumors, and it doesn't bother me," Noah said. "I'm not gay, not that anything would be wrong if I were."

"Fair enough," Ava said. "You said Dr. Mason doesn't like you: explain. I mean, it is common knowledge that you are considered one of the best residents at BMH."

"Do you remember Margery, or Meg, Green? She was a surgical resident almost three years ago."

"I remember her," Ava said. "What about her? As I recall, she left rather suddenly."

"She certainly did," Noah said. "She was dismissed from the program. What no one knew was that she and Dr. Mason were having some sort of an affair. The full details were never revealed, but it had to be the case."

"She was dismissed because she was having an affair with an attending? That doesn't seem right."

"No, the affair aspect came out after the fact. She was dismissed because she was abusing opioids, and I was the person who outed her. I was the messenger, so to speak, and Dr. Mason has never forgiven me. Ergo, I'm terrified I'm going to be the messenger again at the upcoming M&M. I want to avoid antagonizing Dr. Mason as much as I possibly can. But it is going to take some planning and diplomacy because I think you are right: The two people mostly responsible for Bruce Vincent's death are Dr. Mason and the patient."

"Okay, I understand where you are coming from," Ava said. "What it boils down to is that 'Wild Bill' is not fond of either of us."

"I'd use a stronger word for his opinion of me," Noah said. "And what makes that so worrisome is that he is an associate surgical residency program director. As vindictive as he is, I would not be surprised if he tried to get me fired."

"I don't think you have to worry about that," Ava said. "You are much too respected by everyone else."

"I know that is the case generally," Noah said. "But it doesn't make me feel any better. Unfortunately, I've had a rather exaggerated fear of authority figures for as long as I can remember, particularly once I decided I wanted to be a surgeon way back in middle school."

"And you see Dr. Mason as an authority figure?"

"Certainly," Noah said. "He's definitely an authority figure."

"If you don't mind my asking, did you have issues with your own father?"

"My father passed away when I was in high school," Noah said.

"Now, there is a coincidence," Ava said with a slight, disbelieving shake of her head. "So did mine."

"I'm sorry," Noah said.

"I'm sorry, too," Ava said.

"Well, let's get to the topic at hand and talk about specifics," Noah said. "Just so you know, I have gone through Bruce Vincent's EMR, and I have spoken with all the key people except Dr. Mason. The wimp that I am, I am leaving that ordeal for last."

"That's smart," Ava said. "Having a conversation with him might turn out to be as difficult as the M&M itself."

"That's exactly how I see it," Noah said. "I've got to be prepared for both. What I need from you is anything at all you might feel is important that I might not have gotten from other sources."

Ava thought for a moment, pursing her lips. "You noticed there was no resident history and physical in the EMR."

"Of course," Noah said. "Martha Stanley explained to me that the resident was backed up when Mr. Vincent showed up forty minutes late."

"And you noticed that in the history and physical that had come from Dr. Mason's office, there was no mention of reflux disease or obstructive symptoms from the hernia."

"Well, that is not entirely true," Noah said. "Both were mentioned."

"They weren't," Ava said with sudden emotion bordering on anger.

"They were, but they were added after the fact," Noah said. "I could tell because they are in a different font than the rest of the H&P. I think they were added later to cover up that the H&P was one of those copy-and-paste jobs off the Internet."

"Good grief!" Ava exclaimed. "This case keeps getting progressively worse. Do you think Dr. Mason did it?"

"I can't imagine," Noah said. "He certainly would know better. I think it had to have been his fellow, Aibek Kolganov. I can't talk to him because he has already gone back to Kazakhstan. But if the issue comes up, which will not come from me, I will blame him."

"That might be helpful," Ava said.

"It would be a way of diverting blame from Mason, even though he is ultimately responsible for his fellow's actions."

"Maybe you should bring it up at the beginning of the discussion," Ava said. "Since the hospital attorneys would want to stop any talk about it because of the malpractice implications, Dr. Hernandez might insist on moving on to the next case."

"The discussion will surely not be restricted to that one issue," Noah said. "There are too many others that are glaringly important. Case in point: the patient's unknown history of reflux disease. Did you actually question the patient whether he had reflux disease?"

"Of course I did," Ava said. "I wouldn't have put it in the EMR if I hadn't. I always ask about reflux disease. The patient out-and-out lied to me, just like he did about not eating."

"How about obstructive GI symptoms? Did you ask about those?"

"No, I did not. That's what the H&P is for. Tell me this: Do you know that Mason's office specified the anesthesia Dr. Mason wanted?"

"I do," Noah said. "He wanted spinal. And I know the patient had been informed as well by the pre-anesthesia call the day before."

"I considered the anesthesia question seriously, as I always do, and decided there was no contraindication for spinal. And I assume you also know that Mason was not part of the pre-op huddle with me and the rest of the OR team?"

"I do," Noah said. "And I know he didn't appear for about an hour after you had given the spinal on the go-ahead by Janet Spaulding, who had been green-lighted by Dr. Mason. But I am not going to bring all this up because it's going to ignite the concurrent-surgery issue, and Dr. Mason has specifically warned me not to do it."

"It is going to be hard not to bring up an hour delay with the patient under anesthesia," Ava said. "Everybody in the OR knew what was going on, since Dr. Mason had two other patients under anesthesia at the very same time. It was like an assembly line that ground to a halt."

"Don't I know," Noah said. "There's the tightrope for me. I just don't want to bring it up. Maybe someone in the audience will, and they can be the messenger."

"One thing I'd like to say upfront," Ava said. She sat up straight and moved forward in her chair. "Emotionally, I'm a wreck because of this case. As I told you, it is my first operative death and hopefully my last."

"Dealing with death is not easy," Noah said. "I know how you feel, as I went through some agony my first year as a resident. You never get used to it, but you can learn to accept it as a possibility at any time, no matter that you do everything correctly, especially in certain specialties like oncology."

"I didn't expect it in anesthesia," Ava said. "I thought attention to detail and staying up with the latest developments would be enough."

"Death is part of the human condition, as it is with all life," Noah said.

"Well, getting back to this case, I have to tell you that I went over every detail with several other staff anesthesiologists, including Dr. Kumar. And as I said before, apart from waiting to give the spinal until Dr. Mason was physically present, there is nothing I would have done differently."

"I can appreciate that," Noah said. "Let me ask you a question about my part in this fiasco. After going over this case as you have, do you think I was right when I went ahead and put the patient on emergency cardiac bypass?"

"I do," Ava said. "No question. Had you not done so, the patient absolutely would have died before we could have bronchoscoped him and got oxygen into his lungs. His oxygen saturation was awful. He was in cardiac arrest. Putting him on cardiac bypass was a necessary and heroic decision, and you should be commended for it even if ultimately it was unsuccessful."

"Dr. Mason threatened to suggest I was the one who killed the patient," Noah said, with his own touch of emotion.

"Nonsense," Ava snapped. "That's because he was embarrassed he didn't or couldn't do it. He was just standing there wringing his hands as the patient's oxygen level was plummeting."

"Thank you," Noah said. "I appreciate your opinion. It is reassuring."

"So when are you going to talk with Dr. Mason?"

Noah shrugged. "I guess as soon as I can. He has patients in the hospital right now, and when he does, he usually comes in on Saturday. I'll try to work up my courage and talk to him tomorrow."

"Tread lightly, my friend," Ava said with obvious empathy.

A wry smile appeared on Noah's face. "Tread lightly! Those were the same words Dr. Mason used when he warned me about my presentation."

"Sorry," Ava said. "Let me change that to: 'Prepare well'! To help you, we should get together again after you speak with Dr. Mason. I am here this weekend, so let me know if you get to speak with him. Meanwhile, I will give the whole mess more thought. I'm certain you will, too. The more prepared you are, the better. Agreed?"

"Absolutely," Noah said.

"This case is disturbing for both of us," Ava said. "Nonetheless, it's been great talking with you. Thank you for being willing to come over here to my home. I'm really glad you approached me. I had thought about approaching you but felt reluctant. I'm not sure why." She shrugged. "Let's stay in touch. I've given you my mobile number. How about texting me so I have yours? Do you use Facebook or Snapchat?"

"I use Facebook a bit more than Snapchat," Noah said. "Mostly Face-Time, to be honest."

"We can use Facebook. The name I use is Gail Shafter." Ava gestured for Noah to precede her out of the room. They started down the main stairs.

"You don't use your real name?"

"I don't," Ava admitted. "On LinkedIn I do, but on the other social-media sites I don't. I'll explain it more to you sometime if you are interested."

"I'm interested," Noah said.

"I don't think we should be seen talking together in the hospital come

Monday, when I will be back for my next shift. It would surely start the gossip mill we both can't stand. We also don't want Dr. Mason to get wind that we have been talking. Agreed?"

"Absolutely," Noah said. "One last thing: Assuming I am successful in corralling Dr. Mason tomorrow, what time would you like to get together?"

"How about tomorrow night at the same time, at eight," Ava said. "We could even get take-out again if you are up for it."

"That would be terrific," Noah said. "Apart from an unexpected disaster at the hospital, I will be here."

They had reached the front door, and being the social nerd he knew he was, he felt suddenly flustered and self-conscious about how to end this pleasant evening. He hadn't expected to like her as much as he did. Should he shake hands, give her a hug, or what? Luckily, Ava came to his rescue. She leaned forward and pressed her cheeks one after the other against his and made a hushed kissing sound, making him realize how much more cosmopolitan she was than he.

"Thank you again for coming over," Ava said, straightening back. "You have made my evening."

Noah could feel himself blush. "And you mine," he managed. "It's been a delight." Then, gathering up his courage, he said, "One last question: You have a charming accent, but I just can't place it. Where are you from?"

"You're too kind," Ava said with a laugh. "Lubbock, Texas. And you?"

"Scarsdale, New York," Noah said. "Westchester County."

Fearing he was acting like a smitten teenager, Noah mumbled a good night. Halfway down the front steps he turned and waved. Ava waved back and closed the door.

"What a jerk," Noah mumbled, castigating himself for his social awkwardness. Yet he felt great. As he walked back toward his apartment in the soft summer night, he felt an excitement he'd not felt since high school with his very first love, Liz Nelson. Right under his nose had been a person with whom he now felt a strong connection of mutual interests, particularly a 100 percent commitment to medicine, not just as a career but as a way of life. He had been impressed when he overheard her give her mobile number to the nurse in the PACU and when he learned she religiously worked on her anesthesia recertification every day. He was also impressed that she had rescued cats from the animal shelter. And on top of all that, Noah had to admit that she was a pleasure to look at, even seductive. Noah had no idea if their friendship would continue and maybe even grow after the M&M, but if it did, he was confident he would never have to explain to Ava why he had to spend as much time at the hospital as he did. In that important way, Ava would be the opposite of Leslie Brooks, who had never understood.

Arriving at his building on Revere Street, Noah hesitated before keying the front door. For a moment he considered dashing over to the hospital just to check on things. But then he admitted he was being far too compulsive. If there was a problem that the chief resident, Tom Bachman, couldn't handle, he would have called. Noah sensed that his showing up unannounced and unrequested might be interpreted by Tom as a lack of confidence, something Noah did not want to communicate. Once again, Noah was realizing just how much diplomacy and psychology were involved in being the super chief.

After entering his apartment and closing the door, Noah stood for a moment, surveying the room. In comparison with Ava's place, it was a joke. The postage-stamp size, the lack of furnishings and decoration, and, most important of all, the lack of any personal touch were striking. He couldn't help but remember all the framed pictures of Ava in her study, which he could still see in his mind's eye, such as those in sporty venues such as ski areas and scuba-diving locales. There was even one of her about to skydive and another of her about to bungee-jump, activities that Noah thought were certifiably crazy. At the same time, he gave her credit for being adventuresome, since he certainly wouldn't do either one.

Most of the other photos were just smiling selfies Ava had taken at various tourist attractions such as the Coliseum in Rome and the Taj Mahal in Agra. Vaguely he wondered if she went on these trips solo, and if she didn't, why a companion wasn't in any of them.

Thinking about Ava's mansion and the money it represented, Noah again wondered exactly what her business connections were that could support such a lifestyle, since he was certain, the more he thought about it, that her anesthesia salary would not be enough. Her explanation that her business involved "consulting" was unclear. He wondered if her outside work involved anesthesia in some way. If their friendship did blossom, he'd ask her. One of the qualities that he particularly liked about her was her apparent self-confidence and openness in who she was, something Noah felt he lacked except for his role of being a doctor.

Trying to tamp down his excitement of a potential new relationship with an attractive, sexy, and impressively intelligent woman with mutual interests and a similar value system, Noah sat down at his card table and booted up his HP laptop. Hungry for more information, he was eager to check out Ava's Facebook page under the name of Gail Shafter. As the comparatively ancient machine labored through its routine, Noah had to smile at the difference between his computer and Ava's setup. It was as stark as their living styles.

When Gail Shafter's page came up, Noah was fascinated. There were lots of photos going back to Ava's childhood. There were even some of the same selfies that Ava had on the wall of her study, as if Gail Shafter was a globetrotter as well. Looking at the "friends" category, he was duly impressed that she had 641, which made him laugh when he thought about his own page. He couldn't remember exactly, but he thought he had about ten. Then Noah looked at the "about" information and saw that Gail Shafter had gone to high school in Lubbock, Texas, and now worked for a dentist in Iowa. What Noah found most interesting was trying to decide what was real and what wasn't.

Something else caught his attention. There was a fan page listed over to the left on Gail Shafter's homepage. When he clicked on it he found Gail Shafter's Nutrition, Exercise, and Beauty page, where he found multiple videos of Ava significantly disguised, providing tips on all sorts of subjects involving makeup, exercise, and general health. But what surprised him the most was when he clicked on "likes," he found that she had 122,363 followers! No wonder she spent so much time on social media. It was a command performance.

Next he pulled up her LinkedIn page. This was decidedly professional. He was interested to read that she had attended Brazos University in Lubbock, Texas, in a combined B.A./M.D. program with an undergraduate major in nutrition. She then went on to an anesthesia residency at the Brazos University Medical Center. Noah thought that nutrition was an interesting major for a premedical student, as nutrition was one of those subjects that medical school did a poor job teaching. He thought it was a smart choice and wondered if nutrition had anything to do with her consulting business.

Glancing over the rest of the material, Noah suddenly burst out laughing. In the skills and endorsement section, he noticed that Gail Shafter was one of the people who gave Ava a positive endorsement as to her anesthesia skills. "Why not?" Noah remarked out loud. He knew what he had found was an example of sockpuppetry, which some people looked down on, but in this instance he thought it was humorous.

After turning off his computer, Noah got to his feet and stretched. He then headed into the bedroom, knowing that 4:45 A.M. would come all too quickly.

10

So far the morning had gone brilliantly, but Noah knew it was about to head south. He was on his way across the pedestrian bridge that connected the Stanhope Pavilion with the Young Clinic Building, where Dr. William Mason had an office. Noah was facing a semi-impromptu meeting with "Wild Bill" for 11:00 A.M. that had been arranged when Noah had run into the surgeon by happenstance on the general surgical floor less than an hour earlier. When Noah had asked if he could have a moment of his time, Mason had responded gruffly that he would be available around eleven in his clinic office for a short time. Noah didn't know exactly what to expect, but the chances the interaction would turn out pleasant were essentially nil.

Noah had arrived at the hospital as per usual around five and gone straight to the surgical intensive-care unit. He was particularly interested to see how John Horton was getting on, even though he was a private patient under the moment-to-moment care of the critical-care people. It was comforting to see that he was doing reasonably well. The same was true with all the other SICU patients. It had also been nice to hear that Carol Jensen, as a unit supervisor, continued to be complimentary about the new residents.

Leaving the SICU, Noah had met up with the residents who had been on call overnight. No problems there. The Saturday-morning work rounds had gone smoothly, although with the new residents it had taken much longer than usual. When Noah had run into Dr. Mason around 10:00, work rounds were just ending, even though they had started at 7:30. As expected, the newbies had yet to master the technique of quick but thorough bedside presentations. That being said, all in all, Noah felt very good about how the first full week of his super chief residency had gone. He wasn't surprised. He'd always been a fast learner. It was the coming second week that had him worried.

Saturday clinic was a mere shadow of its normal weekday self, and the Young Building was comparatively empty. Noah was the only one in the elevator as he rode up to the fifth floor, home of the General Surgery Clinic. Although he was certainly not looking forward to the next fifteen minutes or so, what bolstered his courage was a sense of secret camaraderie that Ava was now providing. It was reassuring to not be alone in regard to the looming M&M.

Noah walked directly back to where he knew Dr. Mason had a small office that also functioned as an exam room. The man's real office was in the much plusher Franklin Building, which catered to the likes of Arab sheiks, billionaires, and heads of state and had been named after one of Mason's former patients, who'd financed it.

Noah knocked on the open door and stepped over the threshold. Dr. Mason was dressed in a light blue seersucker jacket, a white shirt, a bow tie, and dark slacks. He was sitting at the small wall-mounted desk, typing on a keyboard. To his right was an exam table. Hearing Noah's knock on the open door, he swung around and pointed to one of two generic molded plastic chairs. He didn't say anything but rather tipped back and interlaced his fingers across his expansive chest. His expression was a half-scowl with pursed lips. Noah was not encouraged.

Taking one of the indicated seats, Noah faced his bête noire as he struggled to decide where to begin. The trouble was he was there because of protocol. He was expected to interview the involved surgeon as part of investigating the case. In reality, he didn't expect to learn anything that he didn't already know. "Thank you for seeing me," Noah said, hoping at least to start out the discussion in a friendly, mutually respectful fashion. In the back of his mind he was hearing Ava's characterization of the man. To Noah, her description of him as a serious narcissist seemed spot-on, meaning that under the circumstances there was zero chance for any reasonable interaction. Not only was the man presumably still furious at Noah's outing of his reputed lover, he was clearly challenged by Noah's work ethic and jealous of the kudos Noah was getting in the process.

When Dr. Mason did not respond or even change his facial expression at Noah's pleasantry, Noah took a deep breath and pressed on: "I've gone over the Bruce Vincent record and have spoken with most of the people involved except you. What I'd like to ask is whether there is anything that you might be able to tell me that I might not know."

"I suppose you saw there was no resident admitting note?" Dr. Mason snapped.

"I did," Noah said. "And I know why. I spoke at length with Martha Stanley, who said—"

"Yeah, I know," Mason interrupted. "The poor overworked bastard was backed up. Bullshit on that excuse." Dr. Mason was now stabbing the air with a thick index finger. "He fucked up, plain and simple. I tell you, with the residents nowadays it's amazing any of us senior men get anything done. When I was a resident that wouldn't have happened, and we saw way more patients than you guys do today and were on call every other night."

Noah was well aware that a number of the senior surgeons bemoaned how easy they thought the residents of today had it, but he resisted questioning the idea. Attempting to calm Dr. Mason, who was already riled, Noah said, "My understanding is that the lack of a resident H&P was a decision made by Ms. Stanley. The junior resident was totally unaware and didn't even know that Mr. Vincent passed through Admitting."

"Well, then it's Ms. Stanley who is to blame. If the junior resident had done what he is supposed to do, all this wouldn't have happened."

"The requirement is that there needs to be an up-to-date history and physical, which was the case. Your fellow Dr. Kolganov had done one the day before that Ms. Stanley thought was adequate." Noah thought briefly about bringing up the deficiencies of Kolganov's H&P as a copy-and-paste job with after-the-fact doctoring but quickly decided against it. Dr. Mason was supposed to have been supervising the man's work and was therefore ultimately responsible. Once again the blame would fall on Dr. Mason's shoulders.

"Then the system has to be changed," Dr. Mason barked. "Residents should see all surgical patients prior to surgery, particularly same-day surgery."

"That can be a good subject for the discussion of the case," Noah said.

"You bet your ass," Dr. Mason agreed.

"Let me ask you this," Noah said. "Did you see and examine the patient before surgery?"

Dr. Mason rocked forward in his chair with such suddenness that the chair squeaked in protest. "What the hell are you implying with a question like that? Of course I saw the patient before surgery. I see every one of my patients before surgery."

"I'm not implying anything," Noah said defensively. "I didn't know how much of the pre-op process you delegated to Dr. Kolganov."

"Rest assured, my precocious friend, I examine all my patients thoroughly. Especially since Dr. Kolganov was not going to be part of the surgery. He was needed elsewhere for one of my much more serious cases."

"Then you were aware that Mr. Vincent had had some symptoms of bowel obstruction," Noah said, ignoring Dr. Mason's condescending remark.

"Of course," Dr. Mason said. "It was even mentioned in the referral note from his GP. It was why we were doing the goddamned operation."

"And yet you still favored spinal anesthesia?"

"I didn't favor any particular anesthesia," Dr. Mason snapped. "That is what anesthesiologists are for. They don't mess around in my area of expertise during the surgery, and I sure don't mess in theirs."

"But your office requested spinal," Noah said. He knew this issue was going to come up no matter what, and he had to know the details.

"On the few hernias I have done over the years, spinal was used. I'm sure that was what my secretary was conveying. It is still up to the anesthesiologist to determine what is best."

"You may be right," Noah conceded but held back what he wanted to say—namely, that anesthesiologists needed all the facts, which plainly were not available in this circumstance for a multitude of reasons, least of which was that Dr. Mason was not available for the pre-op huddle.

"What else?" Dr. Mason demanded. He had returned to tipping back in his chair, fingers again interlocked. His earlier anger had dissipated and the pursed-lipped scowl had returned.

"It seems to me," Noah said, trying to organize his thoughts and be as diplomatic as possible, "the patient didn't take his upcoming surgery as seriously as he should have."

Dr. Mason laughed derisively. "That's the understatement of the year. I heard he was forty minutes late to Admitting. The guy was working that morning. I saw him myself. He even parked my car. But worse yet, he ate a goddamn full breakfast and then lied about it. I tell you, you try to do a guy a favor and he kicks you in the teeth."

"Was he informed of the seriousness of what he was facing?"

Dr. Mason tipped forward again and eyed Noah. Instinctively, Noah leaned back as much as his chair would allow.

"I told him I was going to operate on him," Dr. Mason said slowly, emphasizing each word. "What went on in his pea brain, I have no idea.

But listen, my friend. We are wasting time here. Tell me! Did you talk to Dr. Ava London, the uppity bitch?"

"Yes, I have," Noah admitted, trying to maintain a neutral expression. Knowing what he did, he was appalled at Dr. Mason for calling Ava an uppity bitch.

"Well, she is the one mostly responsible for this catastrophe," Dr. Mason snapped. "And to tell you the truth, I don't know if she should be on the staff here at BMH. I don't know if she is qualified."

"She is board-qualified in anesthesia," Noah offered.

"Yeah, well, I don't know how good anesthesia boards are to let someone like her pass. I've never been all that impressed with Dr. London, nor have some of the other staff. I've tried to be nice to her, but there is some disconnect in her personality. Frankly, she is a cold fish."

I'm sure you have tried to be nice to her, Noah thought sarcastically but didn't say.

"I want you to make it crystal clear at the M&M that general anesthesia should have been used on this patient at the get-go. If it had been, we could have gone into the abdomen when we needed to do so. Admittedly, the patient might have regurgitated anyway during induction since his stomach was so full, but who's to know. At least it would have happened at the beginning of the case and not at the middle, and it would have been an anesthesia fatality, not a surgical one. It's aggravating to have this screw up my statistics."

"So you think Anesthesia is solely responsible?" Noah said, trying to keep disbelief out of his voice.

"The lion's share," Dr. Mason said. "Of course the patient didn't help, and Admitting should have discovered the man had eaten a full breakfast. Making sure the patient has been NPO is a major responsibility for them, everybody knows that."

"Thank you for your time," Noah said. He got to his feet.

"Let me warn you once again, my friend. Do not turn this case into a discussion about concurrent surgery. That is not the issue here. The fact that I was held up for a few minutes in one of my major cases because of a congenital abnormality was not a factor in Bruce Vincent's death. You get my point?"

"I believe I do," Noah said.

"Good," Dr. Mason said. "It is nice to have you as our super chief resident. It would be a tragedy if your year was prematurely terminated."

A cruel smile appeared on Dr. Mason's face. He didn't stand up.

Noah nodded a final time, then turned and left. As he punched the elevator button out in the hall he became aware that his heart was racing. Although he knew he shouldn't have been surprised, he had not expected Dr. Mason to be quite so specific with his threat. Noah's worst-case scenario would be losing his position at BMH this close to the end of what had been a long odyssey and practically a lifelong dream.

Once again, he was the only person in the elevator. With trembling hands he took out his mobile phone and texted Ava: *Met with the enemy. Bad as expected. Will fill u in 2nite.* Almost immediately the three little blinking bubbles appeared on his screen. As the elevator door began to open, a message popped up: *At least you got it over with. I can't wait to hear what he said.* The message was followed by a smiley-face emoji.

Feeling relatively chipper from Ava's text, despite the meeting with Dr. Mason, Noah emerged from the elevator onto the second floor of the Young Building, which served as the triage center for the BMH clinical services. His intent was to use the pedestrian bridge to get back to the Stanhope Pavilion. His destination was the fourth floor, to see if he could locate the chief anesthesia resident. For several days he'd entertained the idea of possibly interviewing Dr. Kumar, but after Ava had told Noah that he and Dr. Mason were close friends, Noah decided against it. Although both Dr. Wiley and Dr. Chung had corroborated Ava's interpretation of the Vincent case, Noah wanted confirmation from someone higher up just to be sure.

11

Knowing he was early, Noah slowed down as he entered Louisburg Square. He noticed the ambient light was significantly greater than it had been the evening before with the sun higher in the sky. Sunset wasn't going to occur for another half-hour. There were more children playing in the grass enclosure, and their shouts and laughter echoed in the confined area. Bright sunlight bathed the façades of the town houses on the upside of the hill, whereas those on the lower side, where number 16 was located, were in comparatively dark shadow.

A few doors away from his destination, Noah stopped and looked at his watch and wondered what to do. He was going to be twenty minutes early, and he didn't want to seem too eager. Of course, he was too eager. He admitted it. As the day had passed, he'd gotten progressively more excited about returning to Ava's that evening. And the excitement wasn't just because of the M&M issue, although it contributed. He was looking forward to spending more time with Ava just to be with her, a feeling he couldn't remember experiencing since he'd been a teenager. But as she'd already made clear her reluctance to form social relationships with fellow hospital personnel, he knew he had to proceed slowly, lest he scare her away. Arriving early could send the wrong message.

As he was standing there dithering, he saw Ava's door open. With a sense of panic, he tried to decide what to do and whether he should turn around and flee. Before he could make a move, Ava stepped out onto her stoop, saw him, and waved.

Noah hesitantly waved back and restarted walking toward her. A moment later a second figure appeared from inside her house. It was a light-complected, clean-cut man, maybe forty, but what caught Noah's attention was that he was even more athletic-appearing than Ava, which was saying something. He was wearing loose-fitting black workout pants with a white V-neck T-shirt that appeared to be a size too small. Even from where Noah was, he could see that the man's biceps were straining the fabric. Noah felt instantly inadequate as he mentally compared his own body image to this physical Adonis. It was like day and night. When Noah got to the base of the stoop, the man came down the steps. There was a distinctive spring to his gait. With a slight, friendly smile he nodded to Noah as he passed. Noah nodded back and mounted the granite stairs.

"See you tomorrow, same time," Ava called after the man.

The man didn't answer or even turn around. He merely waved over his shoulder as he climbed into a black Suburban parked in front of Ava's house.

"You're early," Ava said cheerfully as Noah gained the top step.

"Sorry," Noah said. "Fearing I was going to be late, I rushed. I guess I didn't need to, but it was a little after seven by the time I was able to leave the hospital." He had indeed rushed to get home, practically jogging the entire way. He's also taken a very quick shower, fearing for the worst about being late, but then here he was being early. He'd been keyed up all day and still was.

"You made good time," Ava said. "Come in! Sorry about my being in my workout clothes yet again. We went over the allotted time we had set, and I didn't expect you for at least another twenty minutes or so."

"Who is 'we'?" Noah asked as he entered the foyer. The inner door was also ajar.

"That was my personal trainer," Ava said. She followed Noah inside.

"So you believe in personal trainers," Noah said. He felt a sense of relief that the man with the buff body was a hired hand.

"I do. Don't you?"

"Not really. Anybody can say they are a personal trainer. I think there are a lot of charlatans out there." Noah silently chided himself for being jealous.

Ava laughed her sparkling laugh. "So you think you can tell?"

"I can't," Noah said. "That's the problem. There is a legitimate certification, but not all of them have it. I think you have to be careful to get what you pay for."

"My trainer is certified. I'm sure of it. He's very good and very motivating."

They ended up standing at the base of Ava's main staircase. As he had done on his previous visit, Noah made a point of keeping his eyes on hers and not allowing his line of vision to stray elsewhere. He liked the yoga pants but didn't want it to be obvious. The two cats reappeared, sniffed Noah disdainfully, then disappeared.

"So we're back to where we were last night," Ava said flirtatiously. "I need to take a shower and change. You can make yourself at home in whatever room you'd like, or we can do what we did last night."

"Meaning?" Noah asked.

"We talked about doing take-out again tonight. I know you were the one to go and get it last night, so it is unfair to ask you to do it again, but . . ."

"I'd be happy to do it," Noah offered eagerly.

"That would be terrific. Why don't we try Toscano tonight?"

"I didn't know they did take-out." Noah was aware of the Italian eatery on Charles Street as a Beacon Hill favorite and had eaten there with Leslie on several occasions.

"They most certainly do," Ava said. "I've used them many times. Give them a call! Order whatever you want and get the same for me. I'm not choosy. I have some great Italian white wine in the fridge. It will be a treat. How do you feel about your on-call team tonight? As good as last night?"

"They're fine," Noah said. He had checked, trying to plan ahead. The in-house chief resident on call was Cynthia Nugent, who Noah thought was just as competent as Tom Bachman, if not more so. Once again he felt confident he wouldn't be called unless the sky fell in.

"Then you might be willing to have a glass or two of wine."

"I will enjoy it," Noah said. It was an amazing feeling to be with someone who truly understood his responsibilities without his having to explain them.

SLIGHTLY LESS THAN an hour later, Ava and Noah were back at the counter table in the kitchen. Night had fallen and a floodlight illuminated Ava's tiny garden, which included a fountain. Since the sliding glass doors were open, the sound of the water could be heard over the classical music that was quietly playing in the background from hidden speakers. Noah had ordered quite a feast, and Ava had opened a chilled bottle of Falanghina Greco.

"Will it ruin your enjoyment of your dinner if we start talking about serious stuff?" Ava asked with a playful smile. She was dressed in a mostly white butterfly-print summer dress, which Noah thought was charming. In contrast, he was wearing almost the same thing he had the night before. He had agonized for a time after his shower about wearing something different, but his choices were limited. He had briefly thought about wearing his resident whites just because he felt the most comfortable in them and thought he looked his best, but had nixed the idea as totally ridiculous. He'd mocked himself for being so pitifully insecure.

"As you like," Noah said. He, too, was interested in getting it out of the way.

"You said in your text that your meeting with Dr. Mason was as bad as expected. Care to elaborate?"

Putting down his wineglass, Noah took a deep breath. "Just as we feared, we're definitely in his crosshairs. He threatened to have me fired if I turn the case into a discussion of the concurrent-surgery issue."

"Good God," Ava said with emotion. "He literally threatened to have you terminated?"

"Well, not in so many words. What he said was that it would be a tragedy if my super chief resident year was prematurely terminated, which I take as the same thing."

"The bastard," Ava snapped. "I'm sorry. What about me? Did he talk about me specifically or about Anesthesia in general?"

"I'm afraid it was about you specifically," Noah said. "You were so right last night when you described him as having a narcissistic personality problem. The man is a classic case. As you suspect, it's pretty obvious that he was and is insulted by your rebuffing him. The man is out of control."

"So what did he say, exactly? You don't have to mince words. I can take it. I just want to know what I am up against."

"Again, he said you were mostly responsible for what happened," Noah said, lowering his voice as if someone might overhear. "It is so obvious that he is incapable of accepting any blame whatsoever. And by his putting the blame on you, it has him questioning if you should be on the BMH staff."

"Why? Because of my personality or my qualifications?"

"I'm afraid a little of both," Noah said reluctantly. The last thing he wanted to do was hurt Ava's feelings, yet he felt obligated to speak the truth. "Dr. Mason said you were a cold person, which made me bite my tongue, knowing what I know."

"Thank you," Ava said sincerely.

"You're welcome," Noah said. "With respect to your qualifications, I reminded him you had passed your anesthesia boards, at which point he questioned the anesthesia boards. I'm telling you, the man is out of control."

For a few moments Ava stared out at the fountain in her garden. It was obvious to Noah that she was upset and turning the news over in her mind. Noah felt bad for her, but he felt worse for himself. He still didn't think it likely that Dr. Mason could get her fired even if Dr. Mason was good friends with Ava's boss. Whereas with himself, Noah was concerned Dr. Mason could possibly get him dismissed or, at a minimum, make his position tenuous if he put his mind to it. After all, he was an associate director of the surgical residency program and therefore was one of just three people in charge.

Ava redirected her attention back to Noah. "Let me guess," she said. "Dr. Mason thinks I should have given general anesthesia even though it had been communicated that he wanted spinal."

Noah nodded. "He claims not to have asked for spinal, and that his secretary merely included it because it had been used on the last hernia he'd done a hundred years ago. He said it is Anesthesia's job to determine the appropriate anesthesia, and he didn't care which was used."

Ava took a deep breath. "You do have your work cut out for you."

"Don't I know," Noah agreed. "I keep thinking it is going to be like walking in a minefield."

"Did he bring up the patient and his role in this tragedy?"

"He certainly did. Actually, considering everyone involved in this case, Dr. Mason might be the angriest at the patient. He described him as having a 'pea brain' despite the man's beloved employee reputation around the hospital. Deep down, Dr. Mason certainly knows it was the patient's fault by eating a full breakfast and lying about it. But Dr. Mason also faults Admissions for not being more aggressive and finding it out."

"All right," Ava said, suddenly motivated. "Let's talk specifics." She sipped her wine and then took a bite of her dinner. "I've given this situation a lot of thought since yesterday evening," she said. "First off, I think you have to understand it will be counterproductive to get into any kind of argument with this man, because if he gets mad, we can both lose. You are going to have to present the case with that restriction in mind."

"Easier said than done," Noah responded. "He got mad this morning, and I was trying to be as diplomatic as I could."

"So what did he get mad at? Let's analyze it."

At that moment Ava's mobile phone chimed, indicating she was getting a call. She picked up the phone, noticed who was calling. Immediately she pushed back from the counter. "Sorry," she said to Noah. "I've got to take this."

"Quite all right," Noah said. He watched her leave the room, vaguely wondering who could be calling after nine on a Saturday night. For him it would have been easy to guess: the hospital. But he knew Ava was not on call. Noah toyed with his food, thinking it was impolite to eat without her. In the distance, he could just barely hear her voice, although at one point it became decidedly louder, as if she were angry.

After about five minutes Ava returned, placed her phone facedown on the counter, and climbed back onto her seat. "Sorry about that," she said. "I know taking calls makes me a less-than-perfect hostess. But what can you do? Silly business sometimes interferes."

"Is everything all right?" Noah questioned.

"It's fine," Ava said, with a wave of her hand. She smiled reassuringly. "Now, where were we?"

"You were asking what Dr. Mason got mad at when I spoke to him this morning."

"Right. So tell me!"

"I'd have to say he got the maddest when he was talking about the lack of a resident history and physical because the resident was backed up. Dr. Mason is one of those old-school surgeons who is convinced we residents today have it easy while he and his contemporaries worked themselves to the bone."

Ava nodded. "I know the type. But it is interesting that he would zero in on that issue. I think that is important to remember. What else did he get mad at, specifically?"

"When I questioned him if he had personally examined the patient."

Ava laughed. "Knowing what we do about his temperament, are you surprised such a question made him angry?"

"I suppose not," Noah admitted, smiling in the face of Ava's laughter. In retrospect, he lambasted himself for not being more circumspect. He should have worded the question to Dr. Mason differently so it wouldn't have been interpreted as being critical. When dealing with a narcissist it is crucial to avoid any suggestion of blaming. "I was trying to be diplomatic but failing."

"I'd say!" Ava responded. "Tell me this: Did he bring up again any nonsense of you being responsible for the death since you put the patient on bypass?"

"No, he didn't."

"At least that's reassuring," Ava said. "I'm starting to get an idea of how you should present this case."

"Really?" Noah questioned. He sat up straighter. She was impressing him again, and he was eager to hear what she had in mind.

"Keeping him from getting mad is going to be key," Ava said. "That's number one. Number two, you have to steer the discussion away from the concurrent-surgery issue. That's mainly for your sake. And number three, you have to avoid the issue of Anesthesia, meaning me, supposedly making the wrong decision about spinal versus general anesthesia."

"That's easier said than done," Noah complained. "The facts are facts. I can't change them."

"What you will have to do is keep away from the troublesome facts. For instance, there is no reason to mention that the patient had been under anesthesia for an hour or more. As bad as that was, it didn't contribute to the death. Instead, emphasize the two points Dr. Mason is most emotional about—namely, the lack of a resident H&P and that the patient ate a breakfast that Admitting didn't uncover. If you are clever and mildly verbose, those two issues could be an hour discussion in and of themselves. Tell me! How many cases are scheduled for the conference?"

"Five so far," Noah said. "There could be more."

"Perfect," Ava said. "Listen! Save Vincent's case until last. Since the M&M has to be adjourned in an hour and a half without fail since surgery is scheduled and everybody has to get to the OR, you can run out of time. What do you think?"

Noah toyed with his food while he pondered Ava's suggestion. The more he thought about it, the better he liked it, because it could work. The scheduling of the presentations was totally up to him. He had initially thought of doing the Vincent case first since there was so much interest in it, but there was no reason he couldn't do it last, and if no one knew it was going to be last, no one, like Dr. Hernandez, could complain and try to change it. There was a good chance that whatever the discussion was, it could be prematurely terminated.

"I think you have some good points," Noah said.

"I do, too," Ava agreed. She picked up her wineglass and motioned with it toward Noah. They clinked glasses. "We have a few more days to plan, but I think we're making headway. To your success!"

AFTER GETTING the serious stuff out of the way, Ava and Noah switched to more lighthearted banter as they finished their dinner and cleaned up the plates and flatware. Ava dominated the conversation, since she was full of stories about her recent travels and athletic episodes, such as her latest bungee-jumping excursion. Noah had been amazed to hear that she had flown all the way to New Zealand to do it, although she also used the trip to scuba-dive in shark cages off the southern coast of Australia. Noah was fascinated but also intimidated, as it made his life seem all that more insular and hospital-bound. The last trip he had taken had been more than two years ago, and only to New York City. He'd gone with Leslie to see a play, and only for a single Saturday night. At the time he had been reluctant to go, since he had several patients he'd operated on in the hospital. Although he had arranged for people to cover for him, it didn't seem right, since he couldn't help but put himself in his patients' shoes.

"How about we head up to the study and relax?" Ava offered when the kitchen was back to spic-and-span. "We can have a cordial if you'd like."

"Thank you, but I think I'll pass on the cordial. Sorry. Two glasses of wine are enough for me."

"Hey, don't be sorry. I'm impressed with your self-restraint. Your dedication is awe-inspiring. I'd want you to be my doctor any day."

"Thank you," Noah said.

While trailing Ava as they headed up the second flight of stairs from the kitchen level, Noah worked up his courage to ask: "Hey, do you take your trips solo or with friends?" He made it sound as if the idea just occurred to him, whereas he'd been wondering about it since he'd heard about all her travels the previous evening. He didn't know what answer he wanted to hear.

"It depends," Ava said. "My fun trips like to New Zealand and the previous one to India I went alone. With my business travel, I'm usually accompanied."

"Seems to me it would be more fun the other way around," Noah said.

"You have a point," Ava said. "Are you interested in going with me when I go back to New Zealand for a repeat bungee-jump?" She laughed in her unique and charming fashion.

"I wish," Noah said. "If you don't mind my asking, are your business trips because of your nutrition background?"

Ava stopped several steps short of the landing outside the study and turned around to face Noah, who was forced to stop as well. She was smiling, but her tone was accusatory. "Have you been spying on me?"

"In a fashion," Noah confessed. "I looked at your LinkedIn page. I was impressed that you majored in nutrition. I think it is a neglected area of expertise when it comes to doctors."

"I agree," Ava said. Her voice had returned to normal. "That's why I chose it as an undergraduate major. But to answer your question, my business trips do involve my background in nutrition, at least indirectly."

Ava didn't elaborate, but rather turned back around and continued up the stairs. Noah followed her into the study. He was dying to ask her more about her business, which he assumed had to be remarkably successful, but he felt reluctant. He didn't want to push it. While she went over to get a bottle of Grand Marnier and a glass from a bookshelf, he took the same velvet club chair he'd occupied the night before. He watched her, fascinated by the way she moved, which was accentuated by her flared dress. He was hypnotized by her entire persona.

"Are you sure you don't want just a nip?" Ava said, holding up the liquor bottle in Noah's direction. She took the other club chair.

"Thank you, no," Noah said. "I also visited your Gail Shafter Facebook page and the fan page. I was truly amazed at the number of your followers."

"I have to admit I have a lot of fun with it. I've even gotten some offers to advertise products."

"Have you done that?" Noah asked.

"No, I haven't," Ava said. "I do it for pleasure, not for business."

"I got a chuckle when I saw that Gail Shafter endorsed you on your LinkedIn page."

Ava treated Noah to another one of her laughs. "Guilty as charged," she said. "I just couldn't help myself."

"Last night you offered to explain to me why you use a fake name on Facebook. If you're willing, I'd like to hear."

"Purely for a sense of freedom," Ava said. "The beauty of the virtual online world is anonymity. Using a made-up name magnifies that and enhances my freedom. I'm sure you have heard the expression: *On the Internet no one knows you are a dog.*"

It was Noah's turn to laugh. "No, I haven't heard that. But I get it."

"Using a made-up name allows me to avoid my own hang-ups," Ava explained. "I don't have to be me. I can project onto Gail Shafter whatever identities I want. And using my avatar, technoself, I can do it without fear of being judged. If someone doesn't like my digital me and acts like a troll, I can block them. In real life I can't do that. And social media can be wonderfully dynamic, whereas real-life social interaction tends to be static."

"I've never heard the term *technoself*. Is that something new?"

"In the tech world, nothing is new. As soon as something is out, like a new app, the next day it is old. Things are changing at warp speed. So no, it is not new. In fact, technoself studies have become an entire interdisciplinary domain of scholarly research. It is where our culture is going. We are all becoming cyborgs with our devices, particularly with our phones."

"You're making me feel old."

"In the teenage mind, you are old. They are the ones who are driving the pace."

"You mentioned you were addicted to social media when you were a teenager, and it was a disaster. How so?"

"I became obsessed with my digital reputation to the detriment of everything else, including my schoolwork. At one point, I got cyberbullied on SixDegrees to the point I couldn't go to school for a week. Well, it wasn't called cyberbullying back then, just harassment. But it was a disaster. I did so poorly academically that I didn't even think about going to college after high school. I had to work, so I worked for a dentist. Luckily, I quickly saw the light."

"Is that why Gail Shafter works for a dentist?" Noah asked.

"You got it. It's something I know about."

"What about dating apps and websites? Do you use them?"

"Of course. Why not? They are particularly fun. Especially now with the swipe-right-or-swipe-left feature. Hot-or-not, what a great game! It empowers even the most pitiful creeps. Online, anyone who is digitally clever can be popular or even famous. Look at the Kardashians."

"Have you ever met anyone in real life that you met on a dating app?"

"Hell, no! I'd never in a million years do that. Everybody lies on those sites. I like to play around with them, but I'd never actually look for anyone on Tinder or any of the others. We're all becoming narcissistic charlatans to one degree or another. Meeting up with someone you met online would be too risky. Besides, it would defeat the whole anonymity thing."

"Aren't you worried somebody sufficiently enamored with Gail Shafter and armed with technical knowhow could get Gail's address here on Louisburg Square?"

"There was a time when that might have happened because I had a proxy server that turned out to be almost worthless. But my computer people set me up with a proper encryption. There's no worry now. And what about you?"

"What do you mean?"

"Have you ever used a dating app or website?"

Noah didn't answer right away. Like most people, he had, but questioned if he should admit it to Ava. What convinced him to come clean was that she readily admitted she'd used them herself so there would be no judgment. "Actually, I did use OkCupid for a couple of weeks not long after it came out. So I used it once."

"Uh-oh," Ava voiced. She flashed a knowing smile. "This is sounding serious. Did you meet someone online and then meet up with them in person?"

"I did," Noah admitted. "Her name was Leslie Brooks. She was a Columbia undergrad. We ended up living together for the last year of my medical school, and then she came up here to Boston to go to Harvard Business School."

"Sweet," Ava said with sincerity. "I guess there are some successes. Are you guys still together?"

"Nope," Noah said. "She left two years ago for a finance job in New York."

"Four years together; that's impressive. Are you still seeing each other?"

"No," Noah said simply. "She couldn't really adjust to my commitment to medicine, which I don't blame her for. In retrospect, she was counting on my hours getting less as I advanced up the training ladder, like it does for most people. Unfortunately, for me they got more, so she bailed out. She's engaged now."

"I think only those of us in medicine understand," Ava said. "So who are you seeing now?"

"No one," Noah said. Inwardly he cringed, wondering if Ava would think of him as socially hopeless.

"That doesn't seem appropriate for a healthy man like yourself," Ava said with a slight, mischievous smile. "As a fellow doctor, I'd like to ask how you manage."

Noah stared back at Ava. He agonized for a beat, questioning if he should take the bait. "I'm resourceful," he said after a pause. "There is always online porn."

Ava roared with laughter and clapped her hands. "You are a trip, Dr. Rothauser. Now I have to wonder which of us is more addicted to the Internet."

"There's no way I am addicted," Noah said. He found her mirth contagious and was laughing at himself even though he questioned why he had said what he did. He was thankful she had taken the comment in a nonjudgmental, humorous fashion.

After putting down her liquor glass, Ava leaned forward. "Last night I showed you most of my house. But there is one cool thing I did not show you. Interested?"

"Sure," Noah said with a shrug. "Give me a clue."

"I put a deck on the top of the building and the view is to die for. And it's a beautiful summer night."

He followed her up two flights of the central, nautilus-like stairway that spiraled from the very first floor. When they gained the sixth and final floor and pretending to be out of breath, Noah said, "With all these stairs you don't need to work out."

"Sometimes I take the elevator," Ava said.

"Elevator? I didn't know you had an elevator." Noah had never been in a private home that had an elevator.

"The doors are disguised so as not to be intrusive," Ava explained. She pointed to the wall to their immediate right. "Here's one here."

All Noah could see was a door-sized, rectangular, grooved outline that even cut through the dado and its trim. "Wow," he said. "I never would have guessed. But there's no call button."

"It's WiFi," Ava said. "Welcome to the tech world."

As Noah followed Ava into the room, he berated himself for acting like such a simpleton. Looking around, he guessed he was in the master bedroom. It was a large space occupying the entire width of the house. The west wall was a bank of French doors with the lights of the city visible through the multipanes just above the row of buildings that lined the next street down the hill.

"This is my bedroom," Ava said proudly.

"Very nice," Noah said. In actuality, he thought it was a lot more than nice. The room had a high cathedral ceiling, and the bed was at least a king and was set against the north wall; both cats were curled up against decorative pillows. Behind the bed was a trompe l'oeil mural of an open window looking out onto a European mountain scene. The south wall had a period marble fireplace similar to those in the living room. A second door on the east wall led into the marble master bath. The lighting was subdued, giving the room an overall restful ambience.

"And the view is terrific," Noah added.

"You haven't seen nothing yet," Ava said playfully. She opened one of the French doors, stepped out onto a narrow balcony, and gestured for Noah to follow.

Moving from the air-conditioned, dehumidified interior, Noah could feel the summer warmth and moisture. He looked out at the view, noticing he could see into multiple apartments in the buildings on the other side of the alley. "Very nice," he repeated.

"This way," Ava said, as she tugged his arm to follow her. At the northern end of the narrow balcony was a black wrought-iron circular staircase that led up into the darkness.

As Noah climbed after Ava, he felt a touch of acrophobia. Just over the low handrail as he went up he could see down six floors into a neighboring garden. A moment later he was up on the very top of Ava's house, standing on a raised deck with a more substantial handrail. The view was truly spectacular, with a good portion of the city of Boston spread out in front of him. From where he was standing he could see over the tops of the buildings in the foreground. In the middle distance was a wide stretch of the Charles River that made it appear more like a lake than a river. "You are right, this is to die for," Noah said.

"You're looking directly at MIT," Ava said.

"Where?" Although he had spent two years at the famed school getting his Ph.D., it was hard to pick out the details from the panorama he was viewing.

"Straight ahead," Ava said. She pointed with her left hand while she put her right hand on Noah's shoulder to pull him closer. She also pushed against him so that he could sight directly along the length of her arm.

"Okay," Noah managed. But he was no longer trying to distinguish which buildings of the thousands he could see belonged to MIT. Instead, he was acutely aware of Ava's hand in the crook of his neck and shoulder with her forearm pressed against his back. He was even more aware of her body pressed up against his. She was busy describing various buildings so he could orient himself to the MIT campus, but he wasn't listening to her voice. He was listening to his body, which was sending alarm bells to his brain. And the messages were not going to the higher-function areas involved with rational thought.

"Can you see the dome?" Ava asked, referring to the building at the very center of MIT.

As if he were being manipulated by some exterior force, Noah turned toward Ava and looked dreamily into her eyes. As there wasn't that much difference in their heights, their faces were close. Ava responded by also turning her body toward him. "I'm getting the message that you are not all that interested in looking at MIT," she said.

Noah didn't answer. Instead he leaned forward in slow motion, turning his head to the side in the process. Ava's head tipped back. A moment later their lips came together as they embraced.

It was a long, sustained kiss. At its conclusion Noah slowly leaned back, although their arms continued to envelop each other. His eyes were fixed on hers, although in the half-light he could only assume hers were on his. Noah sensed an overpowering urge to make love to her. It had been a long time since he had had such feelings, and the sheer intensity of the desire caught him by surprise. Previously he had worried that arriving early might have scared her off. Now he was worried that if she knew the fierceness of his passion, she would be literally frightened. It was so encompassing that it even scared him to a degree.

"I think we should go down to my bedroom," Ava said. "Will you be okay navigating the stairs?"

"I think so," Noah croaked. Reluctantly, he let go of her.

It was a good thing she had warned him. Going down the tight spiral staircase was more challenging than going up. He took his time, with one hand grasping the steep bannister and the other hand wrapped around the central pole, especially during the portion when he seemed to be looking straight down six stories to a neighboring granite patio.

To Noah's astonishment and relief, once they got into the bedroom and the French doors closed, Ava was as much the aggressor as he was. After getting rid of the decorative pillows and the cats, they quickly made short work of each other's clothes and collapsed onto Ava's bed.

As if regaining consciousness several minutes later, Noah suddenly became aware of the surroundings. The bedroom lights were on and the draperies for the French doors were fully open. Concerned that Ava would find the situation untenable, as it was her house and her neighbors, Noah pushed himself up on an elbow. Looking down at Ava, who smiled up at him, he thought he'd never seen anyone so beautiful and so sexy. "Should I get the lights?" he said, almost in a whisper. The last thing he wanted to do was compromise the atmosphere, but he didn't want her to feel uncomfortable.

"Who cares about the lights," Ava said. She reached up and pulled Noah down onto her.

Her strength and her passion, which seemed to mirror his own, impressed him greatly. *Forget the lights,* he thought, and allowed himself to be lost in the moment.

Almost an hour later, they rested in each other's arms. After a few minutes Ava excused herself. "I'll be right back," she said. And then playfully added: "And don't you move!" Without the slightest concern for her nakedness, she slid off the bed and disappeared into the master bath. She didn't even close the door.

Noah felt delirious with pleasure, almost drunk. He looked around the room. It was like a dream, too perfect to be true. He had never had the pleasure of being with a woman who seemed so comfortable with her body. There was no way Leslie would have been willing to make love with the lights on, and during the few times they had had sex during the day, she immediately insisted on covering herself with the sheet the moment they were done. It wasn't that Leslie didn't have a good figure, because she did. Yet Leslie had always acted somewhat embarrassed about the whole process, the exact opposite of Ava. Vaguely, Noah wondered who was more typical, because as an adult, he'd not had that much experience. He'd had more experience as a teenager, but those episodes were over before they started.

Ava returned after a few moments just as naked as she was when she had left. Noah had half expected her to reappear in a robe or some other covering. Instead, she seemed to revel in her nudity. Noah couldn't have been more pleased, as it made him more comfortable at having resisted the temptation to pull on his own clothes.

Jumping onto the bed, Ava proceeded to tickle Noah, further surprising him with how relaxed and natural she was. It was as if they had been intimate for some time rather experiencing their first episode. It helped that Noah was an easy target since he'd been exceptionally ticklish from as far back as he could remember.

When the tickling was over, to Noah's relief, Ava sat up. "I hate to be a spoilsport," she said, "but sex makes me ravenous. How about we try the elevator and go down to the kitchen for some munchies?"

A few moments later and still as naked as a jaybird, Noah found himself pressed up against Ava face-to-face in the smallest elevator he'd ever been in. They kissed again as they silently and effortlessly descended.

To Noah's surprise they ended up on the ground floor instead of the kitchen floor. "I'm going to get us some terry robes from the guest apartment," Ava explained. "Hold the elevator door open. I'll be right back."

Noah did as he was told. He couldn't believe what had happened. In one unexpected evening he had a sense that the anxiety-producing, upcoming M&M Conference might possibly be under control, and, more important, he might have found a new love. He was hard put to decide which was more incredible. Could it be true, or was this all a dream? If it was, Noah didn't want to wake up.

12

"On to the next case," Noah said into the microphone. "Appropriately enough, it is the fifth and last page of the handout." There were a few titters from the audience reflecting their tenseness about what was coming. Noah had written out the key facts on each of the cases to be presented for the M&M and had provided them to everyone as they arrived.

Noah was back in the Fagan Amphitheater. This time he was alone in the pit, standing at the lectern, looking up at the tiered room whose upper reaches were lost in shadow. As expected, the room was full to overflowing, which had intimidated him at first, especially with all the big guns of the department, including Dr. Hernandez, Dr. Mason, and Dr. Cantor, filling the first and second rows. Ava was there, too, about ten rows back off to the left, dressed in her usual hospital garb concealing her trim, athletic body and a bouffant cap covering her striking hair. All the rest of the seats of the entire amphitheater were occupied as well. There were even people standing way up in the back a full story above, leaning on the railing. Everyone had come for this last case: the Bruce Vincent disaster.

Up until that point the conference had gone extremely well. So far, Noah had presented four cases. The first involved bariatric surgery on a six-hundred-pound man who'd developed a leak where the intestine had

151

been joined to the stomach pouch. Diagnosis of the problem had been difficult and the patient had passed away from complications following reoperation. The second case had been a spinal surgery in which an implant had migrated and caused serious neurological damage. The third involved a gallbladder removal followed by deep vein thrombosis, or clotting, with death from a large clot or embolism traveling up to the lungs. The fourth case had been a multiresistant bacterial infection following an appendectomy in a teenage girl. She had died of sepsis.

What pleased Noah was that the discussions that ensued after each of the cases had gobbled up over an hour of the conference time in their totality. The one that had dominated had been the tragic sepsis case, since everyone was alarmed about the spread of antibiotic-resistant bacteria and unsure what to do about it. That discussion alone had used up more than thirty minutes, and now, as Noah was about to begin the Vincent case, there was just slightly over twenty minutes of the conference left. What Noah planned was taking almost half of the time for the presentation, leaving a mere ten minutes for the discussion. Although he was well aware that a lot of trouble could still occur in ten minutes, he was counting on controlling the discussion as much as possible by steering away from difficult topics.

Over the three days before the conference, Noah and Ava had gone over the methodology he was to use, honing it after she had suggested it Saturday night. Every evening after leaving the hospital he would secretly head over to her house, staying with her every night except last night, which he had to spend in the hospital, dealing with multiple trauma victims following a major car crash on the Massachusetts Turnpike.

All in all, it had been an incredible three days for Noah. During his invariably busy days he and Ava would occasionally run into each other in the hospital, since Ava also had to work the weekend. She covered one weekend approximately every other month, sharing the burden with the rest of the Anesthesia staff. But when Noah and Ava would cross paths in the hospital, they made it a point to give only a casual offhand greeting, and only if it was appropriate. Otherwise, they ignored each other. Noah found their playacting strangely titillating, as it contrasted so sharply with their nightly passion.

As Noah proceeded to present the Bruce Vincent case, he took advantage of its intricacies to use up as much time as possible, describing step by step Bruce's extraordinary activities on the morning in question, including parking cars, solving the problem of an absentee garage employee, and, worst of all, eating a full breakfast. Noah even carefully enumerated each item Bruce had consumed, which included French toast, fruit cocktail, orange juice, bacon, and coffee. Noah was able to do this because he had interviewed the cashier who had taken Bruce's money on the fateful morning and, astonishingly enough, had remembered exactly what Bruce had had on his tray.

After a surreptitious glance at his watch, Noah described Bruce's admission process. He purposely did not mention any names so as not to cast any blame. What he did do was mention exactly how many times Bruce was asked whether he had followed orders to be NPO, and how many times Bruce had lied. Next Noah brought up the issue that no junior surgical resident history and physical had been done, explaining that Bruce had been forty minutes late when he arrived at Admitting and that the resident was busy seeing those patients who were not late. Noah concluded that section of the presentation by saying that there was a history and physical that had been done within the previous twenty-four hours that fulfilled the hospital's standing pre-op requirements. He did not make any reference to the quality of the H&P nor that it had been doctored, but he did say that the review of systems was negative, including the gastrointestinal system, as that had been the way it was when Ava had read it.

Noah paused at this stage of his presentation and glanced around at the audience, hoping someone would comment on the admission process or Bruce's behavior, but no one did. Noah was a little concerned that Dr. Mason might chime in even though it was a BMH tradition that the surgeon involved in the case being presented did not make statements unless asked specific questions. Noah avoided even looking at Dr. Mason, lest it encourage him to break the precedent.

When no one raised a hand to be recognized, Noah continued on by describing in detail the difficulty the surgeons encountered during the operation in attempting to release a small portion of the wall of the large intestine caught up in the hernia, which necessitated a decision to go into the abdomen.

"This is a crucial fact in this case," Noah said. "To go into the abdomen it was necessary to switch from spinal anesthesia to general anesthesia. The first step of this process was to place an endotracheal tube. When this was attempted, the patient regurgitated his stomach contents and aspirated a massive amount of undigested food."

Noah again paused briefly at this point in his presentation to allow what he had just said to sink in. He and Ava had decided it was particularly critical that the audience recognize the unfortunate and critical role the patient had played in his own demise, something they knew Dr. Mason felt strongly as well.

Noah then went on to describe the cardiac arrest, the briefly successful resuscitation, followed by a second cardiac arrest as the oxygen content of his blood fell precipitously. "At that point," Noah said, "it was clear to everyone the patient was on the brink of death with nonfunctioning lungs and that the only way possible to save him was to put him on emergency cardiac bypass." Noah did not mention that it had been only he who had made this decision. Instead, he said that once the patient was on bypass his blood oxygenation was quickly restored to normal, making it possible to clean out the aspirated food from his pulmonary system by bronchoscopy. "Unfortunately," Noah continued, "even though the lungs were now functioning normally, the heart could not be restarted, no matter what was tried by a skilled cardiac surgeon over a several-hour period. At that point the patient was declared dead. Why the heart would not restart is not yet known. An autopsy was carried out by the medical examiner as required of all operative deaths, but the findings are not yet available as of yesterday afternoon."

Noah again paused for a moment and glanced around the room. No one moved. Everyone was clearly caught up in the emotion of the circumstance.

"This was a very disturbing case for everyone involved and for the entire hospital," Noah said reverentially. "Bruce Vincent was an enormously respected member of the hospital community. In keeping with the goals of the Morbidity and Mortality Conference, it would be fitting to Mr. Vincent's memory if we could come up with changes that could be instituted to avoid deaths like his in the future. What I propose we discuss is the need for we healthcare providers to impress on our patients the absolute necessity for them to be NPO for at least seven to eight hours prior to surgery and why."

Almost immediately, Martha Stanley raised her hand to be recognized. Noah called on her.

"I couldn't agree more," Martha said. She then launched into a protracted self-reproachful statement of how it wasn't enough to go through a list of questions just to check them off as she had unfortunately done when she had tried to speed Bruce Vincent through the process.

As Noah listened and occasionally nodded in agreement, he felt like running up the steps and giving Martha a hug. She was doing exactly what Noah and Ava had hoped someone would do—namely, chewing up the minutes on an issue everyone could agree on. Furtively, he glanced at his watch. There were only three or four minutes left before he could announce that the M&M was over. Already he saw a few people leaving who had been standing at the railing. He allowed himself to glance in Ava's direction. For an instant they locked eyes. She flashed a brief thumbs-up, keeping her hand pressed against her chest so as not to be obvious. Noah nodded.

When Martha finished her monologue, a number of hands went up. Noah recognized a woman sitting to Martha's immediate right.

"I agree with Martha," the woman said. "But I think we should add to the list of what we ask. We always ask about whether they have eaten and if they have any allergies to medication and if they have ever had surgery and anesthesia, but we never ask if they have reflux disease. It seems to me that is an important piece of information."

"I certainly agree," Noah said. He then pointed to the person sitting on the opposite side of Martha who waved her hand insistently. Only then did he recognize who it was: Helen Moran, who had cornered him in that very pit after the welcoming ceremony. Noah's heart skipped a beat as she began talking. He knew what was coming but couldn't think of any way to stop it.

"Excuse me, Dr. Rothauser," Helen said, "but I think you have left out an important aspect of this case that certainly could be used to memorialize Mr. Vincent. Isn't this a prime example of the problems associated with concurrent surgery? My understanding is that Mr. Vincent was subjected to over an hour of anesthesia time before Dr. Mason showed up because he had two other people under anesthesia at the very same time. That's atrocious. It would serve Mr. Vincent's memory if concurrent surgery was eliminated here at the BMH."

All at once the almost somnolent atmosphere of the room exploded in conversation. A few people even yelled out their opinion on the issue. Articles in the lay press, particularly *The Boston Globe*, had ignited the general public's opinions either for or against, but on average mostly against.

Out of the babble, one nurse yelled out: "Dr. Rothauser. Is it true Mr. Vincent had to wait an hour under anesthesia?"

Noah raised both hands and fanned the air in an attempt to quiet the crowd. He avoided looking at Dr. Mason as he scanned the audience. "Please," he said into the microphone several times. "Allow me to explain." The effect was immediate, and for the most part the crowd settled.

"There was a delay," Noah said. "Yet—"

He planned to say that the delay had no impact on the unfortunate outcome, but he was drowned out after Helen shouted: "I think an hour is more than a delay. If it had been me or a member of my family on that table, I would have raised holy hell."

A number of people clapped. Nervously, Noah looked at his watch. It was now 9:00. Did he dare to conclude the conference under these circumstances? He didn't know. Glancing back up at the restive audience, he saw that Dr. Hernandez had gotten to his feet and was climbing down into the pit. Noah gladly stepped from the lectern when the chief approached and indicated he wanted to speak.

"Let me say a few words," Dr. Hernandez said over the commotion. He had to repeat the phrase several times before the audience finally calmed down enough for him to be heard.

While the chief of surgery was waiting to say a few words, Noah's eyes scanned the audience to find Dr. Bernard Patrick, an orthopedic surgeon who had strong feelings against concurrent surgery. When their eyes briefly met, the man nodded. At least he was pleased the issue had been raised.

"I would like to say that I wish this last case had been the first case," Dr. Hernandez said, causing Noah to wince. He couldn't help but worry that the chief might guess the reason it was last. "Obviously, this tragedy has touched all of us here at BMH. The Surgical Department spent many hours looking at this case very carefully, as we do all deaths, but particularly so because the patient was a friend and colleague of ours. It is unfortunate that there was a delay in the arrival of the surgeon, Dr. Mason, but it is felt by all that the delay did not contribute to the unfortunate outcome and the cause of the delay was a legitimate complication elsewhere.

"The concurrent-surgery issue has been looked into with considerable care by the Surgical Department, the BMH administration, and by me, as well as the American College of Surgeons, and we will continue to do so.

We strongly feel it is in the best interests of our patients but will be monitored. The Massachusetts Board of Medicine agrees but has demanded that our surgeons document when they enter and when they leave various ORs in situations requiring concurrent surgery. With that said, and since it is after nine A.M., this M&M Conference is adjourned."

The audience immediately erupted into pockets of animated conversation as people got to their feet. Dr. Hernandez turned to Noah. "My sense is that you put the Vincent case last to limit discussion. Am I right?"

With his mind racing around for a noncommittal answer but not finding one, Noah guardedly admitted the truth. "I suppose that was the intent," he said. "I knew emotions were high because of the patient's reputation."

"I don't know whether it was clever or stupid," Dr. Hernandez remarked. "I'll have to think about it more." With that said, he left the amphitheater.

Taking a deep breath, Noah turned to see if he could catch Ava's eye. As upset as he felt at the concurrent surgery surfacing, at least he thought she'd be pleased that he had managed to avoid the whole anesthesia choice issue and any blame that could be directed toward her. But she was already on the stairs, heading away from him, on her way to the main exit on the upper level. It was at that moment that Noah saw Dr. Mason climbing down into the pit. For a brief second Noah considered bolting out the exit that Dr. Hernandez had used. But it was too late. Dr. Mason would have caught him one way or the other, so he stayed where he was.

With a kind of rolling gait because of his girth, Mason bore down on Noah. His heavy face was set in his typical scowl. "You are your own worst enemy, Dr. Rothauser," Mason snapped when he came up to Noah, crowding him and forcing Noah to take a step back. "I warned you not to skew the facts, which you most certainly did. You didn't even mention that Anesthesia gave the wrong fucking anesthesia, a key point in the whole case. Who the hell are you protecting and why?"

"I'm not protecting anyone," Noah said, knowing he was lying. "Least of all the patient, despite his popularity. He was the one mostly responsible for what happened, and I made that very clear. I also talked about the Admitting people and their role. Those are the two parties that you brought up to me when we spoke."

Dr. Mason cocked his head to the side, looking at Noah askance and twisting his face into a wry smile. "You're a goddamn liar. When we talked about this we were standing right here in this pit and then in my clinic office. I said specifically that Anesthesia screwed up plain and simple on both occasions. That's what I said. Then I added something about the patient and Admitting, but it was Anesthesia's fault, stupid, and this death should have been an anesthesia death, not a surgical one!"

"I did the best I could," Noah said. He didn't know what else to say. He had the sense that if he apologized, it wouldn't help and would maybe even make things worse.

"Bullshit," Dr. Mason snapped back. "Worst of all, you let the discussion disintegrate into the concurrent-surgery issue, something I specifically warned you not to do. If this thing blows up again around here, I'm going to hold you responsible, and you are out of here. You understand what I'm saying?"

"I think so," Noah croaked.

"You know what really irks me about you is that you are one of those holier-than-thou, prissy snobs who thinks he is better than everybody else, like Meg Green, for instance, one of the best goddamned residents we had around here. You got her busted because she was taking Oxycontin for her shoulder."

"She was abusing it," Noah said.

"So you said," Dr. Mason said, lowering his voice. "You are on thin ice, my friend. Just keep that in mind."

13

After using a disposable nail cleaner and tossing it into the toe-operated waste can, Noah began to scrub his hands for his final scheduled case of the day. He was with his assistant at the scrub sink between operating rooms 18 and 20 with a hood and surgical mask in place. He had been in 18 since coming up to the OR after the M&M Conference and had been busy and efficient. Already he'd completed a colectomy, or the excision of a portion of the large intestine, a removal of a benign but sizable liver tumor, and a hemorrhoidectomy. The first two patients were doing well and back in their respective rooms. The only one who wasn't was the last case. He was still in the PACU, or post-anesthesia care unit, but he had been cleared to leave and was only waiting for a bed to become available on the general surgical floor. The next and final case on Noah's schedule was a breast biopsy with a possible full mastectomy, depending on the results of the biopsy.

As the day had progressed, he'd felt better. Noah loved being in the operating room. With his natural technical ability and confidence, it was in the OR that he felt the most at home. It was his sanctuary where everyday concerns faded. Although the interaction with Dr. Mason after the M&M had been unnerving, it could have been worse. His warning was contingent on the concurrent-surgery issue blowing up again, but the chances of that happening, in Noah's estimation, were close to nil. As Dr. Hernandez had mentioned in his short speech that morning, the matter had been fully vetted by the BMH hierarchy, the Massachusetts Board of Medicine, and even national surgical organizations, despite a number of patient advocate people being emotionally against it. What was clear to Noah was that the sticking point in his relationship with Mason was Meg Green's departure and Noah's role in that regrettable episode.

"I enjoyed the M&M Conference this morning," Mark Donaldson said, interrupting Noah's thoughts. Mark had been tapped to help Noah for the upcoming case. On the previous three cases that day, Noah had been assisted by one of the new first-year residents, but since she was scheduled for clinic starting at 3:00 P.M., Noah had called on Mark to come up and relieve her.

Over the previous week and a half, Noah had made it a point to assign the new residents to assist him in surgery so that he could evaluate their skills. So far he'd been exposed to a third of the group and was pleased with their performance. There was no doubt in his mind that they were a solid, talented bunch, which boded well for Noah's tenure as the super chief. Often it was the new crop of residents who gave the super chief the most headaches as they adjusted or didn't adjust to the demands of the program.

"I appreciate you telling me you enjoyed the conference," Noah said, continuing his scrub. It was the fourth time he had done it that day, but he remained compulsive about following protocol, just as he did with everything else in medicine. But with hand washing he was particularly careful. The specter of postoperative infections was Noah's biggest worry. He did everything possible to avoid them.

In between his surgeries, Noah had kept an eye out for Ava, surreptitiously, so as not to call attention. He certainly wasn't about to ask anyone about her whereabouts. When he didn't happen to run into her, he checked the scheduling monitor. When he didn't see her name, he checked out the Anesthesia schedule. It was there that he learned why she wasn't on the surgical monitor. It was her turn to supervise anesthesia residents and nurse anesthetists in rooms 6, 8, and 10. This kind of supervisory role was done on a rotating basis among all the staff anesthesiologists except the chief, Dr. Kumar.

Noah had no intention of talking with Ava even if he ran into her, for fear of starting rumors. Janet Spaulding, the OR supervisor, had an uncanny ability to be aware of everything that was going on in the department, professionally and otherwise. It hadn't been a coincidence that she had come over to chat when she had noticed Ava and Noah sitting together in the surgical lounge the previous Friday.

Just before Noah had started scrubbing for this final case, he managed to catch a glimpse of Ava by glancing into OR 10 as he passed by. Although it had been a fleeting glimpse, he was certain it was she, standing behind a nurse anesthetist who was busy intubating a patient. Noah doubted that she had seen him. For a host of reasons he was eager to see her that night, especially to get her take on the M&M. He was certain she had to be pleased.

Holding his hands up, Noah began scrubbing his forearms as the final part of the process. He was close to finishing when the intercom system suddenly came to life. A disembodied but urgent voice called out: "Code blue in OR number eight!"

Nearing the end of the scrub process but continuing to keep his hands aloft to avoid any potentially contaminated water from running down onto them, Noah took a step back from the sink so he could look in the direction of OR 8. Almost immediately, a couple of anesthesia residents appeared, running toward the room in question. One was Dr. Brianna Wilson, pushing the cardiac crash cart with a defibrillator as well as a collection of medications and other equipment. The other resident was

Dr. Peter Wong, who pushed a second cart that Noah was later to learn was specifically for difficult airway-management situations.

By reflex born of a willingness to help in any emergency, Noah tossed his scrub brush into the sink and took off toward OR 8, realizing that it was one of the rooms in which Ava was supervising either a resident or nurse anesthetist. He hoped that she wasn't involved directly in another major complication, knowing just how emotionally traumatic the Bruce Vincent case had been for her.

Using his shoulder to push through the OR door, Noah kept his scrubbed hands raised just in case he was called on to jump into the operation. Just inside the door, he paused to assess the situation. The ECG alarm was going off and the monitor showed ventricular fibrillation. The pulse-oximeter alarm was also going off, adding to the cacophony in the room and urgently announcing the blood oxygen was low.

The patient was a significantly obese Caucasian woman who Noah would later learn was a thirty-two-year-old mother of four named Helen Gibson. Instantly, he could tell it was an emergency trauma case. There was a compound fracture of her right lower leg, suggesting an auto accident of some kind. A bit of bone protruded through the skin.

Ava stood at the head of the table. She was struggling with an advanced video laryngoscope, trying to intubate the patient, who Noah could tell was not breathing. To Ava's right was a first-year anesthesia resident named Dr. Carla Violeta, who attempted to aid Ava by pushing down on the patient's neck at the point of the cricothyroid cartilage. Normally a bit of pressure at that location would make the entrance to the trachea easier to see. The problem was that a second anesthesia resident was giving external cardiac massage by forcibly and rapidly compressing the woman's sternum, causing the entire body, including the head, to bounce around. Getting an endotracheal tube into a difficult-to-intubate patient under such conditions was almost impossible. Noah could tell the patient fit the difficult category by her head being tilted forward rather than back, suggesting a cervical neck problem.

The anesthesia residents who'd rushed in with the two carts were busy getting the defibrillator prepared. Standing to the side all gowned and gloved and ready to operate was Dr. Warren Jackson. Noah knew him all too well. He wasn't quite as bad as Dr. Mason, but he was no polished gentleman, either. He, too, was an old-school, demanding, and temperamental surgeon who had trained back in the good old days when he apparently had been abused and now felt it was his duty to abuse. Noah could sense the man was irritated, as usual.

By some coincidence, the circulating nurse was Dawn Williams, who'd been in OR 8 on the Vincent case. Seeing Noah burst in, she immediately rushed over. "We got another doozie of a problem," she said. "The first-year resident went ahead and tried to intubate the patient before Dr. London got in here. Dr. London was supervising another intubation in the next room."

"Let me guess," Noah said. "Dr. Jackson pressured her."

"You got it," Dawn said. "He was really on her case something awful."

"Okay, clear," Dr. Wilson called out. She was holding the paddles of the fully charged defibrillator and moved to the side of the patient. The resident giving the cardiac massage lifted his hands in the air. Ava stepped back from the head of the table, and Carla stopped pushing on the woman's neck.

There was a distinctive thud as the defibrillator discharged. Simultaneously, Helen's body lurched on the operating table as the electric charge spread through her and caused widespread muscular contractions. All eyes were glued to the ECG monitor except for Ava's. She immediately reinserted the tip of the video laryngoscope and went back to trying to get an endotracheal tube placed.

Noah hurried over to Ava's side while a subdued cheer arose from the residents who'd brought the crash cart. The fibrillation had stopped. The patient's heart was now beating with a normal rhythm.

"What's the problem?" Noah quickly asked Ava.

"We can't respire this patient," Ava shouted. "She's paralyzed and can't be bagged for some reason. And I can't get an airway because I can't see what the hell I'm doing."

"It looks like her neck is flexed," Noah said.

"It is, and it's fixated. In terms of visibility of the trachea, it's the worst I've ever seen: Mallampati Class Four Grade Four."

"What the hell is Mallampati?" Noah said. He'd never heard the term.

"It's a grading system for visualization of the trachea," Ava snapped. Then to Carla she said: "Try pushing on the neck again. I almost had it a moment ago, before the shock."

Feeling a rising panic, Noah glanced at the ECG monitor. He didn't like the looks of it, fearing the heart was about to fibrillate again. He looked at the pulse-oximeter readout, whose alarm was still sounding. The oxygen level in the patient's blood had barely changed. In fact, the patient's color, which had been a slight shade of blue when he'd arrived, was getting worse. There was no doubt in Noah's mind that the situation was rapidly deteriorating. To his right was the second cart, with various laryngoscopes, tracheal tubes, and other intubating equipment, plus an emergency cricothyrotomy kit that contained the paraphernalia needed to create a new opening into the lungs through the neck, bypassing the nose and the mouth.

With the same resolve that Noah had demonstrated when he'd stormed in on the Bruce Vincent case, he suddenly knew what he had to do. He snapped up the cricothyrotomy kit and tore it open. Without taking the time to put on sterile gloves, he grabbed a syringe outfitted with a catheter from the kit's contents, pushing around to the patient's right side, crowding Ava and Carla out of the way. Angling the tip of the catheter toward the patient's feet, he placed its needle end into the depression below the patient's Adam's apple and decisively pushed it directly into the patient's neck. There was a popping sound. When Noah pulled back on the syringe's plunger and the syringe filled with air, he knew he was in the right place. Quickly he passed a guide wire through the catheter, then a dilator to enlarge the opening, and a moment later a breathing tube.

"Okay, good," Ava said. She connected the newly created breathing tube to the anesthesia machine and began respiring the patient with 100 percent oxygen.

Just as the entire team was beginning to feel upbeat, disaster struck. Without warning, the patient's heart reverted back to fibrillating, causing the cardiac alarm to resound. The oxygen level in the blood that had been rising now reversed course, necessitating a flurry of activity. After a short period of external massage that required one of the residents to climb up and kneel on the operating table, Helen received another shock from the defibrillator.

Once again there were some restrained cheers while everyone watched the cardiac monitor. The fibrillation stopped. But any sense of celebration quickly evaporated when the heart's normal rhythm didn't reinstate. Instead, the heart was stubbornly electrically silent, and the cardiac monitor traced a flat, unchanging straight line. Now there was no heartbeat, a situation known as asystole, which was disturbingly reminiscent of Bruce Vincent. Quickly the resident climbed back up onto the OR table to recommence closed-chest massage. At the same time the anesthesia team started various medications in hopes of restoring a heartbeat.

A few moments later, cardiologist Dr. Gerhard Spallek entered the OR, struggling to secure his surgical mask. After hearing the details, he said: "My guess is that we have had what amounts to a major heart attack secondary to the low oxygen levels. It doesn't bode well, but here's what we can try."

Under his direction a few more drugs were used in an attempt to stimulate the heart. Meanwhile, the external cardiac massage was continued, as was the 100 percent oxygen, keeping the blood oxygen levels reasonable. When the additional medication wasn't successful, Gerhard proceeded to thread an internal pacemaker wire in through the patient's right internal jugular vein. Even that wasn't successful to initiate a heartbeat.

"That's it," Gerhard declared. "The heart is not responding in the slightest. There's no doubt it was severely damaged. I'm afraid the patient is gone. I'm sorry I could not be of more help. Thank you for allowing me to participate." With a respectful half bow, he pulled open the door and left the room.

The resident who had been giving the external cardiac massage climbed down from the operating table.

"This is an outrage," Dr. Jackson said the moment the door closed behind the cardiologist. Throughout the ordeal he'd been totally silent, standing off to the side with his hands clasped across his chest, watching with growing concern but apparently keeping hope alive that he would be repairing the patient's damaged leg. "Just so everyone knows, I am going to be talking with Dr. Kumar about this"—he struggled for words—"this disaster. This patient is a thirty-two-year-old healthy mother of four. I'm appalled this could happen here at the BMH. We're not out in the boonies someplace."

Noah was sorely tempted to bring up the issue of his inappropriately pressuring the first-year anesthesia resident to begin the case before Ava as the supervisor was in the room, but he held his tongue. He felt it wasn't the time or place, as the man was already irate and it would serve no purpose other than to inflame the situation.

"In all my experience I have never seen a more difficult patient to intubate," Ava said with a voice that seriously quavered. Noah understood immediately that she was making an attempt to support Carla, which impressed him because he could tell from getting to know her that she was devastated by the episode herself. Up until the Vincent case she'd never had an operative death. Now she had been involved in two.

"What made it so goddamn hard?" Dr. Jackson spat. "You're supposed to be professionals at putting in endotracheal tubes."

"It was a combination," Ava managed. Her voice broke with emotion, almost anger. She took a deep breath to calm herself.

"It is apparent that her neck is deformed," Noah said, coming to Ava's rescue. He didn't want the conversation to get out of hand. "It is flexed and fixed. And the patient is moderately obese. That contributes. Isn't that right, Dr. London?"

Ava nodded.

"Well, wasn't that taken into consideration?" Dr. Jackson snapped, looking directly at Ava. "This is your specialty, for God's sake."

"I didn't know about the neck," Carla said. From the sound of her voice, she was as anguished as Ava.

"You mean to tell me it wasn't in the ER resident admitting note?" Dr. Jackson demanded.

"It wasn't," Carla managed. "There was nothing about neck problems."

"Good God!" Dr. Jackson voiced. He turned to Noah. "This morning we hear about a resident who didn't even do an admitting note. Now we hear about a resident leaving out a mighty important finding that's indirectly caused this patient's death. That's your department, Mr. Super Chief. Sounds like I'll need to talk to Dr. Hernandez as well as Dr. Kumar."

"I will certainly look into it," Noah said. Inwardly, he groaned. At that morning's M&M he'd barely avoided a personal disaster, and now he was facing another potential one for the next M&M.

"You'd better!" Dr. Jackson barked. He tore off his gloves and threw them to the floor. He did the same with his surgical gown. After that juvenile show of misplaced anger, he left the room.

While Doctors Wilson and Wong gathered up the cardiac-arrest paraphernalia and Dawn disgustedly picked up the discarded gloves and gown, Noah turned to Ava and Carla, particularly looking at Ava. He wanted to say something supportive if not give her a reassuring hug, but he didn't dare. Instead he merely nodded, hoping to communicate his concern in some nonverbal way. "Sorry," he said simply. He held her eyes for a moment with his own, but she didn't react. Then he, too, left the room.

As Noah hurried back to room 18 he thought again of the next M&M, wondering if they were going to be his bane for the entire year. At least on this case he wasn't going to be harassed by the concurrent-surgery issue, which was a definite plus. On the negative side, he would be dealing with an unleashed Dr. Mason, who normally was an active participant in M&M discussions. Noah knew full well that during the next one, Dr. Mason wouldn't be constrained as he had been that morning in his role as the involved surgeon. What Noah was already worrying about was Dr. Mason's reaction to Ava's being involved in yet another death, because he obviously still blamed Vincent's on her.

Intent on getting back to OR 18 as soon as possible to apologize and explain his absence in case they hadn't heard, Noah practically collided with Dr. Mason, who had just emerged from room 15. He was in the process of removing his surgical mask and not looking where he was going. Noah's heart skipped a beat.

"Ah!" Dr. Mason exclaimed, seeing who he was confronting. "Just the person I wanted to find."

Instantly, Noah's fears were confirmed. Mason knew. It was confirmation that bad news traveled quickly around the OR, especially when the PA system played a role.

"I've got a case in room number eighteen and I'm awfully late," Noah said. He tried to detour around his antagonist, but Dr. Mason blocked his way.

"So, my friend," Dr. Mason said sarcastically, "are you proud of yourself now?"

"Excuse me?" Noah asked. He was confused. Proud? Why would he be proud after what had happened?

"You get to take some credit for what just happened in OR number eight," Dr. Mason explained. He was sporting a nasty smile. "You more than anyone else have been supporting that incompetent bitch of an anesthesiologist, and now you are being rewarded with another unnecessary death."

"Dr. London was only the supervisor on the case," Noah said, but as soon as he said it, he wished he hadn't.

"And you think that exonerates her? Bullshit. She shouldn't be supervising anyone. Somebody needs to supervise her. We're supposed to be one of the best hospitals in the whole damn country, if not the best, and we lose two healthy young people in two weeks? There's something wrong with this story."

"There were complications," Noah said.

"Complications, my ass. I heard that she couldn't even get a goddamn endotracheal tube in. Simple as that. I never heard of an anesthesiologist who couldn't get an endotracheal tube in, not with all the tricks they have up their sleeve."

"Dr. London wasn't even in the room when the problem began," Noah snapped.

"That's an explanation? Give me a break! Where the hell was she?"

"She was supervising an induction on another case," Noah said. "It's an Anesthesia rule that the supervising anesthesiologist be in the room throughout the induction process. The attending surgeon on the case in question was insistent a new first-year anesthesia resident start even though the supervisor wasn't immediately available."

"So it was Dr. Jackson's fault?" Dr. Mason questioned superciliously. "That's bullshit. That's like me being to blame for the Bruce Vincent fiasco."

"I'm not saying it was Dr. Jackson's fault," Noah said. "But what I am saying is that he shouldn't have been encouraging a new resident to break the rules."

"Let me ask you something, Dr. Rothauser," Dr. Mason said. "Why do you protect this bitch? I don't understand. You're a smart man. I mean, I've been asking myself this question over and over."

"I'm not protecting anyone," Noah said. "I try to see the whole picture and get all the facts. I will certainly be investigating this case, as it will obviously need to be presented and discussed."

"Wait a second!" Dr. Mason said. A slight smile formed with his narrow lips. "I'm suddenly seeing the light. I bet I know why you are protecting her. You want to know what I think?"

"I'm not protecting her," Noah said. "I don't protect anyone who doesn't deserve it."

"Here's what I think," Dr. Mason said. "Have you been banging her? Tell me straight! Have you and she been getting it on? One thing I can give her credit for is having a decent body, and she's got a house in a hell of a neighborhood."

Noah's mouth went dry, and for a moment words abandoned him. He stared at Dr. Mason with shock, wondering just how he had known. He and Ava had been so careful, almost obsessed with their secrecy.

"Okay," Dr. Mason said derisively, noticing Noah's deer-in-the-headlights response. "Why didn't I guess this before, I haven't the foggiest, but it all makes sense. Of course, I don't know how you got to first base since she is such a cold fish. So I have to give you credit where credit is due."

"This is ridiculous," Noah managed. He realized Dr. Mason was guessing, and Noah lambasted himself for hesitating to respond.

"I should have guessed," Dr. Mason snapped, ignoring Noah's attempt at denial. "You're so transparent it's a joke. And let me tell you this: It doesn't help your image in my mind. I don't know why, but it really pisses me off big-time."

I know why, Noah thought but didn't dare say. As a narcissist, Dr. Mason would see Noah's success with Ava as the reason she had spurned him, and that was probably the reason he'd come up with the accusation. It was better than admitting Ava might not find him attractive.

"Maybe you'd better start packing your bags," Dr. Mason said, reverting back to poking Noah in the chest with one of his thick index fingers as he'd done in the past. "I'm going to make sure that Dr. Hernandez knows about this."

Dr. Mason then literally pushed Noah out of the way and continued down the OR corridor, heading toward the surgical lounge.

Noah watched him go, feeling a mixture of anger and disgust toward the man. His threat to tell the chief about his suspicions of Noah and Ava having an affair could have serious consequences. Although Noah couldn't imagine it could threaten his job, it would certainly affect his relationship with Ava. She had made it clear that she prized her privacy, and Noah agreed with her. But was it a legitimate concern over the long haul? Noah doubted that their being circumspect about their interactions in the hospital was going to be enough to shield their affair. Eventually someone in the hospital community was bound to see him coming or going from Ava's Louisburg Square home since a number of them lived in the Beacon Hill neighborhood. It was only a matter of time.

"What a bastard," Noah mused out loud as he hurried toward OR 18. Ava described a narcissist like Dr. Mason as a bull in a china shop. Noah thought the simile should be a lot stronger and be about people, not dishes. Spontaneously he came up with a rabid gorilla at a picnic. The thought made him smile. It was to be the last time he smiled for the day.

14

Noah had hoped to get out of the hospital much earlier, but it wasn't to be. At around 5:30 he'd been informed that several organs were available because of a motorcycle accident on the Cape that afternoon and that a kidney was on its way to the BMH. Noah had been pleased, although certainly not for the motorcyclist. Although he'd ridden one as a teenager, as a resident he'd learned to see motorcycles as a method of nonintentional suicide for the riders and, as a result, a gift to those needing organs.

Once it had been confirmed that the organ was on the premises, the sixteen-year-old girl recipient was inducted under anesthesia, and by the time the gifted organ arrived in the OR, Noah was nearly ready for it. It was a happy time for everyone, including Noah, who had known the patient for several years as she had waited. What made it particularly exciting was that the organ was a particularly good match, with an outstanding prognosis for the patient.

The kidney operation had been the highlight of Noah's day. It was one of those episodes that confirmed for him that he had made the right career choice and more than justified all his efforts. It had even nearly erased the bad feelings associated with the unfortunate death of Helen

Gibson and the confrontation with Dr. Mason, although Noah had yet to communicate on any level with Ava after the disaster in OR 8.

Noah had tried between surgeries to casually run into Ava to be assured she was okay, a shrug or a nod to suggest she was coping, but he hadn't seen her. After he'd finished his last scheduled case, he'd made a concerted search for her around the entire OR area. It wasn't unusual for anesthesiologists to remain after hours, even though it wasn't Ava's habit. Noah finally went so far as to ask for her in the Anesthesia office, where he was told she had left for the day. It was at that point that Noah had resorted to digital means to contact her.

The first thing he had done was text her. While he waited for her response, he'd started afternoon work rounds with the residents on the surgical floor. When rounds were done and she hadn't responded, he texted her again, indicating it was urgent that she respond. Meanwhile, he'd started seeing his own inpatients, including the patients he'd operated on earlier. Between the colectomy and the hemorrhoid, he'd tried to call her. Not only had she not answered, but after listening to her stock outgoing message, he'd been told that her voice-message box was full.

Feeling frustrated by the technology that promised immediate contact but wasn't delivering, Noah tried Facebook messaging, then went back to seeing his post-op patients. It wasn't the best time to visit, since most were eating dinner, but still they were glad to see him. More important, there were no complications such as fevers or complaints of pain, and they were even complimentary about the food. Noah wasn't surprised. Hospitals today, even tertiary teaching hospitals like the BMH, knew they were in competition and made an effort with their food service. It was just as Noah was seeing his last patient that the kidney notification had come through.

With the surgical call team prepared to take over for the night, Noah left the hospital through the main entrance. It was a warm summer evening and the sidewalks were busy. He crossed the green space created

when the Big Dig had put the main north-south traffic artery underground. From there he walked through a portion of downtown Boston to
emerge at the northeastern tip of the Public Garden. It was Noah's usual
route when heading home. But he wasn't heading home. He was heading
to Ava's house.

He entered Louisburg Square from the opposite direction than when
he was coming from his apartment. Ava's building looked dark and uninviting.

Noah climbed her stoop. He entered the foyer. There was an overhead
light, but it wasn't on. To find the doorbell he had to go by feel. He pressed
it and listened. In the far distance, he could hear a phone ringing, which
was the way Ava's doorbell worked, since it was tied into the phone system. It rang six times. No one answered.

"Shit," Noah said. "Where the hell are you?" Out of frustration he
pounded on the door. The moment he stopped, a heavy silence returned.

After a long sigh, he went back through the outer door. Stepping into
the street, he walked over to the fence that circled the greensward and
then looked back up at Ava's house. There had been no change. All the
windows were dark, including the three dormers on the top sixth floor.
Although he couldn't see any of the windows in the L portion of the house
nor the workout room, he felt confident she was either not home or hiding
from the world. Knowing what he did about her, he doubted the latter.
There was nothing about her that suggested she was the depressive type.
Besides, what could he do even if she was keeping to herself? It was her
house. He couldn't break down the door and look for her.

For a moment Noah debated what to do, but ultimately he recognized
he didn't have much choice. He had to either go back to the hospital if he
wanted any companionship whatsoever or go back to his apartment.
Under the circumstances, both destinations seemed pathetic. If he went
back to the hospital, as the super chief resident he would be hard put to
explain why he was there, and people would most likely ask. He had no

idea what he would say, and it might turn out to be embarrassing. As for his apartment, at least he wouldn't have to explain himself, although the idea of being there was far from enticing for a multitude of reasons.

Finally, as the least bad idea, he decided on his apartment and began to head in its direction. As he walked he found himself back to wondering if Ava could be seriously depressed, but then dismissed it again. He was convinced she was a doer like himself. When the chips were down and things weren't going your way, you didn't cry and mope. You sucked it up and worked harder.

As he climbed the stark stairs in his building, he couldn't help but compare the experience with going up the stairs in Ava's home with its mahogany handrail, hand-turned balusters, and custom carpeting. Yet the thought surprised him. Had four days and three nights spoiled him?

When he got into his unit, the comparisons were even more dramatic. It was like night and day. He couldn't quite believe the barrenness and impersonal nature of the place.

Trying to ignore the decor or the lack of it, he sat down at the miserable folding table and booted up his HP, still wondering when he'd hear from Ava and wishing he'd inquired about her schedule when he'd visited the Anesthesia office. Quite suddenly, the disturbing thought came to him that she might have some time off and be away on one of her frequent trips without telling him.

After quickly checking if he had gotten any emails or Facebook messages on his computer that might have mysteriously eluded his phone, Noah sent another email to her. He struggled with the phrasing so as not to sound as irritated as he felt. In many respects, it was rude and unempathetic of her to ignore him like this. She had to know he would be beside himself with concern.

Then he picked up his mobile phone, and against his better judgment, he typed her yet another short text, urging her to text back and included a sad-face emoji. But then he held up for a moment with his finger poised to hit the send button, trying to talk himself out of doing it. He'd already sent her a half-dozen unanswered texts.

In an attempt to salvage a modicum of self-esteem, he deleted it instead and tossed the phone onto the table in disgust. He wondered when he would hear from her, whether the next day or the day after that or if at all. Could the next time he saw her be in the OR corridor, ignoring each other and passing like two ships in the night? He had no idea, but he realized it was a possibility, as were a half-dozen other scenarios. Not since high school when his first love had suddenly turned her affections elsewhere had he been quite so confused, irritated, and worried all at the same time.

"Maybe I'm in love," Noah questioned out loud. As lonely as he'd been over the last two years, he knew he was possibly a needy, love-starved nerd who'd been swept off his feet over the previous three or four days by an exceptional woman who had been hiding out in plain sight.

BOOK 2

15

The next four days did not rank among Noah's favorites. To try to avoid obsessing over Ava's disappearance and her total lack of communication, he buried himself in work. Not only did he do more surgery than his usual amount and see far more people in clinic, he found the time to plan the basic science lectures and Journal Club meetings for the entire next month. He also met with each first-year resident to hear his or her complaints and raves.

Even though he told himself he wasn't going to hear from Ava, every time he got a text message or an email or even a phone call he thought it might be her and his heart quickened. Unfortunately, every time he was disappointed. In order to avoid looking for her in the OR each day, he made it a point to go back to the anesthesia office the day after she'd disappeared and ask the secretary when Ava was due back. To avoid stoking any gossip, he'd used the excuse that he had to talk with her about the Helen Gibson case. What he had learned was that she wasn't scheduled until Monday.

Noah left the hospital by the main entrance and crossed the swath of greenery that covered the freeway tunnel on his way home. Once he was out of the hospital with all its demands on his attention, time, and energy, he was unable to stop his mind from mulling over his problems. Dr. Mason had made good on his threat to tell Dr. Hernandez about Noah and Ava possibly having an affair. Noah had become aware Thursday morning when he had gotten a message as he was scrubbing for his final surgery that he was wanted ASAP in the chief of surgery's office.

The meeting had not been pleasant. It got off on the wrong foot because Noah had gone ahead and finished his last case and didn't show up in the chief's office for almost two hours. Clearly miffed despite Noah's explanation for the delay, Dr. Hernandez started out by saying the hospital administration didn't condemn fraternization or romance between hospital employees, as they are grown-ups, but it did frown on such relationships if they affected performance. He went on to say that it was Dr. Mason's strong opinion that Noah had deliberately shielded Dr. London from blame in the Vincent case during the M&M Conference by not bringing up the fault of Anesthesia choosing to use a spinal rather than general anesthesia.

Noah had tried to defend himself by denying any attempt to shield Dr. London and by mentioning that Dr. Mason's secretary had requested the spinal. But his attempts seemed to fall on deaf ears. Instead of listening, Dr. Hernandez had gone on to criticize Noah's role in reawakening the concurrent-surgery debate, which had already been adequately vetted and cleared. At that point, Noah tried to remind the chief that the issue had been raised by a member of the audience and not by him.

"Let's not quibble about the details," Dr. Hernandez had said with a wave of his hand. "The point here in both these circumstances is that we expect you to side with the Department of Surgery as a potential member of the staff. Now, I don't know what you have done to get under Dr. Mason's skin, nor do I want to know. But whatever it was or is, I think it would be in your best interest to rectify it. You have been a wonderful resident, Dr. Rothauser. I would hate to see you ruin it in this final sprint to the finish line. Do I make myself clear?"

As Noah thought again about this brief meeting, it irritated and scared him. It was disheartening to see how blind the administration was to Dr. Mason's personality flaws just because of his exceptional surgical skills. Noah had had to fight with himself not to bring up the Meg Green dismissal issue as the real cause of Dr. Mason's discontent. That unfortunate affair was still a sore subject, and Noah feared bringing it up might make the situation worse.

Noah reached the eastern corner of the Boston Common and began to cut diagonally across the park, heading in the direction of the gold-domed Massachusetts State House. In contrast with the downtown area, which had been relatively deserted, the park was full of people enjoying the Sunday summer evening. Despite it being after nine P.M., there were still children in the kids' playground. Noah felt distinctively out of place in his hospital whites, surrounded by healthy, normal people who he knew thought of his world as a scary place.

As bad as the meeting with Dr. Hernandez had gone, the meeting with Dr. Edward Cantor, the surgical residency program director, had been worse. Noah had been summoned a few hours after the meeting with the chief. As soon as Noah had arrived in the director's office, it had been obvious that Dr. Mason had also passed on to him the story of Noah and Ava's possible romance and his possible shielding of her at the M&M Conference.

"I don't like this one bit," Dr. Cantor had snapped. "It is not the role of the super chief surgical resident to protect a possibly incompetent anesthesia attending because of an affair."

"Dr. London is far from incompetent," Noah said before thinking. In retrospect, he should have stayed mostly quiet, as he had with Dr. Hernandez. By denying Ava's incompetence, he was in a fashion affirming the allegation that he'd been protecting her.

"Her competence or lack thereof is not for you to decide," Dr. Cantor said. "It is a different department. We wouldn't tolerate anesthesia residents protecting possibly incompetent surgeons. Don't do it. If you do, we will find someone else to take your place. It is as simple as that. And I want to remind you that any screwup by a junior resident, such as the lack of an H&P on the Vincent case, is on your shoulders. As super chief, you are responsible for junior resident performance, plain and simple. Are you clear on this?"

As Noah walked he had to smile wryly as he remembered this portion of the meeting. At the time, he'd considered reminding Dr. Cantor that he had not been the super chief when the Bruce Vincent case had occurred. It had been Dr. Claire Thomas. Luckily, he hadn't done it, as it might have pushed the already upset man over the top.

Suddenly, Noah stopped. He was close to a flight of stairs that led up to Beacon Street that ran along the north side of the park. He had just by chance glanced behind him to take one more quick look around the pleasant summer evening scene in the Common. What had caught his attention was a man in a dark suit and tie. There weren't many men in suits at that time of the evening. In fact, as he glanced around again, he didn't see another.

What had caught Noah's attention was more than just the suit. It was that he had the impression he'd seen the same man earlier, with his impressively trim physique and short, light hair. Noah had noticed the man, who had been standing alone at the side of the circular drive at the hospital's main entrance. It was the suit at that time of night that made the man stand out, but Noah quickly forgot the incident until by chance he had taken this one last glance around the Common. Was it the same man? Noah didn't know. But if it were, was it just a coincidence, or could the man be following him?

"Good grief," Noah said out loud, mocking himself. "Now you're having paranoid delusions. What a pathetic lame-brain." Without giving the man in the suit another thought, Noah went up the stairs, taking them in twos and threes. At the top, he had to stop for the traffic on busy Beacon

Street, joining a group of people waiting for the light to change. Most were dog walkers with their pets.

When the walk sign came on, the group surged forward. As Noah allowed himself to be carried along, he managed a quick glance behind him down the flight of stairs. At the bottom, he caught a fleeting look at the man in the suit. He was bent over, seemingly tying a shoe.

Noah paused on the other side of Beacon Street where it met Joy Street. His normal route took him up Joy Street to Pinckney, where he took a left. But at this time of night, Pinckney Street was quiet, with few pedestrians. Noah decided to continue on Joy Street and make a left on Myrtle, which was busier, with multifamily buildings and a playground. If he was being followed, as crazy as that sounded, he preferred people around.

A moment later the man in the suit appeared across the street. He was now waiting for the walk signal just as Noah had done. Noah turned and ascended Joy Street at a rapid walk. Since there was plenty of pedestrian traffic, he felt reasonably relaxed. He still thought that he was being paranoid in thinking that this man, whoever he was, was following him. It all had to be a coincidence. Why would someone be following him, a surgical resident? It made no sense.

But then a few minutes later when Noah ventured a look behind him, the same man was there, walking in the same direction as Noah and seemingly at the same pace.

At Myrtle Street Noah turned left. As he had expected, there were lots of pedestrians. There were even a few families still in the playground using the swings. As Noah crested Beacon Hill and started down on the other side, he looked behind him. The man was still there. Could it be a coincidence? Noah didn't know, but he felt the chances were getting progressively slimmer. Revere Street, his street, ran parallel with Myrtle one short block to the north. There were several streets Noah could have taken, but he waited until Anderson Street because there was a convenience store on the corner, meaning more people.

Once on Revere Street, Noah had only a short way to go. Remembering hearing stories in the past about people being mugged when they paused at their front doors, searching for their keys, Noah made sure he had his in his hand. As he turned to his front door, he looked back. The man was still there, coming toward him, walking quickly.

In a rapid fashion, Noah keyed his front door, pushed it open, entered, and slammed it closed. He heard the reassuring click of the lock and breathed a sigh of relief. He'd not been aware he had been holding his breath. Then, going up on his tiptoes, he was able to see out one of two small glass panes in the upper panels of the building's front door. In a moment the man in the suit appeared, but as Noah watched, he didn't pause or even look in Noah's direction. Instead, he passed by in a flash, heading down Revere Street, which meant the whole episode had been a product of his emotionally overwrought state.

Noah laughed at himself. He felt like a fool as he climbed his utilitarian staircase, heading for his lonely apartment. At that moment, he really missed Leslie Brooks and wished he'd made more effort in their relationship. If he had, maybe she would still be here. He keyed his apartment door and pushed it open. Inside he turned on the harsh overhead light, which was a cheap fixture with two hundred-watt bulbs.

After taking off his white coat, hanging it up, and kicking off his shoes, he went into the small kitchen and opened the refrigerator door. There wasn't much in there, and what was didn't appeal to him. It was to be another night without dinner. Instead of eating, he sat down at the folding table, booted up the old HP laptop, and went on Facebook. Although he knew it probably wasn't an emotionally healthy thing for him to do, he had in mind to look over the many photos of Gail Shafter, including a couple baby pictures. But what he found was more interesting. It was a brand-new selfie of Ava pouting at the camera with the caption: *Relaxing after a hard day's work.* She was clad in a luxurious terry-cloth robe. There was a logo on the breast pocket, but Noah couldn't make it out. Checking the background, he thought it looked like an upscale hotel room. He wished there were some indication where it was. As he looked at it, it seemed awfully cruel to him that she had taken the time and effort to post a photo on Facebook for her myriad Facebook friends but didn't have the time or inclination to send him a single text.

Looking down at the likes and comments, he was surprised at the number of people who reacted to the post. Most of the comments were short, like "hot" or "aesthetically flawless" or just a thumbs-up emoji, as if they were from teenagers. Noah shook his head at the inanity of it all. Knowing what he knew of Ava's intelligence, education, and training, he couldn't explain her attraction to such a superficial activity. Why did she bother? Did she get enjoyment from the responses she got, in particular the three comments saying her photo was hot?

Wondering if his suspicion that the authors of the short comments were as young as he envisioned, Noah decided to look at one of the commenters' Facebook page. He chose Teresa Puksar's because she was one of the people who wrote "hot" and because the surname jumped out as being unique. He'd seen the name before on his previous visits to Gail Shafter's homepage, as she was one of a half-dozen or so people who were loyal followers of Gail Shafter and commented on every post.

"Just as I thought," Noah mused when he had Teresa Puksar's homepage on his screen and saw that Teresa Puksar was thirteen. Then he noticed some of the young girl's photos as being overly provocative. There were even a few nudes with her coyly covering nipples and the genital area. Even so, Noah was shocked that Facebook allowed them, as they could be considered by some conservative people as child pornography.

At that moment, the silence in his apartment was shattered by the raucous sound of his front door buzzer. Concentrating as he was, Noah leaped at the sound. "What the hell?" he questioned when he recovered. No one ever rang his doorbell, especially not after ten on a Sunday night.

Confused, Noah got up and went to the window. He pressed his face against the glass to see what he could on the sidewalk in front of his building, but he didn't see anybody. He wasn't surprised, because there was an alcove at his building's front door where the apartment buzzer was located. Whoever had rung was most likely standing in there. Raising his line of sight, he saw that there was a dark SUV pulled over to the curb on the opposite side of his street with its blinkers going. That wasn't normal, either.

Noah straightened up. Who the hell could be visiting? All at once the memory of the man in the suit came back in a rush. He'd decided that the episode had been all in his paranoid imagination. But was it? Could this strange visitor somehow be associated?

Then the buzzer sounded again. Knowing that he wasn't going to find out anything unless he went down to the front door, Noah put his shoes back on. He looked around for some sort of weapon to defend himself if need be, but then dismissed the idea as coming from a sick, paranoid mind.

When he got down to the front door, he debated what to do. Should he just open the door and face whoever was there? It seemed more prudent to call through the door and get some idea before opening up. "Who is it?" he yelled.

"It's Ava," a woman's voice responded.

For a second, Noah was startled. It was as if his brain was momentarily scrambled. "Ava? Is that really you?" he asked incredulously. What he was doing was playing for time to recover. Without waiting for an answer, he struggled with the door to undo the dead bolt that was used after nine. A moment later he was staring at Ava, dressed in a businesslike pantsuit. The blond streaks in her hair gleamed in the harsh overhead entrance light.

For a moment neither spoke. Finally, Ava said, "Well? Can I come in?"

As if waking from a trance, Noah said, "Sorry! Sure, come in."

"Upstairs?" Ava asked.

"Yes," Noah said. "One flight."

He followed her up the stairs, feeling confused. While he was thrilled to see her, he was furious that she had disappeared and totally ignored him. "The door is unlocked," he said as they reached the landing.

He followed her inside his apartment and closed the door behind them. She had stopped a few feet from the door and let her eyes roam around the small, sparse room. "I'd describe this as minimalist," she said.

"That's being kind," Noah said.

For a beat, they stared at each other. Noah was still fighting his emotions. All at once tears appeared in Ava's eyes and spilled out onto her cheeks. Her hand shot up and covered her eyes, and for a moment she sobbed quietly, her shoulders shaking.

Noah was beside himself with indecision. He didn't know how to respond. But then charity won out and he stepped forward and enveloped her in his arms. They stood that way for a few moments until Noah led her to the small couch and encouraged her to sit down.

"I'm sorry," she managed. She wiped her tears from her cheeks with a knuckle, but it was a losing battle.

"It's okay," Noah said. He went back to his bathroom and brought out a small box of tissues. She took one and noisily blew her nose. She took another and wiped her eyes. This time she was more successful.

"I want to apologize to you for not contacting you," she said when she was more in control.

"Thank you," Noah said. "Why didn't you?"

"I don't know exactly," Ava said. "At first I was just too distraught after being involved with another death. I'm still distraught, obviously. Anyway, I just wanted to get away and forget everything. I thought about quitting anesthesia."

"No!" Noah said without hesitation. "Don't say that. Not after all your training and effort. You are a talented anesthesiologist. You wouldn't be on the BMH staff if you weren't."

"I never expected to be involved with one death," Ava said. "Suddenly, it's two. I thought that by constant studying, by constant attempts to make myself better, it wouldn't happen. But it has."

"You know the expression 'medicine is more art than science,'" Noah said. "It's true. As a doctor, even if you do everything exactly right, things can disintegrate into chaos. There are too many variables. It's part of the human condition."

"I thought I could be different. I thought dedication and commitment would be enough."

"We are all in this together," Noah said. "We do the best we can. That is all that can be expected of us. You didn't do anything wrong on either case. I know. I was there."

"You really think so? Honest?"

"Absolutely! No question. I think you are a terrific anesthesiologist."

"Well, thank you. Your support means a lot to me."

"But it's not going to be easy to put all this to rest," Noah said. "I had several run-ins with Dr. Mason. The first was right after the M&M and the second after the Gibson death. I'm afraid he's still on our case." Noah went on to tell Ava the details about the two confrontations, particularly about Dr. Mason's accusation that Noah was purposefully protecting her. He then went so far as to tell her that Dr. Mason suspected that they were having an affair.

"Oh, no," Ava said with consternation. "Why? How?"

"He has no evidence," Noah said quickly, alarmed at Ava's reaction. "He came up with the idea out of the blue when he was talking with me, saying he couldn't understand why I was protecting you. He wants to put you down because you've rebuffed him, and obviously, he saw through my ruse at the M&M of avoiding the anesthesia issue entirely."

"Do you think he has told anyone about his suspicions?"

"I know he has," Noah admitted. "I got called on the carpet by both the head of the Surgery Department and the head of the surgical residency program."

"They had the nerve to reprimand you for possibly having an affair with me?" Ava questioned with disbelief. She didn't know whether to be insulted or more worried about the inevitable rumors.

"The possibility of an affair was just mentioned in passing," Noah said. "The hospital doesn't care. What both of them were irritated about was Dr. Mason's complaint that I have been protecting you."

"Oh my goodness," Ava said. "This keeps getting worse. I hate to think we'll become a source of gossip. What did you end up saying?"

"Not much," Noah admitted. "I denied that I was protecting you, of course, because the implication was that I was doing something underhanded. I'm not doing anything I don't think is right. You were certainly not to blame in either of these unfortunate cases, and I'm more than happy to say so."

"Thank you again."

"You're welcome," Noah said. "We need to get busy and plan the next M&M like we did for the last one because the Gibson case will need to be presented, and Dr. Mason most likely will be a bear. On the Vincent case his hands were tied because he was the surgeon. With the Gibson case, there's no such luck. You'll have to gird yourself. It might not be pretty, but at least the concurrent-surgery issue is not involved."

"I'll help you plan however I can," Ava said. "Does this mean you've forgiven me?"

"Why didn't you contact me? Why not a simple text saying you were all right?"

"At first I was just too overwrought and knew you wouldn't be satisfied with a simple text. Then after a day or so I felt embarrassed I'd been so emotional. I thought it best to apologize to you in person. That's why I'm here. I just got back to Boston and came straight here. I haven't even been home yet. I'm sure you have been concerned, and I would have been concerned if it had been the other way around."

"Where were you? It looked like a fancy hotel in your selfie."

"Oh, good, you saw it. I really posted it for you to show you that I was all right."

"I saw it," Noah said. "But I couldn't tell where you were."

"Washington, D.C. It was the Ritz."

"Were you playing tourist or working?"

"I was working," Ava said. "The trip had been scheduled months ago. Actually, the timing was good. Being busy helped pull me out of an emotional nosedive."

"What type of consulting do you do, if I can ask?"

Ava regarded Noah for a few beats. He sensed she was debating whether she wanted to tell him, which only fired up his curiosity. Whatever she was doing had to be exceptionally lucrative. Not every consultant stayed at the Ritz.

"I'm hesitating because I think you're not going to approve," Ava said.

"If you think telling me that is going to make me less interested, you're wrong. Why would I not approve of your consulting work?"

"I consult for the NSC."

"Really," Noah said. He didn't know if he was more shocked or impressed. "You consult for the National Security Council?" The National Security Council was the U.S. president's principal forum for national-security and foreign-policy matters.

Ava had recovered enough from her earlier tears to laugh her usual laugh. "I wish. No, I work for the Nutritional Supplement Council. I'm a combination spokesperson/lobbyist. My NSC is a lobby group lavishly funded by the nutritional-supplement industry."

"Okay," Noah said. He nodded. "Now I understand why you questioned if I would approve. As a doctor, I do have strong negative feelings about the industry, which I equate to a bunch of snake-oil manufacturers and salesmen."

"But on the positive side, they pay well," Ava said.

"How did you happen to start working for them? I would think as a doctor you'd find it problematic. It's a little like colluding with the enemy."

"I started working for them from the day I received my combined M.D. and B.S. nutrition degree," Ava said. "I'd run up a big debt from college and medical school. I had to pay my own way after my father died of a heart attack in my junior year of high school. The NSC and its deep pockets have been kind of a savior."

"I suppose I can relate," Noah said. "I've had my share of economic problems, some of which are still going on. As you know, my father also died of a heart attack when I was in high school, and I've got a huge debt as well. My mother helped when I was in college, but when I got to medical school, she came down with early-onset Alzheimer's and lost her job. At that point the tables were turned, and I had to support her."

"I'm sorry to hear that," Ava said. "Sounds like you had it harder than I."

"I guess your bosses at the NSC were pleased that you had both a B.S. and an M.D.," Noah said. "Especially now, with you being on the BMH staff."

"You have no idea," Ava said. "They love me and treat me like a queen. My life would be totally different if it weren't for the NSC. At the same time, I do them a big service. I'm probably the main reason the 1994 law that took the FDA off their back hasn't been amended. That's the law that absolves the industry from having to prove efficacy or even safety. It's kind of a joke, really, but who am I to say. Besides, it is fun. I get to dine with senators and congressmen."

"But you're a doctor and a committed one. Why doesn't that keep you awake at night?"

"Believe it or not, it's what the American public wants. They are convinced they don't want government bureaucrats messing with their pills, elixirs, and botanicals, whether they are worthless or not or even dangerous. They want to believe in the magic pill to make up for their unhealthy lifestyle. Taking a pill is a lot easier than eating right, exercising, and getting a decent night's sleep."

"Do you believe the public is that stupid?" Noah said.

"I do," Ava said. "Did you ever see the commercial that Mel Gibson did back when the supplement industry was lobbying Congress to pass the 1994 law?"

"I didn't. Or if I did, I was in the sixth grade, and it probably went over my head."

"I was in the seventh grade," Ava said. "I didn't see it back then, but one of my NSC bosses showed it to me last year. It is a classic. Mel Gibson's house is raided by armed FDA agents acting like a SWAT team, and he's arrested for taking vitamin C supplements. It's hilarious, but it was very effective. The public really thinks the government wants to take away their beloved vitamins. You should watch the video."

"I'll have to check it out," Noah said.

"You didn't answer when I asked you if I've been forgiven for disappearing for a few days," Ava said. "Was that intentional?"

"I suppose you are forgiven," Noah said halfheartedly.

"That doesn't sound so convincing," Ava said.

"I was really worried about you," Noah said.

"I understand, but I'm all right. I've mostly recovered, except for random episodes like when I first arrived here. But I think I am ready to go back to work tomorrow. And I'm interested in starting to plan for the next M&M whenever you are."

"Okay," Noah said, "you're forgiven. I can appreciate how upset you must have been."

"Thank you," Ava said. "Now, what time is it?" She looked at her watch. "Oh, dear. It's later than I thought. But how about coming back with me to my house? I have a car waiting outside."

"That's your SUV I saw earlier with its blinkers on?" Noah asked with surprise. The idea hadn't even occurred to him. The idea of having a driver wait an indeterminate amount of time seemed excessively extravagant.

"It's the car that the NSC arranged to pick me up at the airport. As I said, I came directly here. We could have a snack or a glass of wine if you would like. I'm wide awake."

"Four forty-five A.M. is going to come all too quickly for me," Noah said. "I've been working like a dog. I'll have to take a rain check."

"Fine," Ava said as she stood. "Maybe tomorrow evening you can come over when you get out of the hospital, and we can have a bite. I've missed you."

"Maybe," Noah said. The real reason he was reluctant to take her up on her offer to go directly back to her house was that he wasn't sure how he felt emotionally. He didn't know if he wanted to get right back into the saddle after falling off the horse. "Sometimes Mondays are very busy, and I don't get out until late," he added as an afterthought.

"Well, let's see how it goes," Ava said. "Anyway, the offer stands."

He walked her down to the front door. Like the first evening they had spent together, she surprised Noah by initiating a double-cheek kiss. Then, with him holding the door open, she said: "I'm really glad to see you, but in the hospital I think we should still play it safe and ignore each other. Dr. Mason's suspicions might not be common knowledge, and it would be best not to give them any sort of credence. Okay?"

"Okay," Noah managed. As usual, she had him off balance. "I've missed you as well. Welcome home!"

He watched her run across the street and open the SUV door. Before she climbed in she turned and waved. Noah waved back, then closed and dead-bolted the door. In contrast to her seeming burst of energy, he felt mentally and physically exhausted.

16

Noah entered Toscano and approached the hostess desk. He told Richard, the handsome owner/manager whom he had formally met two nights ago, that he was there once again to pick up a take-out order. As he waited, Noah glanced around at the busy scene. All the tables and the lengthy bar were filled and a buzz of happy conversation and laughter permeated the room. None of the diners were thinking of sickness, injury, or death, which consumed Noah's world on a daily basis. Usually he would have felt jealous of their normal lives and their facility at easy conversation. But tonight he wasn't jealous in the slightest, as he was anticipating another delightful evening of his own.

The past Monday had been busy for Noah, even more than he had expected. So was the rest of the week. But any reluctance he might have entertained on Sunday night, the night Ava unexpectedly appeared at his door, about restarting his secret, intense relationship with her had progressively lessened. Although Monday morning he'd awakened still feeling that the prudent course would be to go slowly, as the day wore on he found himself becoming more and more excited about the prospect of seeing her that evening. Passing her several times in the surgery corridor, where they both scrupulously avoided any recognition of the other, only served to fan the embers of his passion into a full blaze. The secrecy alone lent a delicious libidinousness to the whole situation.

By the time Noah got to her house well after 9:00 P.M. Monday night, he was wound up like an old-fashioned clock. Apparently, it had been the same for her, because they ended up making love on the floor in the foyer just inside the inner door. In the background, they could hear occasional chatter by passing pedestrians out on the sidewalk as they were that close, but it didn't affect their ardor in the slightest. After they were spent they lay for a time on the carpet runner, staring up at the hallway chandelier. It was a tender time as they reaffirmed how much they had missed each other, an emotion augmented by guilt on her part for not having texted him and worry on his part for not having heard from her.

Later, over take-out food, Noah had learned how hard it had been for Ava to do her consulting work while she was in Washington, since it meant meeting with or having meals with senators and congressmen who were members of key committees. She told Noah that she had suffered from a mild form of PTSD, or post-traumatic stress disorder, with persistent GI symptoms and recurrent nightmares about failing to get an endotracheal tube placed. She also confessed how close she'd come to calling Dr. Kumar to say that she was resigning.

Noah's reaction to all this was similar to how he had responded the previous night in his apartment, reminding her of her board certification and that she had been hired by one of the country's most prestigious hospitals. He told her that it had not been an accident that she had handled superbly more than three thousand anesthesia cases at BMH without a significant complication. He also reminded her that she had made several major contributions to the hospital. The first had been playing the key role behind the program of recapturing vast quantities of anesthetic gases rather than venting them into the atmosphere, which saved the hospital money and was also environmentally appropriate. The second had been that she had sat with him on the hybrid operating room committee, whose work resulted in the current remodel of the entire Stanhope Pavilion OR complex.

So far Noah had ended up staying overnight at Ava's for the entire work week, arriving somewhere between 6:15 P.M. at the earliest, which happened on Tuesday, and 9:52 P.M. at the latest, which happened on Monday, and leaving each morning a tad before 5:00 A.M. Every night they had gotten take-out food from a Charles Street eatery and then spent hours talking while they ate and sipped a bit of wine.

In many ways, Noah found getting to know Ava like peeling an onion. Every time he learned something new, he found another layer, something he didn't know or suspect, like the fact that she had a nearly photographic memory or that she was a talented computer coder, a skill she had picked up herself, mostly thanks to her love of computer gaming. Photographic memory and coding were aptitudes that Noah appreciated because he shared them.

Perhaps the most astounding new thing Noah learned about Ava was that she was fluent in Spanish, French, and German and spoke enough Italian to get along traveling the back roads in Italy. Why it surprised him was because language was not one of his fortes, and he had struggled through Latin and Spanish in high school courses. He also came to realize that, in contrast to himself, she had a sixth sense about reading people, something that came in particularly handy with her lobbying efforts. She explained to him how easy it was for her to discover a senator's or a congressman's opinion on a specific issue and then how to change it if it wasn't in line with her NSC bosses' desires.

"You never order dessert," Richard, the restaurant owner, said. He interrupted Noah's thoughts when he brought out the package of take-out food. "We have some delicious selections. How about I throw in some tiramisu on the house just so you can try it?"

"Thank you, but no," Noah said. He doubted Ava would want it, even though she could certainly get away with it, considering the amount of exercise she did every day in her workout room. Noah didn't feel the same about himself. With as little aerobic exercise as he got, he was lucky he hadn't put on significant weight.

"Perhaps next time," Richard said graciously, handing the credit card receipt to Noah.

Noah walked quickly up the hill to Louisburg Square. Now that he had the food he was in a hurry, and not just because he wanted the food to be hot but because he was even more eager than usual to see Ava. Earlier that afternoon they had practically collided with each other, with him pushing into the PACU and her coming out. At first both had been horrified, but when no one seemed to notice since it happened frequently to other people, they had both found it like a bit of slapstick comedy, since they'd been trying so hard to avoid each other.

Noah pushed the doorbell and in the far distance could hear the phone inside the house. The next thing he heard was the door lock clicking open. He'd learned that at any phone extension in the house it was possible to see who was at the door and then release the lock.

Once inside, Noah kicked off his shoes and took the main stairs down to the kitchen. Ava was busy setting out place mats, flatware, and napkins at the countertop table. To Noah she looked as fetching as usual, this time in sweatpants, a mock-neck tank top, and bare feet. Her hair was damp and her skin was glowing from a recent hot shower after her workout.

While Ava opened a bottle of wine and Noah unpacked the take-out food and put it on plates, they had a good laugh about their near collision at the PACU entrance that afternoon and how they'd both panicked.

"It's a good thing Janet Spaulding didn't see us," Ava said, still giggling.

"It's amazing how she seems to know everything that goes on in the OR," Noah agreed.

Once they had started on their meal, Ava said: "I hate to bring up a sore subject, but have you spoken with Dr. Jackson?"

"Not yet," Noah admitted.

"Any reason why?" Ava questioned. "The M&M is coming up quickly. Only three more work days before it's here."

"The same reason I put off talking with Dr. Mason for the last M&M," Noah said. "I'm a coward."

"I can understand," Ava said. "It could be almost as bad as talking with Dr. Mason. He is not as narcissistic, but they share some of the same personality traits."

"I know. That's the reason I've put off having the meeting."

"But it is important to know his mind-set," Ava said. "I'd like to know if he's still mad."

"Me, too," Noah said. "Have you heard anything from Dr. Kumar to make you think that Dr. Jackson complained to him?"

"Not a thing."

"Okay, good," Noah said. "I think his threats to talk with our bosses was just his venting in the heat of the moment. Dr. Hernandez hasn't said anything to me, either. Best-case scenario is that Dr. Jackson realizes some of the blame falls on his shoulders. If that's true, we are in a far better position than with Dr. Mason."

"We need to find out how he feels to plan your presentation," Ava said. "When do you think you will be talking with him?"

"Now that you've reminded me, I'll try to do it tomorrow."

"I hate to be pushy, but it could be important."

Eager to change the subject, Noah said, "The first time I was here, when you were showing me your fabulous computer setup, you said something interesting after admitting how much you enjoyed social media and how much time you spend doing it. You said it's allowed you to learn more about yourself than if you'd done psychoanalysis. Were you being serious?"

"I was very serious."

"You also said that you would be willing to explain it to me sometime. Is this a good time?"

"As good a time as any," Ava said. She sat back in her seat. "First, why I enjoy it so much? That's easy. It fills a social void, which binge-watching Netflix doesn't do, although I do that sometimes, too. I've already explained why I prefer not to socialize with colleagues—you excepted, of course. Since my work is so encompassing and I'm invariably out of town consulting or traveling when I'm off, I know almost no one here in Boston. Online, I have an entire complement of so-called 'friends' always waiting, probably a lot more varied and interesting than if I had acquaintances here in Boston who would undoubtedly be as busy as I am and unavailable when I was available. The online world is so much bigger than the invariably parochial real world, and it is always there, never sleeping and never too busy. And best of all, when you have had enough for whatever reason, you just click it off, no muss, no fuss."

At that moment, Ava's mobile phone filled the room with its raucous sound. After checking to see who was calling, she excused herself and went out of earshot to take the call. It was a typical interruption that Noah had learned to expect but hadn't learned to like. While she was away, he thought about what she had said and wondered if he would rely on social media as much as she if he had as much free time as she did. She averaged a typical 40-hour-per-week schedule, whereas he averaged somewhere in the neighborhood of 120 hours per week at the hospital, far more than he was supposed to be doing.

Noah toyed with his food but didn't eat, preferring to wait for her return. Unfortunately, this episode was longer than the usual. When she finally reappeared thirty-five minutes later, she was appropriately apologetic. While they microwaved their food to rewarm it, she explained that one of her major bosses at the NSC was all uptight about an article coming out in the *Annals of Internal Medicine* the following week. This article, similar to but larger than others that had come out since 1992, would be reporting on a study of almost a half million people over a decade that multivitamins and dietary supplements failed to show any benefits. Perhaps even more damning, it would state that megavitamins had shown a paradoxical increased risk of cancer and heart disease.

"No wonder your boss was upset," Noah said, not bothering to suppress his delight. "That could be a death knell for the industry and maybe for your consulting."

"Not in the slightest," Ava mocked. "We lobbyists have learned how to deal with such studies. There have been others, and like what was done in the past, we'll argue that the wrong amounts of vitamins or the wrong brands of supplements were used. Then we'll say there was something wrong with the way the subjects were selected. After that we'll blame the results on the big drug companies and fan conspiracy theories even to the point of suggesting big pharma was behind the study because they don't want people to keep themselves well with relatively inexpensive supplements. The implication, of course, is that the drug companies want to sell more expensive prescription drugs. The public will eat it up. Besides, something like a medical journal article stays in the news feed for one cycle only, and then it disappears under the next scandal or disaster or tweet."

"God! That's discouraging," Noah said.

"Ultimately, it is what the public wants, meaning an easy way out by taking a few pills rather than making the effort to maintain healthy lifestyles. Of course, for me it means I'll have to go directly back to Washington to do damage control."

With the food reheated, they sat back down at the counter. Night had completely fallen, and thanks to a run of superb weather, it was yet another picture-perfect evening. The glass sliders that lined the kitchen were folded back into their pockets, making it seem like the kitchen and the backyard were one single room. The floodlight illuminated the carefully planted garden. With the help of a few crickets, the fountain provided restful background noise.

"So you were telling me how social media fills a social need for you with no muss and no fuss."

"Right," Ava said. "But it's a lot bigger than that. It gives me the opportunity to explore aspects of myself that I wasn't even aware of."

"Oh?" Noah questioned. Statements like that seemed to him to be on the weird side, especially coming from a fellow physician.

"In real life we're all caught up in the reality of who and what we think we are," Ava said. "We value consistency and so do our family and friends, who are more like us than we usually like to admit. That's not the case in a virtual world. I can be whoever I want to be without any downside or consequence, with the benefit of learning more about myself."

"So Gail Shafter, your Facebook and Snapchat persona, is not you with a different name?"

"No way," Ava said with a unique laugh. "Although we're the same age, she's mired in a world that I was initially caught in right after high school but managed to escape. She's stuck in a small town, working for a dentist who lords it over her, and she's divorced after a failed marriage. She gives me a true appreciation of my life and what I've been able to become in the real world by a combination of hard work and chance. Compared to her, I am so lucky."

"So it's safe to say that when you're on Facebook you're Gail and not you?"

"Of course. It goes without saying, just like when I go on Facebook as Melanie Howard, I'm Melanie Howard."

"Melanie Howard? Is that the name of another sockpuppet?"

"I don't like the term *sockpuppet* or even *smurf*. They are too closely associated with uncivil online behavior. Melanie and I don't do that. We don't engage in any vicious trolling or any flaming whatsoever. That's hardly the goal or the point. Melanie Howard is just another person in the virtual world trying to do the best she can within the limitations of her social circumstances, her personality, and her intelligence."

"What's she like?"

"In general, she's the antithesis of me, or what I am afraid could have been me to some extent. She is the same age but a shy, unsophisticated, and gullible woman who is as desperately looking for love and companionship. Her boring job is as a secretary at a plumbing firm in Brownfield, Texas, working for an unappreciative boss who is constantly trying to hustle her. On the positive side, she's attractive, with a warm, generous, and accepting heart, at least up to a point. Once that point is overstepped, she is as hard as steel."

"Wow," Noah said, not quite knowing what else to say. His original thought was that Ava used the name Gail Shafter just to protect her privacy, not because she wanted to experience a virtual life completely different from her own.

"Does this shock you?" Ava asked, looking at Noah with her head tilted slightly. She was smiling and obviously challenging him. "This is the twenty-first century," she reminded him. "Almost two billion people use Facebook alone."

"I'm just surprised," Noah said. "Does it make you feel at all like an imposter with all these Facebook identities?"

Ava laughed. "Not in the slightest, because the word *imposter* has much too much of a negative connotation. I consider people like Melanie friends of mine and separate, real virtual identities for whom I merely act as the spokesperson so I can explore aspects of my own personality. I know that sounds a bit like 'real artificial diamonds,' but the current-day virtual world is challenging the real world in terms of relevance. What does *real* really mean? But if you insist on using the word *imposter*, remember that almost everyone on social media lies to puff themselves up and make their lives sound more exciting than they are. Even their supposedly candid pics are all Photoshopped. All they care about is the number of 'likes' they get. In that sense, most everyone today is an imposter. And what about you, Dr. Rothauser? Have you ever been an imposter to some degree, say, on a résumé?"

"Absolutely," Noah said with such surety that it was Ava's turn to be taken aback.

"Like all third- and fourth-year medical students," Noah explained, "I had to pretend I was a doctor. If we didn't do it, patients wouldn't have put up with our fumbling antics."

"Ah, yes, I remember it well. There were many times I felt guilty about the deception. But I was truthful if a patient asked."

"Same with me," Noah said. "What about dating websites, which you said you visited? Is that Gail and Melanie who go on them?"

"For sure," Ava said. "I'd never go on a dating website for myself. They are entertaining, but there are too many weirdos out there hiding behind fake profiles. I know you said it worked for you, but that was a few years ago. Today most are just trolling for sex."

"Has Gail or Melanie ever met up with any of the people they have interacted with online?" Noah asked.

"Of course not!" Ava said. "I'm surprised you'd even ask. That would have to be me, and I would never do it, even if I was trying to pass myself off as Gail or Melanie. It would be a huge mistake for dozens of reasons. Besides, it wouldn't surprise me if half or more of the other people are smurfs as well. It's officially admitted that at least ten percent of all the Facebook users are fake profiles. That's somewhere around two hundred million. But as disturbing as that may sound, it doesn't matter. It is the anonymity that is important. As soon as real people are involved face-to-face, anonymity goes out the window."

"It all sounds confusing to me," Noah said. "And not easy to do. When I was a teenager, I learned that the problem with lying was forgetting what you lied about. Do you ever get confused about who you are when you move from one to the other with these virtual identities?"

"I keep extensive files on them, which I update on a regular basis. I even have developed my own algorithms to alert me if I say something out of character. It is part of the challenge to be consistent."

"You are really into this," Noah said. He had trouble believing it was all worth the effort.

"I am," Ava admitted. "As much or more than I was into gaming."

"What about photos and all that? How is that handled?"

"That's easy with all the profiles and photos available on the Internet and the capabilities of photo-editing apps. Believe me, it's not hard."

"One last thing," Noah said. "I remember reading an op-ed piece not too long ago about people coming to believe their lies on social media. Some psychologists were worried about such distortions affecting someone's sense of self. Do you see that as a problem?"

"It depends on your viewpoint," Ava said. "There has always been a certain amount of embellishment that people have done to their histories, even before the Internet and social media. The opportunities are greater now, with technology effectively changing our culture. It is even changing medicine. Everybody is becoming somewhat of an imposter as well as progressively narcissistic. Some people might see that as a problem, others might view it as opportunity."

"I have to admit it's all fascinating," Noah said. "While I've been locked up in the hospital these last five years, the world has changed."

"And the speed of change is accelerating," Ava said. "Listen, after your shower, I can take you up to the computer room and introduce you to Melanie Howard. In a half-hour or so, you'll feel like she's an old friend. You'll know that much about her, and we'll make sure to friend you. I can assure you that she is going to love you."

"I'll enjoy meeting Melanie," Noah said while he and Ava carried their dishes to the kitchen sink. As they rode up squashed together in the elevator, Noah found himself remembering the movie *Her*, wondering exactly how he was going to feel about Melanie Howard. Would he see her as a separate, virtual person even though he knew it was Ava's hand inside the sockpuppet?

17

Keyon Dexter took exit 25 off Interstate 93 to Plymouth, New Hampshire. He was tired since he'd been driving for almost two hours from Boston. He had lost a coin toss with his partner, George Marlowe, that decided who would be the driver. On out-of-town trips, they both preferred to sit with the passenger seat pushed way back and reclined, so they could put their feet up on the Ford van's dash. For almost a year they had been assigned to the Boston area by ABC Security out of Baltimore, Maryland, which had established a branch office in Boston in the Old City Hall building on School Street.

"Man, we are out in the boonies here," Keyon remarked. "I was hoping we were finished with this mickey-mouse stuff after taking care of Savageboy."

"I did, too," George said. He put his feet down and slipped on his shoes, then straightened up the seat and pulled it forward to make it even with Keyon's. "Hopefully once we take care of CreepyBoar we'll have seen the end of it. The virtual proxy network that's in place now should keep this kind of crap from happening in the future."

"I don't know," Keyon said. "These kids are something else. They've grown up with this technology rather than having to learn it the hard way like we did. For them it's second nature. They're all a bunch of hackers in waiting. Maybe they'll find a way to circumvent a VPN."

"I suppose it's possible. They are also clever in their username choices. CreepyBoar is pretty unique."

"Do you think he's going to be as easy as Gary Sheffield?"

"If I had to guess, I'd say yes. Why else would he be spending so much effort trying to meet up with a thirteen-year-old girl?"

"It takes all kinds," Keyon said with disgust. "It also depends on whether he's a faculty member or a student. What's your guess?"

"Faculty member," George said without hesitation. "Students have too much candy within reach. They don't have to go trolling on the Internet."

"I suppose you have a point," Keyon said. "But online he says he's an eighteen-year-old college student."

"I don't care what he says," George snapped. "People make up all sorts of shit online. But maybe I'm just being hopeful. If it turns out to be a student, our job of cleaning up this particular mess gets a lot harder. Teenage boys in particular are always bragging about their exploits, so Teresa Puksar's address and info might already be in lots of smartphones."

"We can only be expected to do the best we can," Keyon said.

They had come to Plymouth as dictated by their target's IP address. But in contrast to Gary Sheffield, whose IP address gave them the man's actual street address, with CreepyBoar, they were able to get only the Plymouth State University network's location. What they needed to do was get on the university's network to get CreepyBoar's computer location, which was why they needed to do it at night. They wanted Creepy-Boar to be at home.

When they came to a roundabout, they headed south on Main Street. It was a modest college town with mostly one- or two-story buildings. The university campus was on their right, stretching up a gradual hill. The center building was a square-shaped brick clock tower.

Using a detailed map they had downloaded from the Internet, they made a circle around the campus, or at least as much of a circle as they could. The architecture was an indeterminate mix, with most of the buildings made of red brick.

"Not a lot of activity," George said.

"It's their summer session," Keyon said. "It's probably a lot different during the normal academic year."

They rode in silence. Each knew what the other was thinking. There was no way they would want to live in such a rural environment.

"All right," George said when they had made a full loop around the college. "Now that we've got the lay of the land, let's find a place to park and see if we get lucky."

Keyon pulled into a spot on Main Street where there were a number of other vehicles. Most were pickup trucks. A few restaurants were still open, including one that looked like a 1950s diner. The other stores were closed.

Both men moved into the back of the van and powered up their gear. It didn't take long once they were on the Plymouth.edu network. As they expected from already knowing CreepyBoar's online habits, the target was busy at the computer. But what they didn't expect was that it wasn't a he. The computer belonged to a Margaret Stonebrenner.

"Well, I'll be damned," Keyon said.

"Let's not jump to conclusions," George said. "Maybe Margaret has a teenage son who is busy using his mother's computer."

"You're right," Keyon said.

They then ran Margaret Stonebrenner of 24 Smith Street through all the extensive databases they had access to. They soon learned she had no criminal record, and that she was an instructor in psychology who had been divorced since 2015 from Claire Walker, whom she had married in 2011. There had been a daughter from Claire's previous marriage, but Claire ended up with full custody.

"There you go," Keyon said. "At least we were right about her being a faculty member."

"And wrong about the orientation," George said. "It never occurred to me the mark might be gay. Why the hell was she trolling a teenage girl pretending to be a teenage boy? I'm shocked, although maybe it's hard being gay in a small rural town. But what do I know?"

"You think you're surprised," Keyon said with a chuckle. "Think how poor Teresa Puksar would have felt if she'd agreed to meet."

Keyon and George had a good laugh.

"I tell you," George said when he had recovered, "I don't know what this world is coming to. I'm only thirty-six, but considering how far out of it I am about all this LGBT stuff, I might as well be twice that. It's crazy."

After consulting their street map of Plymouth, the two men climbed back into the front bucket seats and set off toward Smith Street. It wasn't far, as nothing in Plymouth was far. They first did a drive-by, noticing that 24 Smith Street was a small two-story white Victorian house with decorative bargeboard under the steeply angled eaves. The first-floor windows were illuminated, while those on the second floor were dark.

"Looks encouraging," Keyon said. "Think she lives alone?"

"We can't be that lucky two hits in a row," George said. "But we can always hope."

They parked the van on a neighboring cross street and hiked back. As they walked they checked out the nearby houses, most of which were dark. "People turn in early here in Plymouth," Keyon said. "I guess there's not a lot of nightlife." He chuckled quietly at his understatement.

When they reached their destination, they glanced around at the immediate neighboring homes. Conveniently, they were all dark. Turning their attention to Margaret's house, they could hear a noisy, old-fashioned window air conditioner, which they also thought advantageous. The sound of gunfire in the complete silence of a country town could carry far and wide. With that in mind, Keyon had brought along his Beretta semi-automatic pistol with suppressor. It was a surprisingly quiet weapon. The downside was that it was significantly bulky in its shoulder holster, and he wouldn't have gotten away with wearing it in daylight.

As per usual, they positioned themselves on either side of the door, fake FBI badges at the ready. As there was no doorbell, George knocked. When no one responded, he knocked louder. This resulted in a carriage lamp going on right next to George, which he didn't like. A moment later a female voice called through the door asking who was there.

On this occasion Keyon did the talking, essentially reiterating the FBI-agent spiel they gave Gary Sheffield about being part of the bureau's Cyber Action Team. The difference was that Margaret didn't open the door.

"What do you need to talk about?" Margaret asked.

Again, Keyon followed their usual protocol by explaining that there had been felonious cyber-activity emanating from the house that needed to be investigated.

"I would prefer that you come back tomorrow," Margaret said. "How do I know you're FBI agents?"

Keyon and George exchanged a worried glance. They also heard something else they didn't like, a bark and growl, and it wasn't from a miniature poodle.

"If you would open the door, we can show you our credentials," Keyon said.

"I've never heard of FBI agents coming to someone's door this time of night," Margaret said. "I'm sorry. I'm here by myself."

"Ma'am, we understand your reluctance, but if you don't talk with us, we will have to come back with the local police and have you arrested. We are quite sure that we can clear this all up without that kind of embarrassment. But we can't do it through the door."

For a moment, there was silence marred only by the sound of the nearby window air conditioner. Keyon and George exchanged another glance, sensing they were losing control of the situation. Then they heard what sounded like the musical notes of a mobile phone being dialed.

"Shit!" George snapped, speaking up for the first time since they'd come onto the porch. He stepped back and raised his foot, kicking the paneled door with all the force he could muster just to the side of the doorknob. The old wood splintered and the door burst open. A second later they charged into the room, causing a shocked Margaret Stonebrenner to stumble backward. At the same moment, a large black German shepherd charged at George, who was first through the door.

Thanks to his Marine Corps training, which had included crowd control and dog attacks, George lifted his arms over his head to deny the shepherd a handy target. George absorbed the sizable dog's attack and stayed on his feet. Although the dog was able to get a bite full of George's right jacket sleeve, Keyon had his Beretta out and shot the animal twice in the chest. At first the bullets seemed to have had no effect, since the dog continued to shake its head, trying to tear George's jacket. Then, with the same suddenness that the attack began, the dog let go of its hold on George's sleeve, teetered for a moment, whimpered, and then sank to the floor. A moment later it rolled onto its side.

Seeing what had happened to her dog, Margaret began screaming, even as Keyon pointed the gun in her direction and yelled for her to shut up.

"You bastards," she cried, her face a picture of terror and anguish. She started coming at Keyon with fire in her eyes. Keyon responded by shooting her in the forehead. The result was the same as it had been for Gary Sheffield. Margaret was knocked over backward onto the floor. For a second or two there was some quivering in her limbs. A moment later her sightless eyes stared up at the ceiling.

"Goddamn it," George exploded. "Now we can't question her."

Before Keyon could respond, both heard a male voice coming from Margaret's mobile phone. She had dropped it onto the hall carpet when she was shot. "This is the Plymouth Police Department. Is everything okay there, Miss Stonebrenner?"

Keyon snapped up the phone, turned it off, and pocketed it. "We have to get the fuck out of here."

"We need her computer," George said.

"I see it," Keyon said. He pushed past George into the dining room, where an open computer sat on the table. Keyon slammed it shut and took it under his arm. There was also a woman's purse. He snapped that up as well.

While Keyon was in the dining room, George hurriedly pulled on some latex gloves. Going to an open roll-top desk, he rifled through a few drawers, leaving them open, dumping one onto the floor. Then the two men hurried out into the night, slowing to a normal walk when they reached the street. As they headed for the van, they cast worried glances at the neighboring houses, but nothing had changed. The neighborhood seemed as quiet as it had been earlier.

"That was messy," George said with disgust as he climbed into the van's driver's seat. It was his turn to drive. "Probably our worst job." He snapped off the gloves before starting the engine.

"In this business, you never know what you're going to get," Keyon said. "Let's not own up to what happened unless we are specifically asked. Let's also hope the new VPN is as good as it's claimed to be so this is our last job like this."

"I'll second that," George said. "But you know what surprised me? How normal this Stonebrenner looked. I expected her to be more like the others, like Sheffield. Somebody you wouldn't look at twice, living a boring humdrum life, kinda nerdy and dumb, relying on social media to have a life, even if only virtual. She didn't strike me like that. And she didn't buy our FBI story, not for a second."

"Social media is taking over our culture," Keyon said. "It's not just the teenyboppers anymore. It's everybody."

To avoid driving back through town, George took a circuitous route to I-93 on their way back to Boston.

18

For a bit of variety after exhausting the Toscano menu for five nights in a row, Noah was back in the Thai restaurant called King & I. He'd called in an order after leaving the hospital and talking briefly with Ava to get her preferences, and now he stood by the cashier to wait.

It had been a very busy Friday. It had started earlier than usual because Friday morning's basic science lecturer had canceled, forcing Noah to give the important lecture on postoperative electrolyte maintenance, which required a bit of preparation. To do so, he'd awakened at 4:00 A.M. and managed to leave Ava's without waking her.

Following the basic science lecture, Noah had four surgeries, including a complicated esophagectomy, or removal and replacement of the esophagus. It was a difficult procedure that he'd done only once before. Luckily it had gone well, although he didn't have high hopes for the patient; esophageal cancer was a particularly difficult disease for the oncologists.

Although all the surgeries had gone well, there was one unfortunate occurrence. Although he generally tried to avoid running into Dr. Mason by keeping track of his schedule, that morning it had happened despite his best intentions. Noah had just finished his first case and was accompanying the patient along with the anesthesiologist to the PACU when

Dr. Mason unexpectedly appeared out of a case that was supposed to take four hours yet had been under way for only less than two. Despite Noah's attempts to indicate he was busy, Dr. Mason insisted he talk and pulled him aside. He then proceeded to rail Noah about the quality of residents Noah was assigning to Dr. Mason's cases. "With the kind of patients I bring into this hospital, I shouldn't have to deal with incompetence in the assistants I'm assigned," Mason had spat. "And let me tell you, I'm going to bring this up with Dr. Herandez, Dr. Cantor, and Ms. Hutchinson." Gloria Hutchinson was the president of BMH.

Of course, Dr. Mason's complaints were baseless. If anything, Noah went out of his way always to provide as senior as possible residents for Dr. Mason, anticipating the man's tendency to blame everyone around him whenever something out of the ordinary happened. It was also true that Noah had not received any complaints about surgical resident assistants from any other surgeon, and that included all twenty-four of the first-year people.

Noah had tried to end the conversation by asking Dr. Mason if he might provide Noah with a list of the residents he enjoyed working with so that Noah could attempt to assign those people to Mason. But instead of taking this peace offering, Dr. Mason had switched the subject of the conversation to the upcoming M&M.

"I hope to God you are not planning on shielding your incompetent lover like you so obviously did with the Vincent case," Dr. Mason had snarled. "Because you are not going to get away with it this time. I had to hold my tongue during the last conference because I was the surgeon. Not so on this occasion. No free lunch this time."

Once again, Noah had to endure being stabbed in the chest by Dr. Mason's persistent index finger as the surgeon made his final point before he continued toward the surgical lounge.

"Your take-out is ready," the King & I cashier said, pulling Noah back to the present.

Noah paid and left the restaurant. Charles Street was alive, with people enjoying themselves. As he walked he felt one with this world, which was unique for him. Anticipating spending another pleasant evening with Ava, he didn't feel his usual sense of isolation from normal society, as he now had a life outside of the hospital. He smiled, thinking that maybe there was hope for him after all.

As he trudged up Pinckney Street on his way to Louisburg Square his thoughts went back to his busy day, which had included several important conversations that he was eager to share with Ava. After the run-in with Dr. Mason, which jolted him into remembering exactly how close the M&M Conference was, he first made it a point to investigate which junior resident had been assigned to the emergency room on that particular day. It was Dr. Harriet Schonfeld. He'd found her in the ER sewing up a laceration. He was pleased with what he had learned from her and looked forward to telling Ava.

Next Noah had met with the anesthesia resident, Dr. Carla Violeta, plus the circulating nurse and the scrub nurse on the Gibson case, but he didn't learn anything from the three of them that he didn't already know. Finally, following Ava's encouragement the night before, he had arranged to meet with Dr. Warren Jackson, which he dreaded and had put off just as he had put off meeting with Dr. Mason before the last M&M. As an older surgeon who had trained at the same place Dr. Mason had trained, Dr. Jackson shared some of Dr. Mason's unpleasant narcissistic traits, in particular an easily offended, arrogant attitude and a stubborn reluctance to accept any blame, even if warranted. To his surprise, Noah had found Dr. Jackson much more reasonable than Dr. Mason.

Ava was particularly happy to see Noah when he finally rang her bell and got buzzed in. It was nearly 10:00 P.M., and she admitted to being starved when Noah found her in the kitchen. She had opened a bottle of wine and had already drunk a quarter of it while she'd used her iPhone to go on Facebook while she waited. Noah apologized for being kept at the hospital because of a late-afternoon emergency.

They ate at their usual location, looking out at the garden. Noah was eager to tell her what he had learned but had to bide his time while she told him about several demanding cases she'd had that day that had required more anesthesia skill than the usual. Noah was impressed with how she had handled them. Her encyclopedic knowledge of anesthesia rivaled his command of the minutiae of surgery. After dinner they ended up in the study as per usual. Noah had come to understand why it was her favorite sitting room in the house. It was rapidly becoming his as well. Almost like Pavlov's dogs, each took the exact same chair they'd occupied on previous evenings, as if responding to some internal directive.

"Okay, your turn," Ava said, realizing how much she had been dominating the conversation. "Sorry for carrying on."

"Not at all," Noah said. "I'm intrigued by your command of your field."

"I've had superb training," Ava said, pleased.

"I have some good news and some bad news," Noah said. "Which do you prefer first?"

"Let's get the bad out of the way so we can rest on the good."

"Unfortunately for me, I ran into Dr. Mason in the OR hallway," Noah said. "He cornered me as usual and mouthed off with a complaint about the assistants I've been assigning him, which is all a bunch of nonsense. But more important, he warned me not to shield you during this M&M like he feels I did during the last M&M."

"He said that specifically?" Ava questioned.

"Very specifically," Noah said, "using the exact same words." Noah did not add that Dr. Mason had referred to her as "your lover." "He also remarked that he'd been muzzled at the last M&M, which wasn't going to be the case this time."

"Okay, that's the bad news. What's the good?"

"My meeting with Dr. Jackson wasn't anything like I expected," Noah said. "He actually admitted that he'd made a mistake pressuring the first-year resident into starting the case before you were in the room. He said he'd come to the realization after giving the episode more thought."

"That's terrific," Ava said, her face lighting up. "Do you think he might be willing to say something to that effect at the conference?"

"I think so," Noah said. "I also talked with Dr. Violeta."

"I know," Ava said. "She told me."

"She's willing to confirm being pressured," Noah said. "So I won't mind bringing it up."

"You'll have to bring it up," Ava said. "It has to be established that I wasn't in the room when the patient was given the paralyzing drug and had already arrested. Both are key."

"You are right," Noah agreed. "I'll definitely mention it."

"This is good news," Ava said. "I feel better already about this M&M."

"And I got more significant news today," Noah said. "I talked with the junior surgical resident who handled the case in the ER. When I told her that the neck problem wasn't in the electronic medical record, she was astounded and insisted that she had included it."

"It wasn't in the EMR," Ava snapped. She sat up and moved forward in her chair, ready to do battle.

"It was, and it wasn't," Noah said. He reached out and put a calming hand on Ava's thigh. "What we found were two EMRs for the same patient with an inversion of two letters in the spelling of the name, one with the problem described and another without it. Somehow the computer had made two records. I already visited IT about it, and one of their people is going to look into it, figure out how it happened and how to keep it from happening in the future."

"That's perfect," Ava said. With a sigh of relief, she sat back in her chair. "That alone could eat up a good portion of the discussion time.

Most of the staff are down on the EMR already and will love to offer their opinions."

"Exactly my thoughts as well," Noah said. "It's looking good, like we'll be able to get through this next M&M as well as we did with the first. What I plan to do is leave Helen Gibson for last, just like I did with Bruce Vincent. If I time it right, maybe there won't be any discussion time and we won't have to listen to Dr. Mason carry on."

"I was just going to suggest as much," Ava said. "I love it."

"I do have one question for you, though," Noah said. "Were you familiar with the video laryngoscope you were using that day? I know there are a number of different brands, each a little different." Noah tried to use an offhand tone of voice as he asked this question, as if the idea just occurred to him. It was an issue that had been bothering him in the back of his mind since the event. He'd had the impression Ava had seemed less than adept with the instrument than she should have been, although he was the first to admit he might have been expecting the impossible. When Ava was using the device, the patient's head had been bouncing all over the place from the cardiac massage, which would have made it difficult for anyone. Putting in an endotracheal tube on certain patients with restricted neck motion could be incredibly difficult, as Noah painfully knew from personal experience.

"Of course I was familiar with the McGrath laryngoscope," Ava said with a touch of irritation. "Just like I'm familiar with all the other scopes on the market, such as the Airtraq or the GlideScope. They are all more similar than different, although I do prefer the GlideScope because it has a larger screen."

"I see," Noah said, nodding. That was already more than he knew about video laryngoscopes. But the issue of Ava's struggles bothered him like a pebble in his shoe. He was also mildly troubled by something else he had learned. There was more time than he expected between the moment the first-year resident sent out the alarm that she was having trouble and needed help and Ava's arrival in the room. Of course, Ava was observing another patient being put under general anesthesia at the time. Yet that induction had been carried out without any trouble whatsoever, so why didn't Ava come right away? And why hadn't Ava ordered a tracheostomy immediately when she saw how difficult it was to put in an endotracheal tube and the patient had already had a cardiac arrest from low oxygen?

"Are you aware of the time?" Ava said, interrupting Noah's thoughts.

Noah glanced at his watch. "Oh, my gosh. It is almost midnight."

"I don't know how you function on so little sleep," Ava said. "I need to go to bed. What do you say?"

"Fine by me," Noah said agreeably, and he meant it, realizing he'd been on the go for just shy of twenty hours.

"You know something?" Ava asked suddenly in a sultry voice.

"What?" Noah asked innocently.

"This good news of yours turns me on."

"Oh?" Noah commented innocently. He wasn't sure he had heard correctly, or if he had, what he should do.

Ava solved Noah's immediate dilemma by standing up, and to Noah's surprise peeled off her blouse and dropped her jeans. She stood before him in a dark green, incredibly sexy bra-and-panties outfit the likes of which Noah had never seen, covering the least amount of dermatological acreage he thought possible. She sauntered over to Noah, who was momentarily paralyzed, and sat on the arm of his chair. He was dazzled by her pheromones.

"You know what I think we should do with all this good news?" she asked in the same husky voice.

"I'm beginning to get an idea," Noah said, more than willing to play the game.

"Let's make love right here, right now!"

AN HOUR LATER, they were lying in Ava's king-size bed, gazing up at the ceiling with Oxi and Carbi curled up at the foot. Although feeling great, Noah was struggling to stay awake after having gotten up that morning at 4:00 A.M. and working all day.

"I have to admit something," Ava said suddenly. "I'm totally jealous of your Ivy League education. What a thrill it must have been for you to go to Columbia, MIT, and Harvard. I can't imagine how proud you must be. And getting a Ph.D. like you did in just two years. It is remarkable."

"I was lucky," Noah said. "At the same time, I worked my butt off."

"I wish I had had the opportunity," Ava said wistfully. "Being here at the BMH, I feel embarrassed at having gone to such an unknown school. It seems that most everyone around here trained at a name institution like you."

"I'm impressed with what you have been able to do," Noah said sincerely. "I looked at your educational background on LinkedIn and learned you were in a combined six-year college and medical school program. In many ways, it's more impressive than what I've done. My path was clear from middle school on. You said you weren't motivated to go to college. What changed your mind?"

"Working for the dentist," Ava said. "It made me realize I wasn't going anyplace fast and that I'd be doing the same thing for the rest of my life. It was a rude awakening. Luckily, my boss, Dr. Winston Herbert, was recruited to start a dental program at Brazos University in 2001, which he did in 2002. Brazos U was a new school formed in the mid-nineties in Lubbock that was growing by leaps and bounds. They had started a medical school a few years later. Dr. Herbert brought me along with him when he became dean of the dental school, so I was in reality working for the university. Of course, he was taking advantage of me at the time, despite his being married and all."

"I'm sorry," Noah said. He felt anger at the thought of a man sexually abusing a teenager.

"It's water over the dam," Ava said. "I'm not bitter. In fact, I'm thankful. I wouldn't be where I am today if it hadn't been for Dr. Herbert. Being part of a growing university opened my eyes to so many things. And he was encouraging right from the start. He even started my interest in anesthesia."

"Really?" Noah questioned. "How was that?"

"Dentists often can be very cavalier about anesthesia," Ava said. "They feel comfortable using it in their offices without the kind of backup I demand now. And he let me do it almost from day one. Here I was giving anesthesia at age eighteen, knowing almost nothing about it. It terrifies me now when I think back, but I was fascinated by it. It's what prompted me to go to college and then medical school. When I barely managed to graduate from Coronado High School, I never in a million years thought I'd go on to any form of formal education."

"How did you manage, moneywise? Did your family help?" Noah asked.

Ava gave a short mocking laugh. "Not in the slightest. I never got along with my father."

"Well, that's another way we're alike. I never got along with mine, either."

"My mother remarried after my father died, but her new husband and I were like oil and water. I was on my own right after high school. Working for Dr. Herbert and the university was what made it all possible. I worked for him whenever I could throughout college and medical school."

"What were you like as a child?" Noah asked. Though they shared a commitment to medicine, it was apparent to him that early on they were very different people. Once he'd seen the light in the first years of high school, he'd been overly committed to education and becoming a surgeon. It had consumed him, and it still did.

"I really don't like talking about my past," Ava said firmly. "It brings back too many painful memories. I'd much prefer to talk about the future. Or better still, your past."

"What would you like to know?" Noah said.

"Everything," Ava said. She pushed herself up on an elbow and looked at Noah. "I know we were born the same year, 1982. When I put it all together, I'm missing two years in your history."

"You continue to impress me," he said. "You're correct. Medical school took me six years rather than the usual four. During my second year my mother got sick and had to leave her job, which was supporting me and my disabled sister. I had to get a job. Luckily, I got a job with the medical school so I could stay involved by attending lectures. When my mother passed away, I was able to rematriculate and finish medical school."

"I'm sorry," Ava said. "That must have been a struggle."

"Like you said earlier, it's water over the dam. You do what you have to do."

"And tell me more about your Ph.D. thesis in genetics from MIT," Ava said. "That's really impressive. I've never heard of someone getting a Ph.D. so quickly. How on earth did you manage it?"

"It sounds more impressive than it was," Noah said. "I had started it as an undergraduate project in bacterial reproduction, so I had a jump on it. But to be honest, I didn't do it for the purest intentions. I did it with the hopes it would get me into Harvard Medical School, which it did. I was scared; when I'd finished my undergraduate degree in biology, I was turned down by both Columbia and Harvard Medical School. I knew I had to do something out of the ordinary."

"You're just being modest," Ava said.

"I don't think so," Noah said. "I even fudged on it a bit, at least initially. But that's another story."

"What do you mean?"

"It doesn't matter," Noah said. "The whole project was more busy work than a real breakthrough, and in that sense somewhat of an embarrassment."

"Sounds imposterish, if I can coin a new term, just like we were talking about last night."

Noah pointed at Ava's nose and said with a laugh, "Very clever. You got me! I suppose I am kind of a Ph.D. imposter."

19

"For your first endoscopic gallbladder removal, that was well done, Mark,"
Noah said to Dr. Mark Donaldson in operating room 24. Mark had just
withdrawn the gallbladder out of one of the four tiny endoscopic incisions
in the patient's abdomen. The second-year resident had done a commendable job, and Noah knew it was important for him to be told. When one
was a junior resident, praise from a senior, especially a super chief, was
critical when it was deserved just as much as criticism when that was appropriate.

"Thank you, Dr. Rothauser," Mark said while handing off the small,
diseased organ to the scrub nurse. He then visibly relaxed a degree, as he
had been tense through the entire hourlong procedure. Noah also relaxed.
He, too, had been tense with the instruments mostly out of his hands,
certainly more tense than if he had been doing the procedure himself. It
was part of the strain of teaching surgery. Both residents were looking at
the monitor, which gave them a good view of the raw gallbladder bed
under the edge of the liver.

"You're practically home free," Noah said. "It looks good. All you have
to do is suture up the bed to prevent adhesions, make sure there are no
bleeders, then pull out the instruments."

Mark set to work. Some inexperienced surgeons had trouble with co-ordination when looking at a monitor at eye level as their hands manipulated the instruments below, inside the patient's body. Mark wasn't one of these. Noah had never had any problem, either, which he attributed to his playing computer games where the play was carried out by manipulating a computer mouse off to the side while looking straight ahead at a monitor. This realization had given him some satisfaction that gaming hadn't been as worthless as his mother had complained.

Once the gallbladder bed had been closed, Noah encouraged Mark to irrigate the area with saline and then suck up the fluid. It was the best way to look for any tiny leaking blood vessels that could cause big trouble after the surgery. A few moments later, when Mark was done with this last suturing chore, everything looked perfect. The case was essentially done.

"We are going to be withdrawing the instruments," Noah said to the nurse anesthetist so she could begin lightening up on the anesthesia. Surgery was a team sport, and it was important to keep everyone informed.

At that moment, the PA system suddenly sprang to life. Everyone started and momentarily froze with their attention focused. Announcements over the inconspicuous speakers rarely occurred, but when they did, it meant something critical was happening. It was Janet Spaulding, and her voice was urgent: "We have an apparent malignant hyperthermia in room number ten. I repeat, we have a malignant hyperthermia in room number ten. The MH cart and all available personnel are needed immediately in room number ten."

Although the anesthetist, the scrub nurse, the circulating nurse, and Mark immediately regained their composure and went back to work on the case at hand, Noah felt differently. Despite being involved in an ongoing operation and therefore not expected to respond, he desperately wanted to do so: Ava was the anesthesiologist assigned to room 10 for an emergency appendectomy on a twelve-year-old boy named Philip Harrison. Noah was aware of this because it had been up to him, as per usual, to assign a resident assistant for the surgeon, Dr. Kevin Nakano.

"Mark!" Noah said sharply. "Do you feel confident to close the incision sites on this case?"

"I suppose," Mark said, a bit taken aback.

"It's not hard," Noah snapped. "But you must close the fascia, particularly at the incision in the umbilicus. We don't want her to get a belly-button hernia. Understand?"

"Got it," Mark said.

"I want to get down to room number ten in case I'm needed," Noah said, as he stepped back from the operating table, snapping off his surgical gloves in the process. He nodded to the nurse anesthetist to make sure she knew he was leaving before the case had ended.

As he went through the OR room door, Noah struggled out of his surgical gown. He left it and the used gloves next to the scrub sink and started running down the hall toward room 10. What was propelling him with such urgency wasn't necessarily the patient's well-being but rather Ava's. He had never seen a case of malignant hyperthermia, known as MH, but he knew a significant amount about the condition, a rare but life-threatening problem usually triggered by exposure to certain drugs used for general anesthesia. The body's muscular machinery went into uncontrolled overdrive, potentially leading to organ failure and death.

What was worrying Noah was the possibility that Ava could be facing yet another anesthesia catastrophe so soon after experiencing two others that already had undermined her self-esteem and had her questioning her competence. Noah wanted to be present for moral support, if nothing else. Although he'd never seen a case of malignant hyperthermia personally, he'd participated on numerous occasions in practice sessions spearheaded by the Anesthesia Department for dealing with the critical emergency.

Noah burst into OR 10 and found himself in the middle of chaos. There were twenty people in the room along with the malignant hyperthermia cart, which contained all the potentially needed drugs and hardware to deal with the emergency. About half the people grouped around the patient were anesthesia residents; the rest were nurses, except for two surgical residents. Off to the side was the cardiac crash cart in case it was needed.

The frantic activity was centered on preparing the major treatment modality, a drug called dantrolene. Since the drug was unstable in solution, it had to be prepared on the spot just prior to use. While that was in process, other people were preparing a cooling blanket. Ice was brought in and put in a basin, into which bottles of IV fluid were placed. As suggested by the name of the condition, one of its critical hallmarks was a dangerous rise in body temperature that had to be controlled or, in irreverent resident parlance, the brain would be "fried."

Dr. Kevin Nakano was standing off to the side with his sterile hands clasped over his sterile surgical gown. His eyes had the terrified look of someone who wanted desperately to do something but didn't quite know what. The situation had been commandeered by the MH team. A sterile towel had been placed over the tiny incision site that Dr. Nakano had been in the process of closing when all hell broke loose. The appendix had already been removed.

Noah made his way through the crowd to the head of the table. Ava stood, her stool pushed to the side, tending to the anesthesia machine, which was ventilating the patient with 100 percent oxygen. Even so, the patient's oxygen saturation was low, as evidenced by the oximeter alarm and the patient's color, a mottled blue.

Noah and Ava exchanged a quick but knowing glance. He could tell immediately that she was beside herself with concern but in control, like a competent pilot in an emergency. Noah looked at the ECG and could see the boy's heart was racing.

"What's his temperature?" Noah asked over the tumult of voices in the room.

"One-oh-six and climbing," Ava said. She shook her head. From her eyes alone Noah could sense she knew she was in the middle of a true emergency and was heartsick over the possible consequences. "He's only twelve years old," she managed.

"Scary!" Noah said. He was going to say more, but he was nudged aside by the most senior anesthesia resident who'd responded to the call, Dr. Allan Martin, the designated leader of the assembled MH group.

"Here's the first hundred milligrams of dantrolene," Allan said to Ava.

"Thank God!" Ava said, taking the medication and immediately attaching it to the IV line. "But I'm going to want three more doses prepared."

"It is in process," Allan assured her.

Noah watched as other members of the team properly positioned the cooling blanket for the now completely rigid boy. All his muscles were in tight contraction. It was as if he were made of wood.

The circulating nurse approached Ava from the other side and handed her a piece of paper.

"Allan," Ava called. "The potassium is going up. I'm going to give glucose and insulin."

Allan responded with a thumbs-up.

Noah managed to move back to Ava. After she had given the insulin, she had a moment of comparative calm.

"What was the first sign of trouble?" Noah asked.

"A sudden unexpected rise in end-tidal carbon dioxide," Ava said. She was staring at the temperature readout.

"Oh," Noah responded. He had expected something more dramatic and not quite so esoteric. "That was all?"

"That was just the first sign of trouble," Ava said, staring at the temperature readout as if trying to make it go south by sheer force of will. "Then I noticed his jaw clenching. That was when I knew what was happening and called the alarm. By the time the MH team got here he was completely rigid. It came on really, really fast. I'm afraid it's a severe case, which doesn't make any sense. There's no family history. I even asked the mother pre-op."

"I'm sorry," Noah said, not knowing what else to say. He could feel her anguish.

"The temperature is not responding to the first dose of dantrolene," Ava said.

"Is that bad?" Noah asked.

"Of course it's bad," Ava said, as if angry. "It's climbed to above one-oh-seven."

Ava called over to Allan, asking for the next dose of dantrolene, but before it could be given the cardiac alarm went off. Twelve-year-old Philip Harrison's heart went into fibrillation.

The team responded appropriately, since the cardiac crash cart was already in the room. The patient was successfully defibrillated, and a relatively normal heartbeat returned. The second dose of dantrolene was given. More tricks were also tried to get the patient's temperature to reverse its relentless rise. It was at that point that Dr. Adam Stevens, the same cardiac surgeon who had helped Noah on the Bruce Vincent case, came into the room to see what was happening. He had just finished a case of his own. He saw Noah and made his way over to him.

"What's happening?" Dr. Stevens asked.

Noah gave the surgeon a quick rundown, saying that it was not looking good for the boy. "The temperature is now over one-oh-eight, despite everything that's being done," Noah added with growing alarm.

"I don't like that mottled blue cyanosis," Dr. Stevens said. "That's a super-bad sign, suggesting disseminated intravascular coagulation."

"More dantrolene," Ava desperately called out to Allan. "The temperature is still rising."

"There's only one way to bring the temperature down," Dr. Stevens said. "Put him on the pump and run the blood through an ice bath. That will do it. Of course, we're not sure if his brain hasn't already called it quits. We could do an EEG, but by the time we do that, it most likely would be too late."

"You're willing to put him on bypass?" Noah questioned. After the Vincent catastrophe, Noah was less willing to contemplate such heroics, especially after what Dr. Mason had said to him about it being Noah's actions that had killed the hospital parking czar.

"If you'll help, I'll do it," Dr. Stevens said.

In record time, with both Noah and Dr. Nakano assisting Dr. Stevens, Philip Harrison was put on cardiac bypass. Unfortunately, his temperature had reached 113 before the cooling could be instigated. As the final coup de grâce when the temperature had been brought down into the normal range, the heart would not start, agonizingly similar to the situation with Bruce Vincent. All the effort turned out to be in vain.

"Well, we gave it our best," Dr. Stevens said an hour later. He was speaking to the entire group in the operating room. No one had left.

Everyone felt dispirited, having given their all, and said little as they filed out of the room. Dr. Stevens departed first, followed by Dr. Nakano. No one spoke.

Noah hung back, watching Ava as she shut down the anesthesia machine and made some final entries in the EMR. On several occasions, she cast a fleeting glance at Noah but didn't say anything. Nor did he. The circulating nurse and the scrub nurse were in the area, starting to clean up the room. They didn't speak, either.

Without a word, Ava suddenly turned around, pushed through a side door, and disappeared into the equipment room that housed the sterilizer and surgical supplies. After a moment of indecision, Noah followed her. He found her leaning against the sterilizer for support. She was still wearing her mask, but Noah could tell she had been crying. He approached her, feeling profound empathy for what she was obviously feeling. He put his arms around her and hugged her. She didn't pull away.

"Do you think it's wise for us to be seen like this?" Ava asked after a few moments.

"You're right," Noah said. He let go and looked back through the glass pane in the door. He was relieved, as he half expected to see either the scrub nurse or circulating nurse staring at them.

"He was only twelve," Ava said, her voice faltering. "I don't know if I can take this. This is my third death. I never thought anything like this would happen."

"It's not your fault," Noah said with emphasis. "It has to mean the boy had a genetic predisposition. That's all. You said you even asked about it in your pre-op interview. You can't ask any more of yourself than that."

"He'd had anesthesia a year ago without a problem," Ava said. "I even used the same agents. He had eaten lunch. That was what I was worried about, not malignant hyperthermia."

"There is no way you could have anticipated this," Noah said. "You can't blame yourself."

"Maybe that is true, maybe it isn't," Ava said dejectedly. "But after this third case, I don't know if I can continue with clinical anesthesia."

"I can understand your feeling," Noah said. "But let's not make any snap decisions on the spur of the moment. Medicine is always risky. It's the nature of the calling. Think of how slim the chances are that you had to face this problem. As I remember, it's like one in twenty thousand cases.

"You have been victimized by statistics or, if you prefer, bad luck. It doesn't speak to your competence as an anesthesiologist. Try to remember the thousands of cases you've done with great results and no problems. You are a great anesthesiologist. You wouldn't be here if you weren't. Don't even think about throwing away all your training and effort."

"I don't know what I'll do," Ava said. She looked at her watch. It was after 4:00 in the afternoon. "I want to go home."

"Good idea," Noah said. "Go home and do something to take your mind off all this. Go on social media!"

"Don't make fun of me!" Ava warned.

"I'm not. You've told me how much you like it. Go do it. Do a video post for your Gail Shafter fan page and make your thousands of followers happy. I'll come over as soon as I can tonight, and we can talk more. That is, if you'd like to talk more. Maybe in the short term we should do something completely different to take your mind off it, like go out to dinner and pretend to be normal people."

Ava glanced up at Noah to see if he was being patronizing. "Okay," she said quietly when she realized he was being sincere. Without another word, she brushed past Noah and exited out into the OR corridor. She didn't look back.

Remaining where he was for a moment to get his own emotional bearings, Noah pushed back into the operating room. The cleanup had progressed. The two nurses had been joined by two orderlies. The MH cart and the cardiac-arrest cart were gone. He was mildly surprised that the dead boy was still on the operating table. He'd been covered by a fresh white sheet. Vaguely he wondered what the holdup was.

Stopping in the middle of the room, Noah winced at the thought of facing the parents of this child. He was thankful the job wasn't his. Noah had had his share of deaths over the five years he'd been a resident. Most of them had been expected, but there had been two that were disturbing surprises that had made him more humble about his skills and the unpredictability of medical science. He remembered how it had affected him and how hard it had been to face the involved families. The remembrance made him even more sympathetic toward Ava, especially as his had been separated by more than a year. All three of Ava's had been within a month.

Noah was about to leave the operating room when the circulating nurse approached him. He knew her reasonably well. Her name was Dorothy Barton. Noah thought of her as competent and knowledgeable but also moody and opinionated, such that he generally made it a point to avoid her. He was surprised when he saw her making a beeline in his direction. He wished he hadn't dallied.

"Dr. Rothauser," Dorothy said. She glanced over her shoulder as if concerned someone might be listening. "Can I have a word with you?"

"Of course," Noah said. "How can I help?'

"Do you mind if we go into the supply room?"

"I guess not," Noah said. It was an unexpected request. He followed her back into the room he'd just left. He wondered if she had seen him and Ava in an embrace, and if so, he tried to think up an explanation. But he needn't have worried. She wanted to speak to him about Ava, but not in a way he could have anticipated.

"I noticed something that I think you should know," she said. She was a heavyset woman shaped like a box, with broad features and thick lips. Her face mask was untied from behind her head and draped over her ample chest. "I've had the misfortune of being involved in two malignant hyperthermia cases. The first was at another hospital. So I know something about the condition and what should be done when it occurs. Dr. London did not turn off the isoflurane when the problem started."

"Oh," Noah commented. "Did she leave it on long?"

"No, not long, but it wasn't until I'd come back to her after following her orders to send out the alarm, which I did by using the phone."

"I see," Noah said, but his attention was diverted by an insistent knocking on the wire-meshed glass pane in the door to the OR corridor. Turning his head, Noah caught a glimpse of the last person he wanted to see, Dr. Mason. When the visibly livid surgeon saw Noah look in his direction, he angrily gestured multiple times for Noah to come out into the OR corridor on the double.

"Sorry, but I have to go," Noah said hastily to Dorothy. "Thanks for the info and for being so attentive. I'll certainly take it into consideration. But right now I've got to talk with Dr. Mason."

Bracing for yet another tongue-lashing, Noah abandoned the surprised nurse and stepped out into the OR corridor.

"I hope you are fucking happy," Dr. Mason snarled. "This is the last straw. This poor child's death is one too many, and since you have been protecting this woman whose incompetence is directly responsible, it's now on your shoulders, too."

"This was a case of malignant hyperthermia," Noah said, trying to remain calm in the face of Dr. Mason's fury. He knew that by talking back to Dr. Mason, he was taking a chance of further inflaming the man, but he couldn't help himself. "It was a bolt out of the blue, and it had nothing to do with anyone's supposed incompetence."

"Three deaths in three weeks?" Dr. Mason practically shouted. "If that's not incompetence, I don't know what is."

Noah thought of a good retort for his last comment, but he wisely held his tongue.

"This has gone too far," Dr. Mason snapped. "I'll tell you what I'm going to do. I'm going to have a heart-to-heart conversation with the chief of Anesthesia. I was tempted to do so after the first two disasters, but now I'm going to do it for certain. I want her to be given her walking papers and be gone. And then I'm going to do the same with Dr. Cantor about you. Your days are numbered. Three preventable deaths are totally unacceptable."

Dr. Mason stared at Noah, defying him to defend himself. When it was apparent Noah wasn't going to try, Dr. Mason spun on his heel and stomped away.

Noah watched the man recede and then disappear from the OR suite, presumably heading to the surgical lounge. Noah was momentarily paralyzed. The death of the boy, the worry about Ava, and now these threats from Dr. Mason combined to make him feel drained of emotion. He didn't think Dr. Mason would be any more successful on this occasion in getting Ava or himself fired, but it was anxiety-producing and worrisome because it was making a bad situation that much worse, especially since Dr. Hernandez had specifically ordered him to do something about the poor relationship he had with Dr. Mason.

Noah sighed and shook his head. He had no idea how to deal with Dr. Mason even in the best of circumstances. With the M&M coming up the day after tomorrow, which Dr. Mason threatened to make memorable, combined with this new malignant hyperthermia death, Noah feared things were going to get worse before they got better.

20

As Noah climbed Ava's front steps, he glanced at his watch, realizing that it wasn't the best time for him to be arriving, since she would still be involved with her workout. He'd been held up when one of his post-op patients had spiked a fever.

Noah had not spoken with Ava after she had walked out of the supply room. He'd thought about calling her to ask if he should stop for take-out food as per usual, but he'd decided against it, thinking it best to leave her alone, hoping she had found something to occupy her mind.

After pressing the doorbell, Noah prepared himself for a wait and possibly the need to ring the bell several times. He knew that Ava and her trainer invariably had music blaring in the workout room as they went through their routine. He was surprised when the door buzzed open almost immediately, and even more surprised to confront Ava when he entered.

"Hello," Noah said, giving her a hug. She didn't respond but didn't turn away, either.

"Are you okay?" Noah asked. He stepped back and looked at her. Her face was unnaturally flaccid, almost expressionless.

"I've been better," she said. Her voice was flat and lifeless.

"I thought for sure you'd be working out."

"I canceled the session," Ava said. "I wasn't up to it."

"Are you depressed?" Noah asked.

"Obviously."

"What can we do to cheer you up? Are you hungry? I can bring us back some take-out or we could go out like normal people. What do you say?"

"I'm not hungry. But you can go and get yourself something."

"I can wait. Let's talk. Should we go up to the study?"

"Whatever."

Once they were in their customary chairs, Noah tried to think of what to say. He knew he wasn't particularly good at psychiatry or talk therapy of any sort. As a surgeon who was accustomed to facing problems head-on with action, he'd never given the field much thought or credence. Yet he felt he knew a bit about depression, having recently dealt with a mild case himself after Leslie Brooks walked out of his life. More important, he had also managed to deal successfully with the issue when his mother had been diagnosed with early Alzheimer's and he had to drop out of medical school. "Let me ask you this," he began. "Have you ever had any problem with depression?"

"Yes," Ava said. "In middle school, mostly around the time I told you I got cyberbullied. Depression, eating problems . . . I had the usual complement of symptoms associated with poor self-esteem."

Noah inwardly recoiled, sensing he was already out of his comfort zone, the way he imagined a psychiatrist might feel if he were suddenly forced to do an appendectomy. "Other than the online harassment, was there ever any specific event that made you depressed?"

Ava didn't answer right away but rather stared at Noah while nodding almost imperceptibly, as if she were struggling with Noah's question and debating how or whether to respond. Noah resisted a strong impulse to say something to ease the moment, but he was glad he didn't.

"There was an event that really bowled me over and made me seriously depressed," Ava said finally. "It was when my oil-executive controlling bastard of a father committed suicide by blowing his brains out. I was just sixteen, a junior in high school."

Almost as if he had been slapped in the face or sloshed with ice water, Noah felt himself start, shocked at being reminded of his metaphor that getting to know Ava was like peeling an onion. Here was yet another peel, another layer, and another surprise. He cleared his throat, frantically thinking of how he should respond. "I thought you said he died of a heart attack?"

"That's what I have told anyone who has asked," Ava said. "Maybe I've even told myself at times, but the reality is that he shot himself, and I got really depressed and almost lost it. The whole mess embarrasses the hell out of me, and I don't like to talk about it."

"My goodness," Noah said, to say something.

"The other time I got truly depressed was when I was twenty," Ava said. Her flat facial expression began to morph into anger. "I was recently married, and my new husband just walked out. Men didn't treat me very well when I was young and vulnerable."

"To say the least," Noah said, thinking about her dentist boss taking advantage of her.

"And you wonder why I stick to a virtual life on social media?" Ava said with a wry smile. "It is infinitely safer to be the one controlling the mouse."

"I guess I understand better now," Noah said. "Were you married for long?"

Ava laughed derisively. "Just long enough for my husband to get a green card. He was in the country on a student visa but wanted to stay. I was merely a means to an end."

"Did you meet him at Brazos University?"

"I did, days after I got there with Dr. Winston. He was a surgical resident like you, but from Serbia."

"I'm sorry," Noah said. Her former husband being a surgical resident made him feel weirdly complicit.

"It feels like it happened in another life," Ava said. "How about you? Have you ever had some major life-changing episode make you depressed?"

Happy to get Ava out of her shell and talking, Noah was willing to be equally open. Like she, he didn't like to talk about such things, and he said as much, but then went on to describe how depressed he felt when his mother started showing signs of dementia and he had to take a leave of absence from medical school. And more recently he mentioned how disconsolate he'd felt following Leslie Brooks's unexpected departure.

"Did Leslie leave totally out of the blue like my bastard of a husband?" Ava asked irritably.

"No," Noah admitted. "For quite a while she had been upfront about my work hours and never having any time for her, and it was getting worse, not better."

"Still, it is a blow to self-esteem."

"Tell me about it," Noah said with a self-mocking laugh.

"Self-esteem is critical," Ava said. "I've been thinking about it all afternoon. I realize it's why I can't leave clinical anesthesia even after these three unfortunate episodes. For me, being a practicing anesthesiologist is too much of my self-image."

"I'm glad to hear you say that," Noah said. He repeated what he'd said before about how good an anesthesiologist she was and what a tragedy it would be for her to throw away all the training she had been through.

"Thank you for saying that," Ava said. "Your support has certainly influenced my thinking. But on all three cases, I truly believe I did all the right things . . . Well, maybe I should have waited for Dr. Mason to get into the room before starting the anesthesia on the Vincent case . . . but even so, I think I did everything as well as anybody in the department, even Dr. Kumar."

"I'm sure you did," Noah said.

"The problem is there's still a chance I could become a departmental scapegoat with Dr. Mason on my case. Is that still your impression?"

Noah thought quickly how he should respond after having just spoken with Dr. Mason. Since Ava seemed to have pulled herself out of her most current nosedive, he didn't want to give her reason to regress, yet she needed to know the truth. "He's still upset with both of us," Noah said. "Not only did he warn me Friday about not protecting you at the M&M, he sought me out this afternoon after the malignant-hyperthermia episode. He said he is going to speak with Dr. Kumar."

"As if he hasn't already," Ava said. "The bastard. I tell you, one of the reasons I'm concerned about being dumped is that I didn't train at one of the overrated Ivy League institutions like most everybody else."

"That doesn't matter," Noah said. "In many ways it is a myth about Ivy League institutions being better than other places. You and Brazos University are a prime example. Tell me about your residency training! How many cases did you do in total?"

"I don't like to feel I have to justify my training," Ava said indignantly. "Nor justify myself. It irritates me to death, as if I'm struggling to stay in a discriminatory, old-boys' club. I'd rather talk about my grades on my Anesthesia boards, which were better than most of my BMH colleagues, and my daily progress with anesthesia MOC. I put in more effort to stay current than anyone else in the entire department. Trust me! On Anesthesia rounds I'm always the one who brings up new developments, not the Ivy League graduates with their supposedly gilded diplomas."

"Okay, okay. I understand completely," Noah said, raising his hands as if he thought he needed to defend himself. Ava always seemed to surprise him. Only on Friday she had voiced the wish that she had had an Ivy League background, and now she was decrying it. "Some people do feel their training makes them superior. All of which means we must protect you from this narcissistic, spiteful blowhard, Dr. Mason. In specific terms, it means being prepared for this next M&M."

"Are you prepared?" Ava asked.

"I think so," Noah said. "As we talked about Friday night, I'll present it last after four other cases. Dr. Hernandez suspected I had presented the Vincent case last to limit discussion. Still, I think it is important to take the risk. With the IT Department talking about how two separate electronic records were created and Dr. Jackson being reasonable about his role in the outcome, I think we should be okay. Those two issues should use up the discussion time. Of course, a lot depends on Dr. Mason and what he says. Whatever it is, I'm going to have to make an effort to sound neutral. I hope you understand that."

"Do you think today's MH case will even be mentioned?"

"Not by me," Noah said. "If it does come up by Dr. Mason, I'll say that I haven't investigated it yet, and it will be presented at the next M&M."

"In a way it is too bad," Ava said. "I couldn't have handled a case of MH any better than I did, despite the terrible outcome."

"That reminds me," Noah said. "Are you friendly with the circulating nurse on the case, Dorothy Barton?"

"Nobody's friendly with Dorothy Barton," Ava said. "She's an odd duck. She even asked me one day if I was gaining weight. Now, that is one hell of a catty thing for a woman to say to another, especially someone who obviously struggles with her own weight."

"Well, she's not a fan," Noah said. "After the MH case she took me aside to tell me that you didn't turn off the isoflurane immediately, which I guess is crucial."

"What?" Ava practically shouted. Her legs dropped off her ottoman, and she slid forward in her chair. "What the hell is she talking about? Absolutely I turned off the isoflurane instantly, the absolute second I noticed a sudden jump in the end-tidal carbon dioxide. And of course it is crucial. It was probably the isoflurane that triggered the whole problem in the first place."

"I figured as much," Noah said. "But I've never seen a case."

"You don't have to have seen a case to know that," Ava snapped. She gave Noah a ten-minute monologue about the rare condition, demonstrating an extraordinarily in-depth knowledge of MH and how to treat it. Noah was both taken aback and impressed, especially as someone who prided himself as a source of medical minutiae helpful for making points on teaching rounds. She was even able to quote the latest statistics and cited the last lengthy review article about the condition in *The New England Journal of Medicine*.

"Wow!" Noah said when Ava finally fell silent. "I'm amazed at your knowledge about MH, as rare as it is."

"I know anesthesia," Ava said, as she slid back in her chair and raised her feet onto the ottoman.

"But to have that much information at your fingertips is truly unique. Did you handle a number of cases during your training?"

"No, I've never seen an actual case until today," Ava admitted. "But I was well schooled in how to handle it because of the simulation center that we had at Brazos University Medical Center. It's called the Weston-Sim Center, as it was named after a West Texas oil baron who donated it. It's truly state-of-the-art. In comparison, it makes the simulation center here at BMH seem as antiquated as a pinball arcade."

Noah had to laugh. He knew the simulation center at BMH wasn't up to par, as the hospital hadn't designated adequate space or computer time. It was a problem he was working on.

"The anesthesia mannequin had a malignant hyperthermia program, which I took advantage of many times when I was a resident."

"I guess it paid off," Noah said. "And I guess Dorothy Barton is envious of your ripped figure."

Ava laughed with real humor, which made Noah feel like he had accomplished what he had hoped—namely, to pull her out of her depressive thoughts.

"That must be the explanation," Ava said.

"Any chance your appetite has improved?" Noah asked.

"It has," Ava said. "And you?"

"I could eat something," Noah said.

"Let's not do the take-out thing," Ava said. "I don't have a lot of food in the house, but there are eggs, bacon, and toast. How does that sound?"

"Perfect," Noah said, and he meant it.

21

"Okay," Noah said. "Let's move on to the last case. This is a thirty-two-year-old woman who had been hit by a car on the corner of State Street and Congress Street and suffered a compound fracture of her right tibia and fibula. If everyone can turn to the final page of the handout, I will begin."

Noah was back in the Fagan Amphitheater facing another packed M&M Conference. It wasn't as crowded with standees as the previous conference, but most of the seats were taken. As was the case two weeks ago, the first two rows front and center had all the big guns of the department, including Dr. Hernandez, Dr. Mason, and Dr. Cantor. As far as Noah was concerned, they were the big three.

The previous day in the middle of the afternoon, Noah had been ordered again to Dr. Hernandez's office, which had made his heart race, as such an ordeal always did. After the run-in with Dr. Mason the afternoon before, it wasn't hard to guess the reason for the call. When Noah arrived, he was moderately surprised to find Dr. Cantor there as well. Although he had expected the worst, the meeting turned out not to be as bad as it could have been. Dr. Hernandez had done most of the talking, with Dr. Cantor merely nodding at key points. The message had been simple and to the point. Dr. Mason wanted Noah gone.

"I can tell you straight out," Dr. Hernandez had said with Noah literally standing on the carpet in front of the man's desk, "I don't totally understand Dr. Mason's reasons for his beliefs, but he is convinced that Dr. London is incompetent and you are complicit in protecting her and therefore bear some responsibility for three deaths. Be that as it may, I made a point to talk privately with Dr. Kumar, mentioned Dr. Mason's feelings, and asked him straight out if Dr. London was up to snuff, and he has assured me that he personally had vetted her and is completely confident of her performance.

"Which brings us to your circumstance . . ."

Expecting the worst, Noah remembered having cringed at that point, but it wasn't necessary. Dr. Hernandez had gone on to say that because of Noah's meritorious record as a resident, he and Dr. Cantor could currently prevail over Dr. Mason's wishes, meaning Noah would not be dismissed. Yet he warned Noah to be extremely careful and not rock the boat, particularly in regard to Dr. Mason. He went on to add that the surgeon wasn't the easiest person to deal with, yet because of his skill and reputation he was a force to be reckoned with.

"Dr. Cantor and I want to be certain," Dr. Hernandez had concluded, "that you will not treat Dr. London's role in the upcoming M&M tomorrow with anything but factual truth and candor."

"Absolutely," Noah had said without hesitation. There was no way he was prepared to lie. As he left Dr. Hernandez's office he'd been thankful that he hadn't been asked if he was having an affair with Ava. If he had been asked, he had been prepared to be honest, although he had no idea what he would have done or said if he were ordered to break it off.

"Does anyone have any questions so far?" Noah asked after a pause a few minutes into his presentation. He looked up from his notes and let his eyes roam around the audience. Briefly he made eye contact with Ava. So far he had just given Helen Gibson's complete medical history, which included four normal pregnancies and a serious bike accident resulting in a cervical neck fracture. As he had done when presenting the Vincent case, he was trying to use up time even though there was only a smidgeon more than fifteen minutes left before the conference would have to end.

When there were no questions, Noah went on to present the rest of the case, beginning with Helen Gibson's arrival in the ER up to her untimely death. He recounted everything that had happened without embellishment just as he had promised Dr. Hernandez, including the two salient facts: that the attending surgeon had pressured the first-year anesthesia resident to begin anesthesia before her supervisor was in the room and that two separate EMRs, with slightly different names and slightly different information, had been inadvertently produced so that the anesthesia resident was unaware of the patient's cervical problems. He pointed out that according to an international rating system, the patient represented the worst-case scenario in regard to placing an endotracheal tube because of her prior history of neck trauma and moderate obesity.

Just as Noah was about to turn over the discussion to the IT representative who was going to talk about exactly how the two separate EMR records had been created, Mason loudly demanded to be recognized. Reluctantly, Noah gave him the floor.

"Excuse me, Dr. Rothauser," Dr. Mason said in his booming voice. "You have put off this particularly tragic case to last to limit discussion time. I know this, and I am certain other members of the faculty do, too. And we know why." He then went on to do his best to fault Ava's performance, throwing the usual accepted academic decorum to the wind by personally disparaging and discrediting her and openly accusing Noah of protecting her and possibly carrying on a secret liaison.

A muted collective gasp emanated from the otherwise passive audience. Everyone was stunned, no one more so than Noah. He was expecting trouble from Dr. Mason, but this was ridiculous. When Mason continued on with his ad hominem outburst, a number of people hissed, as most everyone in the audience knew Ava on some level, liked her, and thought of her as totally competent. Up until these last two M&Ms, her name had never come up in a single adverse-outcome case.

When Dr. Mason finally fell silent, Noah struggled with what he should say. Luckily, Dr. Kumar stood up and worked his way to the aisle before descending into the pit. He was a tall, handsome man with a heavy mustache who had grown up in the Punjab region of India. Noah was more than glad to step aside and allow the chief of Anesthesia to take over the lectern.

In sharp contrast to Dr. Mason's muckraking style, Dr. Kumar lavished praise on Ava, citing her incredible performance on the anesthesia boards as evidence of her terrific training. He also mentioned that he had personally observed her providing anesthesia on numerous occasions when she first joined the staff and found her performance to be exemplary. He said it was his professional opinion that the way she handled the current case and the Vincent case were similarly commendable. Then, to everyone's surprise, he lavished equivalent praise on Dr. Mason, calling him a brilliant surgeon and a tribute to the hospital, and he offered to meet with him to discuss his concerns about Dr. London or about anyone on the anesthesia team.

At this point, most of the people in the audience clapped.

"The woman was involved in yet another death just two days ago," Mason blurted out. "That's three deaths in so many weeks. I find that unacceptable."

There was more hissing.

"I have already reviewed the case from Monday," Dr. Kumar said calmly. "It was a fulminant malignant hyperthermia episode. Again, it is my belief that Dr. London and the entire MH protocol worked admirably."

Dr. Kumar then went on to give an extended explanation of how the Anesthesia Department handled supervising residents and nurse anesthetists. He did this to explain why Ava was not in the room at the time when Helen Gibson's anesthesia was initiated, because she was in another room supervising another resident. Staff anesthesiologists were expected to supervise up to two residents and four anesthetists simultaneously.

While Noah listened to Dr. Kumar's staffing explanations, he thought back to when he'd first burst into the operating room when Helen Gibson was already in extremis. The fleeting impression of Ava fumbling with the advanced video laryngoscope nagged at him. Should he have perhaps mentioned this impression to someone like Dr. Kumar, or was the fumbling due to the patient's head bouncing around from the external cardiac massage? And what about why she hadn't ordered an emergency tracheostomy or used a large-bore needle with jet ventilation?

"Thank you for allowing me to speak," Dr. Kumar said to Noah, stepping away from the lectern and interrupting Noah's thoughts.

"You are entirely welcome, sir," Noah said hurriedly. He returned to the lectern and looked up at the restive audience who'd erupted into many individual whispered but animated discussions.

"I'd like to say something," a voice called out.

Noah looked in the direction of the request. It was Dr. Jackson. Noah pointed to him, giving him the floor.

"I know it is generally not the involved surgeon's role to speak at an M&M unless asked a specific question, but I feel I should do so in this case. I never did get to operate on the deceased, even though I am the surgeon of record. What I'd like to say is that I made a mistake by actively urging the anesthesia resident to start the anesthesia before her staff supervisor was present. In my defense, the case involved a compound fracture. In such circumstances the chances of infection increase the longer the surgery is delayed. Nonetheless, I shouldn't have forced the issue."

There was a smattering of muted applause as people appreciated Dr. Jackson's mea culpa, since it was as unexpected as Dr. Mason's inappropriate comments. For a second, Noah locked eyes with Ava. She was one of the people who was quietly clapping. Noah wondered if it was for Dr. Jackson or for Dr. Kumar. Both had helped exonerate her.

After a quick glance at his watch and seeing it was already after 9:00 A.M., Noah concluded the M&M. The audience stood up immediately. Most everyone had to get to surgery, as they were already late for their scheduled 9:00 A.M. cases.

Stepping away from the lectern, Noah turned to the representative from the IT Department. She had been sitting in the lone chair in the amphitheater's pit for the entire conference, waiting to speak her piece about the Helen Gibson case.

"I'm terribly sorry," Noah said. "I didn't expect we would run out of time."

"No problem," the woman said graciously. "I actually enjoyed listening. I've never been to an M&M Conference. As a layperson, I'm glad to hear these tragedies are not ignored."

"We try our best to learn from each one," Noah said. "Thank you for coming and for your time. I'm sorry we didn't get to hear your presentation."

Noah turned to look up, in hopes of catching Ava's eye. He was certain she had to be pleased. Instead, he found himself facing an angry and empurpled Dr. Mason, who was beside himself with barely contained rage. He was heedless of all the other bigwigs, who had already descended into the pit and were standing around, socializing in small groups.

"You think you are so goddamn smart," Dr. Mason jeered, poking his face within inches of Noah's. "Maybe you've gotten your prissy girlfriend off the hook because she is in a different department, but let me assure you, I'm sure as hell not finished with you. Not by a long shot. If I have anything to say about it, you are out of here!"

Sensing it was best to remain silent, Noah just blankly stared back. Dr. Mason glowered at him with narrowed eyes. Then, with even more ostentatious drama than after the prior M&M, he stormed out of the room.

By reflex, Noah hazarded a glance in the direction of the nearest group of surgical attendings and caught them rolling their eyes for his benefit. It was apparent they had overheard Dr. Mason and were being supportive. It gave Noah a modicum of confidence that staff members were cognizant of Dr. Mason's personality shortcomings, but Noah was still nervous. As Dr. Hernandez had said the day before, Dr. Mason was a force to be reckoned with. Unfortunately, Noah had no idea how to help his case, as he was caught in the web of Dr. Mason's narcissistic ego.

22

It had been a busy day for Noah. After the M&M Conference, he'd headed over to the Stanhope and up to the OR along with a good portion of the rest of the attendees. En route he'd had several people compliment him on the program, and even a few had remarked how surprised they were about Dr. Mason's outburst, which was reassuring.

Despite Dr. Mason's comment to him after the conference was over, Noah felt very good about how things had gone in general, and he imagined Ava did, too. For Dr. Kumar to have supported her the way he had was certainly a tribute to her standing in the department, and it had to have buoyed her lagging self-confidence about her clinical abilities. And Dr. Jackson had certainly come through in a commendable fashion.

After making certain all was copasetic with the day's surgical-resident assist schedule, Noah had started his own four operative cases. As his assistant for the day, he had chosen third-year Dr. Dorothy Klim. She was a terrific resident with whom Noah enjoyed working. This was the first time they'd operated together since Noah had assumed his super chief role. They made a good team, as she could anticipate Noah's technical needs as any good assistant does, so the cases proceeded apace. Such efficiency always made the nurses happy, so it ended up being a pleasant day for all involved, including the patients.

In between each case, Noah dictated the procedure as he always did. Some surgeons put off the dictation until their last case was over, but Noah liked to do it right away to be certain he didn't forget any details. During each round trip to and from the surgical lounge where the dictating booths were located, Noah kept an eye out for Ava on the rare possibility they could interact on some superficial level, but it wasn't to be.

Leaving his final scheduled case for the day, an open cholecystectomy, or gallbladder removal, Noah again looked for Ava. Seeing that it was past 3:00 when her shift ended, he checked the PACU, where he had run into her the day they had their first real conversation. But she wasn't there. Checking the scheduling board, he saw that her last case had finished almost an hour earlier, meaning she'd most likely left the hospital on time.

Disappointed not to have even made eye contact during the day, Noah looked forward to seeing her that evening at her house. Although he'd been staying with her almost every night since she'd gotten back from Washington, he hadn't the previous night, due to emergency surgery that had kept him in the hospital. As he sat down in one of the dictating booths, he found himself fantasizing about the upcoming evening. There was a wine shop on Charles Street appropriately called Beacon Hill Wine, and he planned on stopping in and getting a bottle of champagne to celebrate the outcome of the M&M. At least she was out of the woods, even if he wasn't.

Just before Noah began his dictation, he made up his mind to call Ava a bit later to find out her thoughts about take-out that night. He even entertained the possibility of their going out to an actual restaurant, either that night or over the coming weekend. He had no idea how she might respond, but it seemed like a fun idea. And why not? Wasn't the cat out of the bag? With what Dr. Mason had publicly said at the M&M, it probably wasn't possible to maintain the secrecy of their affair even if they continued overtly to ignore each other in the hospital.

When Noah was finished with the dictation, he went back into the PACU to make sure everything was fine with the cholecystectomy patient. When he had left the OR, the operation hadn't been totally over. The six-inch incision in the right upper abdomen was still open. This was standard protocol in a teaching hospital. With the open gallbladder removal, Noah had brought in a first-year resident to provide traction. When the key part of the operation was done, it was standard protocol for the most senior resident, meaning Noah, to leave so that the next senior resident, Dr. Klim, could teach the first-year resident basic suturing technique.

Noah briefly glanced over the postoperative orders, which the first-year resident had written, again under the auspices of the third-year resident. This was par for the course and hadn't changed in years. Medical education in general hadn't altered much over the last century, despite everything else involving medical science and technology being drastically different.

Noah hurried back to the surgical lounge to change into his whites. He had an enormous amount of work to do above and beyond work rounds and seeing his private patients. Now that the M&M was over, there was a lot of catching up to be done, which he intended to do and still leave the hospital close to 6:00. If it was at all possible, his hope was to get to Ava's before she started her workout so that by the time she was finished showering, he'd have their celebratory feast, including champagne, ready to be enjoyed.

Almost at the exact moment he hurriedly pushed into the men's surgical locker room, Noah felt his phone buzz with a text. Curious who might be texting him on his phone rather than his hospital tablet, which was where he received the vast majority of his messages, Noah pulled out his phone and was happy to see it was a text from Ava. With a mixture of titillation tinged with relief to finally connect with her, he opened it.

Noah stopped in his tracks, his euphoria evaporating. With almost total disbelief, he read over the message multiple times. It was brief: *On a business trip for a few days. Will text when I return.*

Noah sank down on a low bench, still holding the phone in his hands, staring at the screen in dismay, amazed that Ava would be insensitive enough to send such a short, emotionally unexpressive text. Under the circumstances, it seemed almost deliberately cruel. Either that or she lacked empathy, although either explanation seemed equivalently heartless. Immediately, the question rose in his mind about how long she had known about this trip or whether it was something that had happened that afternoon as a response to a lobbying emergency, if there was such a thing. He hoped it was the latter, because if it wasn't, she should have told him she was going the moment she'd heard about it.

As Noah thought more about this totally unexpected development, he realized she must have some days off, as she had worked more than a week straight, including the entire past weekend. At the time, Noah hadn't questioned it, because he worked every day and every weekend as a matter of course. The idea it was rare for her to work more than five days in a row hadn't even entered his mind. But why didn't she bring it up last night that she was scheduled to be off tomorrow?

"It must have been an emergency," Noah said out loud in a vain attempt to buoy his sagging emotions. "Surely she must have been in a rush, and I'll be hearing from her with all the details." But the attempt to make himself feel better didn't work. It would have been so easy for her to express some emotion; even just a few words would have made a complete difference.

He tried to rally his injured self-esteem by coming up with another potential explanation. With all the time she devoted to social media, maybe it didn't even cross her mind that he might be sensitive about not being told in advance. Her constant communicating in a virtual world without all the rich, nonverbal aspects of real-time, face-to-face interaction had probably made her less sensitive to nuances of other peoples' feelings. By her own admission, she spent most of her free time in a world where everything could be handled by a mere click of the mouse, and whatever interaction was in progress was gone without consequence. Considering all the wonderful intimacy they had enjoyed together that week, there was no way she would have wanted to upset him. It had to be more oversight than purposeful.

Feeling a strong need to be proactive rather than just sitting there feeling sorry for himself, Noah leaped to his feet. He quickly changed out of his scrubs and into his normal hospital clothes. He even decided to stop by the laundry and get a freshly cleaned and pressed white jacket to look his best. For Noah, work had always been his fallback. It had been the way he'd handled Leslie's departure.

Fifteen minutes later, Noah was on the surgical floor, rallying the troops by calling for afternoon work rounds to begin earlier than usual. With a burst of energy, he goaded all the residents to the max, demanding particularly thorough and up-to-date presentations on all the patients as they went room to room. He quizzed everyone on the latest journal articles apropos of each case, turning afternoon work rounds into teaching rounds.

When rounds were done, Noah visited each of his own inpatients and had lengthy conversations about their progress and what they should expect over the next few days, discharging three of them. Noah then visited two patients who were scheduled for surgery the next morning. Both had been transferred from hospitals in the western part of the state, where their surgery had been botched and needed to be redone.

With no more work to be done on the surgical floor, Noah retreated down to his desk in the surgical residency program office. Since it was now well after 5:00 P.M., he happily found the place empty. His intent was to read the journal articles for the following day's Journal Club, but instead of calling them up on the monitor as planned, he had a different idea. Although his initial intention was to visit the *Annals of Surgery*, he googled Brazos University instead.

The website was impressive. There were more than two hundred photos of modern buildings of red brick, concrete, and glass. He was surprised to see as much grass as he did, since he thought of West Texas as being desertlike. He could see the flat terrain surrounding the city and the horizon with a sky that seemed larger than life. He had never been to Texas, and there was nothing about the pictures that beckoned him. He wasn't much of a traveler. The farthest south he'd ever been was South Carolina, but that was when he was a teenager.

Next Noah looked at the Brazos University Medical Center website. The hospital appeared even more modern than the rest of the university, suggesting that it was a relatively late addition. Within the website, the WestonSim Center had its own section, advertising itself as one of the world's premier robotic-simulation centers for medical teaching after its opening in 2013. When Noah clicked on it and looked at the exterior photos of the extremely modern glass-sheathed building and read the description of the 30,000-square-foot behemoth, he had to agree. It was a sweet setup, a quantum leap better than what was available at BMH, which had to fight for space in the Wilson Building's basement. Looking at the many photos of the WestonSim Center interior, Noah was even more impressed by the mock-up sets that looked amazingly realistic, including two fully functioning operating rooms, a delivery room, an intensive-care unit with multiple beds, and three ER trauma spaces. Noah could easily imagine Ava in all of them, taking advantage of their potential for teaching anesthesia technique and how to handle such emergencies as malignant hyperthermia.

Next Noah checked if the hospital and the medical school had all the appropriate certifications from the various accreditation organizations. It did, including the ACGME, or Accreditation Council for Graduate Medical Education. That was the key one, meaning the medical school and the residency training program were entirely qualified.

After several hours of frantic activity since leaving the OR but with nothing but busy work left to keep him occupied, Noah glanced at the time. It was now almost seven-thirty in the evening, and still there had been no additional text from Ava. With painful resignation, Noah began to accept that he wasn't going to hear any more from her like he had hoped. It seemed that the curt, original text might be all he was going to get until she returned.

Feeling exceptionally weary, depressed, and confused, Noah stood up from his desk. He hadn't felt this bad since Leslie Brooks had bailed out and left him with a denuded apartment. He struggled with the question of what he should do, whether he should go back to his bleak apartment or stay in the on-call facilities in the hospital. Technically, Noah wasn't on call, but he knew there was plenty of room if he wanted to stay. Since he was in no condition to make a rational decision, he ended up staying in the hospital by default.

23

After spending Wednesday, Thursday, and Friday nights in the on-call facility in the Stanhope Pavilion, Noah finally felt the need to go back to his apartment Saturday afternoon when he finished everything he could think of doing in the hospital. By then he was entirely caught up in all aspects of his wide-ranging responsibilities as the super chief surgical resident. Even the basic science lecture and the Journal Club agendas for the following two weeks were already done, as was the resident on-call schedule for the months of August and September.

In his whirlwind of work energy, Noah had accomplished more than he thought possible but had run out of things to do, and he began to feel as if people were wondering why he was still hanging around. To make matters worse, on Thursday and Friday nights the on-call chief residents had pointedly asked Noah what he was doing in the hospital on-call room facility, which had a lounge area as well as multiple bedrooms. It was clear both residents were concerned that their competence was being questioned by his presence. In both instances, Noah had reassured them they were doing fine and left it at that, but there was a lingering sense they didn't believe him.

Unfortunately, for the entire period, he'd not heard a word from Ava.

He'd hoped he'd get a text or something, but by Friday he acknowledged it wasn't going to happen. On several occasions over the last three days he had pointedly argued with himself whether he should text her or even try to call her, but on each occasion his pride had won out. He felt it was her responsibility to get in touch with him, since she was the one who had left. Under the circumstances, his reaching out would undermine the small amount of social self-esteem he was trying vainly to maintain.

But coming back to his sparse apartment did little to buoy his spirits. To him it looked worse than usual in its emptiness, which magnified his loneliness and reminded him how much he missed Ava. At the same time the situation was forcing him to question if his feelings for her were being reciprocated, as he could not imagine leaving her such a curt message if the situation had been reversed. Yet he urged himself to cut her a little slack, remembering that she was a unique, extraordinarily self-motivated individual who came from a background completely different from his, who had suffered a father's suicide when she was in high school and a failed marriage around age twenty. He knew it was important for him to keep all this in mind because it was how he explained what he termed her "teenagelike" attachment to social media.

Thinking about Ava and her self-centeredness, he wondered if social media was making people narcissistic because of the opportunities for self-promotion or if narcissists were attracted to social media for the same reason. He knew that one of the hallmarks of narcissism was a lack of empathy, which was still how Noah viewed Ava's terse text and her lack of follow-up communication. If Ava's love of social media was making her egocentric, he could hold out hope that she had no idea how much emotional distress she was causing him and might very well be sincerely apologetic when told.

With nothing better to do and thinking that it would at least make him feel closer to Ava, he booted up his old laptop and went to Gail Shafter's homepage. To his chagrin he immediately saw that Gail had posted on Friday, which meant that Ava had enough free time to be on social media yet not enough time or inclination to send him a simple text. The post was about Gail having an "OMG fabulous" opportunity to visit Washington, D.C., complete with a smiling selfie of Ava with a baseball hat covering her blond-streaked hair in front of the Lincoln Memorial and another in front of the new National Museum of African American History. At least he now knew that Ava had indeed gone back to Washington for her lobbying work. After studying the photos, which reminded him of the many in her study, Noah clicked on Gail Shafter's fan page. He was relieved to see that at least Ava hadn't found the time to do one of her beauty tips.

Returning to the homepage, Noah reread the post, which talked about what a treat the city was for tourists, how many fun things there were to do and see, and how it was possible to run into famous politicians, with a list of those Gail had managed to see. He then read some of the comments. It was surprising how many people responded in a single day. There were ninety-two likes and almost three dozen comments. Noah read the comments, which were interesting in their banality and how they all seemed paradoxically to exalt simultaneously individualism and tribal group think. There were even replies to the comments and even a few replies to the replies. There was no doubt in Noah's mind that the dialogue in the virtual space was far different from how it was in the real world.

Suddenly Noah laughed in disbelief. He noticed that one of the particularly favorable comments was from Melanie Howard, meaning Ava had taken the time to comment on her own post. And then Gail Shafter had replied, praising Melanie. Knowing how intelligent Ava was, he was mystified by her behavior.

Progressively fascinated, Noah began looking at the various home pages of the people who had commented on Gail's post, reading some of their posts, looking at the groups they favored, and clicking on their friends. It was like following a geometric progression in an endless, ever-expanding universe. In the process, he came across comments about all sorts of things, including the newsfeeds and even discussions about some of the ads that Facebook had inserted to expand their bottom line.

Since Gail Shafter and Melanie Howard were Ava's fake profiles and not real people, he wondered if Ava had any more fake characters, and if she did, why would it be worth the effort? Following in that line of thinking, Noah began to wonder how many of the profiles he was looking at were also fakes. There was no way to know.

Going back to Gail's homepage, Noah looked at the gender makeup of those people who had commented on Gail's latest post. Surprisingly, he saw that it was approximately even between males and females. He had expected it would be mostly females without questioning why. Then he found himself glancing at the thumbnail photos accompanying the comments and noticed that the age of those who used photos of themselves rather than pets or infant children were roughly in the twenty-to-forty range until his eye stopped on one that he recognized. It was Teresa Puksar, a family name that Noah had never come across except on a previous visit to Gail's Facebook page, and he wondered about its ancestry. Clicking on the photo, he went back to Teresa's homepage. Glancing again at her risqué photos and looking at her friends, he noticed that there were very few around her age. Noah was both perplexed and put off. He questioned if Teresa's parents had any idea what their daughter was doing on social media.

As Noah spent more time in Ava's virtual world, he couldn't help but start questioning who was the real Ava London. Prior to their relationship, did the social-media world he was now visiting truly take the place for her of real-time, normal, face-to-face interactions? That was what she had implied, yet it hardly seemed possible, considering the vast difference between what he and Ava had been sharing over the previous three weeks and what he considered a vacuous substitute. Yet the issue raised a worrisome idea: Maybe Noah was wrong. Maybe they hadn't been sharing what he so wanted to believe. Being "in love" certainly didn't mesh with her flying off with essentially no explanation or the slightest endearment like "I'm sorry I have to go" or "I miss you." And what about there being so little apparent gratitude for the considerable effort he'd made for her regarding both M&M Conferences, particularly after this last one?

All at once Noah's eye rose from his laptop, and he stared blankly out the window. Suddenly, an even more disturbing thought entered his mind. Was this whole relationship with Ava a sham? Could Ava have been merely using him to navigate the rough waters of the M&M Conferences because of her irrational fear of being terminated from her dream position on the BMH anesthesia staff?

"Hell, no!" Noah blurted out with conviction. Almost as soon as the idea had occurred to him, he rejected it as a pathetic reminder of his own social insecurity. He'd never been with a woman more open, giving, and comfortable with her body than Ava. Thinking that such intimacy could be less than sincere reflected more on him than on her.

Yet as Noah went back to staring out the window, he couldn't keep his mind away from those nagging misgivings that continued to trouble him about tiny aspects of Ava's professional behavior in all three anesthesia deaths. In the Vincent case, did she truly do her own careful questioning of the patient regarding whether he'd eaten or whether he had any GI symptoms with his hernia? Did she critically evaluate the kind of anesthesia to use or just blindly follow Dr. Mason's secretary's wishes? During the Gibson case, was she struggling with the advanced video laryngoscope or was the problem that the patient's head was bouncing all over from the cardiac massage? Why did she not do a tracheostomy? And concerning the Harrison case, did she turn off the anesthetic agent immediately or was there a delay, as suggested by the circulating nurse?

As soon as these questions resurfaced, Noah couldn't help but remember Ava's response when he'd mentioned the nurse's comment on the Harrison case. The remembrance made him smile. Ava had been irate and had launched into a detailed monologue of malignant hyperthermia that had put his knowledge and understanding of the condition to shame. She had even said that it had probably been the anesthesia gas that had triggered the condition, so certainly she would have turned it off the second she suspected what was happening. He remembered she'd told him what had alerted her. It had been something so esoteric about carbon dioxide that Noah couldn't even remember.

Just to reassure himself, Noah went back on his laptop and googled *malignant hyperthermia*. A few minutes later he confirmed that she had been right. It probably had been the isoflurane to blame. Since she said that she had learned about the condition by using the WestonSim Center at Brazos University Medical Center, Noah went back to their website. He reread all the material that was available. He was again impressed, especially since Ava had validated the concept that simulation experience was tremendously valuable. He thought he'd bring the issue up at the next Surgical Residency Advisory Board meeting as he was a sitting member. Stimulating the hospital to expand the BMH simulation center would be a valuable contribution of the board.

It was at that moment with the WestonSim Center still on his laptop screen that Noah's mobile phone rang. Trying to rein in his hopes that it would be Ava, he struggled to get it out of his pocket. As soon as he did, his heart sank. It wasn't Ava. It was Leslie Brooks making her bimonthly FaceTime call. When she did it, it was always on a Saturday afternoon. For a moment Noah held the phone in his hand, wondering if he should answer. His disappointment it wasn't Ava was so strong that he worried Leslie might sense it, and it would then be an unkindness to her, who he knew only had his best interests at heart. He wasn't in the mood to hear how great things were for her in New York or how happy she was with her fiancé, who showered her with attention. Thinking it would only make his circumstance that much worse by comparison, he hesitated, but by the fifth ring he relented and answered. He was, after all, desperate for companionship.

He propped his phone up against the laptop. She looked terrific as usual. He could always tell she made sure her hair was in place and her makeup was perfect when she called. After their initial hellos, Leslie was sensitive enough to comment that he didn't look like he had been getting enough sleep. He agreed, saying that he had averaged only four or five hours over the last few nights.

"That's ridiculous," Leslie said. "You are in charge now. You are supposed to be delegating work to others, not doing it all yourself."

"The reason I haven't been getting enough sleep is not because of work," he said, deciding to be forthright. He was in the need for some sympathy, and Leslie was the only person in the world with whom he felt he could be honest as she already knew his weaknesses. "I've met someone and started a rather intense relationship for the last three weeks."

"That's terrific!" Leslie said without hesitation. "Who is she, if you don't mind my asking?"

"She's a colleague," Noah said, being intentionally vague. "She's also a doctor and is as committed to medicine as I am."

"That is a good start," Leslie said. "You guys should get along fine. The only problem might be finding time together outside of the hospital, if she's as busy as you are."

"She's an attending on the faculty," Noah said. "So she has predictable hours. It's my schedule that's still the problem, but she completely understands the demands on me."

"So now I understand why you look sleep-deprived," Leslie said with a laugh. "That's not the Noah I remember from our last few years together."

Noah laughed himself as he understood Leslie's implication. "That's not the reason I'm sleep-deprived. I'm afraid I've been jilted just when I thought everything was going terrifically."

"If you want my opinion, which I'm sensing, maybe you should tell me what's happened with a bit more detail."

Noah described his relationship with Ava as openly as he could. He also explained what sparked his current distress. What he left out for privacy reasons were Ava's name, her medical specialty, her personal history, and where she had gone on her recent trip. Noah did want Leslie's opinion, in hopes that she would tell him that he was reading more into Ava's lack of communication than he should, and that Ava would return and all would be back to normal. Unfortunately, that wasn't what happened.

When Noah finished his brief monologue, Leslie merely stared at him, slowly shaking her head.

"Well?" Noah questioned. "Aren't you going to say something?"

"I'm not sure what I should say," Leslie admitted. "I can guess what you want to hear."

"I can guess what I want to hear, too," Noah said. "But I think I need honesty."

"Okay," Leslie said. She pointed at him as if lecturing. "Now, don't get mad at me when you hear my opinion. Promise?"

"Promise," Noah said, sighing. He sensed what was coming, and he felt like terminating the call.

"I would advise you to be careful with this person," Leslie said. "Suddenly disappearing twice with no real explanation after you and she had been intimate and essentially living together, even if only for weeks, is not normal behavior by a long shot. And having it happen right after you made significant efforts on her behalf makes it even more bizarre. She sounds to me like a manipulative person, and if she is as manipulative as she sounds, she might have a personality disorder. What you have been describing is not normal behavior in the very beginning of a romantic relationship.

"Now," Leslie continued, "I know I might sound as if I'm going out on a limb here when my only qualification is having taken an introductory 101 psychology course in college, but I can't help it. I don't want you to be hurt."

"That's not what I wanted to hear," Noah said. He looked away. For a second he did not want to see Leslie's knowing expression. He also knew Leslie was coming to her conclusions without being aware of any of the significant details of Ava's life, which he didn't feel comfortable revealing.

"I'm just trying to be honest with the facts you've given me," Leslie said. "I hope I am wrong. But you didn't tell me what she was doing on these two occasions she disappeared. Do you know?"

"Generally, I know," Noah said. "She moonlights as a lobbyist for the nutritional-supplement industry."

"Now, that is truly ironic," Leslie said. Having lived with Noah and knowing full well his low opinion of what he called the thirty-four-billion-dollar-a-year snake-oil industry, the idea that he was dating someone who worked for them was farcical. "Where did she go?" she asked.

"On both trips she went to Washington, D.C.," Noah said. He was thinking he wanted to get off the phone. His talk with Leslie wasn't helping but rather making him more depressed, as she was lending credence to his own fears.

"From all that you have told me, it seems oxymoronic for a doctor to be working for the nutritional-supplement industry," Leslie said. "At the same time, they must love her. Her credentials give them credibility they don't deserve."

"You got that right," Noah said. "I think they keep pretty close tabs on her. Almost every night she gets at least one call, and apparently they pay her a king's ransom. She could never afford the house she occupies on her faculty salary, nor the pleasure travel she does. But they get what they pay for. She is extremely intelligent, attractive, personable, has a good sense of humor, and has an undergraduate degree in nutrition, an M.D., and is on the BMH faculty. My sense is that she, and maybe she alone, keeps the politicians from altering the 1994 law that freed the industry from any sensible control by the FDA. She said as much."

"Sounds like they hit a gold mine with her," Leslie admitted. "I wish I could say the same for you. For self-preservation, I think you should take things slowly and very carefully and not let your needs and emotion overshadow your judgment. That's my advice."

"Thank you for your insight, Mother," Noah said with obvious sarcasm, although he knew that she was most likely right. He hadn't realized how much he needed love in his life before the chance meeting with Ava.

"You asked me to be honest," Leslie said.

After he had terminated the FaceTime session, Noah tossed his cell across the room onto the threadbare couch as a controlled gesture of displeasure. The conversation wasn't what he had hoped, and it stimulated him to remember other things about Ava that seemed mildly inconsistent, such as her keen social skills and ability to read people that contrasted with her mildly antisocial behavior in the hospital. It also seemed to clash with her professed preference for social media over face-to-face interactions. As their relationship grew, Noah had become progressively aware that she was not friendly with anyone in the hospital except him. At first he took this as a compliment and thought of it as another way they were similar. But as time had passed, he began to realize there was a difference. Noah was superficially friendly with everyone, whereas she kept everyone at arm's length. And such thinking reminded him of something else he'd noticed reading her entries in the EMRs of Vincent, Gibson, and Harrison. Her syntax was somehow vaguely unique, which he had ended up attributing to her having trained in West Texas and not in one of the more mainstream academic medical centers.

Noah stood up and retrieved his phone. He almost wished the hospital would call him to give him an excuse to go back. Here it was almost seven o'clock on a Saturday night, and he had nothing to do. It was pathetic. He was even caught up on all his medical journal reading for the first time in his life. Finally, out of desperation he decided he'd go down to the popular bar at Toscano's that he'd seen on all those evenings when he'd picked up take-out food. Maybe he'd feel hungry enough to eat something. Maybe he could even find someone who might be willing to talk with him.

24

Despite being caught up with all his work, Noah managed to spend the entire Sunday in the hospital. There had been some interesting emergency surgery involving a group of bicyclists who had been run into by an aged driver who claimed he hadn't seen them. He'd also reviewed all the surgical inpatients in the hospital by reading every EMR in their totality, which was something he had never done. He was amazed and disturbed at the number of minor problems he uncovered, which resulted in a flurry of emails to the involved residents demanding they be more attentive to details.

As Noah finished up Monday's resident-assist surgical schedule, his phone buzzed in his pocket. Getting the phone out, he was taken aback to see it was a text from Ava. The text was equally terse as the one that he had gotten on Wednesday. All it said was: *Arrived home. Exhausted but come over if you can.*

For a few minutes Noah just stared at the nine words. He didn't know what to think. There were certainly no endearments, but there was an invitation. The question was should he go, and if he did, when? Ultimately, he decided he would go but would keep Leslie's cautionary words and his own misgivings in mind. Wishing to sound nonchalant and

270

maintain some self-respect, he typed: *Will be finishing up shortly. Will stop by.* After reading it several times and deciding it was as emotionally noncommittal as her message, he sent it.

Almost immediately the thumbs-up emoji flashed onto his screen.

Noah didn't break any records getting to Ava's house. He'd finished up with the surgical schedule and then rounded on his four private patients, including one scheduled to have surgery the following morning. By the time he climbed the steps in front of Ava's house and rang her bell, it was almost 6:15.

The door buzzed open, and Noah entered the inner foyer. Ava was nowhere to be seen, but several minutes later she appeared at the top of the main stairs. She came down quickly. "Hey!" she called out, bubbly. She was in her black yoga pants and tank top. Without a second's hesitation, she gave him a double-cheek kiss as if everything was entirely normal and nothing had happened. "Sorry! I was on the computer."

"No need to apologize."

"I'm glad you made it before I got on the exercise bike. Do you want to work out with me? My trainer isn't here."

"I think I'll pass," Noah said. He had exercise clothes there at her house, but he was in no mood to exercise.

"Do you want to come down to the exercise room with me or wait up in the study?"

"I'll come down," Noah said. "If you don't mind."

"Mind?" Ava questioned. She looked at him askance. "Why would I mind?"

"I don't know," Noah said, being truthful. He didn't know why he had said it. Ava already had him off guard. He hadn't known what to expect from her, but certainly he didn't expect her to act so normal.

Still looking at him sideways, she asked: "Are you okay? You're acting a little . . . strangely."

"I'm feeling a little strange," Noah said.

"Why? What's happened?"

Noah let out a sigh. "Ava, you disappeared without a word for three or four days. I think it is entirely reasonable for me to act a bit strangely."

"That's not true!" Ava said with emphasis. "What on earth are you talking about? I texted you I was going."

"You texted me, but it wasn't much of a text," Noah said.

"I was in a hurry. I got a call from Washington that they needed me immediately. As soon as I got it, I texted you to let you know I had to leave."

"But you never followed up," Noah said.

"Yeah, well, you never texted me back," Ava said defensively. "I thought I'd get something like 'fly safely' or 'good luck with your meetings.' But I got nothing. It crossed my mind that maybe you needed a little break. To tell you the truth, as hot and heavy as we'd become, I thought I was doing you a favor leaving you alone to get some work done. I'd been selfishly monopolizing all your free time."

Noah stared at Ava with disbelief. Had he manufactured all this emotional turmoil he'd been suffering? Was he that socially inept or was it the ease of current messaging technology that was at fault? Was it that instant connection raised expectations with more chance of misunderstanding? He tried to remember why he hadn't responded to her first text but could only recall it had something to do with childish, hurt pride.

"You knew that I had to go to Washington sometime soon," Ava continued with irritation. "It was just a week ago that I got the call about the damning article coming out in *The Annals of Internal Medicine*. You remember: the hugely unflattering one about a new nutritional supplement study. Don't tell me you forgot!"

"I remember," Noah admitted.

"So you knew I had to go to Washington in the near future, and I texted you I had to leave on a business trip. You don't need to be a rocket scientist to put two and two together."

"Well, maybe I overreacted," Noah said.

"Why didn't you text me or call me to tell me you were upset?" Ava demanded.

"I suppose I should have," Noah said.

"Of course you should have, you ass," Ava said.

"I missed you," Noah said.

A smile appeared on Ava's face. "That's the first nice thing you've said to me."

"It is true," Noah said. "I missed you."

Ava put her arms around Noah's neck and drew herself in close to him. "I'll tell you what I think. I think you work way too hard. You have to give yourself a break. And I think you are stressed out and should work out with me. It will do you a world of good."

"Maybe you're right," Noah said.

A half-hour later they were on tandem exercise bikes, riding through a program projected on a large screen that was supposed to match a portion of one of the stages of the Tour de France. Ava was riding with considerably more resistance than Noah, but that was a given. Both knew she was in far better shape.

"What's the story with Dr. Mason since I've been gone?" Ava said between breaths.

"I only spoke with him once," Noah managed. Hoping that Ava couldn't see, he reduced the resistance of his bike by several digits. "It was right after the M&M. He came down into the pit and was fit to be tied."

"Not at all surprising," Ava said. "By the way, you handled the M&M superbly, just like you did the previous one. Thank you."

"You're welcome," Noah said. He was pleased to hear her gratitude but wished she had texted it while she was away. "But the real credit on your behalf was Dr. Kumar. He couldn't have been more supportive than he was."

"I was humbled," Ava said.

"It was sincere and deserved," Noah said.

"When Dr. Mason came down into the pit after the conference, did he say anything about me specifically?"

"He did," Noah said. "He more or less admitted that he couldn't do anything about you since you were in a different department."

"Really?" Ava questioned with obvious appreciation. "That's terrific! What a load off my mind to get him off my case. We'll have to celebrate."

"I wish I could say the same," Noah said. "If anything, I'm afraid he's even more motivated to get me fired. Obviously, he at least partially blames me for getting you off the hook."

"Oh, come on!" Ava said. "There's no way he could get you fired. Everyone knows what a narcissistic blowhard he is, particularly after his performance at the last M&M. Everyone thinks you're the best resident the BMH surgical department has ever seen. I've heard the rumor myself."

"Rumors are rumors," Noah said. "That's all well and good, but reality can be much different. Dr. Mason is a powerful fixture of the Department of Surgery. Even Dr. Hernandez felt obligated to remind me of that inconvenient fact and advised me to get along with him, as if that was something easy to do. I'm going to be on thin ice until Dr. Mason finds another target. Right now, I'm the man."

Without any warning, Noah stopped riding his tandem and let his feet plop loudly to the floor. He was sweating profusely and his thigh muscles burned.

"What's the matter?" Ava asked. In sharp contrast, she didn't even alter her rapid pedaling cadence.

"I'm done," Noah said. "I'm the first to confess I'm not in shape. That's a future goal, maybe next year. Right now, I'm bushed. But this little mini-workout has been good. Thanks for suggesting it. I'm a lot calmer than when I first arrived. I'll shower and go get us some food so when you get out of your shower we can eat."

"Okay," Ava said agreeably. "But remember, I've got to do some floor exercises after I finish with the bike."

"No problem," Noah said. He walked on wobbly legs into the nearby shower.

25

After they finished eating, Noah and Ava cleaned up, keeping the conversation light. Mostly they had talked about Ava's opportunities to do touristy things in Washington. For her it had been unique because on her other visits to the District, she'd always been too busy. Noah had admitted that he'd seen her posts on her Gail Shafter Facebook page and had read all the comments out of desperation to hear about what she was doing. "You should have texted me," Ava had said. "I would have told you directly." Sensibly enough, Noah had not responded to that comment.

When Ava was finished rinsing the dishes they had used, she leaned back against the sink, drying her hands. "For me the sudden trip to Washington turned out to be a godsend," she said. "This last MH death almost put me over the top. Getting away was what I needed. The fact that the patient was a twelve-year-old boy made it so much harder for me to accept. Not that the others were easy, mind you."

"I can understand," Noah said, as he put the plastic containers into the recycling bin. "I've always found pediatrics harder to deal with than other specialties. Life can be unfair, everyone knows that, but it seems particularly unfair when the patients are kids."

"I was again seriously considering giving up clinical anesthesia," Ava said wistfully.

"You mentioned that."

"While I was away I decided I'm going to use these three deaths to motivate me to work even harder than I have been on my anesthesia MOC."

"That is a very healthy way to deal with these tragedies," Noah said. "There is always something more that we doctors need to learn for our patients."

"The one thing that makes this last case easier than the first two is that we don't have to worry about the M&M. I don't believe there is a single thing in this case that I would change. Nor is there anything that some-one like Dr. Mason could challenge."

"Good point," Noah said, but he couldn't keep his mind from remembering Dorothy Barton's remark about Ava not turning off the isoflurane when she should have. He wasn't going to bring that up again but the remembrance keyed off another issue. "You said that the reason you knew so much about how to handle a malignant hyperthermia case was from using the WestonSim Center."

"Absolutely," Ava said. "I ran the MH program a bunch of times." She hung up the kitchen towel on the oven handle.

"While you were gone, I went on the WestonSim Center website," Noah said. "I was impressed with the building and the setup. It makes what we have at BMH seem rather pitiful. But while I was looking at their facts and figures, I noticed it didn't open its doors until 2013."

For a few moments Noah and Ava stared at each other. Suddenly there was a sense of unease in the air like static electricity.

"Are you doubting what I told you?" Ava asked challengingly.

"I'm not doubting anything," Noah said. "I just noticed the date, which is the year after you and I started at the BMH."

Ava laughed derisively. "Two thousand thirteen is the year that the center moved into its new building. The robotic human mannequins had been in the main hospital building since I was in college and had been regularly upgraded. I started using them way back when."

"Oh," Noah said. "Okay. That explains that."

"Any other questions about my training and timing?" Ava said challengingly.

"Well, since you asked, I'm still curious about how much experience you had during your residency training with the advanced video laryngoscope? Did you use them a lot?"

"That seems like a pointed question," Ava said. "Is this issue coming back? Why are you asking this?"

"I'm just curious," Noah said breezily. He could tell that Ava was annoyed again.

"I don't buy that," Ava said with a definite edge to her voice. "What's on your mind? What are you implying?"

"Nothing in particular," Noah said, struggling to come up with an explanation. "I'm just wondering if there are differences in anesthesia programs like there are in surgery."

"Are you suggesting that my training at Brazos University might not be as good as your Ivy League background? I'm appalled. You were the one telling me it was all a myth just last Monday, and now you are questioning me because I didn't train at a known medical center? Give me a break!"

"While you were away I checked out the Brazos University Medical Center and the medical school. It was a way to feel closer to you because I missed you. And I was impressed. It looks like a terrific facility."

At that moment Ava's phone rang. She snatched it up from the countertop and looked at the screen. "Oh, damn! It's my NSC boss. He's going to want to debrief me about the weekend. Do you mind? I should talk with him, but it might take a while. I'm sorry."

"Not a problem," Noah said graciously. In truth, he felt a little like a boxer being saved by the bell. "Do what you need to do."

"It might take as long as an hour," Ava said as the ringing continued. "I ended up seeing a lot of congressmen, including over dinner with two very important senators, including Orrin Hatch."

"Take your time!" Noah said. "I'll head up to the study. You've got enough coffee table books up there to keep me busy all night."

"Okay," Ava said. "I'll be up as soon as I can." She then clicked on the phone and held it to her ear. "Howard, hold on just a second." Then to Noah she mouthed, "See you!" and gave him a wink.

As Noah headed for the main stairs, he was aware of Ava already describing her dinner Saturday night at the Washington, D.C., Capital Grille as she headed over to the sitting area of the expansive kitchen. He was glad to put a bit of space between them. He'd not expected her to react so sensitively to the laryngoscope issue. All he wanted to know was if it was in common use during her residency. Her response made him wonder just what she would say if he voiced all his misgivings.

In the study Noah pawed through the books on the coffee table. It was an eclectic selection of large-format hardcover travel and art books. He picked up one that was both. It was an encased two-volume extravaganza called *Venice: Art and Architecture.* As he went to sit down, another idea occurred to him. He remembered Ava saying she'd been on the computer when he had arrived. He glanced at his watch. It had only been five minutes or so since he had left the kitchen.

Placing the books on the ottoman, Noah walked back out into the hall and peered down the main stairs. He strained to hear Ava's voice as she talked on the phone, but he couldn't. The house was still except for an almost imperceptible hum of the air-conditioning system. Advancing a few feet more, Noah glanced into the computer room. From where he was standing he could see the machine was on but apparently in sleep mode. After yet another glance down the stairs and a brief listen for any sign of

Ava, Noah quickly made a beeline for the computer chair. Although he knew he shouldn't do what he had in mind, he couldn't help himself. Her reaction to his simple questions about her residency training had fanned his curiosity about how extensive it had been. Although having been selected for a staff position in the BMH Anesthesia Department spoke volumes concerning the quality of her training, Noah was eager to get some specifics. Anesthesia residents, like surgical residents, at least at BMH, had to maintain case logs. Noah wanted to see hers, and see if it compared with those at BMH in terms of number of cases and type. Noah kept his case logs as a Word document and constantly updated it. He assumed Ava would have done the same and trusted it would still be on her system.

With a sudden impulsivity born of a nagging confusion about Ava and her training, Noah woke up the sleeping machine. It was easy, by merely typing 1 six times in lieu of a security code, which he knew from his first visit that Ava had never bothered to install. Expecting he'd have to go to documents to search, Noah was surprised to find the screen filled with an uncompleted letter to Howard Beckmann of the Nutritional Supplement Council. Unable to help himself, Noah began reading the letter. What caught his attention was the reference to the 1994 Dietary Supplement Act, or DSHEA, in bold letters. This was a law that Noah knew all too well, as it promoted quackery for profit by giving the supplement industry free rein to avoid effective monitoring by the FDA.

To Noah's utter dismay, the letter talked about the need to launch political and personal defamatory targeting of those few congressmen and senators who had voiced opposition to the DSHEA and wanted to repeal it or significantly amend it. As engrossed as he was in reading, he was totally unaware when Ava appeared in the doorway. He wasn't even aware when she charged into the room and looked over his shoulder.

"What do you think you are doing?" she screamed. She grabbed Noah's arm and spun him around in the swivel chair to face her. Her face was a ghostly pale blue, as the only illumination in the room was from the central computer screen.

"I was just going to . . ." Noah began, but in the press of the moment, he couldn't decide whether he should be truthful, and his hesitation enflamed Ava even more.

"That is personal correspondence you are reading," Ava yelled, pointing over Noah's shoulder. "How dare you!"

"I'm sorry," Noah managed. "I thought you were going to be occupied for a time, and after our discussion downstairs, I had it in mind to look at your resident case log, or at least see if you had one."

"Of course I have one," Ava snapped irritably. "So you are still looking down your nose at where I got my anesthesia training. That adds insult to injury, making this violation of my privacy even worse. I can't believe you."

"I'm sorry," Noah repeated. He started to get up, but Ava reached out and forced him back down on the computer chair.

"I've trusted you," Ava yelled. "I've opened my home to you and this is how I'm rewarded? If I were a guest in your apartment, it wouldn't even dawn on me to go into your computer."

"You are right," Noah said. "I don't know why I did it. Well, maybe I do. I think you are a terrific anesthesiologist and have said so many times. But there are some . . . I don't know exactly how to word this . . . but I have some misgivings that I'd like to get off my mind."

"Like what?" Ava snarled.

"Maybe this isn't the best time to talk about this," Noah said. He tried to stand again, but Ava wouldn't let him. She was in a rage, hovering over him.

"It's now or never," Ava snapped. "Explain yourself!"

"It's just a few little things," Noah said with a sigh. "Like with the Gibson case, it seemed you were struggling with the video laryngoscope.

Now, I know the patient's head was bouncing around from the cardiac massage, but it just looked like you weren't as familiar with the instrument as I would have guessed."

"What else?"

"On the same case, I wondered why you hadn't secured an airway some other way, like with a needle tracheostomy with high-pressure oxygen."

"Anything else? Let's hear it all!"

"With the Harrison case I keep wondering why Dorothy Barton told me you hadn't turned off the isoflurane as fast as you should have."

"Are you saying you take her word over mine?" Ava questioned with disbelief.

"No, not at all. It's just . . . what can I say? They are misgivings. That's the only word I can think of, and I'd rather get them off my mind."

"I'm the anesthesiologist, not you," Ava said angrily. "When I got in on the Gibson case the patient had already arrested. A needle tracheotomy wouldn't have sufficed, especially since I didn't know what the problem was and couldn't be sure that expiration would have been adequate. An endotracheal tube would have been immeasurably better, and I came close to getting one in. As for Miss Barton, I think her problematic personality speaks volumes. I turned that damn isoflurane off the second I suspected malignant hyperthermia. But you know something, I shouldn't have to justify my professional behavior to you. My anesthesia peers went over these cases, and they were discussed at our rounds. You, of all people, are supposed to be on my side. This is absurd."

"I am on your side," Noah said. "I've been on your side from the beginning. As proof, look how I handled both M&M Conferences. I couldn't have been any more on your side than I was. I wouldn't have done that if I didn't believe in your competence."

For the first time since Ava had surprised Noah, she broke off, angrily staring at him. She was furious and breathing heavily. A moment later, she looked back down. "You shouldn't have gone into my computer, especially reading my correspondence. I have a right to privacy in my own home."

"I know," Noah admitted. "I'm sorry. You are perfectly justified to be upset. I don't know what came over me. It won't happen again."

"It better not," Ava warned. "And now I want you to leave."

It was Noah's turn to be shocked. He had not expected to be dismissed, even though he recognized he was guilty of a serious faux pas. The idea of returning to his depressing apartment seemed harsh punishment indeed.

"Are you sure?" Noah pleaded.

Ava nodded. "I need some space to calm down. I've been betrayed before by a cunning, scheming husband, and I don't like the feeling." She backed up, giving Noah some room.

"I haven't betrayed you," Noah said, getting to his feet. "I think you are a great and exceptionally motivated anesthesiologist. And certainly my personal feelings for you haven't changed one iota."

"I want you to leave," Ava said. "Violating my trust and questioning my training feels like a betrayal."

Noah did not want to leave. He'd missed her terribly over the previous four days. For a moment, they just stared at each other, with Noah trying desperately to think of a way to make amends. He'd been caught with his hand in the cookie jar and was now being banned to his room. "You'll call or text if you change your mind?" Noah said. "I can just come back." Inwardly, Noah cringed. It was a pitiful, pleading comment, and he hated himself as soon as it escaped his lips.

"I'm not going to change my mind," Ava said.

Twenty minutes later, when Noah entered his apartment and collapsed dejectedly onto his tiny couch, he was furious with himself for not resisting the temptation to go on Ava's computer. How could he have been so stupid? And then, to make matters worse, how could he have been even stupider to bring up his misgivings about her professional performance as an explanation? It had been like adding fuel to a goddamn fire.

"You are fucking hopeless," he said out loud to himself while he knocked his head multiple times with the knuckles of his fist. He knew he was terrible at navigating relationships, but this evening's performance was a study in ineptitude, especially since they were just getting over a major misunderstanding, for which he now realized he was as guilty as she was. He should have responded to her initial text and let her know how he felt.

Noah wondered how long it would take for Ava to come around, if she was going to come around. He recognized there was a chance she'd decide he wasn't worth all the angst, preferring her social media activities as much easier and cleaner. Gloomily, his mind switched over to the letter he'd read on her computer screen. In some ways having graphic proof that she was figuratively in bed with the nutritional-supplement industry was almost equally as disturbing as being sent home. Prior to reading the letter he'd made a specific effort to ignore her involvement. Now he couldn't. She was recommending defaming people who he felt were on the responsible side of the issue. That was serious.

26

The melodic alarm on Noah's smartphone went off, breaking his concentration. He was on the eighth floor of the Stanhope Pavilion in what was still called the chart room, even though charts were relics of the past. Now all the information on each patient was in their EMR stored in the central computer, so the chart room should have been called the monitor room, but tradition played a significant role at BMH and the old name stuck. Noah had been busy going over all the appropriate inpatient records in preparation for work rounds that would begin at their usual time of 5:00 P.M., but in his usual compulsive manner, he liked to be up on all the patients even before rounds began.

Noah had set his alarm to meet with Dr. Kumar, chief of Anesthesia, and he didn't want to be late or, worse yet, forget. Noah stood up and pulled on a freshly pressed white jacket. He was nervous about the upcoming meeting. Deciding on doing it had not been easy, and he had argued the pros and cons for almost two days before making the plans.

Clicking off the monitor, Noah headed for the elevators. Dr. Kumar had scheduled the meeting in his department chair office in Administration on the third floor. Although Noah would have preferred to meet someplace on the surgical floor to keep things more casual, Dr. Kumar had insisted, and Noah had been forced to agree, so even the formal setting was adding to Noah's unease.

The past week had not been Noah's favorite. As a disturbing replay of the previous weekend, Noah had not heard from Ava. To avoid any repeat of the misunderstanding that had contributed to that unpleasant situation, Noah had sent her several texts, starting Sunday night. Each time he'd thrown any pretext of pride out the window and had apologized effusively for what he had done and, more or less, pleaded to get together to talk it out. Ava had responded once, late Tuesday afternoon in her signature terse style: *I need a break.*

Wednesday Noah had changed tactics. He texted her that he thought they should at least get together to plan the following week's M&M Conference, but she didn't respond. It was becoming perfectly clear what she meant by "a break" was no contact. When they had had encountered each other by chance in the OR, she'd even avoided eye contact.

In the beginning of the week Noah had struggled with a mixture of regret and remorse, but by Wednesday, when she chose not to respond to his text about the M&M, his feelings began to shift. Although he admitted he'd made a mistake violating her trust by accessing her computer, he began to sense the punishment was more than the offense warranted. The idea resurfaced that there was a disconnect with her current behavior and the intimacy he thought they had shared. Such thinking brought back Leslie's warnings and his own concern that Ava might have been using him. It also reawakened his nagging misgivings about her training and competence. Feeling a flash of irritation over her lack of communication, he found himself wondering something he never thought he'd question: Could Dr. Mason be right about Ava?

From Noah's perspective, the problem with such an idea was that she had been hired by one of the best anesthesia departments in the country, which meant that she'd been seriously vetted way beyond having just passed the anesthesia boards and obtained a Massachusetts medical license. At a minimum, a complete file of her training, including letters of recommendation, would have been required. It was that fact that made him overcome his reservations about approaching Dr. Kumar.

Noah pushed into the crowded elevator, which was occupied mostly by nurses leaving the hospital at the end of their shift. In contrast to the usual elevator silence, there was a lot of conversation. Noah stayed near the door, as he was only going to the third floor and not the ground floor.

As the elevator descended, Noah thought more about the past week and why it was going to go down emotionally as one of his worst. Although he had tried the same defense mechanism for his heartache that he had used over the weekend, namely by concentrating on his work, he'd had less to do because he had done so much from Thursday through Sunday. He'd also felt reluctant to stay in the on-call room again, so he'd gone back to his apartment each night. The result was comparatively too much free time on his hands to keep from mulling over the situation with Ava. And on top of that, he'd had another one of his paranoid reactions.

Although Noah couldn't have been certain, it seemed to him that the same man in the dark suit who had followed him a couple weeks earlier reappeared and followed him again late Tuesday evening. This time Noah had taken a particularly circuitous route, going through Louisburg Square to gaze longingly up at Ava's lighted study window. Each time he had turned a corner and glanced back the man had been there, seemingly talking on a cell phone. Noah had first noticed him in the Boston Common. When Noah had arrived back at his building on Revere Street, he'd pulled off the same maneuver of getting his door quickly locked behind him, only to see the man again walk by without so much as a glance in Noah's direction.

Although Noah had again attributed this episode to his overwrought emotional state, he didn't impute it to his imagination when he got upstairs to his apartment to find his door had been forced. Since it had happened five times over the past two years, most likely thanks to the woman college student who lived above him and who had a lot of after-hours fellow-student male visitors to whom she gave front door keys, he wasn't terribly surprised or concerned, a testament to how the human mind could adapt to an inconvenience if it happened often enough. After the first four episodes, he'd complained to the landlord, who'd patched his door, but after the last he hadn't even bothered to do that. After all, there wasn't much to steal in his unit beyond his aged laptop. He didn't even have a TV. Although he'd been initially thankful his computer was still on the card table on this occasion, he did become moderately concerned when he realized someone had been using it!

As a surgeon, Noah had some compulsive traits, like a lot of his colleagues. One of the traits involved how he dealt with his tools, and in his mind tools included electronics. He was very particular about the way he handled his laptop, which had caused a good deal of merciless teasing by Leslie, who thought it silly that he insisted it be lined up with the edges of the table. Frequently she'd move it just to playfully aggravate him. Tuesday night it was as if Leslie had been there.

Recognizing someone had been on his computer, Noah had immediately checked his bank account information. When that had seemed okay, he'd checked his browser's history to find that it had been wiped clean, including what he had done the previous night. It was apparent someone had used his computer and then had covered his tracks. After checking all his documents, including his surgical case log, which thankfully didn't include any personal patient information, Noah hadn't known what to make of the incident and had tried not to dwell on it, although it had fanned his paranoia.

When the hospital elevator arrived on Stanhope 3, Noah got out. As he hurried along the administration corridor, he checked his watch. He still had a full five minutes before the scheduled 4:00 meeting.

It turned out that Dr. Kumar was about twenty minutes late, but he was gracious about it. He came directly over to where Noah was waiting in a common waiting area and apologized. He explained he'd been called in on a problematic cardiac surgery case and had come down as soon as he was free. Noah assured him there was no problem, explaining he'd enjoyed the brief respite from a typically busy day. Dr. Kumar then led Noah into his office, the decor of which had an Indian motif. There was a collection of framed Mughal miniatures on the walls.

"Please have a seat," Dr. Kumar said in his charmingly melodic Indian accent. He was dressed in a long white coat over scrubs that emphasized his darkly burnished skin tone. He went around and sat behind his desk, putting his elbows on the surface and clasping his hands below his chin.

"I assumed when you requested this meeting that the subject would be Dr. Ava London," Dr. Kumar said. "That's why I thought it best to meet down here rather than upstairs. Let me say at the outset, there is no need for you to worry about her tenure here at BMH, despite Dr. Mason's recent comments. He is a passionate man, but I have spoken with him about Dr. London since his outburst at the M&M, and I believe he feels differently now. Does that put your mind at ease? And, by the way, I believe you handled both M&M conferences superbly, from the Anesthesia Department's point of view."

"Thank you," Noah said. "I tried my best to present the facts."

"You did a superbly diplomatic job."

"I thank you again," Noah said. "I did want to talk with you about Dr. London, but for a different reason."

"Oh?" Dr. Kumar questioned. He visibly stiffened. His clasped hands lowered to the desk surface.

"There were a few aspects of Dr. London's performance that I did not mention in my presentations but which I feel is my ethical duty to bring to your attention."

"I'm listening," Dr. Kumar said, with his voice changed. It had hardened a degree, but Noah pressed on.

Noah started with the Gibson case, followed by the Harrison and then finally the Vincent, describing in as much detail as possible his mild, and purely subjective, misgivings about Ava's performance. When he was finished, a heavy silence reigned. Dr. Kumar stared back at him with his penetratingly dark, unblinking eyes, making Noah uncomfortable. The man had not shown any reaction during Noah's monologue.

Noah felt an irresistible urge to add: "With the Gibson case I was directly involved, meaning I saw the situation. With the other two cases, what I'm relating is hearsay from a circulating nurse or Dr. London."

When Dr. Kumar still didn't respond, Noah said: "My motivation for coming to you is for you to hear my concerns and either substantiate them or dismiss them as you see fit. I haven't said anything to anyone else and don't plan to do so."

"I find this all very troubling indeed," Dr. Kumar snapped. "These are all very vague and, as you say, subjective observations. Our department and I have looked into these three cases with close attention to detail and found nothing wrong. If anything, Dr. London handled them very appropriately, if not superbly. Consequently, I can't help but take your comments as a value judgment of my leadership skills and my competence as an administrator, since I was personally responsible for hiring Dr. London."

Noah was flabbergasted. Instead of being thankful of his efforts, Dr. Kumar was taking his visit as a personal affront.

"There is only one question about Dr. London's résumé," Dr. Kumar said angrily, "and that is that she trained at a new, relatively unknown institution. But because of that, I and the faculty hiring committee went over her application with great care. And something else you might not know: Dr. London scored remarkably well on her anesthesia boards, both written and oral. I spoke to several of the examiners directly. She's also passed muster with the Massachusetts Board of Medicine."

"I certainly knew she had passed her anesthesia boards," Noah said. "And I had heard she had done exceptionally. I am not surprised. She knows the science remarkably well."

"We wouldn't have hired her otherwise," Dr. Kumar said with obvious annoyance. "And let me say this: If you continue to defame Dr. London by talking with others about these unsubstantiated and, frankly, vague impressions, you could be putting yourself and the hospital in a difficult legal situation. Am I making myself clear?"

"Perfectly clear," Noah said. He stood up. It was painfully obvious that coming to Dr. Kumar had been a big mistake.

"Dr. Mason told me that it was his impression that you and Dr. London were having an affair," Dr. Kumar added. "Is that now on the rocks, and are you coming to me out of spurned lover's spite? Honestly, that's what it sounds like."

Noah stared at the Anesthesia chief with total disbelief. It was such an outrageous idea that Noah suddenly questioned if Dr. Kumar himself was a spurned lover of Ava's. And what about Dr. Mason? Could his anger be from spite based on more than just having his advances rebuffed? From the little Noah had told Leslie about Ava, she had classified Ava as a manipulative person with a possible personality disorder. Could Leslie be right? Yet the moment the shocking idea of Ava's possible promiscuousness occurred to him, Noah immediately dismissed it out of hand, sensing his paranoia was running away with itself. Dr. Kumar was not behaving like a spurned lover in the slightest. He wasn't putting Ava down but rather the absolute opposite. He was truly convinced of Ava's competence, as well as his own leadership abilities for having hired her. And it was his leadership that Noah was challenging by voicing his misgivings.

"My only motivation is my ethical duty," Noah said. The last thing he wanted to do was get into any kind of discussion about his relationship with Ava. "Thank you for your time."

Noah started to leave, but Dr. Kumar stopped him. "One last piece of advice: In the future, if you have any concerns about people in my department, I advise you to go through channels. You should speak with your chief, Dr. Hernandez, and not to me. Am I making myself clear?"

"You are," Noah said. "Thank you for seeing me." He turned and left. As he headed back to the elevators, he mocked himself for previously thinking that he was making progress in the diplomatic arena. It seemed that handling staff egos at the BMH was certainly not his forte. In retrospect, there was no doubt in his mind that it had been a remarkably poor decision to seek out the Anesthesia chief. Worriedly, he wondered if Dr. Kumar would mention their tête-à-tête to Dr. Hernandez. Unfortunately, he thought the chances were better than good.

27

Mondays were always difficult for Noah, even though he'd spent the entire weekend at the hospital, searching for things to do to avoid obsessing over Ava's continued silence. Although he was completely caught up on all his responsibilities, the Monday surgical schedule was particularly heavy as every attending wanted OR time and pressured Noah to provide it. Everyone felt it was far better to get their cases done earlier in the week, the better so that by the end of the week patients could be sent home, which was more pleasant for patients and surgeons alike. To add to his burden, Noah had three of his own cases. Luckily, those had gone well, so he now had time to finish one of the projects he'd started over the weekend.

Changing out of his scrubs, Noah headed to the surgical residency program office. The administration area was in full swing, especially around the hospital president's massive corner office. As Noah passed the anesthesia office he cringed, thinking of the unpleasant meeting he'd had with Dr. Kumar Friday afternoon. So far there had been no fallout, but Noah was quite certain it would happen, maybe even later that day.

Noah's goal was to pick up some files from Shirley Berenson, the surgical residency program coordinator, who managed the complicated resident evaluation process upon which the program's accreditation depended. Every month each resident was evaluated as to his or her progress in a wide variety of arenas, such as surgical skills, patient care, medical knowledge, attendance, timeliness, and a host of other subjective attributes such as professionalism and communication skills. As super chief, it was Noah's responsibility to get the completed forms from all chief residents evaluating the residents under their tutelage for the month. Noah had done this on Saturday. On Sunday, he had used this material to help him fill out his own evaluations of all fifty-six residents, including all the chief residents, and put all the paperwork in Shirley's inbox. Since it was Noah's first attempt at this process, it had taken him longer than he'd expected. And he wasn't finished.

Shirley had told him that she would collate all the material, fill out the required regulatory forms, make four separate copies of the complete report, and have them all done by noon. At that point it was Noah's job as super chief to deliver a copy to Drs. Hernandez, Cantor, Mason, and Hiroshi. Why it had to be the super chief to act as delivery boy, Noah didn't know, but he assumed it was a holdover from days past, when a certain amount of hazing was part of surgical training. The next year, by tradition, Noah was to become a member of the BMH staff, and accordingly he had to be appropriately humbled before he joined the august community.

Noah had no problem with tradition and liked it to a degree. There was something reassuring about it as a direct connection with the hospital's venerable past. Delivering copies of the resident evaluation report to Dr. Hernandez and Dr. Cantor was easy. Their offices were right there in the administration area, and Noah handed copies to their secretaries, who were literally around the corner from the surgical residency program office. It was the last two heavyweights that required a certain amount of effort because their offices were in the swanky Franklin Building.

Noah looked at his watch as he crossed the pedestrian bridge. It was a little after 3:00, so he was confident that he wouldn't run into Wild

Bill at his office, since he'd still be in surgery, having been scheduled for three big cases. Even though he was a remarkably fast surgeon who relied on his fellow to open and close, Noah was relatively certain he'd still be occupied.

As he walked, Noah thought about Ava and how he hadn't seen her that morning, nor even her name on the surgical schedule, suggesting that she was not working that day. On Saturday night, after he'd left the hospital later than 9:00 P.M., Noah had again detoured through Louisburg Square, even though he had tried to talk himself out of doing it. En route he'd argued with himself whether he would have the courage to ring her bell if he saw a light in her study, but he needn't have bothered. There'd been no light in the study or in any other window, suggesting she was again out of town, most likely back in Washington. With a heavy heart, yet rationalizing that it was for the best, Noah had continued on to his drab apartment. At least he didn't have the impression he'd been followed, making him feel as if his paranoia was under control.

Dr. Mason's office was on the eighth floor and Dr. Hiroshi's was on the sixth. To speed up the process and get Dr. Mason's delivery out of the way sooner rather than later, he took the elevator to the eighth floor with the idea of then using the stairs to get down to the sixth. Entering Dr. Mason's posh, mahogany-clad domain, Noah headed directly for his secretary, Miss Lancaster. She was somewhere in her fifties, with an impressive ash-blond chignon piled on her head. She had an imperious manner that caused her to treat surgical residents like hired help. Noah had had to deal with her in the past and had never found it pleasant.

As Noah approached, Miss Lancaster was on the phone, angrily dealing with someone who apparently wished to see Dr. Mason as soon as possible. "I'm sorry, but Dr. Mason is a busy man," Miss Lancaster scolded. "No, he will not call you back."

Noah held up the resident evaluation report, which he knew that Miss Lancaster surely recognized, as it was a monthly tradition and had a distinctive red cover. The secretary looked at Noah over the top of her reading glasses. There was no recognition or any semblance of graciousness. Instead, she merely nodded irritably toward the open door into Dr. Mason's inner sanctum and then gestured with her free hand as if shooing away a pest. She didn't interrupt her conversation with what Noah assumed was a desperate patient, most likely dealing with a recent diagnosis of pancreatic cancer. "Have your doctor call me," Miss Lancaster snapped into the phone. "But first make sure that the CT scans are sent so Dr. Mason can review them before speaking with your doctor."

Feeling considerable empathy for the patient, Noah resisted the temptation to say something appropriately harsh to Miss Lancaster. She was treating the caller outrageously. After having recently filled out all the evaluations of the residents, he wished there was a mechanism for doing the same with staff secretaries.

Dr. Mason's corner office appeared to Noah the way he imagined the office of a CEO of a major international corporation would look, as a reflection of the amount of money the man brought to the hospital. It was ridiculously large, commanded an impressive view of Boston Harbor, and was also paneled in mahogany. The furniture in the sitting area was upholstered in a soft, premium leather. Covering the walls were a profusion of framed diplomas, both earned and honorary. The desk size matched the renowned surgeon's ego.

For a second Noah debated where to put the resident evaluation report as he noticed correspondence waiting Dr. Mason's signature on the table in front of the couch. Still, Noah decided to put his report front and center on the desk, but as he approached with the report outstretched something caught his eye. Lying on the desk off to the side was a bound Ph.D. thesis. Noah did a double take. To his shock, he thought he recognized it. It looked like his!

Noah dropped the evaluation report on the desk's blotter, and then after a glance over his shoulder to make sure Miss Lancaster was still preoccupied with her phone conversation, he reached out and snapped up the bound thesis. A second later he confirmed it was indeed as he suspected: *Genetic Control of the Rate of Binary Fission in Escherichia Coli* by Noah Rothauser. Someone, presumably Dr. Mason, had inserted a number of Post-it bookmarks.

After another fleeting glance in Miss Lancaster's direction, Noah opened the bookmarked pages. They marked various tables of data. One table in particular made Noah's heart leap in his chest. For a brief second he thought about taking the thesis to get it out of Dr. Mason's hands, but immediately he decided against the idea. Miss Lancaster's eagle eye would undoubtedly see him carrying it, as it would be difficult to conceal. The only way possible would be to hold it under his white coat, but that would be awkward and most likely wouldn't work. And even if he succeeded in getting it by her, she'd remember it had been sitting on the desk when Noah had visited. Reluctantly, Noah replaced the thesis, convinced that taking it would only serve to call attention to it and probably make things worse.

28

"Dr. Rothauser?" the OR intercom announced. "This is Janet Spaulding. I just got a call from Dr. Hernandez. He wants to know how long you might be. He would like you to meet with him as soon as possible."

Noah straightened up suddenly, as if a bolt of electricity had descended his spine. Once again he was being summoned to the principal's office, and it made his heart race. It had been two weeks to the day that he'd been texted to see Dr. Hernandez out of the blue. Although that meeting had gone well, Noah had no idea why the chief wanted to see him yet again, but it couldn't be good news. It was certainly out of the ordinary for such a request to come through the OR intercom. "Tell him I'm finishing up now and I'll be available in a half-hour or so. Where does he want to meet?"

"His departmental office," Janet said.

"Got it," Noah replied. He tried to calm himself, but it was difficult. He was watching Dr. Lynn Pierce, a first-year resident, sew up the skin under the watchful eye of Dr. Arnold Wells, a third-year senior resident. Dr. Pierce was doing a credible job even though it was her first time doing so. She had spent her first month in the SICU, or surgical intensive-care unit, where she had done a superb job. Now she was rotating on the gastrointestinal service.

The operation had been a pancreatectomy, Dr. Mason's specialty, and Noah was pleased with his performance. He'd used Dr. Mason's technique to the letter and had accomplished the difficult surgery almost as quickly as Dr. Mason, a tribute both to the technique and Noah's dexterity. Noah was known as one of the fastest residents when it came to doing surgery. It wasn't that he rushed. It was just that he knew the anatomy cold and had exceptional hand-eye coordination. There was never any wasted motion.

"Would you guys mind if I duck out?" Noah asked. He couldn't stand the tension of not knowing why the chief wanted to see him, especially by having him paged in the middle of an operation.

"Not at all," Arnold said. Lynn didn't respond, as she was concentrating on her suturing.

After a quick chat with the anesthesiologist about post-op orders on the patient, Noah hurried toward the men's locker room to change out of his scrubs. As he powerwalked the length of the OR suite, it occurred to him that the most likely explanation was that Dr. Kumar had finally gotten to Dr. Hernandez to complain about Noah's importunate Friday-afternoon visit. Racking his brains, Noah tried to think up some elaborate explanation of why he had gone directly to the chief of Anesthesia bypassing Dr. Hernandez. Unfortunately, Noah didn't feel very creative, since he was exhausted and already on edge.

The previous night Noah had slept little, unable to stop fretting about his Ph.D. thesis being on Dr. Mason's desk. For the life of him, he couldn't figure out why or how it had gotten there and why there were bookmarks at various data tables. Recalling Dr. Mason's threat to do his best to have Noah dismissed, there could be only one explanation. Was that something Noah had to worry about? He didn't know, but it had made him feel extremely agitated.

Unable to sleep with his mind in turmoil, Noah had gotten up at three in the morning and had returned to the hospital. For lack of anything else to do, he'd started his prep for the next M&M Conference, even though by doing so he'd also had to contend with thoughts of Ava. When he had done the Tuesday resident surgical schedule, he'd seen that she was assigned to cases on Tuesday, meaning she was back from wherever she had gone. It had made him wonder if he'd run into her by chance, and if he did how he would react, but it hadn't happened.

Noah took the stairs to get down to the third floor, once again anxious about heading to a confrontation with someone who had the power to derail his career ambitions. Obviously, it was a fear he was never to outgrow.

When Noah presented himself in front of Dr. Hernandez's charming secretary, Mrs. Kimble, who was the antithesis of Miss Lancaster, he was asked to take a seat in the common administrative waiting area. She said she would come and get him when Dr. Hernandez was ready. Her pleasant attitude seemed entirely normal, which Noah took as a good sign. As he sat down he felt a bit more at ease. Another idea had occurred to him. Maybe Dr. Hernandez wanted to congratulate him on his first resident evaluation report, which Noah had turned in the day before. Noah did feel confident the report had been done with appropriate attention to detail, and it was entirely positive, which was unique. Contrary to most years, none of the first-year residents were having any difficulty adapting to the rigors of the program.

With these thoughts in mind, Noah was feeling confident until a small parade of additional authority figures appeared, including Dr. Cantor, Dr. Mason, Dr. Hiroshi, and, strangely enough, Gloria Hutchinson, the president of the hospital. Chatting together, all of them trooped into Dr. Hernandez's office and disappeared behind a closed door.

Now Noah's anxiety returned in a rush as the minutes ticked by. Were all these bigwigs going to be part of the meeting with Noah, or was Noah merely waiting until their meeting with Dr. Hernandez was over? If it was to be the former, something rather extraordinary was afoot, especially with Dr. Mason's presence. If it was the latter, things might turn out okay. Noah took his pulse, which was normally in the sixty-per-minute range. Now it was one hundred and ten, and he could feel it in his temples.

Tossing aside an old issue of *Time* magazine, Noah concentrated on Mrs. Kimble. He'd concluded that her behavior was key. To his dismay, a few minutes later, after hanging up her phone, she pushed back from the desk and stood. As she started in Noah's direction, he could feel his pulse rate jump from its already fast pace.

"Dr. Hernandez can see you now," Mrs. Kimble said with the same pleasantness she'd used before. This time Noah wasn't fooled. The meeting was going to be with the whole group.

When Noah got into the inner office, his worst fears seemed justified. Dr. Hernandez did not get up as he usually had in the past, and he exuded an alarming intensity. Dr. Cantor and Dr. Hiroshi were sitting by the window in side chairs. Gloria Hutchinson was on the couch, looking as serious as Dr. Hernandez. Next to her was Dr. Mason with an expression of pompous self-satisfaction. But worst of all, from Noah's viewpoint, was catching sight of his wayward thesis perched on Dr. Hernandez desk. This impromptu meeting was not about the resident evaluation report, or his misguided meeting with Dr. Kumar, but something far more serious.

With no seat available and no verbal direction from Dr. Hernandez, Noah stopped in the middle of the room. He felt agonizingly vulnerable, facing not one but four authority figures. His heart was racing. When no one spoke or moved, Noah felt pressured to break the silence: "You wanted to see me, sir?" The pitch of his voice was higher than he would have liked.

"That's correct," Dr. Hernandez snapped angrily. Then, in his signature bombastic style, he launched into a mini-lecture about how seriously the surgical department took ethical breaches, emphasizing that the

BMH, as one of the country's premier tertiary-care and teaching programs, was obliged to set a high standard for professional integrity and honesty.

As Dr. Hernandez droned on, Noah glanced at the other people in the room. Most had assumed a glazed look, except for Dr. Mason, who was enjoying every second. A sudden slapping sound yanked Noah's attention back to Dr. Hernandez. The chief's hand was now resting on the top of Noah's Ph.D. thesis.

"With these standards in mind, we are faced with a major problem," Dr. Hernandez continued. He picked up the slender volume and held it aloft, reminiscent of a preacher with a bible. "It has been brought to the department's attention that there is falsified data in this thesis, which we understand played a significant role in your acceptance to Harvard Medical School. Is that your understanding, Dr. Rothauser?"

Noah stared with disbelief at the chief. He couldn't believe this was happening. He felt like he was teetering on the edge of a precipice. "Yes," he said after a short pause. "I believe that my thesis made the Admissions people look more positively at my application."

"Then perhaps your acceptance was based on falsehood," Dr. Hernandez said. "If that is the case, we have a serious dilemma that requires attention. So I ask you directly, does this thesis of yours contain falsified or contrived data?"

"To a degree," Noah said, struggling to decide how to answer.

"That seems inordinately evasive," Dr. Hernandez snapped. "I think the question deserves an unambiguous answer. Yes or no!" He glowered at Noah.

"Yes," Noah said reluctantly. "But let me explain. By working day and night I was able to complete my Ph.D. work in two years. For it to be officially part of my medical school application, I had to hand in my thesis on a specific date. To make that date, I was forced to make some very modest outcome predictions for my final confirming experiment, whose results had already been proven by previous work. Those estimates remained in the hard copies I submitted, one of which you are holding. When the final data was available within the month, which was more positive than my conservative estimates, I changed the digital version, which is the version that is online and cited in the literature."

"In other words," Dr. Hernandez said while still holding Noah's bound thesis in the air, "there is definitely falsified data in this work."

"Yes," Noah repeated. "But—"

"I'm sorry," Dr. Hernandez said, interrupting Noah in a tone of voice that was the opposite of being sorry. "This is not the time for explanations of why purposely falsified material exists in a Ph.D. thesis. The fact that it does forces our hand. From this moment, Dr. Rothauser, you are suspended from your duties as super chief resident pending an ad hoc hearing of the Residency Advisory Board. The board will adjudicate the situation and determine if the suspension will be reversed or made permanent. The board will also decide if the Massachusetts Board of Medicine should be advised.

"That will be all, Dr. Rothauser. Needless to say, we are all shocked and disappointed."

Noah was the one who was the most shocked. He couldn't believe he was being summarily dismissed and, worst of all, suspended. He was momentarily paralyzed. He'd expected something bad, but more in line of being formally censured for ignoring proper channels and meeting with Dr. Kumar to question the competence of one of his staff members.

"That will be all, Dr. Rothauser," Dr. Hernandez repeated irritably. He tossed Noah's bound thesis onto his desk in an overt display of indignation.

"What about my patients?" Noah pleaded, finding his voice. He had six post-operative patients in the hospital at that moment, several still in the PACU, and he had surgical cases scheduled for the week.

"Your patients will be taken care of by others," Dr. Hernandez said.

"You should leave the hospital until this issue is resolved. Dr. Cantor will be in touch with you in due course."

Noah literally stumbled out of the chief of surgery's office, totally stunned. In a semi-trance, he walked the length of the corridor toward the elevators. He couldn't believe that Dr. Mason had succeeded in accomplishing what he had threatened. As Ava had reminded him, his reputation as a resident among staff, fellow residents, and patients was sterling. The whole situation was a nightmare.

For Noah, the potential implications of being permanently dismissed from his residency and losing his medical license was the worst news imaginable, akin to being diagnosed with an untreatable cancer. Suddenly, everything he had worked for since he'd decided on medicine as a career was in jeopardy. It was as if his life was unraveling.

BOOK 3

29

Noah felt oppressively hot as he stepped out of his Beacon Hill building into the hazy summer sunshine. Typical of Boston in mid-summer, the humidity had climbed along with the temperature. As he walked up the few steps to the corner of Revere and Grove Streets, he could feel perspiration run down his back despite his summer attire of T-shirt, shorts, and flip-flops. Heat radiating up from the brick sidewalk seemed equal to the heat streaming down from the sun above.

At the corner, Noah stopped and turned around suddenly to look behind him. As he expected, there was a man trudging up Revere Street in his direction. He was dressed in a shirt and tie and had a summer-weight jacket slung over his shoulder. In deference to the heat, the shirt was unbuttoned at the neck and the tie loosened. He was African American with closely cropped hair and a trim, athletic build.

Noah believed he had seen this individual before. It had been on Thursday when he'd emerged from his apartment at about the same time with the same destination in mind, Whole Foods on Cambridge Street. Since the cataclysmic meeting in Dr. Hernandez's office on Tuesday, Noah had been holed up in his tiny apartment, paralyzed by a combination of depression and anxiety, believing his life was in the balance. Beginning on Wednesday, the only thing that had driven him outside was the knowledge that he needed to eat, even though he didn't feel particularly hungry. Each day he'd made the trip to the prepared-food section of Whole Foods to bring home some selections that would serve for both lunch and dinner. He felt totally incapable of preparing anything, and the idea of going to a restaurant in the presence of happy, normal people didn't even occur to him. Breakfast, he'd ignored.

On Wednesday, when he came out on his way to Cambridge Street, he soon had the perception he was being followed. Curiously enough, he had the impression it was the same person who he felt had followed him home on two nights, although he couldn't be certain, since it had been night and he'd never gotten a particularly good look at the man. What made Noah think it could be the same person was the suit, the same thing that had caught his eye on those nights. That and his particularly trim build, similar to the African American's.

Although Noah initially attributed the idea of being followed to delusional paranoia, he went out of his way on Wednesday to follow a circuitous route. Without fail, the man reappeared after each turn, even to the point of going in a full circle, forcing Noah to recognize he wasn't suffering a delusion. He was indeed being followed. Yet the man didn't seem to mind that he stood out like a sore thumb, which made no sense. If someone wanted to follow him, wouldn't they try to conceal it? But why would anyone want to follow him? The only possible idea that came to mind was the hospital wanted to make certain that Noah stayed away as he'd been told. Noah admitted that he'd been sorely tempted on several occasions to sneak back to check on his in-house patients.

On Thursday, Noah had thought it had been the same man following him who was now coming up Revere Street. On Friday, it had been the Caucasian man. It was as if they were a tag team, sharing the burden by alternating days.

Motivated by an equal amount of curiosity and irritation, Noah made the snap decision not to move. He thought the man would surely stop and pretend to be occupied with examining something as the Caucasian fellow had done on several occasions, but he didn't. He kept coming, not in a hurried way but certainly without the slightest hesitation. It seemed that Noah's standing still didn't faze him in the slightest.

When the man got to Noah and motioned to go around him, Noah reached out and stopped him by lightly grabbing his upper, heavily muscled arm. They regarded each other. Noah estimated he was in his thirties. Up close, he was clean shaven, handsome, and clearly in excellent physical shape. The man didn't move except for his eyes, which lowered to look at Noah's hand that was grasping his arm. Noah sensed that the man was tense, like a tightly coiled spring. Noah quickly withdrew his hand.

"Why are you following me?" Noah said. He tried to make his voice sound casual, even though he was suddenly afraid of this individual.

"I'm not following you, man," the individual said calmly. "I'm just hanging out here in Boston, taking in the sights. Now, if you'll excuse me, I'll be on my way."

Noah stepped aside. With a slight nod, the man continued along Revere Street. Noah watched him until he was about a half block away, then Noah turned down Grove Street, more confused than ever. He walked quickly, occasionally looking over his shoulder, fully expecting to see the man reappear.

It had been a difficult three days for Noah. Being isolated in his depressing apartment and having nothing to do was torture. Accustomed to working fifteen hours a day seven days a week and always behind, the change was intolerable. He couldn't remember when he'd been so idle, unable to stop obsessing about what was happening to him. And, disturbingly enough, he'd learned Wednesday afternoon that there were many more days of boredom to be endured. It had been then that he'd gotten a call from Dr. Edward Cantor's office, and, as a further humiliation, it hadn't been the surgical residency program director himself. It had been his secretary, informing Noah in a disinterested monotone that an ad hoc meeting of the Surgical Residency Advisory Board to decide his fate was scheduled for 4:00 P.M. on Wednesday, August 23. She also gave Noah the name and phone number of an attorney that the hospital had retained for him, in accordance with existing labor laws.

The idea that Noah would need an attorney, which hadn't even occurred to him, didn't help his terror about the upcoming meeting. For him, having lawyers involved made the whole situation much more threatening and serious. He'd been hoping the problem might resolve itself when people realized he didn't manufacture data but rather just conservatively estimated the results to make a deadline and replaced them as soon as the real data was available.

The other issue that weighed heavily on Noah's mind was learning how long he would have to suffer the uncertainty of his fate. Initially, when he left Dr. Hernandez's office, he'd assumed the meeting would have been scheduled within a day or two at most. He had not expected two weeks! For him it was an added torment to drag it out.

Reaching busy Cambridge Street, Noah glanced behind him. He didn't see his follower, but he sensed that the man would reappear just as his partner managed. Noah still could not imagine why the hospital was keeping him under surveillance but accepted he just had to live with it despite its absurdity.

Once Noah was in the supermarket, he went directly to the prepared-foods section. Since he didn't feel the slightest bit hungry, it took him quite a while to pick out a few items from the vast array available. At least it was cool in the store. After he paid for his purchases, he started back up Beacon Hill. He looked for the African American but didn't see him. Since he no longer thought of it as any kind of threat, he was beginning not to care.

Noah's legs felt heavy as he trudged up Grove Street, which seemed to have become steeper than he remembered. He was dreading returning to his sparse, lonely apartment. Late Wednesday afternoon, Noah had finally swallowed his pride and had tried again to get in touch with Ava in hopes of eliciting some sympathy. He'd expected to hear from her as soon as the word of his suspension spread through the operating room, which he assumed would have been almost instantaneous following the meeting with Dr. Hernandez Tuesday afternoon. He'd fully expected she'd call or at least text between her cases, considering the seriousness of the situation. When it hadn't happened by 4:00 P.M. Wednesday, he'd first tried to call her landline, thinking she'd be at home. When she hadn't answered, he'd tried her mobile. When that was unsuccessful, he'd texted and waited for a full half-hour. Ultimately, he tried both email and Facebook messaging. Nothing had worked.

All day Thursday and all day Friday, he had hoped to hear from her, and when he hadn't he'd become progressively more depressed. It seemed totally out of character. She would have known immediately the depths of his despair since she had firsthand knowledge of his total commitment to surgery, which was as strong as her commitment to anesthesia. Considering their physical intimacy, how could she not feel an irresistible urge to get in touch with him, just to be sure he was all right? Noah knew that if the tables were reversed, he'd be the very first to make sure she was okay, even if he were irritated with her over some other issue.

By Friday night he'd reached his emotional nadir. Could she still be that upset and angry over his violation of her trust? Apparently so, even though it didn't seem possible to Noah, especially after his sincere apology, and once again his yearning to hear from her morphed into anger at her apparent lack of empathy. Such a mind-set had led to another even more disturbing possibility. He'd recalled several weeks earlier in responding to Ava's questions about his Ph.D. by admitting that he had fudged it a little. Since she'd been the only person in recent years to whom he'd mentioned his thesis, could she possibly have anything to do with the issue being raised by the surgery department?

One thing that Noah was certain about was Dr. Mason's role in the affair. His self-satisfied smile alone during the fateful meeting in the chief's office had made that clear. Noah was certain it had been Dr. Mason who had gotten the bound copy of his Ph.D. thesis from MIT, apparently studied it as evidenced by the Post-it notes, found the discrepancy between the submitted hardcopies and the online version, and had sounded the alarm. Could Ava have been so low as to communicate to Dr. Mason to look for discrepancies in the thesis?

When this thought had occurred to Noah Friday night, he had dismissed it out of hand as he'd done other suspicions. Noah was absolutely confident that Ava detested Dr. Mason, so the idea that she would help him was ludicrous. Yet how did Dr. Mason know about the issue? Noah had no idea.

Arriving at the corner of Grove Street and Revere, Noah was about to turn right when he glanced over his shoulder down the hill. He started. Almost a block away was the African American. He was coming in Noah's direction once again with his jacket still slung casually over his shoulder.

"Taking in the sights, my ass," Noah said under his breath, his anger at Ava finding a convenient target even though he'd resigned himself to being under surveillance. He hurried down Revere Street to his front door and quickly entered. A moment later he was in his apartment and rushed to the front window. He was certain the man would appear, and when he did, Noah planned on opening his window and loudly embarrassing the man. Noah even briefly thought about calling 911 to complain about being harassed.

After ten minutes of watching, Noah gave up. He carried the bag of prepared food into the kitchen and pushed it into his refrigerator without opening it. Now he was less hungry than when he was at the store despite not having eaten since the previous night. It was a little after 3:00 in the afternoon.

Returning to the living room, Noah again looked out the window. There were a few pedestrians going in both directions as there had been before, but no athletic-appearing African American with white shirt and tie carrying a suit jacket over his shoulder. Just like on Wednesday, Thursday, and Friday, the person he thought had been following him just disappeared, making him question his sanity.

Sitting down on his couch and gazing at his blank walls, Noah felt adrift and intensely lonely. It was as if the weight of the world was pressing down on him. He needed some human warmth, and unfortunately, Ava was not coming through. The only person who came to mind was Leslie Brooks. He looked at his watch again as if he'd forgotten he'd just checked it. It was almost 4:00. He wondered if Leslie would be available. For the entire two-years-plus that they had been apart, it had always been Leslie who called, and it had always been on Saturday afternoon. Maybe she might be available. After all, it was Saturday afternoon.

In his depressed state, Noah found decision making difficult. Should he call, and if he should, should he use FaceTime or not? As a doctor he was always decisive, but in the social arena, he was not, especially now, under these extraordinary circumstances. After going back and forth several times, he heaved himself to his feet and went into the bathroom to get a look at himself in the medicine-cabinet mirror. He didn't like what he saw. He hadn't shaved since Tuesday, hadn't slept well, and accordingly looked like death warmed over. No, he wouldn't use FaceTime if he called. He didn't want to scare Leslie, even though he craved sympathy.

After flip-flopping on whether to call or not, he impulsively clicked her number. He felt great relief when she picked up on the third ring. Noah had been counting.

"Will wonders never cease?" Leslie said. She was a little out of breath. "This is the first time you've called me since I don't remember when. What's up?"

"Can you talk, or is this an inconvenient time?"

"I'm on the street, walking back to my apartment," Leslie said. "I'll be home in five minutes. Can I call you back?"

"I suppose," Noah said. Now that he had her on the line, he didn't want to lose her.

"You don't sound good. Is something wrong?"

"Call me back," Noah said. "But don't use FaceTime. I don't want to scare you." He disconnected without waiting for a response.

As Noah impatiently waited, he found himself imagining how her apartment looked. Undoubtedly, it was the opposite of his, with all sorts of decorative, feminine stuff, including colorful curtains and soft rugs. When he lived with it, he'd never appreciated it. Now he missed it.

True to her word, she called back. It was more like ten minutes than five, but Noah was happy to hear her voice.

"Okay," Leslie said in a serious tone. "What's wrong? Have you broken up with your new girlfriend?"

"Worse," Noah said. "I was suspended from my residency position. In a week and a half I have to go before the Surgical Residency Advisory Board to see if it is going to be permanent. One of the ironies is that I sit on the board, so I need to recuse myself."

"Good God!" Leslie exclaimed. "How? Why? This has to be a misunderstanding."

Noah told her the whole story. It felt good for him to voice it all, especially to someone who knew him and whose opinion he trusted. Leslie was well aware of Dr. Mason, as she had been around during the Dr. Meg Green fiasco and the resulting fallout. Noah included that Ava, whose name he now used, had not so much as texted him since the event, which she surely would have learned about. He admitted she was justifiably angry with him and described why. As a final point, he mentioned that Ava had been the only person in years to whom he had mentioned anything about his Ph.D. thesis.

"First let me say how very sorry I am this has happened," Leslie said when Noah fell silent. "Knowing you, I can understand how devastated you are. I'm sure it will be reversed at the advisory meeting. Clearly, from what you have told me, no one has put more of themselves into being a surgical resident than you."

"I wish I could be so sure," Noah said, his voice breaking.

"With your record and your level of commitment, it is an inexcusable reason to dismiss you. I'm sure of it. It has to be reversed. I think their motivation is merely to play along with Dr. Mason and make a statement about ethics."

"I hope you're right," Noah said. "It's possible it was done to humor Dr. Mason. Dr. Hernandez did specifically tell me a week ago that Dr. Mason had to be reckoned with. Well, we'll have to see. Regardless, I appreciate your sympathy and thoughts."

"Now for the rest of my response, which I assume you want because you made the effort to call, how honest do you want me to be? I know on our last conversation you weren't too happy with what I had to say."

"I need you to be honest," Noah admitted. "I might not like it, but I need to hear it."

"I think there is a very good chance that Miss Ava was the source of raising this thesis issue, especially after you telling me how angry she was catching you snooping in her computer."

"But I apologized profusely," Noah argued. "It doesn't seem reasonable she'd do such a thing, even as it smacked of betrayal to her. The punishment doesn't match the crime, and she hates Dr. Mason, and I believe she truly cares for me. And she knows how much surgery means to me because I think she cares about anesthesia to the same degree."

"Again, you are asking for my opinion, and I am giving it," Leslie said gently. "If you listen to this story that you are telling me about this woman, there seems to be a disconnect. You even questioned yourself if she was being manipulative, and she has used this silence routine before. In my mind, I don't think there is any question. But more to the point, have you asked yourself why she should be so damn sensitive about her computer? I mean, you said you apologized."

"Good point," Noah admitted. "I have asked myself that question. I think it has to do with her lobbying for the nutritional-supplement industry, which supports her lifestyle. When she caught me at her computer, I was reading a letter she was in the process of writing to her boss. It was serious stuff advocating dirty tricks associated with the law that keeps the FDA from interfering with the industry. We're talking about billions of dollars.

"And there is another reason for her to be sensitive about her computer. Incredibly enough, her major social activity is social media. It is a significant part of her identity."

"You are joking," Leslie said.

"I'm not," Noah insisted. "She's on all forms of social media every day, from Facebook to Twitter to Snapchat to dating sites. She even has a fan page with over a hundred thousand followers." What he purposefully avoided saying was that she used sockpuppets, except for LinkedIn.

"Noah!" Leslie exclaimed. "What you're describing is a media-crazed preteen girl inhabiting a grown woman's body. Are you sure this is a healthy relationship for you?"

"There are extenuating reasons for her interest in social media," Noah said. He didn't want to hear where Leslie was going, since it mirrored too closely his own reservations about Ava that he'd been trying to ignore. "She is reluctant to socialize with hospital colleagues, somewhat like myself. And her lobbying job takes her away most weekends, so social media fills a void. She lives in Boston but doesn't seem to know anyone in particular."

"I don't know," Leslie said with resignation. "I wish I could be more positive about this woman, since you obviously care for her. But I think you should be careful."

"She also has a history of having been emotionally injured," Noah said. "She was abandoned by a new husband who was a surgical resident from Serbia who needed a green card. I've never been married, but I think I can relate to that."

There was a pause in the conversation, with the issue of abandonment hanging in the air.

"Is there anything you can do to prepare for the Advisory Board hearing?" Leslie said to change the subject.

"The hospital has assigned me a lawyer," Noah said. "I haven't called him yet. I'll do that on Monday. I suppose it will be interesting to get his take. But it scares me the hospital thought I needed a lawyer. It certainly suggests they are taking this seriously. They even have me under surveillance."

"What do you mean?"

"Every time I go out there's a guy in a suit following me. There's two of them and they trade off."

"Are you sure they're following you?"

"I'm pretty sure," Noah said.

"You think it is the hospital?"

"I do. Who else would it be? The only problem is that I think it might have started before my suspension."

"That doesn't make any sense."

"Tell me something I don't know."

"But why would they be watching you?"

"Your guess is as good as mine," Noah said. "I guess they want to keep tabs on me to make sure I don't sneak back into the hospital. It's true that I considered doing it. I can't imagine what my patients are thinking. I don't know what they have been told. Maybe there are some serious legal issues I don't understand."

"I'm so sorry all this is happening to you," Leslie said. "You don't deserve it. I still think it will work itself out, at least in respect to the hospital. I'm afraid your girlfriend might be another story."

"I appreciate your listening to me," Noah said.

"Call me whenever," Leslie said. "And good luck. I hope everything turns out okay. I really do."

After appropriate goodbyes, Noah disconnected the call. For a moment, he sat staring at the blank wall. His calling Leslie had been a toss-up emotionally. He appreciated her sympathy and support, but she'd aggravated his concern for Ava's possible involvement in his suspension.

Thinking about his thesis got him up from the couch. He went into the surprisingly large walk-in closet where he kept several heavy cardboard storage boxes. He rummaged through them until he found the large portfolio with an elastic closure containing all the material relating to his thesis—all his notes and copies of the various drafts. He brought it out into the living room and began to go through it to refresh his memory. He hadn't opened the file for more than ten years.

30

The lawyer that the hospital had retained for Noah was not the warm-and-fuzzy person Noah had hoped for. His name was John Cavendish, a thin, young man with gaunt features and lank blond hair who Noah guessed was in his late twenties. He was not particularly personable. Although he was a member of a large law firm housed on the fiftieth floor in an elegant high-rise building on State Street, he had only junior status. His office was an interior one without a window and was as small as Noah's living room.

Noah's appointment had been for 3:00, but as eager as he was, he'd arrived around 2:30 and had been kept waiting for forty-five minutes. John had come out to the waiting room when he was ready to see Noah and had stiffly introduced himself. The lawyer was now going through Noah's Ph.D. file page by page, his expression neutral.

Taking a deep breath, Noah settled back into his chair. It was the first time he'd ventured out of his apartment since going to Whole Foods Saturday afternoon. He was still depressed and anxious, hoping the visit to the lawyer might buoy his mood. So far it didn't seem promising.

The weather was as hot as it had been on Saturday, and Noah felt it more acutely, because he was now dressed in his only jacket and tie. As he had expected, he'd been followed, this time by the Caucasian, who was significantly more subtle in his surveillance technique than his African American colleague.

"Thank you for bringing in this material," John said as he slid the papers back into their folder. "Unfortunately, there doesn't seem to be anything of particular value in the present circumstance.

"Let me ask you again, just to be sure. It is my understanding that you stated in front of witnesses that the bound volume of your thesis contained falsified information. Is that correct?"

"It is," Noah said. He then went over the entire problem for the second time to make sure the lawyer knew all the details. Watching the man's expression as he talked made Noah feel he was trying to go up a down escalator.

"I can appreciate what you are saying," John said when Noah finished, "but you did admit to falsifying data. It would have been far better if you hadn't done that.

"Just so I am not blindsided, have there been any other similar ethical lapses in your academic career that if revealed would influence this current problem?"

"Only one," Noah admitted. "Once while I was a freshman at Columbia University, I bought a paper off the Internet and handed it in as my own work."

"Was there any fallout at all at the time?"

"No," Noah said.

"Does anyone know of this incident?" John asked.

"No," Noah said. "I don't believe I've ever mentioned it to anyone other than you."

"Good," John said. "If the question of other ethical lapses comes up during the Advisory Board meeting, I don't want you to answer. I will answer for you. Understand?"

"I suppose," Noah said. The meeting with the lawyer was not helping his anxiety.

"All right," John said, standing up behind his desk. "I will do my best. Thank you for coming in. If you think of anything else germane, please let me know. Otherwise, I will see you on the twenty-third of August."

A few minutes later Noah walked out into the August heat onto State Street. He felt so depressed he didn't even bother to look for his tail until Court Street. He wasn't sure what prompted him to look back over his shoulder, but he was surprised not to see the Caucasian, so he stopped to look more carefully. When he still didn't see him, he felt somehow let down, like his life was in such dire straits that even his mysterious followers were abandoning him.

Thinking the man was being more subtle than usual, Noah continued at a slower pace to the northeastern end of the Boston Common. The route required a number of uniquely Boston twists and turns, due to the city having been designed more for horseback than cars. On each corner, Noah checked behind him, expecting to see his follower, but he was nowhere to be seen.

Suddenly feeling relieved rather than abandoned, Noah wondered what he should do to take advantage. Since he had no idea why he was being followed, it wasn't a totally rational thought. Nonetheless, the idea of visiting Louisburg Square occurred to him, maybe even ringing Ava's doorbell. What could he lose? Since his conversation with Leslie Saturday afternoon, his confusion about Ava had weighed on him. Although he had thought about trying to contact her again, he hadn't. The idea of confronting her seemed appropriate, although there was the question if she would even talk to him. He decided it was worth the risk.

Arriving outside her house, Noah climbed the half-dozen stairs of her stoop and entered her foyer. Since he knew she had a camera at her front door as part of her security system, he purposefully stood to the side to avoid being seen. He rang the bell. Staying perfectly still, he could hear a phone ring in the distance. When she didn't respond, he tried again. This time he heard her voice from a hidden speaker asking who was there.

"FedEx," Noah said in a falsetto, making him cringe at the absurdity of it all.

"Just leave it," Ava's voice said.

"I need a signature," Noah said in the same falsetto. He was embarrassed for himself and suppressed a nervous chuckle about the antics he was capable.

A moment later the door swung open. Ava was back to her yoga pants and tank top, presumably in anticipation of her afternoon workout. Within a fraction of a second her expression morphed from ennui to irritation when she caught sight of Noah. She started to close the door, but Noah inserted his foot like an old-fashioned door-to-door salesman.

"I need to talk to you," he said.

"I'm still angry with you," Ava said. She pushed the door against him, but not with much resolve.

"That's obvious. I want to know if you're aware that I have been suspended from the hospital."

"Of course I know," Ava said. "Everybody in the hospital knows, and no one can figure it out. You are a popular person. I give you that."

"Can I come in for a moment?"

Ava reluctantly opened the door, leaving it ajar. It was apparent she expected it was to be a short visit. Both cats appeared and sniffed Noah's leg.

Noah and Ava eyed each other. Finally, Noah spoke: "Knowing my commitment to surgery, I thought I would hear from you. I could have used some sympathy. I'm devastated, and I'm having trouble coping."

"As I said, I'm still really, really mad at you."

"But I apologized sincerely about violating your trust. I'm so sorry, Ava. I admitted my mistake of going on your computer. I thought you could forgive me and be supportive, considering how close we've become. If the tables were turned, I guarantee I'd be on your side."

"I'm not so sure about that," Ava said.

"Why not? Why would I lie to you?"

"You betrayed me. Not only did you go into my computer because you had misgivings about my anesthesia training, you went to my boss, Dr. Kumar, questioning my competence in regard to the three deaths. And you did it behind my back. You know how I know? He told me. He has that much confidence in me. How dare you?"

Noah felt his mouth go dry as he realized she was partially right. He had betrayed her in both circumstances. "I felt it was my ethical responsibility as the super chief resident to voice my concerns to the proper person. You weren't willing to talk to me about them. I'm not an anesthesiologist. In retrospect, it was a mistake to go to your chief. I should have gone to mine and let him talk to Dr. Kumar. I'm sorry for that, too."

"It seems that your ethics function selectively," Ava snapped. "The rumor is that you were suspended from the hospital for falsifying data on a thesis that helped get you into medical school."

"How did you know that?"

"Dr. Mason told Janet Spaulding, which is a sure way to get it all around the OR."

Noah knew there was no way Dr. Mason would have told the whole story. He worried how such rumors might affect the people on the Advisory Board.

"Dr. Kumar advised me to break off our relationship," Ava said. "He strongly suggested I avoid fraternizing with you."

For almost a full minute Noah and Ava stared at each other. Both were overwrought. Noah broke the silence: "So is this the end of our little romance?"

"I don't know," Ava said. "I'm trying to digest it all."

"If it is the end of our relationship," Noah said irritably, "there is one thing that I'd like to know. Were you the one who raised the Ph.D. thesis with Dr. Mason and got the damn thing from MIT?"

Ava threw her head back and laughed derisively. "Hell, no. I can't stand the blowhard. There's no way I would want to help him. Why would you even think such a thing?"

"Because you were the only person I've talked with about my thesis for years. And you are certainly the only person I've said anything to about 'fudging.' Dr. Mason wouldn't have come up with the idea on his own."

"It wasn't me," Ava snapped. "Maybe it was your old girlfriend who you ignored. Maybe she wanted to get back at you."

"It wasn't Leslie," Noah snapped back.

"Then I don't know who the hell it was," Ava said. "Now I want to work out. So if you don't mind, I'd like you to leave."

His emotions in turmoil, Noah walked out of Ava's house. When he'd entered, he'd felt perplexed, depressed, and anxious. Now he felt perplexed, depressed, and angry. Despite Ava's protestations to the contrary, she had to be the one who brought the stupid thesis issue to Dr. Mason's attention. Yet her suggestion about Leslie ate at him even though he was sure she could not be involved. She'd never acted angry when she left. If anyone had been angry, it had been Noah, but even he had been angry at himself not Leslie.

He pulled out his mobile phone as he headed up Revere Street toward his building and called her. He had no idea if she'd answer, but at least it was after 5:00, so he was reasonably confident he wouldn't be disturbing her at work.

"What's up?" Leslie responded after only two rings. "Are you okay?"

Noah assured her he was okay and explained that the reason for his call was just to ask her if, by any chance, she had ever said anything to anybody about his Ph.D. thesis, particularly recently.

"Absolutely not," Leslie said. "To tell you the honest truth, I completely forgot the whole story about your thesis until you brought it up on Saturday. I'd never given it any significance that you'd had to estimate some figures to get it in on time since you made the effort to replace them with the real ones when they were available. Besides, I'd never say anything to anybody about your thesis. I don't even remember the name."

"Okay, good," Noah said. "I just wanted to be sure."

"I've been thinking about your situation ever since we hung up on Saturday," Leslie said. "Are you interested in what I've been thinking?"

"I guess," Noah said.

"The more I think about it, the more certain I am that your erstwhile friend Ava has to be responsible for raising the thesis issue."

"I thought the same thing, since you and she were the only two people I'd ever confided in about it. Five minutes ago, I asked her point blank whether she'd done it, and she denied it."

"So she finally contacted you?" Leslie said.

"No, I went to her house and rang the bell." He was too embarrassed to mention the FedEx ruse.

"Was she at least friendly?"

"No. She said she was still angry at me."

"Did you believe her denial?"

"To some degree," Noah said. "She didn't hesitate in the slightest. She even mocked me for suggesting such a thing."

"Well, I certainly didn't do it," Leslie said. "And if she was the only other person who knew about this thesis issue, it would have had to have been her who spilled the beans. Yet it does seem out of keeping with how you described your relationship and certainly out of proportion to your going on her computer without permission."

"I did something else that I didn't tell you about," Noah said. He went on to admit that he'd gone to her boss behind her back with minor but nagging concerns about her professional performance in a couple critical situations.

"Ouch," Leslie said. "To my way of thinking, that could be interpreted

325

as betrayal more than accessing her computer, especially if she is as dedicated to her work as you say. How did she find out you went to her chief? Do you know?"

"He told her."

"Double ouch," Leslie said. "Now all this is making more sense. If she did blow the horn on your thesis, it could be a kind of sick tit-for-tat by forcing the surgery department to question your ethical competence."

"That's gone through my mind," Noah said.

"Is there a reason to question her competence?" Leslie asked.

"No," Noah said, "not really. She's a well-trained anesthesiologist who is religious about keeping up with her specialty. She's done thousands of cases at the BMH over the last five years. I've been told she passed her written and oral anesthesia boards with flying colors, which is no mean accomplishment. And to be hired by the BMH, she had to be seriously vetted. There is no doubt about her general competence."

Noah reached his building but hesitated going inside. He was afraid he'd cut Leslie off.

"Did you see the lawyer today?" Leslie asked.

"I did, but it was a bust. He must have just graduated from law school and got assigned all the crap cases. I can't imagine he'll be any help."

"I'm sorry."

"Thank you."

After saying goodbye, Noah hung up. Once inside his building he began to slowly climb the stairs. His legs felt strangely heavy again, as if they didn't want to return to his apartment any more than he did.

31

After getting into his apartment, Noah peeled off his damp shirt and tie, turned on the window air conditioner in the bedroom, and collapsed on his couch. It had been a discouraging day. Even the phone call with Leslie hadn't cheered him. Instead it had increased the anxiety and irritation he felt about Ava. And Ava's continued overtly defensive reactions whenever he tried to voice his misgivings about her three anesthesia deaths only heightened the concerns he had about her anesthesia training. It could have been so easy for Ava to reassure him, and if she had, he never would have even considered the misguided idea of going to Dr. Kumar, which ended up aggravating the situation. One way or another, Noah thought that the issue of Ava's sensitivity to questions about her professional training and competence demanded more attention if for no other reason than to take his mind off his own problems. It was also a type of therapy for his smoldering resentment in how Ava was treating him.

The question for Noah was how to go about doing it. Since Dr. Mason was the only other person who questioned Ava's competence, Noah thought for a fleeting moment about approaching him to ask if his opinion was based on anything other than using Ava as an easy mark for the Vincent case. The idea of attempting to have such a conversation brought a smile to Noah's face as he considered the absurdity of it. He doubted if the vain blowhard would even talk to him other than to gloat that he'd succeeded in getting Noah dismissed, and Noah couldn't imagine the conversation staying civil. Noah knew that he'd be unable to resist demanding to know who had alerted him to the Ph.D. issue.

And how the hell did his bound Ph.D. thesis end up on Dr. Mason's desk? The main MIT library where the bound theses were stored did not allow them to circulate now that all Ph.D. theses were available online. If people wanted to see the originals, they had to go to the library.

Noah checked the time. It was quarter past seven. He couldn't remember the summer hours of the main MIT library on Memorial Drive, but he assumed it would be open until at least 8:00 and possibly as late as midnight. Impulsively, he decided to visit as a way of getting out of his apartment. He knew the place well from having spent considerable time there when he was writing his thesis. What he had in mind was to find out who had borrowed his thesis and how it had been arranged.

Since it was a hot, muggy summer evening, a T-shirt, jeans, and tennis sneakers without socks sufficed. A few minutes later he was heading down Revere Street. His goal was the MBTA station at Charles Street. There were a lot of people out and about, particularly on Charles Street. When Noah restricted his life to the hospital and his apartment, it was always a minor shock to be reminded he was in the middle of a world-class city.

The subway station at Charles Street was elevated above the street at the Boston side of the Longfellow Bridge. Noah used the stairs instead of the escalator for a bit of exercise. Except for the trip to the lawyer's office and several excursions to Whole Foods, Noah had been vegetating in his apartment since Tuesday afternoon.

The platform was crowded, particularly at the head of the stairs but less so at the far end. Still, Noah held back, knowing it was best for him to be toward the rear of the train. He was only going one stop to Kendall

Square. It was for that reason that he had a view back down the stairs he'd just come up. With a minor start, he once again caught a view of the African American fellow who was on his way up on the escalator. When Noah had first emerged from his building, he'd looked for his followers but didn't see them. He didn't care one way or the other, as he'd become inured to their presence. If they had meant him harm, it would have already happened.

Noah studied the man as he approached. For a brief moment their eyes met. There was no sign of recognition on the part of the African American. Whoever he was, it was becoming clear to Noah that he was a professional, even if not as subtle in his technique as his colleague. When the man reached the platform, Noah toyed with the idea of approaching him and asking him if he was working for the hospital but then discarded the notion. Intuitively, he knew the man would deny trailing Noah just as he had the last time Noah spoke with him. Instead, Noah merely watched the man as he disappeared into the waiting crowd farther along the platform.

After detraining at the Kendall Square stop, Noah searched for his tail but didn't see him, at least not immediately. It wasn't until he was a few blocks away from the MIT Library that he saw him again when he looked over his shoulder. The man was at some distance but coming in Noah's direction. He was clearly not in a hurry but rather moving at Noah's moderate pace, seemingly content to keep Noah in sight. Noah shrugged, finding it mildly curious that the man's presence no longer caused him any concern, although he was still puzzled about the situation. The hospital would only care if he was on the hospital grounds, not what he was doing elsewhere.

As Noah reached the front door of the library, he noted it was open until 11:00 P.M. so there was no need to rush. He used his hospital ID to be admitted, which worked, since there was general sharing of research facilities among several of the academic institutions in the Boston area. Once inside he went directly to the library office to talk with one of the librarians on duty. The sole person available was named Gertrude Hessen.

"You are correct," Gertrude said in response to Noah's question. "Bound Ph.D. theses do not circulate. It has been a policy in place since all of them have been digitized."

Noah explained that he was a surgical resident at BMH and had been surprised to see a copy of his MIT thesis on a professor's desk. "Is there an exception to the rule for professors?" he asked.

"Not to my knowledge," Gertrude said. "Are you quite sure it was an original copy of your thesis?"

"There was no doubt," Noah said. "Would you mind if I checked the thesis room?"

"Not at all," Gertrude said. "Let me get you the key."

A few minutes later Noah was in the subterranean stacks of the library, standing at the locked wire cage that contained all the MIT theses going back to the nineteenth century. The key was attached to a wooden paddle by a short chain. Once he was inside, the heavy steel-and-wire door swung closed on its own. The click of the lock seemed loud in the total, mausole-umlike stillness. Noah noticed that the key was needed even to get out, giving him a creepy feeling. With so much material available online, few people ventured into library stacks anymore. Noah wondered how long it would take for him to be rescued if something went wrong and he couldn't get out of the cage, especially if Gertrude forgot she'd given out the key.

With some mild unease about his being isolated and locked in, Noah searched quickly for the section where his thesis would be located. The works were filed alphabetically by author rather than by subject matter. It didn't take him long to find the R's, and when he did, he was soon looking at the spines of two copies of his bound thesis. There was space for a third copy, but it was empty. Someone had managed to get the volume out of the library against the rules.

Happy to be back in the library office, Noah told Gertrude one of his bound volumes was definitely missing.

"I don't know what to say," Gertrude admitted with a flutter of her eyelids. "But what I will do is leave a note for the day people to investigate the matter. If you want to leave your mobile number, I can have someone get back to you."

When Noah emerged from the library, the sun had set but it was still light. The view of Boston reflected in the Charles River was stunning from the library steps. Noah hesitated for a moment to appreciate it and then scanned the area for his tail, but he was nowhere to be seen. Somewhat surprising himself, he again felt oddly ignored, similar to how he'd felt on leaving the lawyer's office. As lamentable as it sounded, his followers had been Noah's main connection with the outside world since Tuesday afternoon.

Several times on his way back to the subway stop at Kendall Square, he glanced over his shoulder, but there was no one there. Once he'd gotten to the underground station, Noah was happy his tail had disappeared. On his way to the library when he'd been followed, it had crossed his mind that he'd feel vulnerable on the way home, thinking that if anyone meant him harm, a deserted inbound platform would have been a perfect location. Now, as he waited for the subway, there was only one other person, and he was way down at the other end.

Noah felt a certain relief when the train thundered into the otherwise silent station, and he was able to board the front car with its complement of people. Ten minutes later he was on busy Charles Street, feeling comfortable being back in his neighborhood. As he passed the Thai restaurant that had supplied many of the take-out dinners he'd enjoyed with Ava, he hesitated. For the first time since the meeting in Dr. Hernandez's office, he felt hungry. After a moment of indecision, he went into the crowded restaurant and ordered what he'd eaten with Ava on so many occasions.

As the only solo diner in the entire restaurant, Noah felt out of place and wished he'd ordered take-out. He ate quickly and was soon back out on the street. It was now dark, with the iconic Beacon Hill gaslights providing the bulk of the ambient light. Hiking up Revere Street, he paused several times to look back, strangely hoping he'd see the African American. There were plenty of people. A neighbor whom he recognized from having seen over the years said hello to him as he passed in the opposite direction even though they had never spoken.

As he neared his building and dreaded being alone, he thought about returning to Ava's to see if she might relent and be willing to iron out their problems. But remembering her attitude, he thought the chances were slim and just showing up again might make things worse.

Climbing the stairs, he fished out his key so that by the time he was standing at his door he had it ready. Unfortunately, he didn't need it. Once again the door had been forced, and on this occasion, it hadn't just been forced. This time it was apparent a crowbar or something similar had been used, as there was a split between the doorknob and the jamb, with a portion of the jamb missing.

A wave of anger spread through Noah. Busting his door seemed unnecessarily aggressive, adding insult to injury. Using just his index finger, he pushed it open slowly. He reached within and flipped on the light. From where he was standing, everything seemed entirely normal. He listened intently for fear whoever had broken in might still be there, but the apartment was silent. All he could hear was some music with a heavy bass coming from the unit above.

32

Noah stepped over the threshold and went immediately to the folding table. He was relieved to see that on this occasion his laptop had not been moved. It was still positioned exactly as he had left it, aligned perfectly with the sides of the folding table. Quickly, he flipped open the computer and booted it up. A moment later he was able to check his browser's history. He wanted to see if it had been cleared as it had been on the recent break-in. It hadn't. He could see all the websites he'd visited that day. At least no one had been using his computer as had happened on the previous occasion.

After checking the kitchen for his few appliances, since a toaster had disappeared in the past, he was relieved to see that none were missing. Moving into the bedroom he immediately noticed that a small stack of spare change and a few single-dollar bills were gone. Otherwise, the room seemed the same as he had left it, including his rumpled bed that hadn't been made in more than a week.

Moving on into the bathroom, he noticed the mirrored medicine cabinet door was slightly ajar. He opened it and looked inside. Immediately, it was apparent that something else was missing. On the second shelf there had been an unopened prescription for Percocet that he'd been given after breaking his nose during the hospital softball game that spring. Now it was gone.

Believing his life was unraveling in all sectors, it took Noah some time and a hot shower to calm down from the trauma of yet another violation of his personal space. What bothered him the most on this occasion was the unnecessary physical damage to the door and the jamb. In the grand scheme of things, losing some spare change and an unwanted vial of Percocet was small potatoes in comparison to having to take the time and effort to convince the landlord to do a decent repair and do it immediately since the door couldn't be secured in its present state. And while he was in contact with the landlord, he was going to demand that the woman tenant above be strongly advised to limit her open-door policy with her many boyfriends. On the positive side, Noah was thankful the intruder didn't trash the apartment in frustration of finding so little of value.

When he was able to relax enough to think, Noah returned to his computer to learn more about Brazos University, its medical center, and its medical school. Comfortably clad only in his skivvies, he rebooted his machine.

Captivated by the extent of the material available, he learned that the university had grown at an impressive rate during the nineties, thanks to the beneficence of a large group of wealthy West Texas oilmen. Sam Weston, honored by the eponymous simulation center, was one of them. The medical school had opened in the mid-nineties upon completion of the nine-hundred-bed hospital, whereas the dental school had to wait until the early aughts. The medical school initially started with only thirty-five students, drawn mostly from West Texas high schools, although they did actively recruit American students who had been forced to attend medical schools in the Caribbean and Europe.

Noah went on to read that the Brazos University School of Medicine quickly had reached its present class size of 145 students. Graduate residency programs were started the same year the hospital opened its doors but initially limited to family practice, surgery, anesthesia, and internal medicine. Within just a few years a full complement of graduate education programs were added in all the specialties associated with a major tertiary care academic medical center with the openly stated goal to supply a wide range of medical talent for West Texas.

Next Noah turned specifically to the Brazos University Department of Anesthesiology, learning that it had recruited professors from a good number of the topflight medical centers around the country. The chief of Anesthesia had been brought in from Johns Hopkins, one of the USA's top academic medical centers, which impressed Noah considerably. He ascertained that all aspects of anesthesia were quickly integrated into the residency program, including sophisticated cardiac surgery, neurosurgery, and transplantation medicine. He also learned that twenty residents were admitted each year, and all residents were required to have performed at least twenty thousand cases during their training.

Noah rocked back from leaning over his laptop. As he stretched, he stared up at the ceiling. He no longer had any doubt that Ava had trained at a fully accredited institution with probably more than adequate supervision, especially considering that the Brazos University Medical Center handled more than twenty thousand major surgeries per year, which was about the same as the BMH. Brazos University might not be Ivy League, but from Noah's perspective, he thought it sounded perfectly adequate.

Noah wasn't completely satisfied, however, thinking it wasn't enough to learn she had been in an okay program. He craved more personal information, like exactly how many cases she had handled personally, what was the breakdown of the types of anesthesia, and if there had been any problems. After all, wanting to find out her residency case load had been his misguided motivation for going on her computer. Of course, he did recognize that her being hired by the BMH suggested she had done extraordinarily well, and Dr. Kumar had bragged that she had passed her anesthesia boards with flying colors. Yet Noah found himself motivated to find out more for three reasons. First, he was bored silly from being locked out of the hospital; second, he was infatuated with her and maybe even in love and eager to find out anything he could; and third, he was lonely, frustrated, and, most important, seriously pissed off at her for the way she was treating him despite his effusive and sincere apologies and his willingness to throw pride to the wind by ringing her doorbell. Whether she had anything to do with the thesis issue he tried not to even think about.

Rocking forward again, Noah suddenly had in mind to check what kind of firewall Brazos University had, if they had one, and if they did, whether it had ever been upgraded. It had been Noah's experience that young, rapidly growing institutions like Brazos U often lagged in cybersecurity, often relegating it to a low level of priority with a constant demand for funds elsewhere. Although Noah guessed that the hospital most likely had up-to-date digital security to satisfy HIPAA regulations, he thought the rest of the institution might be a relative pushover.

With his natural computer aptitude, Noah had engaged in some innocent hacking in his teenage years, purely for fun. Now he had the opportunity to apply these skills. What he was hoping to find were details of Ava's medical school and residency records, which he imagined were going to be stellar. Having just finished the resident evaluations for the BMH crew, he knew what kind of information was potentially available.

Going back to the websites of Brazos University School of Medicine and the Department of Anesthesia, he had it in mind to request application forms be emailed to him from both. Once that was done he planned to use the email headers to see if he could get into their systems. But as he waited for the first website to come up on his screen, alarm bells went off in his brain, reminding him that what he was about to attempt was illegal and certainly not ethical. If there was good security, there was a slight chance he could be discovered. With his upcoming Surgical Residency

Advisory Board meeting, being caught committing a cyber-felony was hardly advisable. In fact, it was downright stupid.

Suddenly, Noah had an idea. He knew he could not risk hacking into the Brazos University computer system, but that didn't mean someone else couldn't possibly get the same information in another, legal fashion. Noah had never thought of hiring a private detective. He'd never even met one and only knew of their existence from watching crime movies, where they seemed to play an oversized role. But here was a situation where a local private investigator would probably be able to get a significant amount of information and do it entirely aboveboard. The idea was, under the circumstances, decidedly appealing on a multitude of levels.

Having no idea what to expect, Noah googled *Private Investigators in Lubbock, Texas*. An instant later he was astounded at the selection of both PI firms and PI individuals. He looked at a few websites of the firms and decided they were too imposing and probably not sufficiently private for his comfort zone. If Noah was going to employ someone, which he hadn't completely decided, he wanted just an individual, not an entire organization, and one who worked out of the home and didn't even have a secretary. Although Noah knew what he was proposing was legal, he didn't want it to get back to Ava. As mad as she had been about his talking with Dr. Kumar, he certainly didn't want her finding out he'd hired a private investigator to look into her training. Yet he was progressively warming to the idea. He didn't see any other way to get answers without putting himself in jeopardy.

After looking over the websites of a dozen individuals, Noah found one that seemed promising. Her name was Roberta Hinkle. Part of her attraction was that she advertised she had gone to Brazos University where she had obtained a degree in Criminal Justice. Another plus was that she listed "background check" as one of her specialties, which was essentially what Noah wanted. He also appreciated that she listed her hourly rate, whereas most of the other people did not. Although Noah initially thought $60 per hour was high, it was less than most of the other sites that did list their fee. Impulsively, he decided to find out more.

Roberta Hinkle's website invited either phone or email contact for more information. Since it was after 11:00, Noah opted to use email. To make it easy there was an online form to be filled out with his name, email address, and the kind of investigation desired. Along with his name he included his title of M.D. In the investigation section to make it sound like a group effort, he wrote: "We are interested in a strictly confidential, full background check on an anesthesiologist on our staff by the name of Dr. Ava London. We need to know more details of her professional training and her earlier schooling. All information made available will be appreciated including psychosocial factors. Dr. London grew up in Lubbock, attended Brazos University School of Medicine and trained at the Brazos University Hospital but now works in Boston, Massachusetts."

In the section of the form labeled "payment preference," Noah wrote "PayPal" to make it simple. In the section labeled "start date," he wrote "ASAP if it is decided to move forward."

After Noah clicked send, he again felt a letdown similar to when he realized the idea of his hacking the Brazos University computer system was off the table. Again, with the PI idea, he had gotten himself worked up, and now he had to sit on his hands and wait. He wondered when he might hear back from Roberta Hinkle, understanding it depended completely on her schedule. If she were busy, it might be days. If she wasn't, then it could possibly be within twenty-four hours. Vaguely, he wondered how busy Lubbock PI's were in mid-summer. Unfortunately, there was no way to know answers to any of these questions. The only thing he could do was call Roberta's phone number in the morning.

For lack of anything else to do, Noah decided to go on Facebook to see if Gail Shafter or Melanie Howard, meaning Ava, were online. Yet he didn't want to do it as Noah Rothauser. Instead, he decided to create his own sockpuppet, calling himself Butch Cassidy, in deference to one of his favorite old movies. That would make it such that Ava wouldn't know she was dealing with him if she happened to be on Facebook. But then he changed his mind about the name. As smart as Ava was, he was afraid she might recognize the name as too much of a coincidence, as they had talked about movies on several occasions. Instead, he decided to call himself Harvey Longfellow, which he just pulled out of the air. At least it sounded appropriately New England.

As Noah was creating the profile of a thirty-year-old love-starved insurance salesman who hated Ivy League snobs, a point he thought Ava might appreciate, he was alerted to an incoming email. Since he wasn't finished with Harvey's profile, he used his phone to see who had emailed him, hoping it might be Roberta Hinkle, and it was.

> Dear Dr. Rothauser: Thank you for your inquiry about possibly retaining my services to undertake a confidential, in-depth background check of Dr. Ava London. I can start tonight with my online sources if you decide to move forward. If you know actual dates of her personal history and the name of her high school, it would be helpful to make sure I am researching the correct individual. Any other pertinent information you might have would also be of assistance for the same reason.
> Respectfully yours, Roberta Hinkle.

Amazed at the rapidity of Roberta's reply, Noah minimized his profile of Harvey Longfellow and immediately began a long email back to Roberta:

> Dear Ms. Hinkle, I appreciate your rapid reply. Here is what I know, although all the dates might not be accurate. She was born in 1982. I do not know where she went to elementary or

middle school, but I was told she went to Coronado High School, where she was a cheerleader and took AP courses. I believe she graduated in 2000. Between 2000 and 2002 she worked for a dentist by the name of Winston Herbert, who became dean of the newly created Brazos University School of Dentistry. She then attended Brazos University for a six-year combined B.S./ M.D. curriculum from 2002 to 2008 with a major in nutrition. After obtaining her M.D. degree, she took a residency in anesthesia at the Brazos University Medical Center from 2008 to 2012. Following her residency, she was offered a position as a staff anesthesiologist at the Boston Memorial Hospital beginning in 2012. Some of these dates are guesses, but they should be close. Other important information: her oil-executive father committed suicide when she was a junior in high school, and she was briefly married around 2000 to a Serbian medical doctor. Although we will find all information about her pertinent, what we are mainly hoping to learn are details about her residency training, and the more detailed the better. We would be particularly interested in whatever any of the faculty remembers about her, which seems would have to be significant for her to get the kind of recommendations needed for her to be hired by the Boston Memorial Hospital. If anyone asks, you can say that she has earned high praise from the BMH chief of Anesthesia. Last point of information is that she is a devotee of Facebook, which she avowedly uses daily but only via aliases named Gail Shafter and Melanie Howard. For a current picture of Dr. Ava London, please check out her LinkedIn page. Does this sound like a job you would be interested in accepting? I must emphasize that confidentiality is key.

Sincerely yours, Dr. Noah Rothauser

After rereading the email and making a few minor changes, Noah sent it off. He then brought up the profile he had been creating for his fake Facebook account. No sooner had he reread what he had written about Harvey Longfellow when a second email came in from Roberta Hinkle.

> Dr. Rothauser: Thank you for the information. I am very interested in accepting your proposed investigation, and I can assure you that it will be done in strict confidentiality, as is the case with all my work. Let me know if you want me to begin.
> Roberta Hinkle

Noah went back to staring up at the ceiling, trying to decide what to do. He had an immediate good feeling about Roberta Hinkle and liked that she was eager and could start right away. With the same impulsivity that had encouraged him to respond to Roberta's website, he decided to go ahead with hiring her. He knew that if he changed his mind overnight, he could stop her efforts. He emailed her back to give her the go-ahead. Almost immediately a reply came back:

> Dear Dr. Rothauser: I am looking forward to this project and will start immediately. I will email you tomorrow what my initial inquiries uncover. This should not be a difficult assignment as I also attended Brazos University and have maintained close contacts by continuing to teach an introductory criminal justice course.
> All the best, Roberta Hinkle

Impressed with Roberta's rapid responses and seeming professionalism, Noah emailed her back that he would be looking forward to her email. Once again, he cautioned her that discretion was paramount. She responded that she understood perfectly and emphasized that strict confidentiality was the nature of the business. She told him not to worry.

After the final email with Roberta, Noah tried to go back to his fake profile, but found he couldn't concentrate. He kept wondering what Roberta might find above and beyond all the complimentary stuff he expected, since Ava certainly had to have done extremely well. Despite Roberta's reassurances, he worried if her questioning might somehow get back to Ava and, if it did, what effect that might have. Would Ava suspect that Noah was behind it? He doubted she would, but who was to know? For a few moments, he thought about emailing back and canceling the investigation, but then he changed his mind again. He'd wait for her morning email. Tonight, Roberta was only going to see what she could learn online.

At that point, Noah noticed it was after midnight. More important, with the feeling he had done something that was potentially promising to dispel once and for all his misgivings about Ava, he felt as if he could finally sleep. He turned off his laptop and the overhead light in the living room, pushed his couch against his broken door for an attempt at security, and went into the bedroom.

33

For the first time in a week Noah had slept reasonably well and woke up refreshed. He attributed it to having hired the private investigator in Lubbock. Engaging the PI gave him the feeling he was doing something positive about Ava, and he was comfortable with the decision. He would have much preferred she was willing to discuss the nettlesome questions he had about her performance in her three deaths, but clearly that wasn't going to happen. Short of his hacking into the Brazos University computer system, it was the only way it might be accomplished. He justified it as ultimately being in her best interests. Just as he expected to be reinstated at the Advisory Board meeting, he was hopeful that Ava was going to ultimately accept his heartfelt apologies and let bygones be bygones. They were too well suited for each other and had been too close in mind and body for any other outcome. And the next time she voiced any thoughts about leaving clinical anesthesiology, he wanted to be sure of her competence.

At 8:00 A.M., Noah surprised himself by going out for eggs and bacon at a local greasy spoon. He'd even read *The New York Times* like a normal person. He'd also gotten some bread and cold cuts for a later lunch before returning to his apartment. His plan had been to finish creating his Harvey Longfellow sockpuppet and then go on Facebook to try to friend both Gail Shafter and Melanie Howard. His hope had been that, come evening, he could be messaging back and forth with an unsuspecting Ava.

It was at 2:52 in the afternoon that the reasonably pleasant day started to fall apart when his mobile phone went off, startling him. Snapping it up, he looked at the screen, hoping it might be Ava. But it wasn't. It was the MIT Library.

"Is this Dr. Rothauser?"

"Yes, it is."

"This is Telah Smith calling. I got a note from Gertrude Hessen that you were interested in finding out why a copy of your bound thesis had been removed from the thesis room. Are you still interested? Because I was the assistant librarian responsible for letting it circulate."

"I am," Noah said, impressed that they were getting back to him so quickly.

"Several FBI agents had come into the library and requested the volume, saying it was needed for a short time as part of an ongoing investigation."

Noah was stunned. He couldn't believe what he was hearing. "FBI?"

"We get occasional requests of this sort," Telah explained. "It is less frequent now that all theses are available in digital form, but it does happen."

"Did they have a warrant?" Noah asked. He was astounded that Dr. Mason would go to the extreme of involving the FBI. And he was even more astounded that the FBI would be interested in becoming involved.

"No, they didn't," Telah said. "They spontaneously mentioned getting a warrant if it was necessary, but they preferred to keep the case on a low-key basis as it was not a criminal investigation. They said that although the material was available online, it would speed things up for them to have the hard copy, and they would be extremely careful with it and need it for only a few days. I brought the issue up with the head librarian, who authorized it to be released for one week, as the library has had good relations with the FBI in the past. The two agents were very nice about it. They were very young and personable and rather handsome." Telah laughed. "I know that doesn't sound very professional, but the visit was a nice break from what normally goes on around here."

"Thank you for letting me know about this," Noah said, searching for something to say. After he disconnected the call, he stared out the window for several minutes, totally taken aback by involvement of the FBI. He couldn't help but feel nervous about such an unexpected development, and it unpleasantly undermined the optimism he had been recently feeling about the Advisory Board meeting. The mere involvement of the FBI gave the accusation that he'd fabricated data a credibility it did not deserve.

In the middle of this new confusion, Noah's phone chimed to indicate he'd just gotten an email. Trying to calm down, he saw it was from Roberta Hinkle. Hoping for some more comforting news, he used his laptop to read what Roberta had written. It didn't take long for his hopes to be dashed.

> Dear Dr. Rothauser: Things have not been going as smoothly as I had anticipated. First, there was no Ava London in the Coronado High School class of 2000. In fact, there had been no young woman by the name of Ava London attending Coronado High School going back fifty years from 2005. I then checked all the other high schools in Lubbock and found that there had been no Ava London for the same fifty-year interval. I then began searching high schools in the surrounding metropolitan area, where there are high schools in most of the larger towns.

After considerable effort, I did find an Ava London in the class of 2000 in Brownfield High School, about an hour's drive from Lubbock. Apparently, she was a very popular cheerleader, and took a number of AP classes, and was consistently on the honor roll. She was also a member of the student council and her father was an oil executive who committed suicide, so it sounds like the same Ava London you have retained me to do a background check on. At this very moment, I am in the Kendrick Public Library in Brownfield, and I am looking at the high school's yearbook for 2000, which has a number of photos of Ava London that conform with the photo of Dr. Ava London on her LinkedIn page. However, a major, unexpected problem has come up that I think you should know about, especially if you want me to continue.

Respectfully, Roberta Hinkle

Noah shook his head in frustration, wondering why Roberta would not have told him directly what the problem was. As he typed a reply asking to be told the problem, he tried to imagine what the PI had uncovered. Whatever it was, it must have been surprising and off-putting. Roberta responded immediately with another email.

Dr. Rothauser, I have uncovered a major complication with Ava London's life story. Perhaps it would be best if we talked directly as it is all rather strange.

Respectfully, Roberta Hinkle

Snatching up his phone, Noah called Roberta's cell phone number. Impatiently, he waited for the call to go through. He couldn't help but feel irritated that she was dragging out telling him what she had learned. Even when she answered, she didn't tell him right away but instead asked him to hold on while she went outside the library. As he waited, Noah began restlessly drumming his fingers on his folding table.

"All right, I'm back," Roberta said. She had a pleasant voice with a slight twang that appropriately reminded him of Ava's voice. "I apologize if this all sounds rather mysterious. Here's the problem: Everything you said about Ava London's high school experience was true except that she had gone to Brownfield High School and not Coronado. But, more important, she did not graduate."

"Excuse me?" Noah questioned. He wasn't sure he'd heard correctly.

"Ava London committed suicide during her senior year exactly twelve months after her father and used the same gun in the same fashion and in the same room of the house. After I discovered this unexpected fact from the memorial in the high school yearbook, I went back and looked at the appropriate issue of the local newspaper published during the week following the event. There were a lot of articles because the tragedy was a major, upsetting episode for the entire town and sparked an investigation by the local authorities. Both the father and the daughter were popular figures in the town. Although no one was ultimately blamed or charged for the tragedy, it was thought by many that Ava's suicide might have been an early case of cyberbullying. Of course, it wasn't yet called cyberbullying, but that was what they were describing. At least three of Ava's classmates were named, and it was considered probable that more were involved. The names of the three were Connie Dugan, Cynthia Sanchez, and Gail Shafter."

For almost a full minute neither Roberta nor Noah spoke. Noah was stunned for the second time within the hour, and even more so than learning the FBI had been responsible for Dr. Mason getting his thesis. It was Roberta who broke the silence after giving Noah enough time to absorb what she had told him. "Do you want me to continue my investigations?"

"Hold off for now," Noah said. "Let me digest this weird revelation. I'll call you back."

After disconnecting the phone, Noah got up to pace in an attempt to get his mind around what he had learned. With the size of the room, there wasn't nearly enough space. After four steps, he had to turn around. But he felt he had to move. For a few minutes as he walked back and forth, he fantasized about confronting Ava that afternoon when she came home from the hospital to tell her he'd discovered that Ava London was the sockpuppet, not Gail Shafter. But he gave up on the idea as a childish urge for a bit of revenge that she, too, had been harboring a secret a lot stranger than his having had to make estimates on his thesis project to get it in on time. Besides, he didn't know for certain if she had anything at all to do with his current thesis fracas.

Instead, Noah picked his phone back up with the idea of reconnecting with Roberta Hinkle. But that turned out to be problematic for the time being. On his screen was a text from her:

> I'm on my way back to Lubbock and the phone signal gets bad.
> Leave me a voicemail if you can't get through, and I will return
> your call. Or you can email me. Roberta

Noah responded by email:

> Ms. Hinkle: Despite this surprising twist to the story, I would
> like you to continue investigating Dr. Ava London's professional
> training record at Brazos University. In keeping with what you
> have learned, I would like you also to check to see if there are
> any court records in and around Lubbock of someone assum-
> ing the name of Ava London around the year 2000. As a final
> request, would you send me photos from the 2000 Brownfield
> Yearbook of Ava London and Gail Shafter?
> Much obliged, Dr. Rothauser

Sending off the email, Noah stared at his computer, wondering what he could find out about Ava using his BMH super chief log-in information. Since he was technically still a member of the surgical staff despite his current suspension, his position allowed him access to a very wide range of BMH data banks, possibly even employee information. Suddenly, he thought it would be ironic after considering hacking into Brazos University if he could get access perfectly legally to Ava's BMH records and possibly see who from the Brazos University Department of Anesthesia had written recommendations for her and possibly read them.

After typing in a bit of information and a few clicks, he was in the BMH computer. A few moments later he was poised to try to go into employee records, but he hesitated. With his computer savvy, he knew that the BMH computer would be recording everything he did while he was logged in. It was standard procedure. His concern was that someone, knowing he had been suspended, might have set it up so that his use of the computer would be flagged. If that were the case, it could reflect badly on him during the upcoming Advisory Board meeting that he had been snooping in employee records. It wouldn't be as bad as hacking into the Brazos University computer, but bad enough.

"Damn!" Noah voiced. It was frustrating to feel thwarted at every turn. Just as he was in the process of logging out from the BMH computer, there was a ping from his phone, indicating that he'd just received an email. Quickly switching to his email inbox on his laptop, he saw it was from Roberta Hinkle. But before he could open it, he noticed that it has been read before he clicked on it. Noah stared in confusion where the little blue dot had been. He looked at the time of the email. As he suspected, it had just arrived, so there was no way he would have read it. Then the blue dot suddenly returned.

Noah froze as a chill descended his spine. He lifted his hands off his keyboard, staring at the blue dot. Slowly he turned his laptop around first one way and then the other, looking at all the expansion slots. He didn't see anything, but that didn't relieve his fear. Knowing what he did about computers, he instantly knew he'd been hacked, perhaps with Spyware and a Keylogger. Someone had read his incoming email, meaning they had also been reading his outgoing email. Someone was spying on him, digitally watching him. Could it have something to do with the two men who had taken turns following him? In his mind's eye, he saw the face of the African American he'd confronted. Then Noah remembered the woman from the MIT library describing the men who had come for Noah's thesis as attractive. Could they have been the same men following him, and if they were, why would the FBI be following him? If they were FBI?

If someone was monitoring his computer use in real time, Noah was relieved he hadn't tried to look up Ava's hospital employee record. His next thought was the realization that the break-in yesterday hadn't been for spare change and a Percocet prescription, but rather to bug his computer. Quickly, Noah reached forward and pressed the power button, turning the blasted laptop off. He got up and went to the window. He couldn't help but worry that whoever had broken into his apartment could be close, watching him physically as well as digitally. There were a few vans double parked on Revere Street. As crowded as Beacon Hill was, it was difficult for electricians, plumbers, and other services to ply their trades. There was never any place to park. So there was no specific reason to suspect any of the vans were there for malicious purposes, but they could have been.

A wave of paranoia spread through Noah, making him painfully aware of his absolute vulnerability. The thought again occurred to him that perhaps the hospital was behind all these shenanigans to buttress their case against him. But he dismissed the thought as totally unrealistic. The issue of a possible minor ethical violation a decade ago on a thesis project hardly warranted continuous and possibly illegal surveillance. Noah searched for something bigger, more sinister, but what? Nothing came to mind other than his questioning Ava's competence, irritating her lobbying boss. But that seemed ridiculously far-fetched. He even mockingly laughed at the idea that the Nutritional Supplement Council might be taking issue with Noah's questioning Ava's ability with an advanced laryngoscope. It was an absurd notion.

But there was one thing Noah was certain about: he did not want to remain a sitting duck in his isolated apartment with its door busted. Anyone could walk in at any moment by just giving the door a forceful push. Besides, if his computer was bugged, which was 99 percent certain as far as he was concerned, the apartment itself could be bugged. Someone could be literally watching him at that very moment. With that thought in mind, he glanced around the room, knowing how small a wireless, wide-angle video recorder could be and how easily it could be hidden.

Making a snap decision to vacate, he leaped up and dashed back into his bedroom. Getting a backpack out of his closet, he tossed in some toiletries and some clothes. He then changed into his whites, or the usual outfit he wore as a surgical resident. Although he hadn't thought of all the potential repercussions, his immediate plan was to go to the hospital and hole up in the on-call suite with its lounge and multiple bedrooms. He didn't know how long he would be able to get away with staying there, as rampant as hospital gossip was, but he thought he'd feel safer than he did in his apartment.

He grabbed his cell phone. His hospital tablet was already in his jacket pocket. He left the laptop on the folding table but took the time to align it as he normally did. He even opened the lid slightly so that when he returned he could tell if someone had disturbed it.

After a quick glance around, trying to think if there was anything else he should take, he went out into the stairwell. It was then that he thought about rigging something so that he could tell if his door was opened while he was away. But then he accused himself of being overly melodramatic. What he'd done with the computer was enough. It was the computer tampering that upset him. It suggested sophistication.

He closed his apartment door gently to avoid further damage. Unless someone looked carefully, the split wasn't obvious as the major jamb damage was on the inside. With his backpack slung over his shoulder, he rapidly descended the stairs. As he neared the bottom, he slowed as the view out onto Revere Street came into focus through the small decorative panes of glass in the upper section of the front door. His view was limited to the car parked directly in front of his building. He didn't see any pedestrians, which concerned him. At that time on a summer afternoon there were usually people all over Beacon Hill.

Descending the remaining steps, Noah opened the door. A young woman in cutoff jeans and a halter top popped into view not six feet away, heading down the street. She warily glanced up at Noah, as if she was wondering why he was standing motionless in an open doorway. In the next instant, she was gone.

From Noah's perspective, seeing the girl was reassuring. Still, he felt decidedly uneasy. Leaving the building door ajar, he descended the three outdoor steps within the building's exterior alcove. His intention was to look up and down the street. Since it was a one-way street coming up the hill, Noah looked in that direction first. What he saw was not encouraging. Three buildings down was a black late-model Ford van with two men in the front seats. It didn't look like the usual service truck. It was too new and shiny and had an out-of-state license plate. Worse yet, the moment Noah appeared, it lurched forward with a squeal of its tires and came rapidly in Noah's direction.

As fearful and keyed up as Noah was, he reacted by pure reflex. A second later he was back inside his building, slamming the door, throwing the deadbolt, and taking the stairs at a run. Outside he heard the Ford van screech to a stop, which only increased his panic. He didn't bother using his key on his own door but rather just broke through it using his shoulder. He slammed the door behind him and pulled the couch over in front of it. He knew it wouldn't prevent someone from coming in, but it might at least slow them down.

Without another second's hesitation, he ran into his bedroom and over to the window, throwing up the sash. A moment later he was out on the rickety fire escape, plunging down the narrow metal steps and leaping into the building's postage-stamp-size yard. After first tossing his backpack over the ramshackle back fence, Noah scaled it himself, dropping into the neighboring yard. He did the same thing with a series of dilapidated fences that defined an entire warren of tiny backyards behind the four- and five-story buildings that lined Revere Street, the adjacent Grove Street, and the parallel Phillips Street. Although Noah had never been in the courtyard, he had been able to see a good portion of it from his bedroom window over the years. What he was counting on was finding an exit that he hoped would eventually lead out onto Phillips Street.

The going was not easy. Not only were the fences in poor repair, which made climbing them difficult, but some of the backyards were filled with all kinds of trash, including discarded baby carriages, mattresses, and old tires. At one point, he had to climb down a short, rocky precipice, since Phillips Street was at a significantly lower elevation than Revere Street. Eventually, he was able to reach Phillips Street by way of a narrow alley that ran alongside a building that was part of the Black Heritage Tour of Beacon Hill.

A few passersby on Phillips Street gave Noah a strange look, but no one said anything or acted alarmed. Noah assumed his medical uniform helped calm any suspicions that he was a burglar. But by the time he had finished his tortuous backyard journey, his white pants and jacket were a bit worse for wear, and he had lost the collection of pens that normally occupied his jacket's breast pocket.

With no late-model Ford van in sight, Noah ran down to Cambridge

Street. There he turned east, heading for the Boston waterfront and the BMH complex. He slowed his gait and tried to act calm even though he didn't feel calm. He kept looking ahead and behind for a shiny new Ford van or for his followers.

After several blocks Noah paused long enough to remove his backpack, dust off his clothes, and straighten his tie in an effort to make himself a bit more presentable. Fifteen minutes later he walked up the circular drive at the front entrance to the Stanhope Pavilion, feeling his pulse quicken. Ahead was BMH security. Though Noah knew many of the security personnel by sight, and they surely knew him, he worried he might be stopped if his suspension was common knowledge, especially since he looked moderately bedraggled, which might have raised suspicions.

Holding up his hospital ID as he normally did but without making eye contact, Noah walked at a brisk clip past the security desk, pretending to be in a rush. At any second he half expected to hear someone calling his name, but it didn't happen. Relieved, he ducked into the first stairwell he passed. He knew better than to use the elevator.

Entering the expansive on-call facility, which was empty at that hour of the day, Noah first went to the laundry room and got clean pants and jacket. Then he put his name down on the master list for one of the dozen bedrooms and took the appropriate key. Before going to the room, he went to his locker. Every resident at the BMH had a locker where they stored their heavy coats during the winter and kept personal items.

The rooms were spartan and windowless but perfectly adequate for a few hours of needed sleep during a busy night. The furniture consisted of a simple single bed, a bureau, and a desk with a hospital monitor. There was a small bathroom with a shower stall en suite. Towels and linen were changed every day.

Noah felt immediately at home. Over the previous five years he had used the on-call facility far more than anyone else, simply because he spent far more time in the hospital than anyone else. Never once in all the times he had been there had all the bedrooms been utilized, which was the reason he thought he could get away with staying there. How long he could get away with it, he didn't know, but he wasn't interested in returning to his apartment until everything was sorted out.

He changed into the clean clothes, then checked his phone to see if Roberta Hinkle had emailed him back. She had:

> Dr. Rothauser, I got your last email and will be happy to continue investigating Dr. Ava London. I'll go to Brazos University tomorrow. I don't see any problem from here on out, and I don't expect it will take very long as I have contacts in the administration. I will also check court records as you requested. About the photos you requested: is there a rush on them or can I wait until I have more time to drive back to Brownfield? Let me know. Otherwise I will be back to you shortly.
>
> Respectfully, Roberta Hinkle

Noah immediately emailed back:

> Dear Ms. Hinkle: Thank you for your efforts. There is no rush on the photos, but we are interested in seeing them whenever it is convenient for you to return to Brownfield. There is also no rush on the court records. We are much more interested in what you are able to learn at Brazos Medical Center. Once again, I would like to remind you that confidentiality is of utmost importance. We look forward to hearing from you. It would be convenient if you give us at least an update on your progress tomorrow afternoon.
>
> With kind regards, Dr. Noah Rothauser

With that out of the way, his mind switched to Ava. He missed her and the relationship that they had, despite his irritation at her behavior. If only he had resisted the temptation to check her computer that evening, he might very well be comfortably staying with her at her fabulous manse instead of at the utilitarian BMH Ritz, as it was jokingly called by the resident staff.

34

The sleek Citation X jet taxied up to the area in front of the General Aviation section of the Preston Smith Airport in Lubbock, Texas. The flight had been chartered by ABC Security and had left Bedford, Massachusetts, a little after 9:00 Tuesday night. Passengers Keyon Dexter and George Marlow had used the flight time to do the necessary due diligence on Private Investigator Roberta Hinkle. They had been informed by their handler that she was considered a threat of the highest order, which necessitated the night flight.

Roberta Hinkle lived in a small ranch-style house to the west of town and just inside the city's ring road. Her main specialty as a private investigator involved domestic disputes and infidelity investigations, which both Keyon and George assumed would have created lots of enemies for her, which would provide a handy cover for what they were about to do. She was also divorced, which increased the chances that she would be alone. The only problem was that she had an eleven-year-old daughter. Both Keyon and George were worried that could be a problem if the child awoke. Although they were both emotionally acclimatized to the nature of their work, they were still squeamish about a few things.

As soon as the copilot opened the plane's door and lowered the steps,

Keyon and George deplaned. A few minutes later they were on their way in a rented Chevy Suburban ABC Security had arranged to be waiting for them. Within fifteen minutes of touchdown, the men were already traveling south toward the city center on Interstate 27.

George was driving, and it soon irritated him that Keyon had almost immediately fallen asleep with his seat cranked back as far as it would go. Out of spite George did a little S-maneuver by yanking on the steering wheel, creating enough force to jostle Keyon awake.

"What the hell?" Keyon blurted. He'd grabbed the armrest to steady himself even though the seat belt would have sufficed.

"Must have been an armadillo," George said, pretending to be looking in the rearview mirror. "I don't know if I hit him or not."

Keyon cast a quick look behind them. The road was clear. He turned back to George. "Are you bullshitting me or what?"

George laughed. "Well, maybe it wasn't an armadillo. Maybe it was a coyote or whatever else they have running around out here in this godforsaken country." The land was desertlike and as flat as a pancake, with only a bit of scrub. It reminded him of parts of Iraq, which wasn't a pleasant memory. "But I would like to point out that this is a two-man job."

"All right, all right," Keyon complained, but he'd gotten the message. He straightened up his seat and took a few deep breaths.

"You know," George said, "I'm really pissed we weren't given the go-ahead to get rid of Rothauser as soon as he was suspended. I thought that was the plan instead of just keeping him under surveillance. The way he was acting, it would have been easy to make it look like a suicide. I knew he was going to be trouble from the word *go*."

"It pisses me off he got away from us," Keyon said. "I wonder what spooked him."

"No way to know," George said.

"I never thought there was a way to get out of that backyard maze, except back onto Revere Street."

"Obviously, we should have checked it out more than we did," George said. "At the same time, there was no way to anticipate him bolting. But it could be worse. At least we know where the hell he is, thanks to pinging his mobile phone."

"But there's not much we can do with him staying in the hospital other than wait for him to come out into the real world."

"I'm shocked he's there at all, considering he was suspended," George said. "It can't last more than a night or so. The hospital admin's not going to tolerate it. I thought he'd go to a hotel or a friend's house."

"Me, too," Keyon said. "But the nerd's got an attitude. He had the balls to confront me when I ended up having to walk past him the other day. He even grabbed my arm."

"I wonder what the hell motivated him to hire a damn PI?" George said.

"No clue," Keyon said. "He's a loose cannon. And the longer we wait, the more trouble he's likely to cause. At this point he's got to be neutralized ASAP."

"I think we should let the higher-ups know how we feel. Maybe they just don't get it, having us dick around for a week like they have."

"I think they finally get it," Keyon said. "It's the only explanation for why they're willing to spend the money having the Citation Jet wait for us. They want us back in Boston tonight. Otherwise, they would have had us go back commercial in the morning."

"How long do you think this job should take?"

"Unless something goes wrong, it shouldn't take us long, maybe an hour at most."

"We're coming up to the Ring Road Two Eighty-nine," George said. "We're supposed to head west, correct?"

"Yup," Keyon said, looking at his Google Maps on his phone. "And then a right on Route Sixty-two and we're almost there."

35

Cocooned in the familiar on-call room and feeling safe, Noah slept like a baby. The previous evening he'd remained in the room and avoided the lounge area for fear of running into surgical residents who would invariably question what he was doing there. He was certain they'd be sympathetic and would not blow the whistle, yet it would invariably start gossip that would go around the hospital like an influenza outbreak, eventually alerting the powers that be. Hunger had finally driven him to make a quick visit to the cafeteria after 11:00 P.M. when he thought it would be mostly deserted. As luck would have it, Dr. Bert Shriver, the on-call chief resident, was also there, having a late supper after being caught in surgery all evening.

Bert was aware of Noah's suspension and had immediately voiced the hope that Noah would be reinstated following the Surgical Residency Advisory Board meeting. Since Noah knew that Bert sat on the board, he had taken the opportunity to clarify the details, which Bert had been unaware of because Dr. Mason had been the source of the gossip. Bert had been under the mistaken impression that it was an established fact that Noah had fabricated all the data for his thesis. When Bert had learned the truth from Noah, he promised to clue in the other resident board members.

When asked why he was in the hospital cafeteria so late, Noah admitted he was staying the night in the on-call room because of a break-in at his apartment. Since Bert was also a Beacon Hill resident in a similar absentee-landlord building with a number of student tenants, he understood immediately why Noah would feel vulnerable.

Although Noah had asked Bert to keep Noah's presence in the on-call room a secret, Noah knew that it was just a matter of time before word got out. As a consequence, the first thing he did that morning when he awoke was call his landlord, demanding his apartment door be replaced and the woman above be warned about giving out front-door keys.

By 9:30 A.M. Noah was ready to try his luck at getting to the hospital cafeteria without being noticed. As he was about to leave his hideout, his mobile phone began to ring. It was an unknown number, yet he recognized the 806 area code as the same as Roberta Hinkle's. Thinking it might be her, he answered.

"Is this Dr. Noah Rothauser?"

"It is," Noah answered. Without knowing why, he immediately felt on edge.

"This is Detective Jonathan Moore of the Persons Crimes Section of the Lubbock, Texas, Police Department. I have a few questions as part of an investigation. Is this a convenient time to talk?"

"I guess," Noah said. Instinctively, he knew he was not going to be happy about this unexpected telephone call. Coming from the police, there was no way it could be good news.

"First and foremost, I would like to ascertain that you retained Roberta Hinkle for investigative services?"

"Why are you asking?" Noah said hesitantly. This was not the confidentiality he had expected.

"Your phone number was found on Roberta Hinkle's phone record," Detective Moore said. "We are calling all her clients. You are the only one from out of town."

"Yes, I did retain Ms. Hinkle," Noah said reluctantly. He had no idea what this was about. His immediate worry was that it had something to do with the hospital, his suspension, and the hacking of his computer. Whoever had hacked his computer would have been privy to his email exchange with the private investigator.

"Was your interest in Roberta Hinkle's services because of a marital or domestic issue of some kind?" Detective Moore asked.

"Absolutely not," Noah said quickly. He was caught off guard by such a question coming out of the blue. "Is she all right?"

"Usually I am the one who asks the questions," Detective Moore said emphatically. "Would you be willing to tell me what kind of investigative work Roberta Hinkle was doing for you? But before you answer, let me remind you that you could be subpoenaed to do so, meaning that it would save time and effort if you are cooperative. Otherwise, you might be forced to come here to Lubbock."

"It was merely an employment background check," Noah said with equal rapidity. His sense was that this unexpected call had nothing to do with BMH.

"Did you know that Roberta Hinkle's main specialty was domestic or marital issues?"

"I did not," Noah said. "Her website said she did background checks, which is what was needed. It also said she had graduated from Brazos University, which seemed convenient. The employee she was investigating attended the same university."

"You found Roberta Hinkle online?"

"I did," Noah said. "And we communicated first by email and then several phone calls."

"Did you ever meet Roberta Hinkle in person?"

"I did not," Noah said.

"What hospital are you with?"

"The Boston Memorial," Noah said. "I am a surgical chief resident."

He purposely did not let on that he was currently suspended from active duty.

"Okay," Detective Moore said. "Thank you for your time and cooperation. And one piece of advice. You'd better find yourself another local private investigator for your background check."

"Why?" Noah asked.

"She was a homicide victim last night," Detective Moore said. "We believe it involved the spouse of one of her marital discord clients. She had standing restraining orders pertaining to several that we know of."

36

Very slowly Noah put his phone down on the utilitarian Formica desk and stared at it as if it were responsible for the shocking news. Any thought of hunger completely vanished. The idea of the private investigator he had retained only the day before being murdered seemed like too much of a coincidence. At the same time, he recognized that he was suffering from a certain amount of understandable paranoia due to what was happening in his own life, which would tend to make him think this new development somehow involved him.

After orienting himself to time, place, and person by taking a few deep breaths, Noah got up from the desk and stumbled into the small bathroom to splash cold water on his face. Then he stared at himself in the mirror while holding on to the edge of the sink for support. What was reverberating in his mind was the idea that whoever had broken into his apartment and bugged his computer would have known he'd hired Roberta Hinkle. Could this individual be responsible for her untimely death? If that were the case, then Noah himself was at least indirectly responsible.

Noah visibly shuddered and looked away from his own image. The idea was horrifying, and he knew he had to get a grip on himself. Such thoughts had to be wild, paranoid conjecture. He understood ever since the awful day in Dr. Hernandez's office, his mind had been in overdrive, and now it was at its worst, like a runaway train.

Looking back at himself in the mirror, he used his fingers to rearrange his hair and straighten his tie as a way of organizing his thoughts. Returning to the bedroom, he sat back down in the desk chair. He even picked up his phone with the sudden idea of calling back Detective Moore to voice his fear about his possible involvement, but then he caught himself. Such a self-implicating statement would have pulled him into the vortex of a murder investigation without a shred of actual evidence. Such a situation would have serious, unknown effects on his own life, which wasn't going that well. With the upcoming Advisory Board meeting to determine if his ethics suspension would be reversed, the last thing he needed was to be involved with a homicide in any capacity.

Quickly, Noah abandoned the phone by tossing it back onto the desk as if it had suddenly become too hot to hold. Yet the shock of realizing how close he had come to causing himself great harm had the unexpected effect of calming him and allowing him to think more clearly. Surely Roberta Hinkle's death had to be due to her marital investigative work as the Lubbock detective believed, especially with there being restraining orders already on file. Finding the murderer would just be a matter of time.

With his mind under a semblance of control, Noah went back to puzzling over his apartment being broken into, not for burglary but apparently to bug his computer. Why and who could have been responsible? It was far-fetched to think it could have been the hospital. And why was he being followed? And why and how was the FBI involved?

The only thing that would incorporate all these disparate aspects, especially if the murder of Roberta Hinkle was thrown in, would be the involvement of organized crime. Ridiculous as the idea might seem, it was in a far-fetched way supported by Ava's moonlighting lobbying job with the Nutritional Supplement Council. Noah had often joked over the years with resident colleagues that organized crime and the nutritional-supplement industry shared some similarities, both operating more or less in the open and making a ton of money robbing the public while thumbing their noses at the authorities. The only difference was that organized crime robbed the public literally while the nutritional-supplement industry did it figuratively.

As was his wont on occasion when deep in thought, Noah got up and paced back and forth in the small room. What he was mulling over was his acknowledged belief the nutritional-supplement industry had to think of Dr. Ava London as a gift from heaven. For her lobbying efforts, she couldn't be better qualified. Considering her credentials, smarts, attractiveness, and outgoing personality, she had enormous and possibly unmatched credibility and effectiveness. In Noah's mind, there was no wonder that they paid her as well as they apparently did.

Suddenly, Noah stopped in the middle of the room as the corollary idea occurred to him that the NSC would understandably be ferociously protective of Ava's well-being and reputation, and they might even do it behind her back. Could his questioning her competence have been the source of all this hullabaloo? If it were the case, it certainly was a major overreaction since Noah truly thought of her as a terrific anesthesiologist. There had been only those few misgivings . . .

Resuming his pacing, Noah's mind veered off in another direction. If what he was thinking was true, maybe it wasn't an overreaction on NSC's part but rather indicative that there was some potential problem with Ava's training. He couldn't imagine what it could be that wouldn't have come out when the BMH Anesthesia Department had done their due diligence before hiring her. Yet it made a certain amount of sense.

Noah stopped again as the idea of hiring another Lubbock private investigator occurred to him. *Why not?* he thought. It could possibly serve the purpose of ruling out something that the NSC was worried about but was inconsequential. After all, Ava had more than proved herself by handling all the anesthesia cases she had without incident before the three recent unfortunate episodes.

Picking up his phone Noah had in mind again to google "Lubbock private investigators" to hire another one, but he hesitated. Thinking about his being under surveillance, possibly by the cyber-proficient FBI and not just some amateur putting Spyware and a Keylogger on his laptop, now he felt reluctant to use any electronic communication, even his phone. There was also the issue that if there was any validity whatsoever of his putting Roberta Hinkle in jeopardy, he didn't want to repeat such a situation. And knowing what he did about the ability of authorities to ping phones and determine their location by triangulation from various cell towers, he removed the battery. He knew it wasn't enough just to turn it off.

So instead of hiring another PI, a new idea occurred to him that two minutes earlier he would never had suspected. Maybe he should secretly travel to Lubbock, as it would solve a lot of problems. He didn't know how long he could get away with staying in the on-call room, so going to Texas would temporarily solve that issue. If he was still being followed and possibly threatened, leaving town had a definite appeal. And he thought he would be far better equipped to check up on Ava's training than any PI. All he would need to do was walk into the Brazos Medical Center and chat up fellow residents, perhaps implying he was looking for a fellowship program. Using the residents as contacts, he was sure he could get to talk to faculty, particularly relatively young faculty. In any residency program, there were always a few who joined the staff, just as Noah planned to do at BMH. Noah imagined there was a very good chance he could even find someone who trained with Ava. As for specifics, he thought he'd start out in Brownsfield and look at the 2000 high school yearbook.

With a new sense of purpose and direction, Noah repacked his backpack, leaving his white jacket and tablet in his locker. Then he headed to the hospital ATM, where he withdrew several thousand dollars. With cash in hand, he went down to the front entrance of the Stanhope Pavilion. Since he was reluctant to use his cell phone and had disabled it by removing its battery, he couldn't take advantage of Uber or Lyft. He didn't even want to use the taxi queue, which required waiting his turn standing outside the door. What he had in mind was to wait for a taxi to pull up to discharge a passenger, which he would commandeer by rushing out and jumping in. The taxi drivers waiting in line weren't going to like it, nor were the doormen or the people waiting in line, but Noah didn't care. He wanted to be sure not to be followed, and he thought the less exposure out in the open, the better. Although he hadn't seen his tails since Monday, he didn't want to take any chances.

37

"Hey! Wake up!" Keyon shouted, giving George a slap on the shoulder. Keyon had lost the coin toss to decide who had to take the first watch. He and George were in the Ford van, parked with the engine idling in a no parking zone across the street from the Boston Memorial Hospital's main entrance. They had arrived back to the Bedford Airport just after 8:00 that morning and had driven directly to the BMH after a quick stop at their office in the Old City Hall Building. A moment after winning the coin toss, George had fallen asleep in the passenger seat. Although both had gotten a few hours of sleep on the plane, they were exhausted.

"Did you see him?" George questioned while sitting up straight. He blinked in the bright morning sunlight, trying to focus on the hospital entrance. There was a lot of activity, with cars pulling up and people coming and going.

"I'm not sure," Keyon admitted, glancing in the rearview mirror to facilitate a U-turn. "I just got a quick glimpse. Whoever it was bolted out of the hospital entrance like they had just robbed a bank and jumped in that white taxi that just pulled away."

"Do you think one of us should stay here in case it wasn't him?" George asked.

"No!" Keyon said without hesitation. "It's got to be him. Who else would leave the hospital like that?"

"Good point," George said. "Of course, it means he's onto us."

"We already knew that was the case," Keyon said. After making the U-turn, he accelerated after the taxi, which now was in the distance. He was hoping not to lose sight of it.

"Has he used his cell?" George asked, raising the back of his seat.

"He got an incoming call, but he hasn't called out. And then I couldn't even get a GPS ping, meaning he knows enough to take out the damn battery."

"That's not a good sign," George said. "If we lose him, it is going to be hard to find him without the help of his mobile."

"As if I didn't know," Keyon said.

"Don't get caught at this traffic light," George said. Just ahead, the light had turned yellow.

"What do you think, I was born yesterday?" Keyon said derisively. Instead of slowing, he accelerated. As they entered the intersection the light was red.

With aggressive, Boston-style driving Keyon was able to close the gap to a degree, and seeing the direction the taxi was going, they could guess it was heading for the Callahan Tunnel to East Boston.

"I don't like this," George said. "Do you think he's going to Logan Airport? If he is, it's ironic he's fleeing town just when we get the okay to move on him."

"I'm afraid there's not much else in East Boston," Keyon said.

By the time they exited from the Callahan Tunnel, Keyon had managed to get within four car lengths of the taxi in question. A few minutes later the taxi bore to the right, heading for the entrance to Logan Airport.

"Shit," George said. "This is becoming a worst-case scenario! Now we've got to find out where the hell he's going, because there's not much we can do to him here with all the security around."

"It's going to be up to you," Keyon said. He smiled inwardly. Earlier, he'd regretted losing the coin toss requiring him to take the first shift; now he was glad. George would have to do the legwork.

The taxi pulled into terminal A and headed for the passenger drop-off area. The Ford was right behind but pulled into the limo line. George quickly got out after it was definitively ascertained it was Noah who had alighted from the cab. "Let's use the radio to keep in touch," he said before slamming the door behind him.

"Roger," Keyon called after him. "Good luck."

George gave Keyon the finger over his shoulder without looking back.

38

Noah climbed into a rental Ford Fusion and started the engine. He then keyed "Brazos University Medical Center" into the GPS. Although he intended to start his investigative work by driving out to Brownfield in the morning, he thought he'd take a quick look around the Brazos hospital complex just to get the lay of the land, since it was still light and relatively early.

It had taken far longer to get to Lubbock, Texas, than Noah had anticipated, mainly because there had been no nonstop flight or even a direct flight. He'd initially gone to the Delta counter to inquire, thinking a flight through Atlanta might work, but he'd learned that the shortest flight time was on American through their principal hub, Dallas.

Since he'd had almost an hour layover in Dallas, Noah had used the time to eat and investigate hotel accommodations in Lubbock. He'd settled on the Embassy Suites, because it had a business facility with available computers. Noah had always known he depended heavily on electronic media, but he wasn't aware to what extent. What he needed was access to the Internet to help with his investigations.

He'd had plenty of time to think about his impetuous decision to take the trip. The more he thought about it, the more appropriate it seemed for so many reasons, although the principal one remained his being the best person for the job. A local PI might have been able to uncover information about Ava's training but not the specifics that Noah was interested in.

Noah's first impressions of the Lubbock area were close to what he imagined. It was hot yet dry and in that sense, less oppressive than Boston at that time of year. As he looked out at the flat desertlike terrain, he wondered if he could live in such an environment, accustomed as he was to hills and lush vegetation.

Driving was easy compared to his limited experience in Boston. Not only was there less traffic, but the other drivers seemed gracious, which was a huge difference. Following the easy GPS directions, Noah soon found himself at the medical center's campus. In contrast with the BMH, all the buildings were modern, appeared to have been designed by the same architects, and looked relatively new. There was lots of bronze-tinted glass and red brick. In contrast with the Stanhope Pavilion, the main hospital building was only five stories tall.

On an impulse, Noah followed the signs directing him to the emergency area. There were a few empty ambulances backed up against a loading dock, but no people visible. Pulling his rental car to a stop in the ER visitor's parking area, Noah debated if he should go in or wait until he'd returned when the hospital was in full swing as he had originally planned. Following the same impulse that had directed him to drive into the ER parking, Noah got out of the car. His thought was that if things were quiet, which they appeared to be, it might be a good time to have a preliminary conversation with the surgical resident assigned to the ER. Having the name of someone might make his job significantly easier tomorrow when the hospital was busy.

The emergency room was as quiet as it was outside. There were only five people in the sitting area looking at cell phones, flipping through magazines, or reading newspapers. Most of the activity was behind the check-in desk, where a number of nurses, orderlies, and a few residents were relaxing and socializing. As Noah approached, he wondered when the last time the BMH emergency room looked equally calm.

"Excuse me," Noah said to the admitting clerk who'd greeted him. "I'm a surgical resident from Boston, and I am interested in talking to someone about fellowships at this hospital. Is there a surgical resident who might be willing to talk with me?"

"I don't know," the woman said. She seemed mildly flustered by the unexpected request. "Let me ask one of the doctors."

Five minutes later Noah found himself in the hospital coffee shop with a third-year surgical resident from Argentina by the name of Dr. Ricardo Labat, who was very impressed that Noah was training at the BMH. He was a handsome, friendly fellow with a charming accent. Noah commented how quiet the emergency room seemed. Ricardo's response was to explain that Lubbock had no shortage of hospital beds, naming Texas Tech's medical center, Methodist, and Convenant as just a few of the hospitals with significant capacity and emergency room services.

"How is the anesthesia department here?" Noah asked casually.

"It gets high marks, as far as I am concerned," Ricardo said.

"I'd be interested in talking with a couple of their residents," Noah said.

"I could go up to the OR and see if any of the on-call residents are available," Ricardo said. "But I doubt it. I happen to know there are several emergency cases under way."

"No problem," Noah said. "I plan on coming back tomorrow. Let me ask you something else. We have a staff anesthesiologist who trained here, finishing up about five years ago. Her name is Dr. Ava London. Does that name ring a bell? My thought is that she must have been a local celebrity of sorts, coming directly from here to the BMH."

"I never heard of her," Ricardo said. "But I'm not surprised. This entire university, including the medical center, has been expanding so fast with residents coming from all over the world. The training is excellent, in my estimation, which is why I am here. Last year one of the surgical residents went to Johns Hopkins for a fellowship, and the year before one went out to Stanford and one to Columbia-Presbyterian."

"I'm impressed," Noah said, and he was.

"I could call upstairs if you want and see if the staff anesthesiologist on call knows of her."

"No need, but thanks," Noah said. "I'll ask about her tomorrow."

Fifteen minutes later Noah was back in the rental car setting up the GPS to get him to his hotel. He had been encouraged by his short conversation with Dr. Labat. Learning that recent resident graduates had been going to big-name tertiary-care institutions suggested that Ava's jump from Brazos to BMH wasn't all that exceptional. His assumptions that her training had been totally satisfactory seemed to be on the mark.

His room was as generic as Noah expected and far more spacious and luxurious than he needed. After taking a quick shower, he went down to the business center to use the computer. He wanted to go on the Brazos University Department of Anesthesiology website to get the names of the principal faculty members who had been there for more than five years. He also wanted to write down the names of the current residents. The more information he had, the more rewarding he thought his visit would be.

Noah was about to leave the website when he thought he'd see if there was a photo of the current residents. There was, and it looked to him like an impressively cosmopolitan group. He then noticed something else of interest. There were archived photos going back to the first year of the residency program. Noah brought up the photo for 2012, the year Ava had finished, and began searching for her. At first he didn't find her, but then he did. She was in the back row peering directly at the camera between two much larger male colleagues. To Noah, she looked exactly as she did currently, although her hair seemed significantly blonder.

After closing down the computer, Noah exited the business center. His plan was to go back to his room and attempt to sleep. As keyed up as he was, he knew it was going to be a struggle, especially in unfamiliar surroundings. In many ways, Noah was a creature of habit. Even when it came to the on-call room in the hospital, he usually always slept in the same one. Not relishing lying in the bed for hours tossing and turning and giving his paranoia free rein, Noah decided to go to the hotel's bar for a beer. It was out of the ordinary for him to do such a thing, but this was not an ordinary time. He thought the diversion and the small amount of alcohol might help calm him.

39

"A bit more than twenty-four hours ago, I had never even heard of Lubbock, Texas," Keyon complained. "Now I've been here twice."

"Who would have guessed," George said.

The same Citation X plane that had taken the two men back and forth the previous day had again been pressed into service by ABC Security and had just touched down at the Preston Smith Airport. The urgency for the second trip was considered just as critical as it had been for the first. Dr. Noah Rothauser had to be sanctioned immediately.

As soon as George had determined Noah had left Boston on a plane bound for Dallas, Texas, the previous morning, he assumed that Noah's ultimate destination had to be Lubbock. Rushing back to Keyon in the van, they had immediately called their controller at the home office to give him the surprising and disturbing news. At first it gave them a sense of vindication, since they had been complaining about Noah for a week without getting the go-ahead to take care of him. But any pleasure was short-lived because they were ordered to return to Lubbock and do what needed to be done. The only problem was that the pilots who were cleared to work for ABC Security had to take their FAA-required rest. To add to the delay, there was a minor mechanical problem with the aircraft that had to be fixed. The result was that Keyon and George had not left Bedford, Massachusetts, until a little after 2:00 A.M.

They had used the delay to good advantage, getting some needed rest and then using their resources in their Boston office to locate Dr. Noah Rothauser at room 504 at Embassy Suites Hotel. They also used the time and the equipment they had to make up a fake Massachusetts driver's license using George's picture.

Again, there was a Chevrolet Suburban waiting for them at the General Aviation terminal, and within twenty minutes of touchdown they were on the Interstate, heading toward Lubbock.

"This place doesn't look that much different in the daytime," Keyon commented, looking out at the vast horizon. He was driving.

"It's as flat as parts of Iraq," George said.

"Don't remind me," Keyon answered.

Arriving at the hotel before 7:00 A.M., there was no activity in the parking lot. George parked as close to the entrance as possible, putting the ignition key behind the visor in case one of them had to leave without the other. Before they got out, both checked their respective weapons, the Smith and Wesson for George and the Berretta for Keyon.

"Ready?" George questioned.

"Let's do it," Keyon said.

They walked quickly but not too quickly, to avoid being conspicuous. There were four taxis waiting in queue, with all four drivers sipping coffee in their respective vehicles. Inside the building, the reception area was deserted except for a single person standing at the front desk being helped by a single hotel employee. George and Keyon walked up and stood in line.

Dressed in their normal suits and ties, Keyon and George were confident that they wouldn't attract any attention. They were just two traveling businessmen like so many others, including the man in front of them.

"Can I help you?" the hotel employee said pleasantly when it was their turn.

"You certainly can," George said with a smile. "I left my room card in the room. My name is Noah Rothauser, and I'm staying in room five-oh-four."

"Certainly," the hotel employee said. "Would you mind showing me some identification?"

"Not at all," George said. He pulled out his wallet and handed over the fake driver's license.

The hotel employee briefly glanced at it and handed it back. After placing a blank room card in the appropriate slot, he produced a room key, and with a few clicks on his keyboard, he handed it over.

"Much obliged," George said, brandishing the key.

George and Keyon went to the elevators, making small talk for the benefit of the employee behind the desk. They boarded the car that was waiting. Keyon pressed five. A moment later the door closed and the car rose.

"It's looking good so far," Keyon said. "Nice and quiet."

George nodded but didn't speak. He was never as calm as Keyon and always felt tense until the action started. He'd had no trouble engaging in the banter, but now that they were alone, he preferred to concentrate on what was going to happen in the next ten minutes and think about possible contingencies.

Arriving at the fifth floor, they stepped out into the main corridor that ran the length of the building. They could see there were exit stairwells at both ends, which could be important if there were problems. No one was in sight.

They exchanged a silent glance, then moved down to room 504 and took up positions on either side of the door. After checking their weapons in their shoulder holsters, Keyon leaned forward and put his ear against the door's upper panel. He listened for a moment, then gave a thumbs-up sign.

Following a final glance up and down the hallway, George inserted the card key. There was a quiet click and a small green light materialized above the handle. After a final nod between the two, George opened the door and the two men rushed inside the room with their pistols in their hands.

They expected to find Noah in the bed, but it was empty. Using hand signals, Keyon pointed toward the closed bathroom door. George nodded and they repeated the maneuver they had used on the outer door. A moment later they were shocked and dismayed to find the bathroom dark and empty.

"Shit!" Keyon snapped.

"I thought it was going too well," George said. "The bastard must be down at breakfast." Both men reholstered their weapons.

They returned to the main part of the room. Keyon closed the outer door, which they had left open in their haste. George took the club chair by the window. Keyon stretched out on the king-size bed after pulling the bedspread up over the pillows. He put his hands comfortably behind his head. They thought it best to wait for Noah's return rather than seeking him out in the breakfast room.

"How long do you think we should wait?" George asked after just a few minutes. "I don't like this. He could be off causing trouble already."

"Let's give him thirty minutes," Keyon said. "If he hasn't shown up, one of us should go down to the breakfast room and reconnoiter."

"Maybe we should let the home office know there's been a hiccup," George said. "Keeping that plane waiting out there at the airport costs a fortune."

"Let's just cool it for a half-hour," Keyon said. "If he doesn't show up, then we switch to plan B."

"What's plan B?"

"Your guess is as good as mine," Keyon said with a laugh. "I suppose we'll just have to stake out the Brazos University Medical Center, where we know he will turn up, unless he's already there, which I doubt. Of course, we can always hope he'll use his cell and give us a location."

40

Noah paid his tab and stepped out into the sunshine in Brownfield, Texas. The temperature had risen considerably since he'd gone into the restaurant.

He'd slept poorly the previous night despite the two beers he'd had at the bar. The problem had been that he couldn't stop his mind from wondering what he was going to learn that day, first at Brownfield and then at the Brazos Medical Center. His intuition was telling him it was going to be significant, and he hoped it would be in a positive way, but he worried it might not be.

By 5:30 he'd given up going back to sleep and had gotten up. Something had awakened him at about 5:00. After a shower, he'd gone out to his rent-a-car and set out for Brownfield around 6:30. Although he'd put the Kendrick Public Library in the GPS, he hadn't needed to because the route was a straight shot southeast down Route 62 that branched off the Lubbock Ring Road, close to where his hotel was located.

Noah seldom had driven on such a straight, flat road, passing through an almost iridescent red, arid landscape. There were several small towns on the way, and Brownfield itself was smaller than he had expected. Route 62, which assumed the name of Lubbock Road and then South First Street once he was in the town, brought him right into the center. The Kendrick Library was on a cross-street.

Noah had pulled up to the library and noticed his was the only car, which he should have taken as a hint he might have been a bit early. Instead he was taken by the library's appearance, which defied classification. It was a unique, single-story, red-brick structure with steeply gabled roofs sporting several purely decorative dormers. Getting out of the car, Noah was so taken with the building's appearance that it wasn't until he got all the way to the front door that he had learned the library didn't open until 9:00 A.M.

Taking the delayed opening in stride, Noah had driven around the town, passing the high school where Ava had gone when she was presumably Gail Shafter. Nearby, he'd come across a pleasant-looking breakfast place. Having an hour and a half to kill, he had gone in for pancakes and coffee and a chance to read the local weekly newspaper, *The Brownfield Gazette*.

Once inside the library, Noah went directly to the circulation desk. The middle-aged woman manning the desk was the spitting image of the prim-and-proper but mildly scary woman he remembered as a young child in his own town library. Despite the similarities appearance-wise, the Brownfield librarian was inordinately friendly, directing him to the end room, which she called the "reading room," to locate the Brownfield High School yearbooks and even offered to accompany him.

"I'm sure I'll be able to find them," Noah said.

In the center of the reading room was a low, two-sided bookcase containing more than fifty years of Brownfield High School yearbooks. Noah took the volume for 2000 and sat down at an oak table.

He first looked at Ava London's photo. He was surprised because the woman in the black-and-white photo did resemble the Ava he knew, with streaked blond hair, remarkably white teeth, a small sculpted nose, and a strong chin line. She also reflected Ava's confident stare. Beneath the photo was an impressive résumé of activities including cheerleading captain, student council, senior play, and many clubs. Below that was a short in memoriam, mentioning her death on April 14, 2000.

Noah's eyes went back to study the photo. He again admitted to himself the individual did look surprisingly similar to his Ava, but he wasn't sure he would have been able to pick her out if there hadn't been a name. But he didn't find that surprising, as it was rare in his experience for someone to resemble their high school photo.

Moving on, he looked at the photo of Gail Shafter. The general features were not too dissimilar, although Gail's nose was larger and appeared as if it were slightly aquiline, and the hair was definitely brunette with just a few blond streaks. Of particular similarity was the way the young woman looked directly into the camera with obvious self-confidence, although with Gail it bordered on brassiness. What was obviously different about the two women was Gail's lack of social activities.

Taking his cell phone out of his backpack, Noah replaced the battery just long enough to take a couple photos of the two women. He had wanted Roberta Hinkle to send him the photos, and now he had them. As he put the yearbook back in the bookshelf, thinking about the private investigator made him wonder what Detective Moore would say if he knew Noah was in the area. It wasn't a pleasant thought, and as best as he could, he put it out of his mind. He didn't want to think about Roberta Hinkle's untimely end.

Noah returned to the circulation desk and asked the librarian where he could find back issues of *The Brownfield Gazette*. She directed him to return to the reading room and to look in the shelving against the near wall. She said there were bound volumes of the paper going back to the year it was founded.

It took Noah only a moment to find the correct volume that contained the April 17, 2000, and the April 24, 2000, issues. He took it back to the same seat. As far as he could tell, he was the only visitor in the library.

As Roberta Hinkle had mentioned in her email, there were many articles on Ava London's suicide, coming as it did almost a year after her father's. It was quickly apparent to Noah that both father and daughter were indeed local celebrities with the father an active town philanthropist and the daughter a popular teen, cheerleading captain, and junior prom queen. It was also said that the two were very close after the death of the wife/mother from breast cancer two years before.

What Noah found the most interesting from his reading was the apparent role the journalists believed social media had played in goading Ava London to follow in her father's footsteps. Numerous emails, messages, and group chats were cited blaming her for her father's suicide and saying she should do the same. The most consistent authors of this progressively relentless harassment were Connie Dugan, Cynthia Sanchez, and Gail Shafter, as Roberta Hinkle had mentioned in her email, although there were other people involved as well, particularly in the group chats. One article claimed that Ava London had become so despondent from this media attention that she had been unable to attend school for the week prior to her suicide. The two social-media sites implicated were Six-Degrees and AOL Instant Messenger.

Noah could only imagine the trauma the small town had endured with the tragic loss of two popular members of the community. The fact that the current Ava's favorite pastime was social media wasn't lost on Noah. There was no doubt in his mind that once things returned to some semblance of normal with her, he would need to bring up all of this. As personally generous as he considered Ava, he thought he had to give her the benefit of doubt and hear her side of the story. It certainly was a bizarre situation.

Noticing that there was an index at the end of the volume, Noah went back to the shelf and got the volume for 2002. Checking the index, he found multiple articles on Dr. Winston Herbert, the dentist that Ava had said she'd worked for after high school. Noah skimmed the articles and confirmed that Dr. Winston Herbert had been drafted to start the Brazos University School of Dentistry just as Ava had said. With that information, Noah felt encouraged. He wanted to believe in Ava despite the oddball name change.

After returning the two bound volumes back to the shelf and thanking the librarian, Noah stepped out into full West Texas summer heat. He had one more destination in Brownfield before tackling Brazos University Medical Center, and that was the Terry County Courthouse.

"HIS PHONE WAS on long enough to get an approximate fix on him," Keyon said, looking up from his laptop screen. "That's the good news. The bad news is that he's already gone back off the grid. At least we now know he's in Brownfield. What are your thoughts? There's only one road between Brownfield and Lubbock, and we know he's driving a gray Ford Fusion."

"What does Google Maps say about driving to Brownfield?" George asked. "How long?"

"About an hour from where we are sitting," Keyon said. He reached back and put away his laptop.

"I think we should just hang here and wait," George said. "If we try to go to Brownfield, we take the risk of missing him, even if Brownfield might be a safer place for us to do what we need to do."

After determining that Noah Rothauser was not in his hotel that morning, Keyon and George had debated their course of action. Ultimately, they decided to drive to the medical center, where they searched for Noah's car in the hospital's parking lot. They'd been relieved when they didn't find any gray Ford Fusions. At that point they'd parked where they could see the front of the hospital and the entrance to the parking lot at the same time, waiting for Noah Rothauser to show up. They had the engine idling to keep on the air-conditioning.

"I think you're right," Keyon said. He lowered the back of his seat and replaced his feet on the dashboard, where they had been before he'd gotten the signal Noah's phone had been turned on. His view out the right of the SUV was of the front of the hospital, which was moderately busy with people coming and going.

From the driver's seat, George could see the parking lot entrance out his side window. Although the lot was almost full, there wasn't as much activity as there had been when they first arrived just before 8:00 A.M. It was apparent that the people coming on duty had arrived, and the people going off duty had already left. It was the doldrums of the morning.

"Do you think we should let Hank know what's up?" Keyon said. Hank Anderson was the controller for Keyon and George. He worked directly under Morton Colman, the CEO of ABC Security.

"No," George said. "We already clued him in there was a problem making contact. He'll get in touch with us if he wants an update."

THE TERRY COUNTY COURTHOUSE reminded Noah of his high school. It was a three-story structure constructed of yellow brick with some engaged columns over the front entrance. In contrast with the few times he'd had to visit government offices in Boston, he found the people in the courthouse in Brownfield pleasant and eager to help. Noah was interested in finding whether there were any court records for Gail Shafter legally changing her name. It didn't take long. There were no such records.

Back out in his rental, Noah retraced his route to Brazos University Medical Center, traveling back up Route 62 toward Lubbock. He felt as if he was making significant progress but knew that the more challenging part was coming up. His plan was to go into the hospital and have Dr. Labat paged. If the Argentine wasn't in surgery, Noah felt he'd be the best way to start getting introduced to some of the anesthesia residents.

41

As Noah pulled into the hospital entrance, he passed the turnoff to the right that went to the Emergency Department. The hospital porte-cochere as well as the expansive, general parking lot was to the left. As he entered the nearly full parking lot itself, Noah slowed, searching for a free slot. There were a few people walking to and from the hospital. A short distance ahead he saw a woman with a small child duck between two cars. Noah stopped. As he anticipated, the woman was clearly about to leave as she opened the rear door of one of the cars and proceeded to put the child into a car seat. She then went around to get into the driver's seat.

Noah put on his blinker to indicate he intended to take the spot once the woman had vacated. Part of the reason he used the blinker was that he'd noticed in the rearview mirror that a large black SUV was coming slowly in his direction, which he assumed was looking for a spot as well. The slot soon to be freed was conveniently located close to the hospital entrance, and Noah wanted it known he planned on taking it.

The moment the woman backed up and then pulled past Noah on her way out of the parking lot, Noah slipped the Ford Fusion into the newly vacated spot.

As he turned off the ignition, he noticed something odd. The black

389

SUV that had been behind him had pulled forward and had now stopped, effectively blocking him from pulling back out if he was so inclined. Noah turned around, confused as to why the vehicle would stop as it did and worried it might be an episode of misdirected road rage over the parking place, something he'd been told that happened in Boston on occasion. What he saw made his blood run cold. A man had exited out of the vehicle's passenger seat even before the vehicle was completely stopped and was now running around its rear. Noah immediately recognized him. It was the African American who had been tailing him around Boston. In the next instant, a man Noah assumed was the Caucasian leaped from the driver's seat. As the African American came along the driver's side of Noah's car, his colleague went to the passenger side.

Noah reacted by reflex and hit the door-lock button to make sure the doors were secure. He then fumbled with his cell phone to get it out of his pocket and try to get the battery back in. There was no doubt in his mind. He needed to dial 911.

"Open the door!" one of the men shouted. "FBI!" Someone pounded on the top of Noah's car.

Noah turned and looked up into the face of the African American who was holding an FBI badge against the car window. Looking in the opposite direction, he saw the Caucasian was doing the same with his badge. Thinking he had no choice with law enforcement involved, Noah reached for the door release handle, but as he did so he heard his phone indicate it was on.

Another glance at the African American's face made Noah hesitate. There was an expression of anger that seemed inappropriate for the situation. Instead of opening his door, Noah hastily began punching 911 into his phone.

Before Noah was even finished with the three digits, there was the sound of shattering glass and small shards rained down along the side of his face. Looking up, Noah could see that the African American was using the butt of an automatic pistol in an attempt to punch through the driver's-side window. Luckily, the window was resisting, but it wasn't going to last. In desperation, Noah threw his torso to the right to extract his left leg from beneath the steering wheel. Placing his foot against the door and releasing the lock at the same time, Noah straightened his leg with as much force as he could possibly muster. The door slammed against the African American, pinning him for a fleeting moment against the neighboring car.

In the next instant Noah was out of the car. His only hope was to get inside the hospital and let hospital security deal with these two men, whether they were real FBI agents or not. But he didn't get far. Although the African American had been momentarily stunned, Noah was aware he'd recovered quickly enough to get a hold of Noah's shirt, slowing Noah enough so that the Caucasian was able to come around the back of Noah's car and join the melee. The Caucasian grabbed Noah's neck with his right hand and Noah's arm with his left. Despite Noah's attempt to free himself, he was forced down onto the hot, dusty pavement face-first.

Noah tried to cry out for help, but a hand was roughly clasped over his mouth, holding his jaw tightly closed. In the next instant Noah's arms were wrenched behind him and his wrists clasped with handcuffs. A moment later he felt a sharp, stinging sensation in his buttocks, followed by a sudden localized pain. As a physician, he knew he'd been injected. Within seconds he felt like he was falling, and then blackness.

"SHIT," KEYON SAID through clenched teeth. "He's feisty!" He and George together hoisted Noah up to his feet using their hands under Noah's armpits. Once they had him upright, they started toward the Suburban. Keyon had to walk awkwardly with his legs apart, since Noah's trick with the car door had caught him in the testicles. Noah was semiconscious from the powerful tranquilizer and would have fallen into a heap had he not been supported. A few people either going or coming from the hospital had stopped to watch the rapidly unfolding spectacle. They were all dumbfounded. It had happened so quickly and unexpectedly.

"FBI!" George called out, holding his fake badge up for all to see. "Everything is under control here. Sorry for the scene. This man is wanted in a half-dozen states."

Reaching the Suburban, Keyon and George quickly got Noah into the backseat and buckled him in with the seat belt. Noah's head lolled forward.

"Do you think he should be kept upright?" George said.

"How the hell am I supposed to know?" Keyon complained.

"That was a walloping dose we gave him. What's that going to do to his blood pressure?"

"Oh, all right," Keyon said with resignation. He lifted the shoulder strap over Noah's head, leaving the waist belt in place. Noah slumped over on his side. "Satisfied?"

"Hey, we both know that if this bastard was delivered as damaged goods, we'd most likely be out of a job."

42

Noah became aware of his surroundings gradually, just the opposite of how he had lost consciousness that morning almost twelve hours ago, something he wasn't going to learn until later. The first thing he realized was that he was on a much more comfortable surface than the macadam he'd been on when the proverbial lights went out. With his left hand he could feel it was a bed. His right hand was shackled over his head, and when he tried to move it, the binding cut into his wrist. He tried to open his eyes, but they refused to open, even when he strained to use his forehead muscles as an additional aid.

Forcing himself to calm down and relax, he took a few deep breaths. It was a good ploy. A moment later his eyes opened on their own, and he found himself looking up at a plaster ceiling. Raising his head, he could see he was in a narrow, elongated bedroom that was tastefully decorated with chintz curtains and flowery wallpaper. A moment later he realized he wasn't alone. There was a man dressed in a dark suit in a nearby club chair, his face hidden behind a newspaper.

Glancing up over his head, he could see that his wrist was in a pair of handcuffs that was also attached to a brass headboard. As Noah's mind continued to clear, he could see he was still wearing the clothes he'd put on that morning, which brought back where he'd been. *My God,* he thought, *I'm in Texas!* Then, like an avalanche of bad memories, he recalled the details of the terrorizing episode of his being boxed in by the black SUV, the men flashing FBI badges at his windows, his car window being busted in, and his vain attempt to flee. It was like reliving a bad dream.

With some effort, Noah tried to shift his position, which caused the handcuffs to rattle against the brass headboard. At the sound, the man in the chair lowered his paper. Noah recognized him. He was the African American, and as Noah watched, he tossed his paper aside and got to his feet. But he didn't say anything. He merely walked out of the room.

"Hey," Noah called out. "Come back here! Where am I? Are you really FBI?" It was adding insult to injury that the man ignored him. If the man was FBI, what in God's name was Noah doing fettered in an upscale bedroom?

Left on his own, Noah tried to sit up by throwing his legs over the right side of the bed. As soon as he did so, he felt a wave of dizziness overwhelm him, forcing him to lie down and raise his feet back onto the bed. He closed his eyes and hoped for the dizziness to subside.

"You have decided to wake up and join us," a familiar female voice said a few minutes later in a solicitous tone. "I'm so pleased. I was a little worried you'd been severely overdosed."

With a sense of shock and fearing he was hallucinating, Noah's eyes popped open. Standing at the bedside, hands on hips, was Dr. Ava London. Noah stared at her, half expecting her to disappear like an apparition, but she didn't. Behind her appeared the African American, whose presence quickly assured him he wasn't hallucinating.

"What are you doing here?" Noah managed.

Ava laughed her unique lucent laugh. "Where do you think 'here' is?"

"Someplace in Lubbock, Texas," Noah said.

Ava laughed again. It was natural and spontaneous. "Sorry to disappoint you," she said. "We're not in Lubbock. We are in Boston—more specifically, in my house. You've been sleeping off your tranquilizer doses in one of my guest bedrooms."

Noah could see that the African American was standing off to the side. "Who is that man?" Noah demanded.

"This Keyon Dexter," Ava said, gesturing over her shoulder.

"Does he work for you?" Noah said.

Ava laughed yet again. "No, he doesn't work for me."

"Is he with the FBI?" Noah asked.

"I don't think so," Ava said. She turned to Keyon. "You aren't with the FBI, are you?"

"No, ma'am," Keyon said politely.

"What the hell is going on?" Noah demanded.

"I'll tell you what is going on," Ava said in a sternly fake voice as evidenced by a simultaneous smile. She waved a finger at Noah as if he were a naughty child. "You have been causing all sorts of trouble and forcing me and a few other people to lose sleep. Thankfully, all that's in the past." Ava's smile broadened. "We need to talk to clear up a few things."

Noah suppressed a strong urge to indulge in serious sarcasm, but he held his tongue as everything that had happened to him over the previous week began to come back to him in a progressive rush, particularly the untimely murder of Roberta Hinkle. He rattled his restraint against the brass headboard. "Why am I handcuffed?"

"I don't know," Ava admitted. She turned to Keyon. "Why is he in handcuffs?"

"He wasn't cooperative in Lubbock," Keyon said evasively.

"Well, take them off!" Ava said.

"Are you sure, ma'am?" Keyon questioned. "George and I think he's a flight risk, and we found him to be on the feisty side."

"Take them off!" Ava repeated.

Keyon did as he was told, then stepped back to his former place, available if needed.

Noah sat up on the bed and rubbed his sore wrist. He was dizzy for a moment, but it cleared quickly. He felt reassured that the African American was taking orders from Ava.

"How do you feel?" Ava asked sympathetically. "I understand they gave you a bit more midazolam than I had suggested and then a few hours later repeated it."

"You suggested?" Noah questioned angrily. "So you are behind all this!"

"Listen, my friend!" Ava said, becoming serious. "If it weren't for my efforts, I'm not sure what shape you would be in, and you certainly wouldn't be sitting here in my guest room. Let's not be judgmental until you've heard the whole story. As I said, we need to talk."

"Does he need to be in here?" Noah asked, nodding toward Keyon. The mere presence of the man had him on edge, whether he followed orders from Ava or not.

Ava shrugged. "Not as far as I am concerned." She turned to Keyon. "Perhaps you could wait out in the hall."

"Yes, ma'am," Keyon said. A moment later he was gone.

"Happy?" Ava questioned.

"Hold the sarcasm!" Noah said. "How the hell did I get here?"

"After Keyon and George met you in Lubbock, they invited you on a private jet that had been chartered for them."

"Invited!" Noah spat. "Ha. They dragged me out of a rental car whose window they busted. What the hell is going to happen to the rental? Jesus!"

"You're incredible," Ava said. "You're really worried about a rental car?"

"I was the one who rented it," Noah said. "The rental company has my driver's license information."

"Good God!" Ava said. "You're so damn compulsive." Without warning, she called out for Keyon, who was back into the room in a flash. From his expression, it was apparent he'd feared the worst.

"Keyon," Ava said with exasperation, "what was done about Dr. Rothauser's rental?"

"Hank Anderson took care of it," Keyon said. "He arranged for an agent to go and get it and turn it in. The agent also took care of the insurance deductible."

"Thank you, Keyon," Ava said. "That will be all."

"Right, ma'am," Keyon said as he touched his forehead with his right hand in a form of salute.

"Satisfied?" Ava asked after turning back to Noah.

"Who is Hank Anderson?" Noah said.

"He is Keyon and George's immediate boss," Ava said.

"This is going in circles," Noah complained. "Who exactly are Keyon Dexter and George whatever his name is?"

"George Marlowe," Ava said. "You've seen him here. I call George my personal trainer. In actuality, he is a security person, but he's into exercise as much as I am, so it seemed convenient to do it together."

Noah nodded. In his mind's eye, he suddenly associated the man he'd known as Ava's personal trainer with the Caucasian who'd been following him and then as one of the men who had attacked him in Lubbock. On a few occasions when he'd caught a decent glimpse of the man's face, he'd had the sense he recognized the man on some level.

"Keyon and George work for a security company called ABC Security," Ava explained. "One of the conditions of my working for the Nutritional Supplement Council from day one has been to accept Keyon and George as my"—Ava groped for the right word—"minders or monitors, or, if you want to be totally pejorative, my babysitters. At first I rarely saw them, but that changed over the last year or so when things with my social media activities got out of hand."

"What on earth does that mean?" Noah said. Although his mind was clearing, he still felt ungrounded as if in a dream state. "How did they help you with social media?" The idea seemed preposterous.

"There had been a few incidents of serious cyberstalking of my sock-puppets, particularly one called Teresa Puksar. Keyon and George had to take care of it before I was directly involved. Truthfully, I don't know what they did, but they solved it and also any future problem by making sure I have proper encryption. And now that the Dr. Mason issue has died down and you are brought into the fold, I imagine I'll see a lot less of them."

"What do you mean when I am brought into the fold?" Noah said heatedly.

"That's what we need to talk about," Ava said. "But before we do, how do you feel, health-wise?"

"Reasonable, I guess," Noah said, forcing himself to calm down. His emotions were all over the map. "I was dizzy when I first sat up, but that's gone. The main problem is feeling totally out of it mentally."

"Let me check your vital signs again," Ava said. "You had quite a dose of midazolam. I'm surprised you don't have more significant anterograde amnesia." She used his right wrist to take his pulse. Then she used a blood-pressure gauge and a stethoscope that had been on the bedside table. Noah watched her as she concentrated, avoiding his line of vision as she wrapped the cuff around his upper arm, inflated it, and then gradually deflated it. A moment later, she was done. "Okay, your vitals are fine. Try to stand up and see how it goes." She extended a hand, and holding on to Noah's, she urged him to slide off the bed.

"Well?" Ava questioned once he was standing.

"I'm okay," Noah said. He teetered a bit. "At least I'm not dizzy."

"So far so good," she said. "Would you like to use the bathroom? Your bladder must be about to burst."

"Now that you mention it, I would," Noah admitted. Until that moment it hadn't occurred to him, but now that it was brought up, it seemed urgent.

In the bathroom with Ava waiting just outside, Noah's mind was progressively moving into overdrive as he urinated. Although he remembered being knocked to the ground in the medical center parking lot, everything else was a blank, and it was disorienting not to have been aware of being transported all the way back to Boston and into Ava's house. It was as if the Lubbock trip had been a dream. But there was one thing he was aware of for certain. Any suspicions he'd entertained about the NSC being ferociously protective of Ava were absolutely on the money. A private jet had been involved in getting him back to Boston, and he couldn't even imagine what it might have cost.

"The reason I had you put in this bedroom is that it's on the same floor as the study," Ava said when Noah opened the door.

Holding on to the jamb to support himself, Noah stepped out of the bathroom.

"If you are up to it, we could go in there to talk," Ava continued. "You might find it more comfortable and familiar. There is also some food and drink that I brought up from the kitchen in case you are hungry. What do you say?"

There were so many thoughts going through Noah's mind that he didn't have the ability to object. He had no idea of what time it was although he'd noticed the windows were dark. Ava urged him forward. Out in the hallway he saw Keyon and George. Dutifully they got out of the way as Noah and Ava passed. Noah glanced at their faces, impressed with their nonchalance. It was apparent they were professionals. And he did recognize George as the reputed physical trainer.

Ava helped Noah seat himself in his usual chair. She put a plate of small cocktail-style sandwiches, water, and Diet Coke within reach. There was also a plate of potato chips.

"I could get you some wine," Ava said, as she watched Noah take one of the sandwiches.

"This is fine," Noah said. After he took a couple bites, he poured himself some Diet Coke over ice. He thought the caffeine might help organize his thoughts, and his mouth was dry. He had no interest in wine.

Keyon and George had quietly followed them into the room and were standing off to the side, leaning against a floor-to-ceiling bookcase. Both had their arms crossed over their chests with the same calm, cool, in-control attitude they'd exhibited in the hallway.

"Do these thugs have to hang around?" Noah questioned, purposefully loud enough for Keyon and George to hear.

"I suppose not," Ava said. "But they are party to all the details of this affair, as they have been the principal investigators. If it makes you more comfortable, they can wait downstairs."

"It would make me more comfortable," Noah said without hesitation.

"Would you mind?" Ava called out to Keyon and George. "If you are worried about him being a flight risk, how about waiting down by the front door?"

"Yes, ma'am," Keyon said. Without another word the two men filed out, and they could be heard tramping down the stairs.

"All right," Ava said. She sat down in her usual chair. "Let's get this over with."

"Fine by me," Noah snapped. "What the hell is going on?"

"Calm down," Ava said. "Keep in mind all this rigmarole has been caused by you and no one else."

Noah laughed mockingly. "I hardly think that's the case," he said. As his mind had continued to clear, his irritation had mounted; so did his fears. "Before we talk of anything else, I want to know if your NSC friends had anything to do with the murder in Lubbock that's been haunting me."

"I don't know anything about any murder," Ava said. "Whose murder?"

"I had hired a private investigator who I'd found on the Internet. Her name was Roberta Hinkle. The night after I'd hired her, she was killed in her own home, supposedly by the disgruntled lover of one of her clients. Her investigative specialty was domestic issues."

"Why on earth did you hire a domestic-issue private investigator?" Ava asked.

"I didn't know it was her specialty," Noah said irritably. "Her website didn't suggest it. I hired her to do a background check."

"Was this background check on me?" Ava asked.

"Yes," Noah said. It was time for the truth, and he expected her to instantly become indignant, but to his surprise she didn't.

"I don't know anything about any murder," Ava repeated calmly, "but I can tell you this: A private investigator nosing around in my personal business at this particular point in time would have made my employers at NSC very nervous and unhappy, to say the very least."

"Are you suggesting the NSC was involved?" Noah said. He was horrified at the implications, as it would mean he, too, was indirectly responsible for the woman's death.

"Certainly not directly," Ava said. "The NSC would never do anything illegal. But what ABC Security might do, that's another question. Do you remember Blackwater, the security company that was active in Iraq during the Iraq War?"

"I think so," Noah said. He had no idea where Ava was going.

"I believe ABC Security is a similar organization, but I don't know for sure. What I *do* know is that this is a highly sensitive period of time for the NSC, and the last thing they would want is for my credibility to be questioned in any way. Currently, I am the key NSC lobbyist dealing with quite a few congressmen and senators who are on the fence about amending or repealing the Dietary Supplement Health Education Act of 1994.

"Remember that article that was coming out in *The Annals of Internal Medicine* that presented a large study that was critical of the nutritional-supplement industry? We talked about it in my kitchen."

"I think so," Noah said.

"It had a big impact and caused a sizable number of legislators to express reservations about DSHEA, and I'm the only person who has been able to get them to reverse course. Ergo, it is a super-critical time for the NSC to make sure the FDA stays out of the picture as far as any regulation of the industry is concerned. It's the reason I've had to spend so much time in Washington. I'm the point person to do damage control."

Noah stared at Ava as his drugged mind wrestled with what he was hearing and began to connect the dots, lending support to his worst fears. Maybe there was some hidden reason to question the depth or quality of Ava's anesthesia training, which the NSC knew about and did not want to be exposed. It was also the reason he'd hired Roberta Hinkle.

As if reading Noah's mind, Ava lifted her legs off her ottoman and moved herself forward to sit on it, bringing her closer to Noah. She leaned toward him and lowered her voice, presumably to keep the men on the floor below from hearing. "Before I tell you what I plan to tell you, I want to ask what the private investigator found that made you suddenly fly the hell off to Lubbock?"

Noah felt himself stiffen. They had reached a critical juncture, a crossroads, a moment of truth. Although he felt nervous about Keyon and George being in the house, emphasizing her home-court advantage, he thought it was time to fish or cut bait, whatever the consequences.

43

Noah debated how to start. He girded himself for what was to come as he settled on presenting the information in the order he had learned it. "I had told Ms. Hinkle you had graduated from the Coronado High School in Lubbock in 2000, so she started there," he said. "Unexpectedly, she found that there had not been an Ava London in the Coronado High School for the last fifty years."

Noah paused, watching Ava and her reaction, which he'd expected would be a mixture of anger and defensiveness as she had been caught in a blatant lie. Instead, she just nodded as if she expected what Noah had said and took it in stride.

"The private investigator decided on her own to look for Ava London at high schools in the Lubbock area," Noah said, watching Ava's lack of response with continued disbelief. It seemed that she never ceased to surprise him. Here was yet another layer of the onion. He went on: "And after considerable searching Ms. Hinkle was successful. She found an Ava London who'd attended Brownfield High School in a small town of the same name about forty miles southeast of Lubbock."

Ava nodded again. "Is that all?" she questioned, in response to Noah's second pause.

"No, it's not all," Noah said. "Ava London was in the class of 2000, but she didn't graduate. Ava London committed suicide on a Friday night, April fourteenth, 2000. It was almost a year to the day from her father's suicide carried out with the same gun in the same room. After the event, it was thought that Ava London had been harassed on social media following her father's death and urged and browbeaten to emulate her father. It seems as if it was an early case of cyberbullying."

"She was a very capable private investigator," Ava said with little or no emotion.

"Ms. Hinkle didn't tell me all those details," Noah said. "I read several issues of the *Brownfield Gazette* that were published after the event. It was big news in Brownfield."

"And I'm sure there must be more tidbits the private investigator discovered," Ava said almost mockingly.

"There were," Noah said. "She found out that there was a Gail Shafter in the same class as Ava London. I had told Ms. Hinkle that was your Facebook user name."

"Very interesting," Ava said with a semi-smile. "What else?"

"That's it," Noah said. "Ms. Hinkle was planning on moving her investigation to the Brazos University Medical Center yesterday, but before she could do so, she was murdered in her home. What worries and horrifies me is that it wasn't a coincidence that it happened when it did."

"I'm afraid I have to agree with you," Ava said, suddenly becoming serious. "The timing is just too coincidental."

Noah shuddered and stared at Ava. Here was yet another surprise. To his utter dismay, she was agreeing with his worst fears that he had played an indirect role in Roberta Hinkle's death. "Who are you?" Noah asked existentially.

"I'm Ava London," Ava said without a moment's hesitation, regaining her aplomb. "I have so completely become Ava London that occasionally I forget that I wasn't always she. As an example, I often truly believe my father committed suicide. It's like what you were suggesting one night when we were talking about how people on social media can get confused with what is true and what they have made up to make their lives look and sound better."

"What about Ava London committing suicide?" Noah asked. "How does that fit in?" He was having trouble understanding how the Ava he knew could be so insouciant about the history she was cavalierly revealing, especially if she had played a role in the online harrassment.

"Obviously, I changed the narrative in that regard," Ava said. "I can imagine you find all this shocking, but understand I had always been jealous of Ava London and had always wanted to be her. Her death was what made it possible, and my need for a new identity was the stimulus. And it was easy. We looked a lot alike, although she was prettier. All it took was a quick nose job, which I always wanted to do anyway, hair color change, and a few forms to be filled out at Lubbock County Courthouse to make it legal."

"Why didn't you do the legal work in Brownfield?" Noah asked. He hadn't thought about checking the court records in Lubbock.

"I'm not sure they would have let me do it in Brownfield," Ava said. "When you want to change your name, the authorities discourage and often deny celebrity names, and Ava was a local celebrity."

"You said you had a need for a new identity," Noah said. "I don't understand. Why?"

"I was being held back by my old identity," Ava said. "When I moved with my dentist boss to Lubbock and got a taste of what an education could do for you, I needed a new beginning. Becoming Ava London was that new beginning. She had had a different outlook on life and a different scholastic record. She would have gone to college and become something more than a dental assistant. She would have at least been the dentist."

"In the articles I read in *The Brownfield Gazette*, you, as Gail Shafter, as well as two other classmates were named as having harassed Ava London after her father's suicide on AOL Instant Messaging to encourage her to follow her father's lead," Noah said. "Was that true?"

"It might have been, on some level," Ava admitted. "But there were a lot of girls who were jealous of Ava London, and she was an entitled snob. What irked me and a sizable number of other female classmates at the time was that she began using her father's suicide to her advantage, looking for more acclaim and status because she was supposedly suffering, the poor dear. It made a lot of us sick, and I wasn't afraid to tell her. But I never encouraged her to kill herself.

"She and I had been friends, or at least as friendly as was possible with the most popular girl in the class who was never satisfied with her status. But when I was honest with her about using her father's suicide as she was, she ostracized me and got me harassed big time about being a slut. And one other thing. When I was in the ninth grade I got harassed so much online I couldn't go to school for a week, and Ava London and two of her then closest friends were the culprits." Ava shook her head. "Growing up is getting progressively more difficult with social media providing instant, nonstop communication. And I think it is harder for girls than boys with the mixed messages we must deal with about sex. If you don't indulge, you're a prude. If you do, you're a slut. I wasn't a slut. I only had one boyfriend in high school and that was short lived."

"And you didn't harass Ava to follow in her father's footsteps?"

"Never," Ava said, "but I was clear about how it was for her to try to benefit from the tragedy."

"Why didn't you tell me about this identity change earlier in our relationship, as intimate as we'd become?" Noah asked.

"I don't know," Ava said. "What might surprise you is that I don't think about it that often. I've adjusted to my new reality, and I much prefer it to the old one. I might have told you eventually, but then I might not have. I don't see it as important. And thinking about what is important leads me to another more serious issue I want to bring up with you."

Ava moved even closer to Noah by pulling the ottoman she was sitting on against his chair so she could lower her voice even more. "Before I say what I plan to say, I want you to know that I like you, Noah Rothauser. I really like you and respect you, which is why we have gotten along as well as we have, and I hope our relationship can continue and hopefully even blossom. I think we were made for each other, but whether or not it happens is going to depend on your cooperation."

"Cooperation on what?" Noah asked hesitantly.

"That you join the team," Ava said "My team! Above and beyond my personal interest, I think you could be a big help to the NSC. You and I together. Understand that I have lobbied for you strenuously, which is ironic, me lobbying a lobbying organization! My success at this particularly lobbying effort is why you are sitting here at this moment rather than having disappeared to God knows where, which would have been easy as no one knew you had gone to Lubbock or why."

A chill descended Noah's spine, making him tense.

"I've had to make a huge pitch to have you brought back to Boston to have this talk," Ava said. "I even essentially ransomed several planned trips to Washington to make it happen, threatening not to go. Now, I want to remind you of the metaphor you used the first evening you visited my home to plan for the initial M&M Conference, and that was when you described us as 'two peas in a pod.' Do you remember?"

"Of course I remember," Noah said. "It was when I learned how similar we were in our total commitments to medicine and our specialties."

"Unfortunately, it seems that the metaphor is not as apropos as I was counting on," Ava said.

"What does that mean?" Noah said. He knew intuitively that something was coming that he was not going to like.

"Believing that you felt as committed to surgery as I feel toward anesthesia, I was sure that if you were suspended from your super chief resident position that you would be so totally consumed by getting yourself reinstated that you wouldn't have time or energy to cause trouble for anyone else—namely, me."

A sudden feeling of anger and betrayal surged through Noah's brain. He regarded Ava with disbelief. "Are you telling me that you were responsible for my suspension?"

"Only indirectly," Ava said. "All I did was tell my babysitters, Keyon and George, that you had somehow fudged or fabricated data on your Ph.D. thesis. I also told them that Dr. Mason was eager to have you fired. With that little bit of information and their considerable resources, they were able to accomplish getting you temporarily furloughed."

Noah could feel his face redden. It was almost too much to believe that he had been jilted by someone he'd felt so very close to and trusted.

"I can see you are upset," Ava continued in the same even tone she'd been maintaining. "But before you allow yourself a paroxysm of righteous indignation, I want to tell you that I wasn't completely confident you would stop causing me potential trouble with your supposed misgivings about my competence even after your suspension. Accordingly, for backup, I encouraged Keyon and George to use the full investigative power of ABC Security to delve into your background. It is fascinating what they have come up with. It seems that you, Dr. Noah Rothauser, like most people, have a few secrets that seem at odds with the persona you present, which might be more like a Facebook sockpuppet than you would have us believe. Who is the real Noah Rothauser?"

The color of Noah's face that had so recently appeared now drained away. It took him a minute to organize his thoughts. "Let me ask you a question," he said in a halting voice.

"Please do," Ava said.

"Why are you and the NSC so against my checking into your training? Initially, I was just interested to know how many and what kind of cases you did as a resident, which is all I was trying to do when I used your computer."

"The NSC doesn't want my training questioned because I told them emphatically I did not want it questioned," Ava said. "It is as simple as that."

"Does the NSC know why you feel that way?"

"No, they don't," Ava said. "My turn for a question. Why are you concerned about my training when I have passed my anesthesia boards both written and oral with honors, and as you have reminded me I've handled upwards of three thousand cases at BMH without a problem."

"It's mostly those niggling questions about the three deaths that I felt ethically obligated to check out. I told them to you."

"And I explained fully that your concerns were without basis in all three instances," Ava said. "What else? Let's clear the slate."

"Okay, I've also wondered about your syntax in your anesthesia notes," Noah said. He felt embarrassed to bring up such an insignificant issue, but it had been bothering him like a pebble in a shoe. "You use fewer acronyms and more superlatives than other doctors."

"That's an absurd notion," Ava said. "If anything, it's mainstream medical snobbery. I write my notes the way notes are written in Brazos University Medical Center in Lubbock, Texas. What else?"

"It surprises me that you have no real friends at the hospital," Noah said. "You keep everyone at arm's length and apparently prefer social media to face-to-face interaction. Why? It seems so strange to me because I know you as warmly personable. It makes no sense, especially with your ability to read people so well."

"Isn't this a little like the pot calling the kettle black?" Ava said. "When it comes down to it, you are the same. Remember: 'two peas in a pod.' Maybe you go more out of your way to be superficially friendly with everyone than I, but you're not close friends with anyone except an alleged girlfriend who no one ever met and who decided she needed more of a relationship, which you weren't supplying. As for social media, I think you don't indulge in it because you don't have the time, at least not until you finish your residency. When you do, the 'gamer' in you is going to reassert itself, and currently there is no better online game than social media.

"Here's the reality. We are both products of the new digital age, where truth and intimacy are becoming less and less important. Thanks to the ubiquity of social media in all its forms, we're all becoming narcissists, maybe not as overt as our friend Wild Bill Mason, but we all thrive on continuous reaffirmation, which is why you work so damn hard and I love anesthesia. Everyone is becoming an elaborate fusion of the real and the virtual, including you and I."

Noah stared back at Ava. Earlier he had had a foreboding about where their strange, digressive conversation was going, but now he was sure, and a deep-seated atavistic fear spread through him. It disturbed him to recognize she was in control and not him. She knew all her own secrets and apparently some of his.

"The growing popularity of Facebook and other social-media sites is a harbinger of the future," Ava said after a pause to see if Noah would speak. When he didn't, she continued: "People can be what they want to be by managing technology, and those who do it the best, like you and I, will thrive despite our pasts."

Ava paused again. This time she resolved to wait for Noah to respond. Her expression was a contented semi-smile of the one in control, in sharp contrast with Noah's clenched, thin-lipped, anxious grimace.

For a moment Noah looked away. Ava's self-assurance and apparent amusement were galling, as he thought of himself as the injured party who should have been treated as such, rather than being toyed with like one of her cats playing with a mouse. When he looked back, he decided once again it was time to go for broke. What he didn't expect was another surprise and an even bigger shock.

44

"Let's stop beating around the bush," Noah said irritably. "I want you to tell me directly why you are so protective of your anesthesia training."

"It's simple," Ava said, her smile broadening. "I don't want people checking into my anesthesia training, because I didn't do it."

Noah's jaw dropped open. Again he stared at Ava, but now it was in total disbelief. "Maybe you better tell me what you mean."

"I am what you might call a modern-day charlatan, which is a world of difference from a charlatan in the past," Ava said. "And I'm not talking about the kind of charlatan everyone is becoming today because of little lies on social media. I'm talking about being a full-blown charlatan but of a different ilk. I am a fully competent charlatan."

"What part of your formal anesthesia training did you not do?" Noah asked with hesitation.

"None of it," Ava said.

"I'm not sure I understand," Noah said, dumbfounded.

"Let me explain," Ava said. "Remember I told you I was giving anesthesia under the supposed supervision of my dentist boss, which wasn't much supervision. What it did was make me very interested in the science of pharmacology and anesthetic gases. When we moved to Brazos University Medical Center, I started going to various lectures and even an anesthesia conference that the school sponsored. My boss was very encouraging. So I started reading in the field online, which turned out to be better for me than the lectures, since I could read with better retention and much faster than professors could talk. I found the information fascinating. I was also impressed with the salary and respect anesthesiologists got and wanted it for myself. I mean, I was kind of doing the same thing but as an assistant in a dental office instead of in an operating room. And I was doing it without the fabulous equipment and support of nurses and residents."

"So let me understand," Noah said with mounting incredulity. "You never did an anesthesia residency?"

"No," Ava said. "I didn't need to."

"What about the anesthesia boards?" Noah asked, his mouth agape. "Did you take them?"

"Oh, yes, of course!" Ava said. "I took the boards and passed them with no problem. I even enjoyed them, as it was an affirmation of a lot of effort I had expended preparing for them."

"But to qualify to take the boards you must do a residency," Noah sputtered.

"That's the usual prerequisite," Ava said. "In my case it was different. I decided to skip the residency part as unnecessary and even exploitive. From my perspective, the residency is a way for the hospital to have people giving anesthesia for three to four years and paying them a pittance in comparison to what the hospital is charging for the service. And the supervision that they are supposed to get is often not all that great."

"How did you manage to be accepted to take the boards?" Noah asked. He was flabbergasted and wasn't sure if Ava wasn't still toying with him.

"It was all relatively easy," Ava said. "The critical event was moving from Brownfield to Lubbock when my dentist boss became dean of the new school of dentistry. As a founding faculty member, he had administrative status with the Brazos Medical Center computer. Using his log-in, I had full access. With my computer skills, it was not difficult to create an entire record for Ava London that matched the other anesthesia residents, complete with grades, evaluations, and letters of recommendation. What helped enormously was that the entire university and the medical center were growing geometrically. It was almost like a revolving door with new personnel, profiles, and résumés being uploaded daily. It also helped that the system had an almost nonexistent firewall, so I probably could have done it all without my boss's log-in. But the log-in made it so easy. I was even able to insert pictures of myself with the real residents for the appropriate years."

Noah found himself nodding. He could remember seeing the photo of Ava with the 2012 resident photo. As astounding as all this was, he was beginning to think she was telling him the truth. "What about your name change?" Noah asked. "When did that happen?"

"That didn't happen until I had to take the U.S. Medical Licensing Examination," Ava said. "That was when I needed the new identity. It was before I took the anesthesia boards."

"So people think that Gail Shafter still exists," Noah said.

"For sure. It was key," Ava said. "Particularly my old boss, Dr. Winston Herbert, who is still dean of the Brazos University School of Dentistry. It's why I keep a Facebook page in her name. Presently, she is working for a virtual dentist in Davenport, Iowa. I mean, at this point I suppose I could kill her off, but why? I enjoy contrasting my old life with the new. It makes me continuously appreciative of what I have achieved."

"Good Lord," Noah said. His head was spinning. "Who got the M.D./ B.S. degree, Gail or Ava?"

Ava laughed. She was enjoying herself. "Of course it was Ava," she said.

Although Noah was surprised at this news, he recognized that he shouldn't have been. "In other words, you didn't go to medical school, either?"

"Of course not," Ava said. "Nor college, for that matter. That would have been a bigger waste of time than doing the anesthesia residency. I wanted to become an anesthesiologist. I didn't want to waste time getting a general liberal-arts education, particularly not the kind you Ivy Leaguers think is appropriate."

"So that means you are not even a doctor," Noah snapped.

"That is a matter of definition," Ava said. "I did take the USMLE as I said, and I did pass it with flying colors in the ninety-fifth percentile because I studied my butt off. According to the State of Massachusetts, I am a doctor. I have an M.D. license. They say that I am a doctor. I feel like a doctor, and I act like a doctor. I have the knowledge of a doctor. I'm a doctor."

"What about the degree in nutrition?"

"Made up as well," Ava said. "That was something I realized later that would come in handy. I just read about the field online."

Noah closed his eyes and ran his fingers through his hair. This was all so incredible he was having difficulty wrapping his mind around what she was telling him. "I'm not sure I believe all this," he murmured.

"Wake up, my friend!" Ava said. "Come and join the digital age in the twenty-first century! The basis of knowledge has changed. It is not hidden away any longer by professional societies, some more secret and restrictive than others. Knowledge of just about everything is now available online for everyone, not just the few who are lucky enough for whatever reason to go to the right schools. Even professional medical experience and expertise is available in simulation centers with computer-driven mannequins that are better in many respects to the real thing. With the mannequins, a student can learn to handle a problem by doing it over and over until it is reflex, like handling malignant hyperthermia. Most anesthesiologists have never handled a case of MH. I've handled seven, to be exact. Six with a simulator and one in real life."

"So you really did use the simulation center?" Noah said. It was a statement more than a question.

"Absolutely," Ava said. "Like there was no tomorrow. Within months of my arriving at Brazos University Medical Center, I started my quest to become an anesthesiologist by using the simulators almost every night when the medical students and the residents had gone back to their beds. I did it religiously. I even started writing programs and to trouble-shoot the system because initially there were a lot of bugs in it. But it was a fabulous way to learn, so much better than the standard methodology. It is almost a crime that medical teaching hasn't been altered for a hundred years, still adhering to a paradigm that started back in 1910, for God's sake. It's almost unbelievable because everything else about our culture and technology has changed drastically. Don't you find it embarrassing that medical education is the most backward of all the pedagogies?"

"I guess I haven't given it that much thought," Noah said.

"Well, I certainly have," Ava said. "Do people really need four years of college to be a terrific doctor? Hell, no! Maybe they did in 1910, but not now. Maybe they think they have a richer life, but even that is open to question. Do people need four full years of medical school to be a terrific doctor? I don't think so. Maybe they did in 1910, when most medical schools were for-profit diploma mills and a bad joke. Do people need to do research for a couple of years? Hell, no, again, unless they choose research as a career. Otherwise it's like treading water. The proof of all this is that I am a damn good anesthesiologist, better than some at the BMH whom I have been able to observe, and I have handled more than three thousand cases and supervised my share of residents and nurse anesthetists.

"Now, I know you have had some misgivings about the three recent deaths I've had. And believe me, they disturbed me more than anyone because they were my first and hopefully my last. But let's reassure you yet again that it wasn't my lack of having had a formal anesthesia residency that was responsible. With Bruce Vincent, we both know that it was the pigheaded Dr. Mason, his fellow, and the patient himself who were at fault. With the Gibson case the problem lay with the departmental rule that it was appropriate for me to supervise two concurrent resident anesthesia cases at the same time and that the resident did not wait for me to be in the room before starting, as I was busy elsewhere. It also didn't help that there was a computer glitch that created two records, one with the information about the patient's neck problem and one without, which was the one that the anesthesia resident got. And the malignant-hyperthermia case could not have been handled any better than it was, despite the outcome. This was determined when it was reviewed. And I can tell you that the majority of the anesthesiologists at the BMH have never handled an MH case, either real or virtual. I don't doubt that they could, but if it were my life on the line, I would rather have me there than them because of my experience. As for why the scrub nurse would tell you I didn't turn the gas off immediately, I have no idea, because for me it was reflex. Maybe she is upset I am an anesthesiologist and she a nurse, or maybe it is that I am younger and more attractive. Who the hell knows . . ."

Ava suddenly threw up her hands as if she were surrendering and sat back. "That's it," she said. "That's the whole story, and you are the only person who knows it." Slowly she lowered her hands, watching Noah expectantly.

"Why have you told me all this?" Noah said. "Why put the burden on me?"

"Two main reasons," Ava said. "First, to save your skin, and second, your career. The NSC sees you as a major threat in regard to me and has let ABC Security know how they feel. Use your imagination for what that might mean! The second reason is that I like you, and we are in many ways 'two peas in a pod.' That is a compliment. I enjoy your company. If you want to know the truth, initially I saw you only as a way to deal with the Dr. Mason problem without involving ABC Security. But that was before I got to know you."

"I enjoy your company as well," Noah admitted. "But—"

"There cannot be any 'buts,'" Ava interjected. "You have to let sleeping dogs lie. I've gone out on a limb for you. I know from your perspective I've gotten to where I am today following a unique path that you don't agree with. But understand that I am the future. Medical education is going to change dramatically in the next five or ten years. It has to change. It took me ten years to get where I am, but I had to work to support myself while I was doing it, and if I didn't, it would have taken half the time. It is inevitable that becoming a specialist like an anesthesiologist will soon take, say, six years or even less from high school to board qualified instead of the current twelve. The costs of healthcare have to go down, and one of them is the cost of training doctors like anesthesiologists. Hell, it's more like a trade than we like to admit."

"I don't think I can do what you are asking," Noah said. "As a real doctor, I'm afraid that I will feel an ethical responsibility to expose you as the charlatan you are. I'm sorry. Maybe you are right about medical education. Perhaps it is behind the times as you say, but I don't think I can be the judge and jury."

"I'm sorry to hear you say this," Ava said. "If you do out me, then I will feel equally obligated to do the same for you."

"What do you mean?" Noah asked hesitantly. The fears he'd felt earlier came back in a rush.

"I mentioned a few minutes ago that Keyon and George, using the investigative powers of ABC Security, came up with a few secrets of yours that are certainly more prejudicial than some temporal data fudging on a Ph.D. thesis. Would you like to hear what they discovered?"

Noah nodded reluctantly.

"First and foremost, it was determined that your father did not die of a heart attack but rather is in prison and will be there for a long, long time, possibly for life for drug trafficking, attempted murder, money laundering, and a few other odds and ends amounting to an impressive felonious résumé. His name is Peter Forrester, and your name was Peter Forrester Jr. until it was legally changed to Noah Rothauser, with Rothauser being your mother's maiden name. I like the choice of Noah, with its biblical connection. Should I go on?"

Noah didn't move, nor did he even blink, yet perspiration appeared on his forehead as evidence of his inner turmoil.

"I'll take your silence as a yes," Ava said. "It was confirmed that you, too, were arrested with your father when you were fourteen for abetting some of your father's activities, and you too went to prison in South Carolina for a time, but as a juvenile offender, since it had been judged that there had been an element of coercion involved. It was also confirmed that you were released at age eighteen and your felony record was sealed. Unfortunately for you but fortunately for us, nothing disappears in the digital age. In the old days, a page was literally torn out of a court log and thrown away. Today, there is no way to make a record such as yours vanish, and the ABC Security investigators, mostly Keyon and George, found all of it. Now, there were some commendable aspects to your backstory, such as you getting your high school diploma with some AP credits while in prison as evidence to your rehabilitation, to the delight of the prison officials. It is also impressive that the warden, hearing of your desire to become a doctor, made great efforts to get you accepted into Columbia University."

"My record is officially sealed," Noah said, finding his voice. "It can't be used against me."

"That is correct, to an extent," Ava said, as the corners of her mouth turned up in a slight but knowing smile. "However, there is the sticky point about the expectation of being truthful. When you filled out the form for your DEA license and there was a place for you to respond to the question of whether you had been convicted of any felonies, you should have marked the box for yes and then on the back of the form in the space provided, you should have explained about having been a juvenile offender and the record sealed. It will be interesting to talk with the DEA about this issue, and see what they say, particularly because your felony involved drug trafficking. The legal opinion is that you will lose your DEA license and thereby make practicing as a doctor all but impossible. It is also interesting to consider how the Residency Advisory Board, which will be ruling on your suspension, will react when they learn that you had lied on your DEA application, which is far more serious than temporarily fudging data on a Ph.D. thesis."

"They cannot use a sealed record against me," Noah repeated, but his voice lacked conviction.

"The Residency Advisory Board is tasked with making a value judgment about ethics," Ava said. "But let's not get into an argument about details, because there is more to your story. It was confirmed that your mother is in an Alzheimer's facility. It was also discovered you have a sister with a chromosomal abnormality who is also institutionalized. It was also confirmed that you were forced to spread your medical school career over six years because of financial difficulties involving supporting your mother, your sister, and yourself, which was all very noble. But since you worked for the medical school administration, it was obvious to me that you would have had special access to the medical school's computer similar to my access to the Brazos University computer. And since we share computer proficiency as part of being 'two peas in a pod,' I recommended that Keyon and George use some IT forensics to look at your record. What was found was not pathognomonic but suggestive there had been some alterations. What I am saying is that at this stage it is not known for certain if you had made any changes to your record to help your application to your BMH residency, and further study would be needed to ascertain it. But here is yet another major area where you are vulnerable."

Ava paused and took a deep breath, watching Noah. She was hoping for more of a reaction, but he just stared back at her, breathing shallowly.

"I can see you are distressed, and for good reason," Ava continued. "So let's talk about a resolution. You want to be one of the world's premier surgeons and have worked stupendously hard to that end. I want to do the same in anesthesia and have worked equally as hard but on a different trajectory. The reason I had you brought back here and have made you privy to all these secrets that no one else knows is that I see our similarities more than our differences, and I like you. I told you all this because there is a solution. What I have intentionally created is a true Mexican standoff, meaning there are three entities pointing guns at each other: you, me, and the NSC. The only way for this to be resolved and we all win is for all of us to agree to the status quo and lay down our weapons. If not, we all lose."

"Every time you say something, it is another surprise," Noah said. "Why do you think the NSC is holding a gun on you? You are their darling."

"If you make an issue about me being a charlatan, I will no longer be their darling but their enemy."

"So the NSC has no idea you are a charlatan?" Noah said, shocked yet again.

"Absolutely not," Ava said.

"And how are you holding a gun against the NSC?"

"That's easy," Ava said. "I could disrupt what I have already accomplished about keeping the 1994 DSHEA from being amended. Also, over the years I have learned enough about the supplement industry to seriously discredit it."

Another silence ensued as Noah struggled to put everything he'd learned over the last half-hour into context. Finally, he said in a subdued voice: "What would you have me do?"

"Nothing," Ava said with a smile. It was clear to her she was making progress. "It is key that you do nothing, but you have to be convincing you are going to do nothing. The NSC has to be absolutely certain that you are not going to try to discredit me in any way at all. As you've guessed, they are enamored of me, which is obvious when you consider this house, my Mercedes, my computer, and all my toys and lifestyle I enjoy. Of course, it would be even better and more convincing if you were willing to help the cause."

"I hope you don't mean me supporting the nutritional-supplement industry," Noah said.

"That's exactly what I mean," Ava said with a chuckle. "Get down off your high horse, Dr. Rothauser! The industry is trying in some ways to clean up its act. Not all companies are bad; it's like everything else, including hospitals and doctors, there's good and bad. The bad ones are really bad, especially the ones who get all their products from China and India, go overboard on their health claims, and really don't give a damn. But with your participation you could be an effective positive force on the inside, trying to get the bad companies to mend their ways by toning down their absurd claims and making them feel responsible for the poisonous crap that's in the bottles they advertise and sell. I can tell you that the good companies, the ones which care about their products and are selling legitimate vitamins and such, are very aware of those companies responsible for all the harm and bad publicity. The reality is that you could do a lot more good on the inside than tilting at windmills from the outside."

Ava paused, aware she was getting carried away. "So what are your thoughts?" she said finally, in a calmer voice.

"I have to think about being supportive," Noah said.

"Okay, you do that," Ava said. "But if you feel as strongly as you say about the nutritional-supplement industry, this could be an opportunity for you to do something positive. The industry is not going to change on its own. The problem is, just like the rest of healthcare, there is too much money involved and the industry has a lot of politicians in their pocket. And as a final note, I imagine the potential remuneration you would receive with your Ivy League credentials from the NSC could easily take care of your educational debt and your mother's and sister's ongoing care. How bad is that?"

EPILOGUE

Dressed in his only jacket and tie, Noah pushed through the revolving door at the entrance to the Stanhope Building. Finally, after several weeks of torment, worrying that his surgical residency was going to be prematurely ended, he felt confident he was going to be reinstated. The day before had been the feared Surgical Residency Advisory Board meeting, but it had gone as well as could be expected. There had been eight members present, which included the program director, Dr. Cantor, and the two assistant program directors, Dr. Mason and Dr. Hiroshi, as well as five surgical residents who had been elected to represent each of the five years of the program. Noah's seat had been empty for obvious reasons. He had served on the board every year he'd been a resident.

Although Noah had been nervous at the outset, it soon became clear to him by the questions asked that his lawyer, John Cavendish, had made it abundantly clear Noah had not fabricated data on his thesis but rather had conservatively estimated results of the final concluding experiment and then replaced them with the real data as soon as it was available, with the motivation being to have his Ph.D. be considered as part of his medical school application. At the end of the meeting, Noah had been told that the board would vote on his case and that he should return in twenty-four hours for the result.

The only surprise for Noah had been Dr. Mason's total silence during the hour-long proceedings. Although Noah had been told by Keyon and George that they had uncovered some potentially compromising information about Dr. Mason, which had been communicated to him, Noah had suspected the worst from his long-time antagonist. He hadn't known why it hadn't happened until last night at Ava's.

As they had eaten their dinner overlooking her garden, she'd explained that Keyon and George had discovered that Dr. Mason had made it a habit over the years to insist that Arab sheiks from the Emirates and Saudi Arabia provide progressively extravagant gifts for the privilege of being seen in a timely fashion, which was important for pancreatic cancer patients. At first these gifts had been mainly in the form of large contributions to his research efforts or to hospital building projects, but then about seven years previously, they became more personal, including his beloved, flamboyant red Ferrari.

After consulting with several knowledgeable tax attorneys, Keyon and George had ascertained that from the IRS's point of view, these gifts had to be considered income, since they were required to secure an appointment and were therefore fee-for-service and not voluntary. Since the amount of money involved was more than 25 percent of Dr. Mason's academic salary, there was the specter of statutory fraud, meaning possible prison time. This information had been provided to Dr. Mason with the advice that it would be best for him to curtail his ongoing harassment of Dr. Noah Rothauser.

Noah took the Stanhope's elevators up to the third floor. Once there, he walked across the sumptuous carpeting toward the double mahogany doors leading into the hospital boardroom where the Advisory Board meeting had been held the day before. He told the hospital president's secretary whose desk was nearby that he was there and then took a seat in the administrative waiting area. It was 1:58 P.M. He had wanted to be exactly on time, not too early and certainly not late, and he could congratulate himself on his timing. Although he'd been optimistic about the upcoming meeting, now that he was waiting to be seen, he felt the old anxiety he'd always felt when forced to confront authority figures. There was always the chance his life could once again be upended. Nervously, he flipped through a magazine that he'd picked up from the low table in front of him.

After the previous night's dinner and following the revelations about Dr. Mason's tax fraud, Noah and Ava had retreated up to her study. He'd been staying with her the whole week, and each night they had gone to the study to continue their conversations. Last night, just when they were ready to call it a night, Noah had said he had a condition he wanted to run by her that involved her babysitters. After explaining what he had in mind, Ava's response had been she'd think about it although a half-hour later she'd reluctantly agreed.

"They are ready for you now," the secretary called out to Noah five minutes later, interrupting his musing.

Getting to his feet, Noah straightened his tie, took a deep breath, and walked over to the imposing, oversized doors of the boardroom. After another slight pause to take yet another deep breath, he entered. He was moderately surprised that only Dr. Cantor, Dr. Mason, and Dr. Hiroshi were seated at the expansive table. None of Noah's resident colleagues were present. Noah's heart skipped a beat. Maybe his optimism had been premature. He closed the door behind him and walked to the near end of the long, boardroom table. The three faculty members representing the executive committee of the Advisory Board were at the opposite end.

"Thank you for returning," Dr. Cantor said. "Sit if you'd like."

"I'll stand," Noah said. He looked at each of the men in turn. Dr. Mason refused to make eye contact, staring at his hands clasped on the table in front of him.

"By a unanimous vote of the Advisory Board with one abstention," Dr. Cantor said formally, "it has been decided that you will be reinstated as the super chief resident."

Relief spread through Noah with such suddenness he had to support himself by grabbing the back of the chair in front of him and leaning on it.

"However," Dr. Cantor continued, "we want to make sure you understand how important we as medical educators feel about the central role ethics play in our profession. We want to make certain that you don't feel that expediency can justify ethical lapses, and furthermore . . ."

Noah was no longer listening to Dr. Cantor. He was already absorbed in thinking about getting himself up to surgery to go over the surgical schedule for the morning to make sure the residents were appropriately assigned as assistants. Then he was going to tour the surgical intensive-care unit to familiarize himself with all the cases. Following that he was going to go to the surgical floor to do the same. The reality was that he had an enormous amount of work to do just to get acclimated back into the system . . .

"Dr. Rothauser," Dr. Cantor said. "We'd like an answer to our question."

"I'm sorry," Noah said clearly flustered. "I'm so pleased to be reinstated that I am already thinking about all that I have to do to get up to speed. I didn't hear the question. Could you repeat it?"

"The question is: Is there anything else of an ethical nature that you would like to reveal to the board? This current problem with your thesis surprised all of us coming out of the blue, and we don't like surprises, especially involving our super chief, who we are considering offering a staff position."

Noah stared back at the program director with his mind in a sudden turmoil. He wanted to say a lot, but how could he? He wanted to explain how difficult it was to be caught in a standoff with an industry he despised and a woman he thought he loved. The truth was that he was caught between the past and the future, between old-school ethics and the new reality of an ever-expanding technological and connected world where the real and the virtual were fusing.

"Well?" Dr. Cantor persisted.

"I don't know," Noah said, stumbling over his words.

"Dr. Rothauser!" Dr. Cantor said sharply. "That is hardly the answer we are looking for. What do you mean you don't know?"

Noah audibly sighed, sounding like a balloon deflating. "Maybe I should sit down," he said. Suddenly his legs felt weak. He pulled out the director's chair directly in front of him and sat heavily. After a deep breath, he looked up, noticing that Dr. Mason was staring at him as intently as the others but with a slight smile of anticipation. Noah was painfully aware that time was passing, and each second was making the situation worse. He should have said "no" immediately and be done with it, but he couldn't. The question had caught him completely unawares, upsetting the unsteady balance he'd been trying to maintain in his mind, sending it into tumult.

"Dr. Rothauser!" Dr. Cantor snapped. "Explain yourself!"

Noah cleared his throat as he struggled to regain control as an idea emerged from the fog of his addled brain. "This thesis situation surprised me as well," he said haltingly but gaining confidence, "and it awakened an old fear that has dogged me since I was a teenager that something unexpected would happen to prevent me from becoming the best academic surgeon my abilities would allow. I had never thought about what I did with my thesis as an ethical issue, but now I can see that it could be considered as such, and I apologize for not having cleared the air on my own accord. But with that thought in mind, there is something else that is more clearly an ethical issue that I believe I should reveal to clear the air."

"By all means," Dr. Cantor said hesitantly with building concern and dismay. He'd never expected a positive answer to what he thought was a pro forma question.

"Once I bought a paper off the Internet, and after doctoring it, I presented it as my own work. I knew it wasn't right, but it was in the very beginning of my freshman year of college, and I was under a lot of pressure to perform."

Dr. Cantor's face, which had hardened considerably from expecting the worst, suddenly softened. He was ostensibly relieved by Noah's benign mea culpa. "That's it?" he questioned with relief. "Early in your college career you bought a paper online?"

"That's correct," Noah admitted. "Others were doing it, too, but I know that is no excuse."

After a quick reassuring glance at his colleagues, whom he judged were as relieved as he, Dr. Cantor assumed a knowing yet condescending smile. "Thank you for your forthrightness, Dr. Rothauser. Although we surely cannot condone plagiarism on any level, I believe we can all relate to the competitiveness we all had to experience early in our lengthy education." He again glanced at his fellow board members to make sure he was speaking for them. Dr. Hiroshi nodded his head in obvious agreement.

"Any other issues besides this freshman-year paper, Dr. Rothauser?" Dr. Cantor asked, redirecting his attention at Noah.

"That's the extent of it," Noah said.

"Okay, fine!" Dr. Cantor said. With a satisfied expression, he sat back, extended his arms, and pressed his palms against the table. "It is good to clear the air. Thank you and welcome back! I know I can say with support of my colleagues, your services have been sorely missed."

"Thank you, Dr. Cantor," Noah said as he got unsteadily to his feet. For a split second, he allowed his eyes to dart in Dr. Mason's direction. He could immediately tell that his erstwhile antagonist didn't share Dr. Cantor's contentment, yet under the circumstances he stayed thankfully silent.

Without another word or even a glance back at the residency program directors, Noah headed for the door on rubbery legs. He felt as if he had dodged a speeding train but needed to do something to control the anxiety that Dr. Cantor's unexpected and open-ended ethical question had unleashed. Luckily, he had just the right antidote. He'd head up to the operating room as he planned and dive back into work.

3:10 P.M.

An eight-ton, intimidating, black Lenco BearCat armored truck with BOSTON POLICE stenciled on its rear panel lurched up onto the curb on School Street in downtown Boston and screeched to a halt. To the shock of several dozen tourists milling about the plaza in front of the refurbished, Old City Hall building, six heavily armed Boston Police SWAT officers, some carrying Colt CAR-15 submachine guns, leaped from the vehicle in a highly rehearsed and synchronized fashion and ran toward the entrance of the ornamental Victorian building. Despite the August heat, they were in long-sleeved black combat gear with military helmets and ballistic vests festooned with additional ammunition clips, flash bang grenades, and Tasers. All but one member of the team were wearing black balaclavas, making them even more sinister.

There was no hesitation or conversation among the group. There didn't need to be. The operation had been planned to the T, with each knowing their position and exactly what was expected. The first officer to reach the building's outer door pulled it open as the others dashed within. He followed immediately on their tail.

Since they had already remotely shut down the elevators, they ran toward the main staircase and entered it on the run. Once inside, they rapidly climbed the stairs in step like a precision dance troop. They exited the stairwell one after the other on the fourth floor and stacked up single-file at the entrance of the ABC Security office. Instantly, the second officer in the line removed a door-breaching Thor Hammer strapped to the back of the first officer who then moved out of the way. The officer with the Thor Hammer stepped to the side and without a second's hesitation swung the heavy hammer so that it hit the door adjacent to the doorknob with as much force as he could muster. With a shockingly loud splintering noise, the door burst open, allowing the next two men in the stack to rush into the room, sighting along their Colt submachine guns with fingers curled about the triggers as they shouted "police arrest warrant." The first man took the right side of the room as his area of concentration, the second man the left as they executed a classic SWAT dynamic entry. Two more officers followed immediately on the tail of the first two while holding Glock automatic pistols out in front of them in both hands.

There were three totally stunned people in the room. George Marlowe was sitting on a couch to the right of the entrance, using a PC laptop. Keyon Dexter was standing at the window, gazing out over the Kings Chapel Burying Ground with his hands in his pockets. Both had removed their suit jackets and had their sleeves rolled up. Charlene Washington, a temp, was at a desk to the left.

"Down!" yelled the first officer into the room, keeping his Colt trained on George. He knew the second man into the room was doing the same for Keyon. "On the floor, now! All of you! Hands extended!"

George and Keyon recovered quickly, their highly trained military minds rushing through the OODA loop of "observing, orienting, deciding, and acting." But it was to no avail. In the split second it took to recover their senses, there was no time to act. Resignedly raising their hands, they obeyed the repeated shouts to lie on the floor. It was different for Charlene, who was frozen in place, paralyzed by fear as she stared into the barrel of a Glock pistol.

The two officers who had been responsible for breaching the door and the last to enter the room now came forward and quickly handcuffed

Keyon and George as they lay facedown. Once the prisoners' hands were secure, the same two policemen removed the weapons from the prisoners' shoulder holsters and their mobile phones and fake FBI badges from their pockets. Once that was accomplished, they hauled the two men to their feet. No one said a word. Only then did the officers with the Colt submachine guns remove their fingers from the triggers and lower their weapons.

The commander of the high-risk-warrant service team and the first person to enter the room stepped forward. He was also the only one not wearing a black balaclava. After handing off his Colt rifle to a colleague, he proceeded to pull out a tattered 3x5 card inscribed with the *Miranda* Rights. Stepping up to Keyon Dexter, he addressed him with his full name, and informed him that he was being arrested for the murder of Roberta Hinkle of Lubbock, Texas, kidnapping, and for impersonating a federal officer. Moving on to George Marlowe, he repeated the charges. When he was done with the arrests, he read both men their Miranda Rights.

Stepping back from the prisoners, the SWAT team leader purposefully fell silent while eyeing the two handcuffed men. As was often the case during an arrest, prisoners frequently said incriminating things as a normal reaction to the stress of the situation even after being informed of their rights to remain silent. But it wasn't to be. Keyon and George were professionals and trained to remain silent, knowing full well that ABC Security would have formidable lawyers on the case within hours of learning of their arrest. They were not intimidated by being arrested, since they were certain they would be quickly out on bail.

AUTHOR'S NOTE

The profession of medicine has always had a problem with charlatans, and there have been quite a number of infamous cases in which the perpetrators literally "got away with murder" after assuming the identity of a real doctor who had either died or moved to another state. Now that the world is engulfed in the digital age, the situation is getting worse and accelerating because of the vulnerability of databases, which make it possible to augment curriculum vitae or even create them completely de novo. Such hacking activities trump the old-fashioned need for identity theft. Compounding the problem is the easy availability of specialized professional knowledge on the Internet, as well as the training potential of virtual reality programs combined with modern simulation systems composed of remarkably realistic, computer-driven mannequins that precisely mimic human pathophysiology and response to treatment. The consequence is that the difference between the physician and the motivated non-physician in terms of apparent basic knowledge and know-how will progressively narrow, effectively blurring the line between the real doctor and the fake.

The origin of the term "charlatan" comes from sixteenth-century French, and it initially referred to a medical quack, although its meaning expanded to include all imposters. Today the word is garnering new significance and meaning. With social media exploding around the world (currently the number of people using Facebook alone is approaching two billion) and the fact that it is estimated that more than 75 percent of the people using Facebook lie to "airbrush reality," there are a lot of new charlatans of varying degree. In a very real sense, being an imposter on some level is rapidly becoming the norm. Indeed, it is generally estimated that 5 to 10 percent of Facebook's almost two billion accounts are "sockpuppets" or fake, online charlatan profiles. Others believe the percentage is significantly higher. Of course, such a situation is hardly surprising considering the attraction. Psychologists think of social media as a virtual-playground for a culture that is becoming progressively narcissistic. The inherent lack of the usual social restrictions of face-to-face interactions creates a dissociative anonymity devoid of any meaningful reprisal, while offering the potential of unlimited and continual egotistical affirmation and gratification. People can be whoever they want to be and say whatever they want to say for whatever reason with both harmless and not-so-harmless consequences even to themselves. It is a "brave new world," and it is evolving rapidly.

Members of the medical profession are no exception in the use of social media, including Facebook, Twitter, Instagram, Snapchat, various dating sites, and other sites. They too fall prey to its allure and pitfalls. Surveys have shown that more than 90 percent of physicians are using it for personal reasons and a lesser percentage for business purposes. This personal use has not been without consequence. More than 90 percent of State Medical Boards have received complaints of inappropriate online behavior by physicians while using social media, and there have been episodes of disciplinary action.

Like society in general, the medical profession is in a state of rapid change due to digitization and associated technologies. No longer is it the major source of medical information for the public since that role has been co-opted by the Internet. A few years from now the entire paradigm of the practice of medicine will change from hospital-centric sick-care that began in the nineteenth century to patient-centric personalized preventive-care built around continuous real-time monitoring and treatment algorithms, and it will take place mostly in the home, workplace, and ambulatory care centers, not in pricey and dangerous hospitals. In response to this tectonic shift due partially to the pressure of runaway costs of healthcare, medical education will have to be dramatically altered to remain relevant, especially since it is one of the most conservative professional pedagogies. The current expensive, long drawn-out, overly competitive path of four years of college, four years of medical school, and up to seven years of hospital-based residency, all of which was instituted in 1910 and hasn't changed much since, will have to be drastically updated. The novel *Charlatans* presages the need for such a change. And on a lighter note, the novel also begs the question: Did your doctor truly get the training he or she so ostentatiously advertises with all those easily reproduced diplomas hanging on the office wall?

ACKNOWLEDGMENTS

I would like to acknowledge my extended family and friends, who are always willing to offer opinions and honestly critique drafts. Thank you all for your invaluable help and support.

SELECTED BIBLIOGRAPHY

Asch, David A., M.D., and Debra F. Weinstein, M.D. "Innovation in Medical Education." *The New England Journal of Medicine* 371 (2014): 794–795.

Diller, Vivian, Ph.D. "Social Media: A Narcissist's Virtual Playground." *The Huffington Post*, March 23, 2015.

Offit, Paul, M.D. "How Lobbyists Will Keep You Hooked on Vitamins." *The Daily Beast*, December 21, 2013.

Sales, Nancy Jo. *American Girls: Social Media and the Secret Lives of Teenagers*. New York: Vintage, Reprint edition, 2017.

Sass, Erik. "People Believe Their Own Lies on Social Media." *MediaPost*, December 29, 2014.

"You're Losing Your Rights to Buy Natural Vitamins" (featuring Mel Gibson), YouTube, 1993..